JOE PICKETT

ORDINARY MAN,
EXTRAORDINARY HERO

"Writing genius... on a par with James Lee Burke."
Library Journal

"I read one book and then hunted out four more...
Box has it all." *Toronto Globe and Mail*

"Joe doesn't let us down... exhilarating."
New York Times

"Box gets better and better with each novel."
Bookreporter.com

"Absorbing... Relentlessly paced powder keg of a thriller."
Publishers Weekly

"Exquisite descriptions... Box's story moves smoothly
and suspensefully to the showdown."
Washington Post

"An absolute must."
Kirkus

"The suspense tears forward like a brush fire."
People Magazine

"A superb mystery series."
Booklist

"Riveting."
USA Today

ALSO BY C.J.BOX

THE JOE PICKETT NOVELS

OPEN SEASON
SAVAGE RUN
WINTERKILL
TROPHY HUNT
OUT OF RANGE
IN PLAIN SIGHT
FREE FIRE
BLOOD TRAIL
BELOW ZERO
NOWHERE TO RUN
COLD WIND

*

THREE WEEKS TO SAY GOODBYE
BLUE HEAVEN
BACK OF BEYOND

BELOW ZERO

C.J. BOX

CORVUS

First published in the United States of America in 2009
by Penguin Group USA, Inc.

This paperback edition first published in Great Britain in 2011
by Corvus, an imprint of Atlantic Books Ltd.

1 3 5 7 9 10 8 6 4 2

A CIP catalogue record for this book is available from
the British Library.

Paperback ISBN: 978-1-84887-993-5
eBook ISBN:978-0-85789-426-7

Printed and bound by CPI Group (UK) Ltd, Croydon, CR0 4YY

Corvus
An imprint of Atlantic Books Ltd
Ormond House
26-27 Boswell Street
London WC1N 3JZ

www.corvus-books.co.uk

For Don Johnson ...
And Laurie, always

PART ONE

Evolution loves death more than it loves you or me ... We are moral creatures, then, in an amoral world. The universe that suckled us is a monster that does not care if we live or die—does not care if it itself grinds to a halt.

—Annie Dillard

1

Keystone, South Dakota

MARSHALL AND SYLVIA Hotle, who liked to list their places of residence as Cedar Rapids, Iowa, Quartzsite, Arizona, and "the open road," were preparing dinner when they saw the dark SUV with Illinois plates drive by on the access road for the third time in less than an hour.

"There they are again," Sylvia said, narrowing her eyes. She was setting two places on the picnic table. Pork cutlets, green beans, dinner rolls, iceberg lettuce salad, and plenty of weak coffee, just like Marshall liked it.

"Gawkers," Marshall said, with a hint of a smile. "I'm getting used to it."

The evening was warm and still and perfumed with dust and pine pollen particular to the Black Hills of South Dakota. Within the next hour, the smell of hot dogs and hamburgers being cooked on dozens of campground grills would waft through the trees as well. By then the Hotles would be done eating. They liked to eat early. It was a habit they developed on their farm.

The Hotles had parked their massive motor home for the

night in a remote campsite within the Mount Rushmore KOA complex near Palmer Gulch, only five miles away from the monument itself. Because it was late August and the roads teemed with tourists, they'd thought ahead and secured this choice site—one they'd occupied before on their semi-annual cross-country trips—by calling and reserving it weeks before. Although there were scores of RVs and tents setting up within the complex below, this particular site was tucked high in the trees and seemed almost remote.

Marshall often said he preferred the Black Hills to the Rocky Mountains farther west. The Black Hills were green, rounded, gentle, with plenty of lots big enough to park The Unit. The highest mountain—Harney Peak—was 7,242 feet. The Black Hills, Marshall said, were *reasonable*. The Rockies were a different matter. As they ventured from South Dakota into Wyoming, both the people and the landscape changed. Good solid midwestern stock gave way to mountain people who were ragged on the edges, he thought. Farms gave way to ranches. The mountains became severe, twice the elevation of Harney Peak, which was just big enough. The weather became volatile. While the mountains could be seductive, they were also amoral. Little of use could be grown. There were creatures—grizzly bears, black bears, mountain lions—capable of eating him and willing to do it. "Give me the Black Hills any old day," Marshall said as he drove, as the rounded dark humps appeared in his windshield to the west. "The Black Hills are plenty."

Sylvia was short, compact, and solid. She wore a sweatshirt covered with balloons and clouds she'd appliquéd herself. Her iron-gray hair was molded into tight curls that looked spring-loaded. She had eight grandchildren with the ninth due any day now. She'd spent the day knitting baby booties and a little stocking cap. She didn't have strong opinions on the Black Hills versus the Rocky Mountains, but …

"I don't like to be gawked at," she said, barely moving her mouth.

"I hate to tell you this, but it's not you they're looking at," Marshall said, sipping coffee. "They're admiring The Unit." Marshall's belly strained at the snap buttons of his Iowa Hawkeyes windbreaker. His face was round, and his cheeks were always red. He'd worn the same steel-framed glasses so long they were back in style, as was his John Deere cap. He chinned toward the motor home. "They probably want to come up here and take a look. Don't worry, though, we can have supper first."

"That's charitable of you," Sylvia said, shaking her head. "Don't you ever get tired of giving tours?"

"No."

"It's not just a motor home, you know. It's where we *live*. But with you giving tours all the time, I feel like I've always got to keep it spotless."

"Ah," he said, sliding a cutlet from the platter onto his plate, "you'd do that anyway."

"Still," she said. "You never gave tours of the farmhouse."

He shrugged. "Nobody ever wanted to look at it. It's just a house, sweetie. Nothing special about a house."

Sylvia said heatedly, "A house where we raised eight children."

"You know what I mean," he said. "Hey, good pork."

"Oh, dear," she said, "here they come again."

The dark SUV with the Illinois plates didn't proceed all the way up the drive to the campsite, but it braked to a stop just off the access road. Sylvia could see two people in the vehicle—two men, it looked like. And maybe someone smaller in the back. A girl? She glared her most unwelcoming

5

glare, she thought. It usually worked. This time, though, the motor shut off and the driver's door opened.

"At least they didn't drive in on top of us," she said.

"Good campground etiquette," Marshall said.

"But they could have waited until after our supper."

"You want me to tell them to come back later?"

"What," she said with sarcasm, "and not give them a tour?"

Marshall chuckled and reached out and patted Sylvia's hand. She shook her head.

Only the driver got out. He was older, about their age or maybe a few years younger, wearing a casual jacket and chinos. He was dark and barrel-chested, with a large head, slicked-back hair, and warm, dark eyes. He had a thick mustache and heavy jowls, and he walked up the drive rocking side-to-side a little, like a B-movie monster.

"He looks like somebody," Sylvia said. "Who am I thinking of?"

Marshall whispered, "How would I know who you're thinking of?"

"Like that dead writer. You know."

"Lots of dead writers," Marshall said. "That's the best kind, you ask me."

"Sorry to bother you," the man said affably. "I'm Dave Stenson. My friends in Chicago call me Stenko."

"Hemingway," Sylvia muttered without moving her lips. *"That's* who I mean."

"Sorry to bother you at dinnertime. Would it be better if I came back?" Stenson/Stenko said, pausing before getting too close.

Before Sylvia could say yes, Marshall said, "I'm Marshall and this is Sylvia. What can we do for you?"

"That's the biggest darned motor home I've ever seen,"

Stenko said, stepping back so he could see it all from stem to stern. "I just wanted to look at it."

Marshall smiled, and his eyes twinkled behind thick lenses. Sylvia sighed. All those years in the cab of a combine, all those years of corn, corn, corn. The last few years of ethanol mandates had been great! This was Marshall's reward.

"I'd be happy to give you a quick tour," her husband said.

"Please," Stenko said, holding up his hand palm out, "finish your dinner first."

Said Marshall, "I'm done," and pushed away from the picnic table, leaving the salad and green beans untouched.

Sylvia thought, *A life spent as a farmer but the man won't eat vegetables.*

Turning to her, Stenko asked, "I was hoping I could borrow a potato or two. I'd sure appreciate it."

She smiled, despite herself, and felt her cheeks get warm. He had good manners, this man, and those dark eyes ...

SHE WAS CLEANING up the dishes on the picnic table when Marshall and Stenko finally came out of the motor home. Marshall had done the tour of The Unit so many times, for so many people, that his speech was becoming smooth and well rehearsed. Fellow retired RV enthusiasts as well as people still moored to their jobs wanted to see what it looked like inside the behemoth vehicle: their 2009 forty-five-foot diesel-powered Fleetwood American Heritage, which Marshall simply called "The Unit." She heard phrases she'd heard dozens of times, "Forty-six thousand, six hundred pounds gross vehicle weight ... five hundred horses with a ten-point-eight-liter diesel engine ... satellite radio ... three integrated cameras for backing up ... GPS ... bedroom with queen bed, satellite television ...

washer-dryer ... wine rack and wet bar even though neither one of us drinks ..."

Now Marshall was getting to the point in his tour where, he said, "We traded a life of farming for life in The Unit. We do the circuit now."

"What's the circuit?" Stenko asked. She thought he sounded genuinely interested. Which meant he might not leave for a while.

Sylvia shot a glance toward the SUV. She wondered why the people inside didn't get out, didn't join Stenko for the tour or at least say hello. They weren't very friendly, she thought. Her sister in Wisconsin said people from Chicago were like that, as if they owned all the midwestern states and thought of Wisconsin as their own personal recreation playground and Iowa as a cornfield populated by hopeless rubes.

"It's *our* circuit," Marshall explained, "visiting our kids and grandkids in six different states, staying ahead of the snow, making sure we hit the big flea markets in Quartzsite, going to a few Fleetwood rallies where we can look at the newest models and talk to our fellow owners. We're kind of a like a club, us Fleetwood people."

Stenko said, "It's the biggest and most luxurious thing I've ever been in. It's amazing. You must really get some looks on the road."

"Thank you," Marshall said. "We spent a lifetime farming just so we ..."

"I've heard a vehicle like this can cost more than six hundred K. Now, I'm not asking you what you paid, but am I in the ballpark?"

Marshall nodded, grinned.

"What kind of gas mileage does it get?" Stenko asked.

"Runs on diesel," Marshall said.

"Whatever," Stenko said, withdrawing a small spiral

8

notebook from his jacket pocket and flipping it open.

What's he doing? Sylvia thought.

"We're getting eight to ten miles a gallon," Marshall said. "Depends on the conditions, though. The Black Hills are the first mountains we hit going west from Iowa, and the air's getting thinner. So the mileage gets worse. When we go through Wyoming and Montana—sheesh."

"Not good, eh?" Stenko said, scribbling.

Sylvia knew Marshall disliked talking about miles per gallon because it made him defensive.

"You can't look at it that way," Marshall said, "you can't look at it like it's a car or a truck. You've got to look at it as your house on wheels. You're moving your own house from place to place. Eight miles per gallon is a small price to pay for living in your own house. You save on motels and such like that."

Stenko licked his pencil and scribbled. He seemed excited. "So how many miles do you put on your ... house ... in a year?"

Marshall looked at Sylvia. She could tell he was ready for Stenko to leave.

"Sixty thousand on average," Marshall said. "Last year we did eighty."

Stenko whistled. "How many years have you been doing this circuit as you call it?"

"Five," Marshall said. "But this is the first year in The Unit."

Stenko ignored Sylvia's stony glare. "How many more years do you figure you'll be doing this?"

"That's a crazy question," she said. "It's like you're asking us when we're going to die."

Stenko chuckled, shaking his head. "I'm sorry, I'm sorry, I didn't mean it like that."

She crossed her arms and gave Marshall a *Get rid of him* look.

"You're what, sixty-five, sixty-six?" Stenko asked.

"Sixty-five," Marshall said. "Sylvia's …"

"Marshall!"

"… approximately the same age," Stenko said, finishing Marshall's thought and making another note. "So it's not crazy to say you two might be able to keep this up for another ten or so years. Maybe even more."

"More," Marshall said, "I hope."

"I've got to clean up," Sylvia said, "if you'll excuse me." She was furious at Stenko for his personal questions and at Marshall for answering them.

"Oh," Stenko said, "about those potatoes."

She paused on the step into the motor home and didn't look at Stenko when she said, "I have a couple of bakers. Will they do?"

"Perfect," Stenko said.

She turned. "Why do you need *two* potatoes? Aren't there three of you? I see two more heads out there in your car."

"Sylvia," Marshall said, "would you please just get the man a couple of spuds?"

She stomped inside and returned with two and held them out like a ritual offering. Stenko chuckled as he took them.

"I really do thank you," he said, reaching inside his jacket. "I appreciate your time and information. Ten years on the road is a long time. I envy you in ways you'll never understand."

She was puzzled now. His voice was warm and something about his tone—so sad—touched her. And was that a tear in his eye?

INSIDE THE HYBRID SUV, the fourteen year-old girl asked the man in the passenger seat, "Like *what* is he doing up there?"

The man—she knew him as Robert—was in his mid-thirties. He was handsome and he knew it with his blond hair with

10

the expensive highlights and his ice-cold green eyes and his small, sharp little nose. But he was shrill for a man his age, she thought, and had yet to be very friendly to her. Not that he'd been cruel. It was obvious, though, that he'd rather have Stenko's undivided attention. Robert said, "He told you not to watch."

"But why is he taking, like, big potatoes from them?"

"Do you really want to know?"

"Yes."

Robert turned and pierced her with those eyes. "They'll act as silencers and muffle the shots."

"The shots?" She shifted in the back seat so she could see through the windshield better between the front seats. Up the hill, Stenko had turned his back to the old couple and was jamming a big potato on the end of a long-barreled pistol. Before she could speak, Stenko wheeled and swung the weapon up and there were two coughs and the old man fell down. The potato had burst and the pieces had fallen so Stenko jammed the second one on. There were two more coughs and the woman dropped out of sight behind the picnic table.

The girl screamed and balled her fists in her mouth.

"SHUT UP!" Robert said, "For God's sake, shut up." To himself, *I knew bringing a girl along was a bad idea. I swear to God I can't figure out what goes on in that brain of his.*

She'd seen killing, but she couldn't believe what had happened. Stenko was so *nice*. Did he know the old couple? Did they say or do something that he felt he had to defend himself? A choking sob broke through.

Robert said, "He should have left you in Chicago."

SHE COULDN'T STOP crying and peeking even though Robert kept telling her to shut up and not to watch as Stenko dragged the two bodies up into the motor home. When the

11

bodies were inside Stenko closed the door. He was in there a long time before tongues of flame licked the inside of the motor home windows and Stenko jogged down the path toward the SUV.

She smelled smoke and gasoline on his clothes when he climbed into the cab and started the motor.

"Man," he said, "I hated doing that."

Robert said, "Move out quick before the fire gets out of control and somebody notices us. Keep cool, drive the speed limit all the way out of here ..."

She noticed how panicked Robert's tone was, how high his voice was. For the first time she saw that his scalp through his hair was glistening with sweat. She'd never noticed how thin his hair was and how skillfully he'd disguised it.

Stenko said, "That old couple—they were kind of sweet."

"It had to be done," Robert said quickly.

"I wish I could believe you."

Robert leaned across the console, his eyes white and wild. "Trust me, Dad. Just trust me. Did they give you the numbers?"

Stenko reached into his breast pocket and flipped the spiral notebook toward Robert. "It's all there," he said. The girl thought Stenko was angry.

Robert flipped through the pad, then drew his laptop out of the computer case near his feet. He talked as he tapped the keys. "Sixty to eighty thousand miles a year at eight to ten miles per gallon. Wow. They've been at it for five years and planned to keep it up until they couldn't. They're both sixty-five, so we could expect them to keep driving that thing for at least ten to fifteen years, maybe more." *Tap-tap-tap.*

"They were farmers from Iowa," Stenko said sadly. "Salt of the earth."

"*Salt of the earth?*" Robert said. "You mean plagues on the earth! Christ, Dad, did you see that thing they were driving?"

"They called it The Unit," Stenko said.

"Wait until I get this all calculated," Robert said. "You just took a sizable chunk out of the balance."

"I hope so," Stenko said.

"Any cash?"

"Of course. All farmers have cash on hand."

"How much?"

"Thirty-seven hundred I found in the cupboard. I have a feeling there was more, but I couldn't take the time. I could have used your help in there."

"That's not what I do."

Stenko snorted. "I *know.*"

"Thirty-seven hundred isn't very much."

"It'll keep us on the road."

"There's that," Robert said, but he didn't sound very impressed.

As they cleared the campground, the girl turned around in her seat. She could see the wink of orange flames in the alcove of pines now. Soon, the fire would engulf the motor home and one of the people in the campground would see it and call the fire department. But it would be too late to save the motor home, just as it was too late to save that poor old couple. As she stared at the motor home on fire, things from deep in her memory came rushing back and her mouth dropped open.

"I said," Stenko pressed, looking at her in the rearview mirror, "you didn't watch, did you? You promised me you wouldn't watch."

"She lied," Robert said. "You should have left her in Chicago."

13

"Damn, honey," Stenko said. "I didn't want you to watch."

But she barely heard him through the roaring in her ears. Back it came, from where it had been hiding and crouching like a night monster in a dark corner of her memory.

The burning trailer. Screams. Shots. Snow.

And a telephone number she'd memorized but that had remained buried in her mind just like all of those people were buried in the ground all these years ...

She thought: *I need to find a phone.*

2

Saddlestring, Wyoming

FIVE DAYS LATER, on a sun-fused but melancholy Sunday afternoon before the school year began again the next day, seventeen-year-old Sheridan Pickett and her thirteen-year-old sister, Lucy, rode double bareback in a grassy pasture near the home they used to live in. Their summer-blond hair shone in the melting sun, and their bare sunburned legs dangled down the sides of their old paint horse, Toby, as he slowly followed an old but well-trammeled path around the inside of the sagging three-rail fence. The ankle-high grass buzzed with insects, and grasshoppers anticipated the oncoming hooves by shooting into the air like sparks. He was a slow horse because he chose to be; he'd never agreed with the concept that he should be ridden, even if his burden was light, and considered riding to be an interruption of his real pursuits, which consisted of eating and sleeping. As he walked, he held his head low and sad and his heavy sighs were epic. When he revealed his true nature by snatching a big mouthful of grass while Sheridan's mind wandered, she pulled up on the reins and said, "Damn you, Toby!"

"He always does that," Lucy said behind her sister. "All he cares about it eating. He hasn't changed."

"He's always been a big lunkhead," Sheridan said, keeping the reins tight so he would know she was watching him this time, "but I've always kind of liked him. I missed him."

Lucy leaned forward so her cheek was against Sheridan's back. Her head was turned toward the house they used to live in before they'd moved eight miles into the town of Saddlestring a year before.

Sheridan looked around. The place hadn't changed much. The gravel road paralleled the fence. Farther, beyond the road, the landscape dipped into a willow-choked saddle where the Twelve Sleep River branched out into six fingers clogged with beaver ponds and brackish mosquito-heaven eddies and paused for a breath before its muscular rush through and past the town of Saddlestring. Beyond were the folds of the valley as it arched and suddenly climbed to form a precipitous mountain-face known as Wolf Mountain in the Twelve Sleep Range.

"I never thought I'd say I missed this place," Lucy said.

"But you do," Sheridan finished.

"No, not really," Lucy giggled.

"You drive me crazy."

"What can I say?" Lucy said. "I like people around. I like being able to ride my bike to school and not take that horrible bus."

"You're a *townie*."

"What's wrong with that?"

"Townie's are ... common. Everybody's a townie. There's nothing special about it."

Lucy affected a snooty, Valley Girl inflection: "Yeah, I'm like, *common*. I should want to still live out here so I can

16

curse at horses, like you. You're the weird one, Sheridan. I keep telling you that but you don't believe me." She flicked a grasshopper off her wrist. "And I don't constantly have *bugs* landing on me."

"Stop talking, Lucy."

Lucy sighed, mimicking Toby. "How long do you think Mom is going to be in there?"

"A long time, I hope," Sheridan said.

Marybeth Pickett, Sheridan and Lucy's mother, had brought them both out to their old house on the Bighorn Road. Their mom owned a business-consulting firm, and she was meeting with Mrs. Kiner, who was starting a bath and body products company using honey or wax or something. Phil Kiner was the game warden of the Saddlestring District, the district their dad used to manage. Because of that, the Kiners took over the state-owned home that was once occupied by the Picketts when the family moved to their Grandmother Missy's ranch for a year, and then to town to a home of their own. Toby had been one of their horses growing up, and when Sheridan saw him standing lazily in the corral, she'd asked if she could ride him around until their mother was done. Lucy tagged along simply because she didn't want to wait inside and listen to business talk.

"I'm getting hungry," Lucy said.

"You're always hungry," Sheridan said. "You're like Toby. You're like his lazy *spawn*."

"Now you shut up," Lucy said.

"*Lucy Pickett,*" Sheridan said in an arena announcer's cadence, "*Lazy Hungry Spawn of Toby!* I like the sound of that."

In response, Lucy leaned forward and locked her hands together under Sheridan's breasts and squeezed her sister's ribs as hard as she could. "I'll crush you," Lucy said.

"You wish," Sheridan laughed.

17

They rode in silence for a moment after Lucy gave up trying to crush Sheridan.

Lucy said, "I miss Dad. I miss his pancakes on Sunday morning."

Sheridan said, "Me, too."

"What's going to happen? Is he ever moving back? Are we moving where he is now?"

Sheridan glanced at the house where her mother was and shrugged, "Who knows? He says he's in exile."

"It sucks."

"Yeah."

"It sucks big-time."

"Mmmm."

"It sucks the big one."

"Okay, Lucy, I got it."

"Ooooh," Lucy said, "I see your boyfriend. I knew he was going to come out and stare at you."

"Stop it."

Jason Kiner, like Sheridan, was set to be a junior at Saddlestring High School. He'd come home from football practice a half hour before in his ancient pickup. He was tall, dull-eyed, and wide-shouldered with shaved temples and a shock of black hair on top, something all the players had done to show their solidarity to ... whatever. He had seen Sheridan and Lucy when he drove up but pretended he hadn't. Playing it cool, Sheridan thought, a trait in boys her age she found particularly annoying. He'd parked near the detached garage, slung his gym bag over his shoulder, and gone into the house.

He emerged now wearing a Saddlestring Wranglers gray hoodie, clean jeans, and white Nikes. He'd spiked his hair. Jason ambled toward the girls in a self-conscious, half-comatose saunter. Waved at them, nonchalant, and leaned forward on the fence with his forearms on the top rail and a Nike on the bottom rail. Trying to make an entrance of sorts, Sheridan thought. They were riding the horse toward the corner of the corral where Jason was waiting. It would be a minute before they'd be upon him.

"There he is," Lucy whispered.

"I see him. So what?"

"Jason Kiner *looooves* you."

"Shut up. He does not."

"I've looked at his MySpace page and his Facebook page," she whispered. "He *looooves* you."

"Stop it."

"Look at him," Lucy whispered, giggling. "There's *loooove* in his eyes."

With the arm Jason couldn't see, Sheridan elbowed her sister in the ribs, and Lucy laughed, "You've gotta do better than that."

When Toby sleepwalked to Jason, Sheridan said, "Hi there."

"How are you guys doing?" Jason said. "I didn't see you when I drove up."

"You didn't?" Lucy asked, mock serious.

Sheridan gritted her teeth and shot a look over her shoulder at her sister, who looked back with her best innocent and charming face.

"It's been a long time since I rode," Sheridan said. "We asked your mom."

Jason shrugged. "Nobody ever rides him anymore, so you might as well. I've been thinking about saddling him up, but with football practice and all ..."

And the conversation went completely and unexpectedly dead. Sheridan could hear the insects buzz in the grass. She could feel Lucy prodding her to say something.

Finally, Jason's face lit up with purpose. "Hey—did that chick call you?"

"What chick?"

"She called here a few days ago for you. She still had this number from when you lived here, I guess. I gave her your cellphone number."

Lucy purred into Sheridan's ear, *"He has your cellphone number?"*

Sheridan ignored her. "Nobody called. Who was it?"

"I didn't know her," Jason said, "She said she used to live here and still had the number for the house."

"What was her name?"

Jason screwed up his mouth and frowned. "She said it, but I can't remember for sure. It was a few days ago. Oh—I remember now. She said something like, 'April.'"

Sheridan dropped the reins in to the grass. *"What?"*

Jason shrugged. "She said something like, 'I wonder if she remembers a girl named April.' Anyway, I gave her your number and ..."

Lucy said to Sheridan, "Did he say what I thought he said?"

Sheridan leaned forward and felt Lucy grip her hard to keep her balance. "Jason, this isn't very funny."

"Who's trying to be funny?"

"If you are," Sheridan said, "I'll kill you."

Jason stepped back and dropped his arms to his sides as if preparing to be rushed by the two girls. "What's going on? What's wrong with you two? You're acting like you see a ghost or something."

Sheridan pointed toward the yard in front of the house but had trouble speaking. Jason turned to where she gestured.

The three Austrian pine trees their dad had planted so long ago in the front yard had all now grown until the tops were level with the gutter of the house. At the time they'd been planted, he'd joked that they were Sheridan's Tree, April's Tree, and Lucy's Tree.

"April was our sister," Sheridan said, pointing at the middle one. "She was killed six years ago."

The door of the house opened, and their mother came out. Sheridan noted how Jason looked over his shoulder at her in a way that in other circumstances would have made her proud and angry at the same time. But now her mother looked stricken. There was no doubt in Sheridan's mind that Jason's mom had just mentioned the call they'd received.

3

Baggs, Wyoming

Wyoming game warden Joe Pickett, his right arm and uniform shirt slick with his own blood, slowed his green Ford pickup as he approached a blind corner on the narrow two-track that paralleled the Little Snake River. It was approaching dusk, and buttery shafts filtered through the trees on the rim of the river canyon and lit up the floor in a pattern resembling jail bars. The river itself, which had been roaring with runoff in the spring and early summer, was now little more than a series of rock-rimmed pools of pocket water connected by an anemic trickle. He couldn't help notice, though, that brook trout were rising in the pools, feverishly slurping at tiny fallen Trico bugs like drunks at last call.

There was a mature female bald eagle in the bed of his pickup bound up tight in a Wyoming Cowboys sweatshirt, and the bird didn't like that he'd slowed down. Her hair-raising screech scared him and made him involuntarily jerk on the wheel.

"Okay," he said, glancing into his rearview mirror at the eagle, which stared back at him with murderous, needle-sharp eyes that made his skin creep. "You've done enough damage already. What—you want me to crash into the river, too?"

He eased his way around the blind corner, encountered no one, and sped up. The road was so narrow—with the river on one side and the canyon wall on the other—that if he had to share it with an oncoming vehicle, they'd both have to maneuver for a place to pull over in order to pass. Instead, he shared the road with a doe mule deer and her fawn that had come down from a cut in the wall for water. Both deer ran ahead of him on the road, looking nervously over their shoulders, until another screech from the eagle sent them bounding through the river and up the other side.

Another blind corner, but this time when he eased around it, he came face-to-face with a pickup parked in the center of the two-track. The vehicle was a jacked-up 2008 Dodge Ram 4x4, Oklahoma plates, the grille a sneering grimace. And no one in the cab. He braked and scanned the river for a fisherman—nope—then up the canyon wall on his right for the driver. No one.

He knew instinctively, *Something is going to happen here.*

THE CALL THAT brought him to this place on this road in this canyon had come via dispatch in Cheyenne just after noon: hikers had reported an injured bald eagle angrily hopping around in a remote campsite far up the canyon, "scaring the bejesus out of everyone." They reported the eagle had an arrow sticking out of it. It was the kind of call that made him wince and made him angry.

Months before, Joe had been assigned to the remote Baggs District in extreme south-central Wyoming. The district (known within the department as either "The Place Where Game Wardens Are Sent to Die" or "Warden Graveyard") was hard against the Colorado border and encompassed the Sierra

24

Madre Mountains, the Little Snake River Valley, dozens of third- and fourth-generation ranches surrounded by a bustling coal-bed methane boom and an influx of energy workers, and long distances to just about anywhere. The nearest town with more than five hundred people was Craig, Colorado, thirty-six miles to the south. The governor had his reasons for making the assignment: to hide him away until the heat and publicity of the events from the previous fall died down. Joe understood Governor Rulon's thinking. After all, even though he'd solved the rash of murders involving hunters across the state of Wyoming, he'd also permitted the unauthorized release of a federal prisoner—Nate Romanowski—as well as committing a shameful act that haunted him still.

Joe had called a few times and sent several e-mails to the governor asking when he could go back to Saddlestring. There had been no response. While Joe felt abandoned, he felt bad that his actions had damaged the governor.

And the governor had enough problems of his own these days to concern himself with Joe's plight. Although he was still the most popular politician in the state despite his mercurial nature and eccentricity, there had been a rumor of scandal about a relationship with Stella Ennis, the governor's chief of staff. The governor denied the rumors angrily and Stella resigned, but it had been a second chink in his armor, and Rulon's enemies—he had them on both sides of the aisle—saw an opening and moved in like wolves on a hamstrung bull moose. Soon, there were innuendos about his fast-and-loose use of state employees, including Joe, even financial questions about the pistol shooting range Rulon had installed behind the governor's mansion to settle political disputes. Joe had no doubt—knowing the governor—that Rulon would emerge victorious. But in the meanwhile, he'd be embattled and distracted.

And Joe would be in exile of sorts. He felt the familiar pang of moral guilt that had visited him more and more the last few years for some of the decisions he'd made and some of the things he'd done that had landed him here. Although he wasn't sure he wouldn't have made the same decisions if he had the opportunity to make them again, the fact was he'd committed acts he was deeply ashamed of and would always be ashamed of. The last moments of J. W. Keeley and Randy Pope, when he'd acted against his nature and concluded that given the situations, the ends justified the means, would forever be with him. Joe's friend Nate Romanowski, the fugitive falconer, had always maintained that often there was a difference between justice and the law, and Joe had always disagreed with the sentiment. He still did. But he'd crossed lines he never thought he'd cross, and he vowed not to do it again. Although he owned the transgressions he'd committed and they would never go away, he'd resolved that the only way to mitigate them was to stay on the straight and narrow, do good works, and not let his dark impulses assert themselves again.

Being in exile could either push a man over the precipice or help a man sort things out, he'd concluded.

DESPITE THE REMOTE location, his lack of familiarity with the new district, and pangs of loneliness, the assignment reminded him how much he loved being a game warden again, *really being a game warden*. It was what he was born to do. It's what gave him joy, purpose, and a connection to the earth, the sky, God, and his environment. It made him whole. But he wished he could resume his career without the dark cloud that had followed him once the governor had chosen to make Joe his go-to guy. He wished he could return home every night to Marybeth, Sheridan, and Lucy,

26

who'd remained in Saddlestring because of Marybeth's business and the home they owned. Every day, he checked his e-mail and phone messages for word from the governor's office in Cheyenne that he could return. So far, it hadn't come.

Life and work in his new district was isolated, slow, and incredibly dull.

Until the Mad Archer arrived, anyway.

By Joe's count, the Mad Archer had killed four elk (two cows and two bulls whose antlers had been hacked off) and wounded three others he had to put down. He could only guess at the additional wounded who'd escaped into the timber and suffered and died alone. It was the same with the two deer and several pronghorn antelope off the highway between the towns of Dixon and Savery, all killed by arrows.

Then there was the dog—a goofy Lab-Corgi hybrid with a Lab body and a Lab *I love everybody please throw me a stick* disposition tacked on to the haughty arrogance of a corgi and a corgi's four-inch stunted legs—who'd suddenly appeared on the doorstep of Joe's game warden home. He fed him and let him sleep in the mudroom while he asked around town about his owner. Joe's conclusion was he'd been dumped by a passing tourist or an energy worker who moved on to a new job. So when the dog was shot through the neck with an arrow outside an ancient cement-block bar once frequented by Butch Cassidy himself, Joe was enraged and convinced the Mad Archer was not only a local but a sick man who should be put down himself if he ever caught him.

The dog—Joe named him "Tube"—was recovering at home after undergoing $3,500 worth of surgery. The money was their savings for a family vacation. Would the state reimburse him if he made the argument that Tube was evidence? He doubted it. What he didn't doubt was that Sheridan and Lucy would grow as attached to the dog as he had. All Tube had going for him was his personality, Joe thought. He was good for nothing else. Was Tube worth the family vacation? That was a question he couldn't answer.

Of course, the best Joe could do within his powers if he caught the Mad Archer would be to charge him with multiple counts of wanton destruction—with fines up to $10,000 for each count—and possibly get the poacher's vehicle and weapons confiscated. Joe was always frustrated at how little he could legally do to game violators. There was some compensation in the fact that citizens in Wyoming and the mountain west were generally as enraged as he was at indiscriminate cruelty against animals. If he caught the man and proved his guilt before a judge, he knew the citizens of Baggs would shun the man and turn him into a pariah, maybe even run him out of the state for good. Still, he'd rather send the criminal to prison.

For the past month, Joe had poured his time and effort into catching the Mad Archer. He'd perched all night near hay meadows popular as elk and deer feeding spots. He'd haunted sporting goods shops asking about purchases of arrows and gone to gas stations asking about suspicious drivers who might have had bows in their pickups in the middle of summer. He'd acquired enough physical evidence to nail the Archer if he could ever catch him in the vicinity of a crime. There were the particular brand of arrows—Beman ICS Hunters tipped with Magnus 2-blade broadheads—partial fingerprints from the shaft of the arrows removed from an elk and Tube, a tire-track impression he'd cast in plaster at the scene of a deer killing, a

28

sample of radiator fluid he'd gathered from a spill on the side of the road near the dead pronghorn, and some transmission fluid of particular viscosity he'd sent to the lab to determine any unique qualities. But he had no real leads on the Mad Archer himself, or even an anonymous tip with a name attached called into the 800-number poacher hotline.

Many of his nightly conversations with Marybeth took place in the dark in the cab of his pickup, overseeing a moon-splashed hay meadow framed by the dark mountain horizon.

JUDGING BY THE call from dispatch earlier, Joe immediately assumed the Mad Archer was at it again, and this time he'd claimed a bald eagle. Although bald eagles had finally been taken off the endangered species list the year before, it was still a crime to harm them. Plus, he liked eagles and it made him mad. So when the call came he checked the loads in the magazine of his Glock and chambered a round, moved his shotgun from behind the bench seat to the front, jammed his weathered gray Stetson on his head, and rushed up the canyon on the two-track, hoping the crime had taken place recently enough that there would be a possibility of encountering the criminal in the vicinity. Since there was only one main road from the valley floor to the campground where the hikers had called in the wounded eagle, he thought he might have a chance.

HE'D FOUND THE bald eagle as described. The hikers—who'd asked a seasonal forest service employee to call it in once the worker cleared the walled canyon—milled about helplessly while the big eagle stood between them and their Subaru with Colorado plates (an inordinate number of complaints were called in by people with Subarus and Colorado plates). The eagle had her wings outstretched an imposing seven and a half feet. Her talons gripped the soft dirt parking lot like a scoop shovel biting through asphalt. Her screech was shrill, chilling, ungodly, as if intended to scare pine-cones out of the trees. Her eyes were as dark, intense, and piercing as hell itself, he thought. He couldn't lock eyes with her more than a few seconds before breaking the gaze.

There were three hikers, two men and a woman. College age, good equipment, scruffy half-beards on the men, the woman a brunette with her hair tied in a ponytail. They told him they'd spent three nights and four days hiking the trails and high-country lakes near Bridger Peak in the Sierra Madres.

The woman told Joe, "We're tired, dirty, and hungry and we need to get out of here. We have a dinner reservation tonight in Steamboat Springs. At the rate we're going, we're going to be late."

"Oh dear," Joe said.

"I'm serious," she said, miffed.

"Did you see anyone in the area other than the forest service guy? Any other hikers or vehicles?"

They all shook their heads no. *Damn.*

The eagle was big, Joe noted, probably fifteen pounds. Females were larger than males. The yellow arrow shaft went cleanly through her right wing and was lodged half-in, half-out, the familiar razor-tipped broadhead winking in the sun. He guessed by looking at the way she held the wounded wing that tendons had been sliced so she couldn't get lift. She'd probably been ambushed while on the ground, he thought, likely surprised while feeding on a fish or roadkill.

As he stood there looking at the eagle with the hikers

gathered behind him, admonishing him not to hurt the bird but to get her out of the way so they could get to their car, he felt a particular kind of bitterness he couldn't give away to them. He knew he was probably looking at a dead bird.

Although there were several rehabilitation centers for raptors and birds of prey, the more reputable of the two being near Sheridan and Boise, there had been a recent departmental memo saying both facilities were filled to capacity. They could take no more birds, no matter the circumstances. Damaged eagles, falcons, and hawks would have to be placed privately or destroyed. Since Joe was in exile of sorts and five hours away from the nearest facility anyway, he knew what the likely conclusion would be. But he didn't dare tell the hikers. So on the spot, he came up with a scheme: tackle the eagle, bind her wings to her body with his spare sweat-shirt, tape it tight, and transport her out of there. To where he would determine later.

The hikers agreed to form a human shield to the side of the eagle and draw her attention (and vitriol) while Joe swooped in from behind her. It worked, except for the part where she slashed down with her hooked beak and ripped a gash the length of his forearm. Spurting blood and holding her wings tight to her body, he managed to slide the arrow out of her wing, slip the sweatshirt over her head, tie the sleeves together around her like a straitjacket, and finish the job with duct tape. Her screech seemed to reach down inside him and tug at primeval fears he didn't even know he had, but he fought through them out of pure terror and eventually gained control of her thrashing body and sharp talons, wrapping the sweatshirt around her with a continuous strip of tape. Finally, as the hikers stepped away, he had her under control except for her screeching, and he picked her up and carried her to his truck. She was surprisingly light with her wings taped tightly to her side, and it reminded him of carrying one of his daughters as babies. It seemed a shame, he thought, to reduce this beautiful and regal creature to a shiny silver papoose. She seemed cowed and harmless—except for the talons, of course.

He used bungee cords to lash her upright to the inside sidewall of his pickup bed. She looked like an insurgent caught in the act and awaiting interrogation, he thought. He avoided looking into her murderous eyes, which pierced him through the curtain of his peripheral vision.

The hikers thanked him and left in time to make their dinner reservation. He watched their taillights recede down the gravel road through the dust kicked up from their tires that hung in clouds and slowly sifted back down to earth. Their problem was now his problem, and they could tell their friends they'd helped save a bald eagle.

Joe stood in the campground bloodied and breathing hard, unable to raise dispatch or get a cell signal because of the height of the canyon walls.

While he bound his bleeding forearm with a compress and medical tape from the oft-used first-aid kit in his pickup, he looked at the eagle and asked, "What am I going to do with you?"

JOE THOUGHT THERE might be enough room on the canyon-wall side of the pickup to get around the driverless pickup with the Oklahoma plates in the middle of the road, but he knew it would be close. The side mirrors of both trucks would likely hit each other if he tried to squeeze through.

Sighing, he put his vehicle into park, got out, and bent both of his mirrors in on their hinges.

"Hey!" he called. "Would you mind moving your truck?"

His words echoed back over the tinkling of the river. Clouds of caddis flies smoked up the river. An aggressive trout smacked the surface of a pocket-water pool to get one.

To be safe, he decided to bend the mirrors of the Dodge in as well so he could pass. It was never a good idea to touch another man's vehicle, but he was sure the missing driver would understand.

As he pushed the driver's side mirror in, he glanced inside the cab and saw a half-empty twelve-pack of beer, binoculars, a pint of tequila, torn empty packages for AA batteries, and a quiver of Beman arrows between the bench seats.

Joe backed away and instinctively rested his right hand on the butt of his .40 Glock semi-auto. His senses sharpened, and he felt his heart beat faster. The rush of blood hurt the gash on his forearm, and dark red blood beaded on the side of the compress. He looked back inside the cab. No keys. He placed his palm on the hood of the truck. It was warm, as if the engine had been running just a moment before. Squatting, he looked underneath the pickup. Two drops of transmission fluid in the dirt and a pink bead of it poised to fall from a black rubber hose. A glance at the tires didn't conclusively confirm the tread was the same as his plaster cast, but it was similar enough. And near the rear tires on both sides, in the loose grit of the road, were two sets of footprints headed down the road in the direction the Dodge had been coming.

He stood.

Flicking his eyes from the river to the canyon wall to the two-track behind the Dodge where the missing driver might walk up, he stepped backward until he was adjacent to the open driver's window of his pickup. He reached in and plucked the mike from its cradle.

"Dispatch, this is GF-fifty-four."

Static.

"Dispatch, this is GF-fifty-four."

Nothing.

"Can anyone hear me?"

No. Still too deep in the canyon for a signal.

Joe withdrew his cellphone from the breast pocket of his red uniform shirt. No bars.

He guessed the scenario: The Mad Archer and his accomplice were coming up the two-track when they either saw or heard Joe's pickup coming down the same road from the campground. Maybe the eagle screech alerted them. Since there was nowhere to turn around and driving the Dodge in reverse around the blind corners was impractical, they'd simply bailed out and run. Since it was approaching dusk, no doubt they hoped Joe would simply pass by their vehicle en route to town. When he passed, they'd come out from where they were hiding.

He ran through his options. None were very good.

Joe thought about the empty packages of AA batteries. And he smiled to himself.

HE GAVE THEM fifteen minutes to show up. They didn't, which didn't surprise him. The shadows within the canyon grew long and dark and the breeze stilled and the temperature dropped twenty degrees. The wounded eagle grew impatient and screamed. Every time she screeched, he flinched and the hair on the back of his neck bristled.

He had the feeling he was being watched, but he couldn't see who was watching him, or from where.

He made a show of checking his wristwatch. Then, with the slumped shoulders of a man who'd just given up waiting, he climbed into his pickup with the pronghorn antelope decals on the door, gunned the engine, and drove

34

slowly forward.

He made it past the Dodge with six inches of clearance to spare, although heavy brush clawed the passenger door and scratched at the window. Back on the road, he turned his headlights on and drove slowly, looking carefully—but not too obviously—from side to side for a flash of color or the dark form of a hidden man. The two-track rose to a crest, and once he dropped over the top, he could no longer see the Dodge in his rearview mirror. The river was less languid on the bottom of the hill, and rallied from its late-summer doldrums into a stretch of fast water that picked up in volume until, spent, it spilled over a small falls into a deep pool. When the rush of water overcame the sound of his motor, he let the pickup coast to a stop and he turned the lights out. There was a narrow meadow to his right—a break in the canyon wall—which he drove into and did a three-point turn in the dark so he was pointed back the way he had come.

Joe kept a small duffel bag of spare clothes in the lockbox in the bed of his pickup and he dug through it until he found a pair of socks.

"Sorry," he whispered, as he slipped one of the socks over the head of the eagle. He'd learned from his friend Nate, who was a master falconer, that raptors went into a state of quiet when their heads were covered by a falcon hood. He hoped the sock would serve the same purpose.

Back in the cab of his pickup, Joe turned on a small radio receiver under the dashboard and waited.

In recent years, the use of handheld two-way radios—mostly manufactured by Motorola—had become standard equipment for hunters, fishermen, and hikers. The radios worked well within a two-to-five-mile range and operated on commercial channels. They were powered by AA batteries. The receiver under Joe's dashboard was designed to scan those commercial channels.

It didn't take long.

"Is that asshole finally gone, Brad?"

"He's gone."

Joe noted the thick Okie accents—he'd heard a lot of them lately in the area.

"Are you sure?"

Brad said, "He's long gone. I seen his truck go over that hill a while back and now I can't even hear it."

"Let's give it ten minutes anyway. If you see his lights or hear anything, shout."

"You bet, Ron. But you know I gotta get back. I'm so god-damned late now Barb's gonna kill me." A little bit of panic in Brad's voice, Joe thought.

"She'll live," Ron said.

"Yeah, she'll live. But she'll make my life a living hell. She's probably throwin' my clothes out into the yard right now."

"Heh-heh," Ron laughed. Then, "What was he doing down there all that time? That game warden?"

"I don't know. But you can bet he got your plate number and he'll know who you are."

"He can't prove nothing, though. All we gotta say is the truck stalled and we walked out trying to get help. That's our story, and we're stickin' to it."

"Yeah." Cautious.

"We're okay." Arrogant. "He can't prove nothin'."

"Yeah." Unsure.

"'Cause he's an asshole," Ron said.

"Yeah," Brad said.

Joe thought, *Ron is the Mad Archer. Brad is his buddy along for the ride. Brad will turn on Ron. Ron is toast.*

Joe felt strangely disappointed. For a month he'd tracked the man, studied his crimes, gathered evidence. In the back of his mind, he supposed he'd built Ron into something he was not. Ron was just a stupid redneck poacher with too much time, too much money, and too many arrows.

WHEN JOE BATHED them with the beam of his Maglite, Ron was reaching for his door handle with one hand while gripping the compound bow with the other. Brad was urinating on the road. Both were wearing full camo and face paint. They were in their early thirties, thick and hairy. Energy workers. Empty beer cans and energy drink containers littered the bed of the pickup.

"Hello, boys," Joe said, the Glock lying alongside the barrel of the flashlight.

Ron and Brad looked nervous and scared. Joe was, too, but he feigned confidence. He knew the blinding beam of his flashlight was his best defense if either of them decided to go for a weapon. He could see them clearly, and all they could see of him was the intense white light.

"Drop that bow," Joe said to Ron. "Toss it into the back of your pickup. The arrows, too."

Ron did. The arrows clattered in the bed of his truck.

"Both of you, up against the truck, legs spread."

"He did it all!" Brad shouted suddenly, reaching for the sky, his spray going everywhere.

"Shut the fuck up, Brad," Ron hissed.

"I never shot once," Brad said, "not a single damn time. I was just along for the ride."

"Would you *shut up*!" Ron said, shaking his head. "Jesus Christ."

"Up against the truck, fellows," Joe said. To Brad, "Zip up first." To Ron, "I'm kind of hoping you make a stupid move since you're the guy who shot my dog."

Ron turned quickly and assumed the position as if he'd

done it before.

"That dog was the worst thing Ron done," Brad said, also turning around.

Ron sighed, "That dog ain't good for nothing."

Joe jammed the muzzle of the Glock into Ron's ear hard enough to make him wince. "And you are?" he asked.

JOE FOUND A .357 Magnum revolver under the pickup seat, but neither Ron nor Brad was armed. There was also a baggie containing two vials of crystal meth. He said to Ron, "I'll stay right on your bumper all the way into town. Don't even think about running. I've caught you boys cold and there aren't enough roads around here to get away on."

"You mean I've got to drive my own self into town to get arrested?"

Joe nodded. "Either that, or I cuff you and throw you in the back of my truck with that eagle you shot."

"Can I ride in with you?" Brad asked Joe.

"Sure you can, Brad," Joe said. To Ron, "Lead on, Mad Archer."

BRAD TEARFULLY CONFESSED into Joe's microcassette while Joe drove toward' Baggs and Ron followed. Every crime had been committed by Ron Connelly, Brad said.

"Why'd he do it?" Joe asked.

"Ron claimed at first he was tuning up for archery season, but things got plumb out of hand. The problem is Ron is as horny as a three-peckered owl. There's plenty of natural gas but there are no women here, you know. I got Barb, and she's no treat, but Ron … Ron is a mess."

"Ah," Joe said. His hands were still shaking from adrenaline, but he hoped Brad couldn't see them in the dark.

"Ron did it all. Every one. Ron should be in prison," Brad

said.

"Don't worry," Joe said, "I'll do my best," knowing jail time was unlikely for the game violations but the meth might be the ticket.

"Good," Brad said.

After a few miles, Brad said, "Jesus, you're that game warden, aren't you? The one from up north?"

Joe didn't respond.

"I heard about you," Brad said.

When Joe cleared the mouth of the canyon in the dark, he heard his radio suddenly gush with voices. He was back in range. At the same time, the cellphone in his pocket burred with vibration.

He took it out, flipped it open.

Three missed calls from Marybeth.

Uh-oh.

4

IN THE THREE hours it took to get the poachers booked and processed into the tiny Baggs jail, the word got out within the community that the Mad Archer was in custody. As Joe hoped, the deputy sheriff added drug charges to Joe's list of game violations, and a quick search of Ron Connelly's history via the National Crime Information Center (NCIC) database showed outstanding warrants from Texas for additional drug-related charges and non-payment of child support. In Joe's experience as a game warden, the bad ones rarely *just* committed game violations. Behind the violation was usually a pattern of serious offenses in other fields. Ron Connelly, the Mad Archer, was a perfect example of the theory. Ron's pal Brad, however, was clean except for a seven-year-old possession charge that had been pled out.

The deputy, a young former Iraq War vet named Rich Brokaw, was new to the job but had the weary old eyes of someone who'd seen things far beyond whatever life in Baggs could bring him. He said to Brad, "You're free to go, but don't even think of missing your court date."

Brad refused to move. He, like Joe, had been noting the number of vehicles gathering outside on the street in front of the jail in the past twenty minutes. He, like Joe, could hear the rumble of men's voices out on the sidewalk and the occasional shout. Apparently, the bars had emptied and the patrons were right outside wanting a piece of the Mad Archer and his accomplice. The new county building, financed with energy money, was under construction across the street. So the jail was located in a temporary modular unit on an empty lot. The modular was cheap and the walls quivered in strong wind. There was a single jail cell inside, open to the deputy's office. The setup reminded Joe of the friendly small-town set for *The Andy Griffith Show.* If the men gathering outside stormed the door, they could be inside in seconds.

"If it's all right with you guys," Brad said, "I'll spend the night in here."

"Pussy," Connelly jeered. "Assclown."

"It's like a damn cowboy movie," Brad said to Joe, pretending he didn't hear Ron. "The mob out there, Jesus. I wouldn't be surprised if they come back with torches and pitchforks and shit."

Joe said, "Neither would I."

"Maybe we can sneak you out the back," the deputy told Brad.

"No way," Brad said, shaking his head. "I ain't leaving tonight. If you want, I'll pay you to stay here. There's got to be a cost for staying the night, right? I'll cover it so the taxpayers don't have to."

Brokaw looked at Joe and smiled, then went back to filling out the paperwork for Ron Connelly. Joe still clutched his cellphone. Three calls were akin to a home-front three-alarm fire, but when he'd tried to connect from the pickup, their home phone was busy. He'd left a message saying he had a man in custody and would call the second he had a moment of privacy. Marybeth knew the drill. He hoped that moment came soon, because he could feel his stomach start to roil. There were so many scenarios he could imagine involving Sheridan, Lucy, Marybeth, his crazy mother-in-law, Missy. Maybe his friend Nate had been apprehended by the FBI?

Someone pounded hard on the front door of the modular building, shaking the walls. Ron Connelly stared at the door, tried to act calm, but failed in his attempt. His hands gripped the bars of the jail door as if to milk them. Brad squirmed in a hardback chair as if he needed a bathroom.

Joe said, "If you guys would have shot somebody or robbed a bank or something minor like that, it would be calm out there. But you killed some nice game animals out of season and you shot that dog. So as far as those people out there go, it's personal."

Ron Connelly nervously raked his fingers through his long hair and chinned toward Joe and the deputy. "Those rednecks out there want blood and there's just the two of you between them and us."

"Yup," Joe said. "And if it were up to me, I'd step aside."

Ron's face twitched. He didn't know if Joe was kidding or not. Joe didn't, either. He disliked Connelly more every minute he was exposed to him. What kind of man shot an eagle on the ground? Or Tube?

"I'll up my offer to stay here tonight," Brad said.

Brokaw finished the page he was working on, looked to Joe, said, *"Okay. Let 'em in."*

Ron Connelly ran in terror to the back of the cell. Brad shrieked.

"Just kidding," the deputy said, standing up and stifling a smile. "I'll go outside and talk to 'em."

Joe watched with admiration as the deputy stepped outside with a shotgun and told everyone to calm down and go home. When a man shouted that the Mad Archer should be released to them, the deputy racked the pump on his shotgun, said, "Go ahead, boys, I got nothing to lose. I don't like this job much, anyhow."

The crowd dispersed, and the deputy came back in and sighed *"Whew"* to Joe.

"Impressive," Joe said.

"I learned in Basra that there is no sound in nature that makes men move along faster than the pumping of a shotgun. Except maybe a chainsaw, but we won't go there."

SIMULTANEOUS WITH THE snap of the jail door on Ron and Brad, Joe opened his phone and speed-dialed Marybeth.

She was anxious. Someone claiming to be April had called their old house.

It took a moment to register. His stomach did a half-turn. Ron, Brad, the deputy, Baggs all faded from his consciousness. "Is this a sick joke?"

"I wish I could say for sure."

"Impossible," Joe said.

"Of course it's impossible," she said. But there was a hesitation—an opening he could sense that maybe she thought it *wasn't* impossible.

"We paid for her funeral. We were *at* her funeral."

"There was never an autopsy."

"There was no need. I *saw* her, Marybeth," Joe said. "She was there."

"You saw her before. You didn't see her after. None of us did."

"Impossible," he said again.

"All I can say is someone called our old house and asked to speak to Sheridan and Lucy. And whoever called identified herself as April and now has Sheridan's cellphone number."

44

"This is the sickest joke anyone's ever played on us."

"It's depraved," she said. "But Jason said the girl asked for 'Sherry.' No one has ever called Sheridan that except Lucy and April."

He waited a moment, said, "Tell Sheridan not to shut her phone off tonight."

"She's a teenager, Joe. She never shuts off her phone."

He tapped out an e-mail to his district supervisor advising him of his decision to take immediate personal time, knowing it wouldn't be received until the next day when he was already gone. Being the governor's unofficial point man had its privileges. He snapped the phone shut.

The deputy was looking at him. "You okay?"

"Not really."

"Did somebody die?"

Joe said, "Just the opposite."

HE DROVE NORTH on lonely state highway 789, where his headlights illuminated sudden herds of mule deer and pronghorn antelope along the road. The adrenaline rush that had surged through him during the arrest and arraignment of the Mad Archer was starting to wear off and a small headache, like a marble-sized ball of black, formed behind his right eye. Wildlife was everywhere, and they all seemed to be restless, on the move, as if anticipating the full-fledged hunting season in two weeks. He had to slow down and stay alert. The night sky was clear and missing a moon and the only lights for the first fifty-one miles were the vertical twinkles from distant natural gas wells. Tube was in the front seat with his head on Joe's lap, where he dreamed and drooled. The eagle was still lashed to the inside wall of his pickup bed with the sock on her head. He felt like he was piloting a traveling freak show in search of rubes who would pay admission.

Maxine, his Labrador who had once been scared white by something she saw in the timber, had passed on the previous winter. Her passing had been traumatic but also a relief of sorts because the old girl went deaf and blind in a remarkable hurry and suffered briefly from the liver condition that took her life. He'd buried her in a howling windstorm in the breaklands she loved, with Sheridan reading a eulogy that was whipped away by the gale. Her loss left a hole in their family that would likely never be filled. Tube might ease some of the pain, he hoped. If nothing else, it was impossible to look at the dog and not smile.

ON THE LONG top-of-the-world drive over the Shirley Mountains in darkness so complete that at times he felt he was in an outdoor tunnel, Joe recalled the incidents of six years before, where they'd lost April in the snow on Battle Mountain.

The Keeley family of Mississippi had played a significant and tragic role in Joe and Marybeth's lives. Ote Keeley, the outfitter father, had turned up dead on Joe's woodpile ten years before. Joe had interviewed his wife, Jeannie, as part of the investigation, and while he was talking with her was the first time he saw April, who was dirty, sick, poorly clothed, and six years old at the time. When Jeannie abandoned April, Marybeth swooped in and took the girl in as their foster daughter. She was nine years old and halfway through third grade at Saddlestring Elementary when Jeannie returned to the valley with the Sovereigns and took her back with a legal maneuver. The Sovereigns were a motley collection of Montana Freemen, survivalists, and conspiracy theorists lead by an old bear of a man named Wade Brockius who chose the Bighorns to establish a mountain outpost during the worst winter of recent memory and make their stand. Although the Sovereigns had really broken no laws other than overstaying their campground permit, a rogue Forest Service district supervisor named Melinda Strickland, with assistance from overeager FBI, BATF, and local police, surrounded the Sovereign camp and forced the issue.

The memories were still painfully fresh because they'd never faded very far beneath the surface, and they came back and he was there again ...

He had been slumped against the outside of the command Sno-cat, but he now stood up. He rubbed his face hard. He didn't know the procedure for a hostage situation—they didn't teach that to game wardens—but he knew this wasn't it. This was madness.

He reached into his snowmobile suit and found his compact binoculars. Moving away from the Sno-cat, he scanned the compound. The nose of Brockius's trailer faced the road. Through the thin curtains, he could see Brockius just as Munker had described.

Then he saw someone else.

Jeannie Keeley was now at the window, pulling the curtain aside to look out. Her face looked tense, and angry. Beneath her chin was another, smaller, paler face. April.

"Fire a warning shot," Melinda Strickland told Munker ...

The slim black barrel of a rifle slid out of blinding whiteness and swung slowly toward the trailer window. Joe screamed "NO!" as he involuntarily launched himself from the cover of the vehicles in the direction of the shooter. As he ran, he watched in absolute horror as the barrel stopped on a target and fired. The shot boomed across the mountain, jarring the dreamlike snowy morning violently awake.

Immediately after the shot, Joe realized what he had just done, how he had exposed himself completely in the open road with the assault team behind him and the hidden Sovereigns somewhere in front. Maybe the Sovereigns were as shocked as he was, he thought, since no one had fired back.

But within the hush of the snowfall and the faint returning echo of the shot, there was a high-pitched hiss. It took a moment for Joe to focus on the sound, and when he did he realized that its origin was a newly severed pipe that had run between a large propane tank on the side of the trailer and the trailer itself. The thin copper tubing rose from the snow and bent toward the trailer like a rattlesnake ready to strike. He could clearly see an open space between the broken tip of the tubing and the fitting on the side of the trailer where the pipe should have been attached. High-pressure gas was shooting into the side vents of the trailer.

No! Joe thought. *Munker couldn't have—*

He looked up to see a flurry of movement behind the curtains inside the trailer a split second before there was a sudden, sickening *whump* that seemed to suck all of the air off the mountain. The explosion came from inside the trailer, blowing out the window glass and instantly crushing two tires so the trailer rocked and heaved to one side like a wounded

48

animal. The hissing gas from the severed pipe was now on fire, and it became a furious gout of flame aimed at the thin metal skin of the trailer.

Suddenly, a burning figure ran from the trailer, its gyrations framed by fire, and crumpled into the snow.

Joe stood transfixed, staring at the open window where he had last seen April. It was now a blazing hole.

The Sovereigns had scattered on snowmobiles, Sno-cats, skis, and four-wheel-drives. It was chaos. He'd chased down Munker and found him mortally injured.

When he returned to the Sovereigns' camp ...

He couldn't even speak. He stared at the smoldering carcass of the trailer. It had scorched the snow and exposed the earth beneath it—dark earth and green grass that didn't belong here. Melted snow mixed with soot had cut miniature troughs, like spindly black fingers, down the hillside. When he stared at the black framework, all he could see was the face of April Keeley as he last saw her. She was looking out of the window, her head tucked under the chin of her mother. April's face had been emotionless, and haunted. April had always been haunted. She had never, it seemed, had much of a chance, no matter how hard he and Marybeth had tried. He had failed her, and as a result, she was gone. It tore his heart out.

Joe stood there, as the snow swirled around him, then felt a wracking sob burst in his chest, taking his remaining strength away. His knees buckled and his hands dropped to his sides and he sank down into the snow, hung his head, and cried.

And he cried now, six years later, hot tears dropping on Tube's head and snout. Joe was always shocked by the appearance of his own tears, as if he'd forgotten he was capable of them. Angrily, he wiped them away.

When he recovered, he called Marybeth. It was after one in the morning, but he knew she'd be awake.

"Where are you?" she asked.

"Nearly to Casper," he said. Which meant still three hours away.

"This won't be like our usual reunion," she said, as if in warning.

"I know." The only good thing about the distance of his district from their home was getting back together. They missed each other and yearned for each other terribly, and seeing each other was still ... wild. Not this time, though.

He said, "You know what's always bothered me about that day on Battle Mountain? I've replayed that day over and over in my head for six years. But you know what's always bothered me the most?"

"What?"

"If it had been Sheridan or Lucy in that trailer, I think I would have gone in after either one of them."

"You could have been killed trying, Joe."

"I know that. But I think I would have *tried*. I think something inside of me would have *made* me go into that camp after them, after my daughters. I wouldn't have waited to see how the situation played out like I did with our foster child. That's always haunted me ..."

There was a long pause. "So what are you saying?"

"That if there's even a remote chance—even a sliver of

50

a chance—that April is alive, I don't want to screw up again. I want to find her and save her. I want to set things right."

"Joe … it's time you let that go. I don't think you did the wrong thing that day. You would have been killed trying, and where would that leave the rest of us?"

He didn't respond, couldn't respond.

After a long time, Marybeth said, "Joe, I can't even imagine a scenario where she's alive. But if she were, if she were …" her voice tailed off. He thought he was losing the signal.

Then she said: "What makes you think she wants to be saved?"

THREE YEARS AFTER the incident on Battle Mountain, a man named J.W. Keeley showed up in Saddlestring seeking revenge on Joe. J.W. was April's uncle. He was also a violent ex-con suspected of murdering a rich couple from Atlanta in his hunting camp. The ending of that encounter still made Joe shudder with guilt.

BOTH EXPERIENCES STAYED with him, messed him up, and made it difficult to concentrate on I-25 as he coursed north. He nearly forgot to acknowledge the memory of Wyoming icon Chris LeDoux as he passed Kaycee.

But he snapped right back when his phone rang at two-thirty in the morning, when Marybeth said, "Sheridan got a text message an hour ago, Joe. From April."

5

Aspen, Colorado

"WHAT ARE YOU doing?" Robert asked her. She quickly jammed the phone between the arm of the overstuffed chair and outside of her leg so he couldn't see it if he looked closely. She hoped her face wouldn't reveal anything, but he'd startled her and she hadn't seen him coming up behind her in the hotel lobby.

"Nothing," she said, hoping she didn't sound guilty.

"I thought I saw you doing something with your hands."

She'd been texting. She was fast, a blur of thumbs. But because Robert was in back of her when he asked, she was fairly certain he couldn't have seen the phone. All he could have seen, she thought, was her leaning forward in the chair, head bent, intent on something. Any kid would have known what she was doing, but despite what he seemed to think of himself, Robert was no kid. She doubted he'd ever sent a text message. Robert thought cellphones were for calls. That's how old he was.

She held up her right hand. "My nails," she said. "I hate my nails. I chew on them too much."

She thought it was a pretty good lie. She *did* hate her nails.

Robert looked at her suspiciously, narrowing his eyes, darting them all over her and around her like a mental frisking. But he skimmed right over her legs and the arm of the chair where the cellphone was.

She'd had the phone for three days, and neither Robert nor Stenko knew she had it. It had been fairly simple to get. She'd asked them to stop at a Wal-Mart as they were passing through Cheyenne on the way to Colorado. She'd said she needed to buy some things. When Robert asked what she needed, she'd said, "Feminine things, if you gotta know," and that shut him up. She knew they wouldn't want to go inside with her to buy Kotex, or whatever else the two of them assumed were "feminine things." She borrowed fifty dollars cash from Stenko and he peeled it off the roll he had taken from the motor home.

The TracFones were located in the electronics section. While standing in line at the cashier's, she bought a 120-minute Airtime card from a display.

She'd activated the phone in a restroom stall by calling an 800 number with the ten free minutes that came with the phone. Following the prompts, she loaded two hours of talk time onto the phone from the code on the Airtime card. Once it was loaded, she muted the ring and placed the call to the number she remembered from so many years ago to the house on Bighorn Road. She didn't recognize the voice of the boy who answered, but he did give her Sheridan's number, which she punched into the memory of the phone before powering it off. Then she threw away the packaging and the charger and slipped the phone down the front of her jeans. She knew that when the battery ran out she could buy another phone at any Wal-Mart or convenience store.

On the way out of the store, she gathered up a large package of Tampax, some nail polish and lotion, and her favorite shampoo. She'd learned years before from one of her many foster brothers that the best time to steal from Wal-Mart was early in the morning, when the employees were lethargic. So she bagged them all up at a self-service checkout and walked out past the staffer near the door who never looked twice.

Outside, she'd offered to give Stenko the change but he smiled and said, "Keep it."

THEY WERE IN the lobby of the nicest hotel she had ever been in. Such luxury! It was warm and comfortable with crowded couches and chairs, bowls of fresh fruit on tables, dark red wallpaper, hanging chandeliers turned low, exposed ceilings with thick wooden beams, deer heads on the walls. It was late, but she couldn't sleep since she'd dozed so much in the car all day getting here. The key card to their suite was on a table in front of her. The sleeve for the card read: HOTEL JEROME. Outside, it smelled of pine trees.

Robert sat down in a chair across from her. He had a large tumbler of amber liquid on ice. He was dressed casually, but in a studied way, as if trying to fit in with the surroundings. Open-collar shirt, sports jacket, chinos, leather shoes without socks. And of course he carried his laptop case.

"Dad's in the bar," he said. "He's likely to be in there awhile."

"I'd like to go to bed," she said. "I'm really tired. It's one in the morning."

"I know what time it is. What, do you have an important meeting tomorrow or something? Besides, all you did all day was sleep in the car." And he laughed.

She really didn't like him at all, she thought. If it weren't for Stenko and what he'd done for her, she would have thought of a plan to get away already. In fact, the thought had crossed her mind in the Cheyenne Wal-Mart when she was alone from the both of them for the first time since they'd left Chicago.

"What's he doing in the bar?" she asked, trying to divert the subject away from what she'd been doing previously.

Robert smirked. "Toasting the groom."

"What groom?" she asked, although she knew.

"*The* groom. There's going to be a big wedding in the hotel in a few days. But you don't need to know anything more about it."

"Why don't you trust me?" she asked.

"Because," he said, taking a sip from his drink, "I think you're a devious little tramp."

"I'm not a tramp."

"Yeah, I forgot," Robert said. "That was a nunnery Dad found you in, not a brothel."

"He saved me," she said. She was so angry she nearly forgot that if she stood up to slap his face he'd see the phone.

"Yeah, I know," he said, rolling his eyes.

"Why are you doing this to him? Making him do these things?"

Robert sat back, steepled his fingers, and stared at her as if weighing how much to tell. "I'm actually helping him."

"How does doing these things help him?"

"You wouldn't understand, girlie."

Oh, how she disliked him.

SHE'D OVERHEARD SOME of the conversation in the car earlier that day as they drove south from Wyoming into Colorado. Stenko and his son, Robert, spoke in hushed

56

tones, but she sensed it when Robert would shoot looks at her in the back seat. She pretended to sleep so she could listen and they'd feel like they could talk freely.

Stenko had said, "So the name of the groom is what again?"

"Alexander Stumpf," Robert said, reading off the screen of his laptop. "Son of Cornelius and Binkie Stumpf of La Jolla, California. Heir to the Stumpf shipping fortune. Reading this, he sounds like a snooty little bastard. The bride is named Patty Johnston. You know, Johnston Cosmetics?"

"I guess I've heard of it."

"Everybody's heard of Johnston Cosmetics, Dad. Sometimes you astound me. They're one of the biggest of the multinationals. They make billions on the backs of Third World workers they exploit so rich women can smell good."

Stenko didn't reply.

"There's a picture of Patty Johnston here. She's kind of a looker. But now she wants to be known as Patty Johnston-Stumpf. Christ Almighty."

"You don't even know her," Stenko said.

Robert snorted. "It sounds like a royal wedding. Guests are flying in from Europe and both coasts for it. Two trust fund babies getting together in Aspen to tie the knot. It's one of the biggest society shindigs of the year, or at least the only one I can find online that's close to us."

"*You've* got a trust fund," Stenko said.

Said Robert, "Considering what you put me through and the dying planet you're leaving me with, it was the *least* you could do. And unlike Patty Johnston or Alexander Stumpf, I'm spending mine in a responsible way, aren't I? At least I'm giving back, Dad. And because of the way the trust fund came about, I have a hell of a lot to account for, don't I?"

Stenko sighed. "Don't be like that."

"How do you expect me to be? How would you expect different, Dad?"

"Maybe you could be a little nicer."

"It's too late for that."

She didn't like the way Robert spoke to his father, the man who had saved her life and been nothing but sweet to her.

"Is she still sleeping?" Stenko whispered.

"Yeah."

"Don't be so loud. You'll wake her up."

"Fuck her."

"Robert, please."

"You're more considerate of her than you ever were of me," Robert said. "Of course, Carmen was another matter. Carmen *loved* her daddy, and you called her Little Angel right in front of me. She was Little Angel and I was what? You never really got around to a nickname for me, did you? I mean, we hardly even saw you growing up. And when we did, you were too busy for us. Remember that time we went to the Wisconsin Dells and got that cabin? You left the first morning and didn't show up for a week afterward."

A long pause. "I had business. We were opening a new casino and there were labor problems. I'm sorry about leaving you kids with your mother for so long."

"But you did," Robert said, triumphant. "But you did. All I can remember about that place is being eaten alive by mosquitoes. It was hot and humid, and the crickets kept me awake all night. Do you remember when I told you I wanted to learn how to fish? Do you remember that?"

Stenko moaned with the memory.

"Right, you remember. So instead of you teaching me dad to son, you get that ape Charlie Sera to take me out on the lake. That goon didn't know fishing from cathedral architecture! He told me to bait my own hook, and he spent the whole time drinking from a flask and shooting at rising trout with a thirty-eight. Boy, what a great bonding experience."

"Sorry. I didn't know about it until later."

"Right, you were *gone* by then. And your Little Angel Carmen—that's when she started hanging out with local losers. That's when it started with her, you know. She missed her daddy so she found other males who liked her. And mom drowning herself in vodka every night. It was a living hell. But you wouldn't know. You *left* us there."

"It was a five-room vacation home, if I recall," Stenko said patiently, "the best available. It wasn't like you were in some shack with an outdoor toilet. Besides, I thought you *liked* nature. I thought that was what this was all about."

"I despise nature," Robert said, "thanks to you."

"But ..."

"I want to save the planet," Robert said. "That's different."

"THERE SHE IS," Robert said, taking the last gulp from his drink and gesturing at a woman checking in with his glass.

"Who?" she asked.

"Patty Johnston, the bride-to-be."

Tall, very thin, thick auburn hair, and green eyes. She had a graceful way of moving and a quick smile. She sure had a lot of luggage, though: two bell-stands worth. The hotel staff hovered around her while she got her key. She was with another woman who looked like an older version of Johnston.

"She just arrived, and that must be her mother," Robert said with a smirk. "She doesn't know her future husband is in the bar with Stenko."

"She's pretty."

"I could have her if I wanted to," Robert said. "The easiest pickings in the world is a woman about to be married. They always want one last blast. And especially if they're going to get married to a guy named Stumpf."

She looked at Robert. His eyes were glassy, and she realized he must have had more to drink than she thought.

"What?" he said, noticing her staring at him.

You're such a prick, she thought.

"Don't look at me that way," he said. "You're just a kid. You shouldn't even be here. And you wouldn't be here if it were up to me."

Robert stood up a little unevenly, smoothed his chinos with both hands and raked his fingers through his streaked blond hair. "Stay put and watch this."

She watched. He shot out his cuffs and detoured on his way to the bar via the front desk. He succeeded in catching the eye of Patty Johnston. Robert flashed his brilliant smile, said, "You must be the bride because you've got a wonderful glow about you."

Patty Johnston looked at him as if he had something in his teeth. Her mother put on a stern face and glared at him.

"I'd be pleased to buy you a drink later," Robert pushed on.

Patty Johnston dismissed him with an embarrassed smile and turned back to the front desk.

Robert's shoulders slumped and his neck turned red. He let a beat pass, then continued his way toward the bar. From her overstuffed chair in the lobby, she almost felt sorry for him. Almost.

When he came back to his chair, the bride-to-be and her mother were gone.

She said, "I guess that didn't work out."

He shook his head as if harboring secret knowledge. "You

didn't see how she looked at me. She looked me over, girlie, and Patty liked what she saw. I could have pursued it, and she would have let me. If she wasn't with her mother, it would be a whole different outcome, believe me."

He sipped his drink, trying to act nonchalant. "But I figure Stenko's working the groom, so why bother?"

Then he did something she was getting used to: he withdrew his laptop from his computer case and opened it on his thighs.

"Stenko got all the numbers from the groom," Robert said, as much to himself as to her. He handed her the spiral notebook opened to a page filled with scrawled words and numbers.

"Read this to me so I can input the data," he said.

"It doesn't make sense."

"It doesn't have to make sense to you," he said, annoyed. "It makes sense to me. Now just start at the top and read out each entry while I put it into the database."

She sighed. "Twenty international guests from Europe."
Tap-tap-tap.

He said, "That's eight thousand nine hundred fifty KM each. Seventeen hundred seventy-two KG of carbon per. Seventeen thousand nine hundred KM total, seventy tons of carbon total. Okay, next."

"One hundred sixty guests from Chicago."

Tap-tap-tap. "Five thousand seven hundred KM. One point two tons carbon each. One hundred ninety-two tons total. Wow. Next."

"Eighty from NYC and LA."

Tap-tap-tap. "Ten thousand four hundred KM. Three hundred twenty tons of carbon total. Then the driving."

"What?" She asked.

"See below where it says rental cars? What are the figures?"

61

She flipped the page back and found more entries. "Two hundred sixty guests driving three hundred twenty miles Denver–Aspen."

Tap-tap-tap. Mumbled, "One hundred twenty-five tons of carbon."

He hit enter with a flourish, then whistled. "One society wedding produces seven hundred and seven tons of carbon into the atmosphere to further choke our planet to death. The offset cost is $7,815.88."

She thought about it for a moment. She was beginning to understand.

"What about the honeymoon?" she asked. "Wouldn't you count that, too?"

He grinned.

She got it, and she felt her scalp crawl. "There won't be a honeymoon."

He waggled his eyebrows. "Our global honeymoon is over, girlie. All for the best," he said.

Then: "Stop looking at me like that. Carmen used to do that, too."

6

Aspen

WHEN PATTY JOHNSTON heard a scratch on the key card entry on the outside of her door and saw the tiny yellow dot of the peephole blink out indicating someone was outside in the hall, she propped up on her elbow in bed and shook her hair so it cascaded into place but not entirely. When a strap from her nightgown didn't fall casually over her shoulder as intended, she squirmed so it did. She tried to imagine what she would look like to Alex when he opened the door, but she was pretty sure she'd look sleepy, soft, warm, inviting—but not too hungry for him. The bathroom lights were dimmed and the door slightly ajar, so there was a soft glow of gold reaching across the bedroom. But not too much. It annoyed her that Alex shut his eyes when the lights were on, that he'd only look at her furtively in casual asides while they made love. She hadn't been working out and dieting until her belly was rock hard for their wedding for him not to look at her.

She was still trying to get over the realization she'd had recently when they were having sex: that Alex closed his eyes because he was a kind of performance artist auditioning for the lead role in his own private movie about himself. The thought still haunted her, but like his tendency to tell his friends and relatives, "I'm getting married," not *"We're getting married,"* it was just one of these quirks she'd eventually grind out of him.

She'd almost fallen asleep waiting. It had been over an hour since she'd slid her extra key under the door of his room so he'd find it when he came in. She'd gone to bed without taking out her contacts, without removing her makeup. Waiting. Her eyes burned but she knew he didn't like her in glasses.

The key card slipped into the lock, was withdrawn, and there was a dull click indicating it was unlocked, but he was too slow grasping the handle—*wasn't he always?*—and she rolled her eyes in the semi-dark while he fumbled with the latch. She breathed in deeply while he did it again. Fumbling, trying to fit the key into the slot. *Wasn't he always?*

Then she heard a deep male voice, not Alex's, say: "Step aside. Let me do it."

She shot up in bed, eyes wide, thinking the front desk had given someone a key to her room.

The door opened and there was Alex's profile. Tall, square shouldered, bad posture, spiked hair. Wearing, as always, an untucked oversized Brooks Brothers shirt so starched it crackled like a wind-filled sail when he moved.

"Alex, is there someone with you?" she asked, making her voice rise toward the end.

Then she saw the profile of the other man in the second it took for the two of them to enter her room and shut the door behind them. The man with Alex was tall as well, but beefy, rounded, thicker, older. His face, illuminated briefly by the hall lights, was jowly. Deep-set eyes, mustache—he

64

looked like that famous writer she never liked. What was that guy's name?

"I'm sorry," Alex said. "This is Stenko."

She dug her heels into the mattress and rocketed back in the bed until her back thumped the headboard. She pulled the comforter up, clutching it under her chin.

Stenko said, "If you scream, you'll both die."

His voice was deep, harsh, but somehow apologetic. It took her a moment to believe what she'd heard.

She said, "Alex, how could you bring someone with you? What in the hell are you thinking?"

"I'm sorry," he said again. The second word was slurred, *shorry*.

"You're drunk," she said. To Stenko: "Get out now. Whatever he told you is *not* a possibility."

"Patty ..." Alex said, stumbling forward in the dark as if pushed, "it's not like that."

"Sit down on the bed, Alex," Stenko said. To her: "I have a gun."

"He has a gun," Alex repeated, bumping into her bed clumsily, then turning and sitting down hard. She barely moved her leg in time to avoid the weight of him.

"What's this about?" she asked Alex. "I can't believe you brought a man in here with you."

"Keep your voice down, please," Stenko said. "I don't want either one of you to get hurt."

"Hurt?" she asked. "What does he want, Alex?"

"He'll tell you," Alex said.

She wanted Alex to stand up and protect her, to charge Stenko, to knock him down to the floor. But Alex just sat there, heavy, his head down and his shoulders slumped more than usual and his hands between his knees.

There was so little light from the bathroom that she could

barely make out Stenko as he grabbed a chair from the desk, turned it backward, and sat down with his legs spread. Stenko rested his arms on the back of the chair and leaned forward, putting his chin on his forearms. He held a long-barreled pistol in a big fist, but it was pointed away from them.

"What do you want?" she asked Stenko directly.

"You're not going to believe it," Alex said, slowly shaking his head from side to side. He smelled of alcohol and cigar smoke. "We met in the bar."

"Obviously," she said, anger starting to replace fear.

Stenko said, "I need you to listen carefully to what I have to say."

She reached out from beneath the covers and hit Alex in the shoulder with her open palm. "Alex, *do something!*"

Alex didn't move.

But Stenko sighed and swung the pistol over, pointed it vaguely at both of them. She saw a smudge of white thumb in the murk and heard him cock the revolver.

"I said listen," Stenko said in a whisper.

She found Alex's biceps, squeezed it hard and not affectionately.

Stenko said, "With the size of the wedding, the number of guests, how far they're all traveling here ... *Wow.* It's quite a big operation."

She shook her head, puzzled.

Stenko said, "When I got married—the first time, I mean—we did it before Judge Komicek at the courthouse. Marie's parents and her best friend, Julie, were there, and I had my mom and all three of the Talich Brothers. That's all—less than ten guests. This was Chicago. The whole thing was over in fifteen minutes. No big deal. Then we moved into a little two-bedroom bungalow off Division Street. And when it was over, we were just as married as you two will be. But it was simple. No impact."

After a beat, she asked, "So?"

"Marie is the mother of my son, Robert, by the way. I've had other wives and other kids, but Marie, Robert, and my daughter Carmen were my first and best family. Marie knew what I did, but she didn't want to know any details, and now that I think about it, that was the happiest time in my life. We were struggling, Marie was pregnant with Carmen, and I was happy but I just didn't realize it at the time. I was too damned impatient."

She cleared her throat. "What does that have to do with us?"

"I'm getting there," Stenko said. "Alex, does she always talk this much? It doesn't bode well, if you ask me."

"No one asked you," she snapped.

"Here's the deal," Stenko said, ignoring her. His voice was soft but flat, midwestern. "Here's the deal. I was a hard-charger. Ambitious, ruthless, I guess. I had a certain affinity for Chicago politics and business, and all the guys I grew up with went into one or the other. Except for the ones who became cops, but they're still friends of mine. So what I did those first few years after marrying Marie was I bull-dozed anyone in my path. I fuckin' ran over 'em, is what I'm saying. I was a force of nature: *Stenko*. No one was safe unless they were on my side helping me get what I wanted. I figured there were two kinds of people—those who sup-ported me and those that needed to be bulldozed.

"But then I got the word from my docs. And I looked up and thought, *Where is Marie? Where is Carmen? Where is Robert?* Hell, I liked Marie. She'd sing to me and she was pretty good. Robert, he was always a little too melodramatic, but he was my first. So when I got the word from my docs,

I thought, *What a selfish bastard I am.* Like you two. I took and I took and I never gave anything back. I *consumed.* Now I've got this deficit I'm trying to pay down. I'm trying to get below zero, but I'm in a time crunch and my friends and associates all cheated me, kicked me when I was down. So the reason I'm here is to help us both out."

She said, "Below zero?"

"You can do it, too," Stenko said. "This is your chance. If only I'd had this opportunity early in life. If only somebody would have shown me how to do it."

Stenko sighed and got quiet. As the seconds went on, her fear returned.

"Anyway," Stenko said finally, his voice still hushed, "that's why I'm here. My son figured it all out. That's what he does. He *cares.* Eight grand—that's how much you owe the planet, and I'm here to collect. Let's start with the eight grand to offset the carbon produced by all the people attending this wedding."

She dug her nails into Alex's arm until he winced and pulled away. She said to Stenko, "What right do you have to say that? This is extortion. You're insane."

Stenko said, "I'm only getting started, Patty. The average American produces twenty tons of carbon a year. I spent a lot of time with my pal Alex tonight and he filled me in on both of you. According to your fiancé, between the two of you, you'll have three homes and an extravagant lifestyle. I got all the particulars from Alex and fed them to my son, Robert. It's pretty amazing. With the homes, the travel you people do on commercial and private jets, your fleet of vehicles at each place, you two will produce *seven thousand tons* of carbon a year. Robert says there are entire villages in Africa that won't produce that much over a decade. To offset that, it would cost over thirty-five K per year helping the environment."

"My God," Patty said. "This is ridiculous. My family contributes to all kinds of environmental causes. My mother *hosts* the Think Green fund-raiser in San Diego every year! Have you ever heard of Think Green?"

Stenko said, "No, I haven't. Robert didn't say anything about that. But he did figure that with your seven tons a year and a life expectancy of sixty more years for Patty and fifty more for Alex, that you two alone will do $2.1 million in damage in your lifetime. That's more than some pissant countries," he said. "I can't remember which ones. They have goofy names I never heard of. Sierra Leone? Burma? Maybe—hell, I don't know which countries. Robert's the expert, not me."

"What is your point?" she asked. "I mean, if you're here to make us buy some of those carbon credit things, I'm sure we can. Will you go away and leave us alone if we do?"

She could see his smile in the light of the bathroom. "Yes," he said. "That's exactly why I'm here."

"We'll do it," she said. "We'll pay the eight thousand for the wedding tomorrow. I swear. Now would you please go away?"

"You'll do it now," Stenko said, his voice hardening. "And you'll have to do the entire amount. Alex has the paper with the wire transfer numbers on it. You can use the phone and call it in."

She shook her auburn hair and rubbed her eyes. "Alex," she said, "send the money."

"From my account?" Alex said, hurt.

"For Christ's sake," she said, "you have eight thousand fucking dollars you can part with if it'll make him go away."

Alex stared at her. "He wants the whole $2.1 million."

"My God," she said, closing her eyes tightly as if it would

make it all go away. "He told you already, Alex? And when he told you, you brought him to my *room*?"

Stenko said, "The place you're sending the money is a legitimate enterprise. From what Robert tells me, they'll use the cash to buy up rain forest, plant trees and shit. And take farmland out of production. They invest in windmills and solar panels. Things like that. It's a wonderful investment in the future of our planet. It's the best thing you could possibly do for yourselves, for me, for all of us."

"You're not kidding, are you?" she said, eyeing him, looking at a ghost in the dark. But one with a gun. And he raised it, straightened his arm, and pointed it at her eyes. The black muzzle was rimmed with silver.

He shook his head. "You owe us," Stenko said. "You owe the world."

"You're crazy," she said.

"Worse than that," Stenko said, "I'm desperate." Was that the glint of tears in his eyes?

"What if we did it in payments?" she asked.

"I don't have the time."

"That's too much," she said with finality.

"Tell that to all of those Third Worlders who died in that tsunami caused by global warming," Stenko said, speaking the words as if by rote, "or those poor stupid polar bears clinging to their last piece of melting ice. What are their lives worth?

"I'll tell you what Robert tells me," Stenko said. "It isn't about you. It's about all of us. We all have to do what we can, not what we want to do."

"But we do so much," Patty said, tears in her eyes. "I told you about Think Green. We recycle, don't we, Alex? And we replaced all of our lightbulbs. You know, with the ones that don't work very well? And one of my cars is a Prius. It's not like I don't care."

70

"Then show me how much you care," Stenko said. "You've got two minutes to make the wire transfer."

They stared at each other in silence for the first minute. She wanted Alex to help her, to agree with her out loud. To stomp the living shit out of this Stenko.

"Do something," she said to Alex.

He sighed.

Through gritted teeth, she said, "Send the goddamn money, Alex. You've got it. It's not like you won't get more."

She leaned forward until her lips brushed Alex's ear, whispered, "Do it. There *have* to be ways of canceling a wire transfer after its been made. We'll call the police and my dad and get it canceled."

Alex snorted, looked away.

"Alex, you've got the money," she said.

"So do you," Alex said, sullen.

She was shocked, and she sat back and glared at the side of Alex's head, thinking that perhaps she hated him.

"I don't care which of you does it," Stenko said, "we're running out of time."

"It'll have to be you," Alex said to her.

She looked at him, openmouthed.

Alex said, "Sorry, Patty."

"My God," she said, "you'd actually choose your money over our marriage? Over me? *That's* why you brought him in here?"

"Don't forget the planet," Stenko said helpfully.

"I'm sorry, Patty," Alex said again.

Stenko said to Patty, "This is the man you want to spend your life with?"

She laughed harshly, more of a bark. "Exactly what I was thinking."

"So," Stenko said to her, "it's up to you. You want the phone?"

She looked from Alex to Stenko and back to Alex.

Stenko said, "Sorry kids. I'd hoped we could come to an understanding, but like I said, I'm impatient. Time's up."

7

Saddlestring

J OE ROLLED INTO town at three-thirty in the morning as the fingers of morning mist began their probing ghost-creep from the river into Saddlestring and the single traffic light at First and Main blinked amber in all directions. There were no lights on yet downtown, and the traffic consisted of a single town cop spotlighting a raccoon in an alley. The only people up, it seemed, were the bored clerk reading a newspaper on the counter of the twenty-four-hour Kum-And-Go convenience store and the morning cook at the Burg-O-Pardner starting on the biscuits and sausage gravy for early rising fishermen.

His street was dark as well except for the porch light burning at his house and the kitchen light next door at neighbor Ed Nedney's, a retired town administrator who'd no doubt arisen early to get a jump-start on late-fall lawn maintenance or putting up the storm windows or plucking the last few errant leaves from his picture-perfect lawn—completed tasks that would make Joe's home look poorer by comparison and Joe himself seem derelict. This is what Nedney lived for, Joe thought.

Joe didn't like his house, and every time he came back, he liked it less. It wasn't the structure or the street; it was simply that he didn't like living in town with neighbors so close, especially after years of waking up on Bighorn Road to the view of Wolf Mountain and the distant river. But it was where his family lived, and that fact far outweighed his dislike of the location.

His neighborhood was new in terms of Saddlestring itself—thirty years old—and had grown leafy and suburban. The Bighorns could be seen on the horizon as well as the neon bucking bronco atop the Stockman's Bar downtown. The houses seemed to have been moved a few inches closer together since the last time he was home a week ago, but he knew that was just his tired eyes playing tricks on him.

He flipped a U-turn and parked behind Sheridan's twenty-year-old pickup—*her first car!*—leaving the driveway open for Marybeth's van. Tube bounded out as if he knew he was home at last, and Joe unstrapped the eagle from his pickup wall and picked the bird up to take to his shed in the backyard. It squirmed when he lifted it up but relaxed as he carried it, either resigned to its fate or calmly looking for an opportunity to blow up and escape. He carefully avoided the talons, aware that if the eagle gripped his hand or wrist it could take him down to his knees in pain. The eagle turned its sock-covered head from side to side as he carried it toward the house.

He didn't hear Ed Nedney come out and stand on his front porch in his robe smoking his morning pipe. And he didn't see him until Ed cleared his throat loudly to indicate his disapproval of Tube, who'd wandered from Joe's lawn onto Nedney's perfect grass to defecate. The pile was huge, steamy.

"Geez, I'm sorry," Joe said. "I'll clean that up."

Nedney snorted, as if to say, *Of course you will.* Then: "So the game warden returns. How is life in *Baggs*?"

He said "Baggs" the way a rich San Franciscan would say "Iowa"—with disdain.

"Fine," Joe said, regretting what Tube had done.

"What do you have there all wrapped up in swaddling clothes?"

"A bald eagle."

"My God. Does it screech?"

"You should hear it. It can wake the dead."

"As long as it doesn't wake *me*."

"I didn't think you slept," Joe said, "with all the lawn maintenance and all."

"Well, I do. What's wrong with that dog? Why does she look so ... ridiculous? She looks like a sausage."

"He's a he. His name is Tube."

"Going to be home for a while?"

"Yup," Joe said, thinking, *Probably not.*

"Maybe you'll get a chance to get the house painted before the snow hits," Nedney said casually.

"It's not that bad," Joe said, wishing he hadn't sounded so defensive.

"Check out the north side under the eaves. The wind is starting to chip away at the paint. Believe me when I tell you this," Nedney said, sighing, the weight of the unkempt world on his shoulders. "I have to look at it every day."

Joe thought, *Tube, go over on Nedney's lawn and take another dump* ...

When Marybeth opened the front door, saw the eagle in his arms wearing Joe's sweatshirt and sock and the huge frankfurter-like dog at his feet who instantly fell in love with her, she said, "Joe, come inside." Then: "So this is Tube. He's very unusual."

75

Joe nodded, "Did I tell you I caught the Mad Archer of Baggs?"

"Yes, twice on the phone. Congratulations, Joe. And welcome home."

AFTER SETTING UP the eagle in the shed with water and rabbit roadkill he had picked up from the highway outside of town, Joe entered the house from the back to avoid seeing Nedney. It was warm and dark inside and smelled of cooking and his family. He was suddenly tired.

Marybeth was sitting on the couch in the front room with her laptop and Sheridan's cellphone. She said, "Do you need to get some sleep? I've been dozing the last couple of hours waiting for you."

"I do," he said. But when he looked into her green eyes and saw the way she was curled up on the cushions of the couch, he said, "But first I need you."

She smiled cautiously and shot a look toward the darkened hallway that lead to Sheridan's and Lucy's bedrooms. "Joe ..."

He took her hand, she squeezed back, and he guided her to the bedroom.

For a few minutes they forgot about the text messages, Nedney, what time it was, and even Tube, who curled up on the rug at the foot of the bed like he owned the place.

"I WAS UP a long time after the text-message exchange last night," Marybeth said at the breakfast table, once Joe had slept hard for three hours but awakened only an hour past his usual time of six o'clock. She had made a fresh pot of coffee, and she poured a mug of it for him. She said, "I read and reread it and I'll walk you through it. Then I got on the Internet and started plugging in the place names April mentioned in the past couple of weeks. You're not going to like what I came up with any more than I do," she said.

He was jarred. "You said April. You said her name. Not 'whoever was contacting us' or whatever."

She returned the carafe to the coffeemaker. When she sat back down she said, "It's her, Joe."

He shook his head.

"You can decide for yourself, then," she said, plucking Sheridan's phone from the table and opening it up.

As she scrolled through the menu Joe said, "*Two thousand text messages?* How is that possible?"

Marybeth smiled. "Where have you been, Joe? Teenagers don't talk. They text."

"But two thousand? In a month? That's crazy."

She shrugged.

He did a quick calculation. "That's nearly seventy texts a day. I don't think I've sent that many in my life, I don't think."

"Are you through?"

"So this isn't unusual?" he asked, thinking that the more time he spent away from his family, the more removed he was becoming from the day-to-day. He didn't like the way it was going. He vowed to see the governor and either be reassigned back home or have to quit. Sheridan's and Lucy's lives were streaking past him, and at this rate he would someday look up and realize they were gone and he'd missed it. Sheridan was seventeen! Lucy was in middle school. In the blink of an eye, they'd be gone if he didn't reconcile his situation.

Marybeth said, "Not at all. In fact, and I hate to tell you this, I've talked to other mothers and two thousand text messages in a month is actually quite low."

He whistled.

"Anyway," she said, scrolling, "Here it is. The first text came in at eleven-eighteen last night. Sheridan was in bed but she heard her phone chime. Remember, we told her to keep her phone on."

She handed the phone to Joe, showed him how to scroll up through the thread:

From: AK
Sherry, is this U? I got your # from a dude named Jason at the old house. U R not gonna believe who this is. Reply by txt but DON'T CALL. DO NOT CALL.
ak
CB: 307-220-5038
Aug 24, 11.18 P.M.
Erase REPLY Options

He read it three times. "No way," he said. "It's a joke."

"That's when Sheridan came out and got me," Marybeth said. "We sat down together on the couch and had a cry. Sheridan was beside herself, and she wasn't sure what to answer or even if she wanted to. But we decided she should answer it for no other reason than to draw her out, to see if she—or he, or whoever—would reveal herself more."

Joe noted the callback number with a Wyoming area code, as well as the exact time and date of the call. He wondered if text messages could be traced like calls could be.

"Scroll up," she said. Joe did.

Sheridan replied:

From: Falconette
I give up. Who RU?
sp
CB: 307-240-4977

78

Aug 24, 11.32 P.M.
Erase REPLY Options

Joe said, "Falconette?"

"It's her user name, I guess."

"Blame Nate," Joe said. Nate Romanowski had taken Sheridan as his apprentice in falconry years before. The lessons had been stop/start, but she'd embraced the cruel and beautiful art of falconry and Nate called her a natural. Since Nate had escaped federal custody a year ago, their lessons had ceased, but Sheridan continued to study up on the sport through books and falconry Internet forums.

"I wonder why she doesn't want Sheridan to call her?" Joe said.

"Read on," Marybeth said.

sherry, this is april. remember me?

You can't be. Come on, who is this?

april keeley no shit.

april's gone. i'm gonna turn this phone off.

this is no joke. ive been away a long time but ya its me.

is this jason? this is NOT funny i'm gonna block yr #.

i don't know jason.

then who R U really?

I told you april.

prove it.

ok. yr 17. yr birthday is May 5. lucy is 13. birthday december 8. howz that?

Joe felt a flutter in his stomach and looked up at Marybeth.

Marybeth said, looking into the living room as if placing herself back there, "Imagine Sheridan and me sitting on the

79

couch when that came up, the birthdays. Sheridan looked at me with tears in her eyes. We both wanted to believe, but at the same time we didn't. I can't remember ever feeling quite like that before. Remember what it was like when we lost April, Joe? My God, those days are still a blur, like being in a car wreck where your mind blots the worst parts out so you won't go crazy recalling the details. And it all came back to me last night—cleaning out her bedroom, the funeral, relearning to say 'the two girls' instead of 'the three girls,' setting one less place at the table."

Her words rushed out. "The mom in me wanted to believe, but I didn't dare allow myself to do it yet. But Joe, I did. And I do. It's like God is giving us a second chance with that poor girl, and I just want to believe even though it doesn't make any logical sense. I wasn't sure what to say to Sheridan."

Joe reached across the table and took her hand. She turned her head, fighting tears.

"Anyone could find out their birthdays," Joe said. "It just means whoever this is has done some homework. I mean, can't anybody get this kind of stuff from MySpace or Facebook or someplace like that? Any kid in their school could know this stuff. After all, it's a Wyoming phone number. It's probably somebody local."

"That thought crossed my mind," Marybeth said, nodding toward the phone. "But we're just getting started."

Joe took a deep breath and continued.

tell me something only april would know.

ok. u used to scare me & luce by saying there was a witch in the closet.

Luce for Lucy. Only April called her that. Just as she called Sheridan Sherry.

80

"What's this about?" Joe asked, his mouth dry.

Marybeth said, "I asked Sheridan. Remember when Lucy and April used to share the same bedroom? For a while—I think it was the November before we lost April—they started asking me to get specific clothes for them to wear in the morning. I remember questioning them why they couldn't get the clothes themselves and they'd just look at each other and neither would tell me why. I knew something was going on but I didn't know what. It wasn't a big deal, and I'd forgotten about it. But now I find out it's because Sheridan told them there was a witch in the closet and that was the reason she moved out of the bedroom and gave it to them. Sheridan also told them that the witch would stay in the closet and not come out to get them unless either they opened the doors or they told anyone about her. That's why they were so secretive."

"That was mean," Joe said, frowning.

Marybeth shrugged. "It was mean, yes. But its what big sisters do to little sisters. And Joe, Lucy's never told me about it to this day. So how could anyone know about it except April?"

"Sheridan or Lucy probably told someone in school about the witch in the closet," Joe said, warming to his schoolmate theory. "Hey—we've been thinking this was someone Sheridan knows. But maybe it's someone Lucy knows?"

Marybeth's lack of response was her signal for him to keep reading.

tell me something else only april would know.

how about the 3 trees? I for each of us. r the trees still there? do U still have Maxine? Is lucy still pretty?

the trees are still there, but maxine died. lucy thinks
she's pretty. She is I guess.
that makes me sad about maxine.
me too. I miss her.
howis yr mom?
she's great.
hows yr dad?
he's great. he's gone a lot.

Joe cringed and tried to swallow. No luck.

is lucy there now?
she's sleeping.
wake her up. I wanna say hi.
just talk 2 me now.
ok.
Where r u?

"At this point," Marybeth said, "Sheridan is pretty sure she's
texting back and forth with April. I am, too. But Joe, it just
can't be, can it?"

"No it can't," he said, his stomach roiling.

aspen
is that where u live?
no.
where do u live?
noplace really. in a car I guess. lol.
W/yr family?
**w/a man & his son. not family. its weird. we've
been all over theplace.**
where?
chicago madison mt rushmore aspen. some

places I dont know. cheyene.

do U have a real home?

**not rly. for 2 weeks its been this car. i used to
live in chicago.**

what r u doing?

**im along for the ride. its weird. They r doing
bad things but im not.**

what kinds of bad things?

rly bad things.

like what?

some pple died.

omg, April! R u ok?

im OK.

Joe sat back, rubbed his eyes. "This can't be true. This
can't be happening."

shld i call the cops? dad knows cops everywhere.

no. 2 complicated.

u shld call the cops.

do u still have toby?

yes. R u safe?

i think so.

Why did u take so long 2 call me?

2 complicated.

Why can't i talk 2 u?

they'll kno I have a phone.

call ME

cant. robert will get mad.

who is robert?

**the son. i don't like him. i like his dad. hes nice
to me. he saved me.**

Why r u in aspen?

Wedding & footprints.
who? what?
G2G. bye.

Joe looked at the time stamp: 12.58 A.M. He sat back, his mind racing, trying to put together what he'd just read. There was a lot there; locations, names (Robert), disjointed facts. "I'm tempted to call the number."

"Don't!" Sheridan said from the hallway. She was in her nightgown and her feet were bare. "If you call they might hurt her, Dad."

"Hurt who?" Lucy asked, looking from her sister in her nightgown to Joe and Marybeth in their robes at the kitchen table. Lucy was dressed for school in a denim mini, a white top, flip-flops. She narrowed her eyes and put her hands on her hips. "Hey, what's going on? Why isn't Sherry dressed for school?"

Sheridan said, "April's alive."

8

"I CAN'T EAT," Lucy said, sitting back in her chair and dropping her fork on the table in front of her with a deliberate clatter. "I just keep thinking about April."

They were at the breakfast table. The morning was dawning crisp, clear, and cool outside. Sheridan and Lucy had met Tube and thought he was sweet and hilarious. Tube showed his astute political instincts by curling up equidistant between their chairs. Joe had never been around a dog that was so self-assured and manipulative. Tube's acceptance was instantaneous, and Tube knew it.

"You need to eat something," Marybeth said. "I can't send you to school without breakfast."

Lucy crossed her arms over her chest and tilted her chin up. "I'm not going to school. Sheridan isn't going, so I'm not going."

"She was up half the night, Lucy," Marybeth said softly.

"And I didn't sleep the other half," Sheridan said.

Joe and Marybeth exchanged a quick look. Had she heard them when they went to bed? Sheridan gave no indication she had. Joe breathed again.

"April calls and no one tells me," Lucy said, looking from Marybeth to Joe to Sheridan, accusing them all.

"It's not like that," Marybeth said.

"It's exactly like that. Sheridan told me she *wanted* to talk to *me*."

Sheridan turned from her sister to Joe. "I wonder what she meant by 'footprints.' Do you think she remembered what you always tell us when we go camping?"

Said Joe, "Leave only footprints, take only memories."

"Yeah—that. Do you think she remembered it?"

Joe was cognizant of Lucy's smoldering at once again being left out of the conversation. He said, "I don't know. What do you think, Lucy?"

She sat back and crossed her arms over her chest and refused to be drawn in by such a transparent ploy.

"Honey," Marybeth said to Lucy, looking to Joe for help, "we weren't sure it was April at the time. We still aren't completely sure."

"Sheridan is. Right, Sherry?"

Sheridan looked away, confirming Lucy's statement.

"Lucy," Joe said, treading into dangerous waters, "we aren't sure. It doesn't make any sense. We're still trying to figure out what's happening."

"You people always leave me out," Lucy said, her face a mask as she fought back her emotions. "My foster sister calls and you don't wake me up."

There was the silence of the guilty.

"She was *my* sister," Lucy said. "I think about her every day. Nobody else does. I never really believed she died."

"Lucy!" Marybeth said, raising her fist to her mouth.

"It's true. I never believed it."

Said Marybeth, "Don't talk like that."

Joe and Sheridan watched the exchange in chastised silence. Lucy had always been happy-go-lucky, fashionable, pretty, and very observant of Sheridan's mistakes so she wouldn't make them herself. In many ways she chose to make herself peripheral. She kept her own counsel. And she was so rarely righteously angry that Joe was slightly stunned.

"I want to talk to her," Lucy said.

Sheridan said, "You can't call. She said not to call."

Lucy glared at her sister and reached across the table and snatched the phone.

"Lucy!" Sheridan said, looking to her mother for help.

"I'm not calling," Lucy said, opening the phone, finding the text thread in an instance, and writing a message so quickly—a blur of practiced thumbs—that she pressed SEND before Sheridan or Marybeth could wrest the phone away. Then she handed the phone back to her sister and gave one last spiteful deadeye to all of them in turn before grabbing her backpack on the way out the door.

There were a few beats of silence.

"Wow," Joe said.

"This will take some work," Marybeth said. "She's got a point. We've got to consider the fact she's growing up. She's not that little girl anymore." She looked blankly at the kitchen window. "Lucy's growing up whether we want her to or not."

Sheridan snorted as she read aloud the message Lucy sent:

april come back. still scared of closet. we need revenge.

love, luce.

LUCY'S BLOW-UP seemed to hang within the walls of the house like a scorching odor long after she left for school. While Sheridan slumped down the hall to take a shower and get dressed—a process that would rarely take less than an hour, Joe knew—Marybeth listlessly cleared the dishes, something on her mind.

When the sound of the shower coursed through the wall, she turned to Joe and said, "Let's go for a drive." He nodded. By her tone and her choice of words, he knew where they were going.

They took her van to the Twelve Sleep County Cemetery, ten minutes away, in complete silence. The cemetery was on the east bank of the river, overlooking a bluff and a shallow bend. During the flash flood three years ago, the river had swollen as if suddenly hungry and had eaten into the soft dirt wall like a beast. The horrified citizens of Saddlestring formed a sandbag brigade that diverted the wall of water before it ate too deeply into the bluff and devoured the coffins. The sandbags were still there, scattered and broken and sunken into the embankment, six feet above the current benign level of the river. Looking at the river, Joe saw violence in remission, a sleeping brute capable of rearing up whenever it wanted if for no other reason than to remind them who was in control.

April's grave was one of those nearest the bluff above the river. The headstone was small and thin, a wafer of granite, all they could afford at the time. It used to be shaded by river cottonwoods, but the trees had washed away in the flood and so had the shade, and the high-altitude sun burned the grass and whitened the stone itself, aging it well past its six years. All it said was:

APRIL KEELEY
WE HARDLY KNEW YOU

And her birth and death dates.

"We used to come here every month," Marybeth said.

"Remember? Then it turned into every few months."

"Yup."

"Joe, we haven't been here for over a year. I feel really guilty about that."

Joe nodded.

"Did we forget about her?"

"No," he said. "Life went on, I guess. Let's not beat ourselves up."

They stood in silence. The only sound was a whisper of breeze high in the remaining treetops that sounded more like the river than the river itself.

She said it: "Is it possible there is someone else in the grave, Joe?"

"I was thinking about that."

"An unknown child? It's too painful to even consider."

Joe said, "I didn't see any other children in that trailer, Marybeth. Only April."

"But we know the Sovereigns had other children with them. We don't know what happened to them after the fire."

Joe remembered the week after the raid when the county coroner and the team from the state Department of Criminal Investigation dug through the charred trailers in the campground. The snow had finally stopped, but in its place an incredible blanket of cold—day after day of twenty, thirty below zero—had descended on the mountains as if to punish them for what had taken place. He had purposely looked away when the investigators cleared blackened sheet metal from the site of Brockius's trailer, when the coroner shouted out that he'd located three bodies—two adults and a child. Joe had no doubt at the time who they were: Jeannie Keeley, April's birth mother; Wade Brockius, the leader of the camp; and April. Joe never looked at the bodies, didn't need to. All he saw were the body bags—one stuffed full like a sausage (Brockius), one stiff and thin (Jeannie), and one with a body so small it seemed empty. The body bags were carried by investigators to an ambulance and taken away. The autopsies of Jeannie and April were cursory—neither had dental records to match up, and the state chose not to run a DNA confirmation because at the time the process was slow and expensive and no one doubted who the bodies were. The decision was made in no small part because of Joe's own eyewitness testimony.

"We could have the body exhumed," Marybeth said. "I don't know how to go about it, but I can find out."

Joe shook his head. "It could take months. We'd need a court order. To get the order we'd need to go to a judge and explain what this is all about. We'd need to try and convince the judge that April might be out there somewhere. We'll need more than those text messages, Marybeth. Even I can't completely convince myself she's alive. We need more."

"We need her to text again," Marybeth said.

"At the very least."

"Joe, there's something else."

He knew there was. She'd alluded to it the night before, when she said she'd been doing an Internet search using the place names from the text thread.

"I DID AN advanced Google search," Marybeth said, seated at her desk in her office. She wore her reading glasses that made her look serious and thoughtful, Joe thought. She tapped the monitor of her computer with an index finger. "I did several combinations of the words Chicago, Madison, Cheyenne, Mount Rushmore and words like crime, murder, killing, police. I got thousands of hits, of course. Then I narrowed down the search to the last two weeks, because

April said she'd been on the road for two weeks, right?"

"Right."

"So since she said she used to live in Chicago, I assumed the two weeks in the car started there. Of course, we don't know for sure, but that's what I'm guessing. So I narrowed it down to the second week of August. Guess how many murders took place that week?"

Joe shrugged.

"Eight. It's a big place. Of the eight, four were 'gang-related,' but I guess we can't rule them out until we get more information from April. The others run the gamut, from the murder of a doctor—wife arrested—to a truck driver in a suspected road-rage incident. And a brothel owner got shot in the head but nobody saw anything. So who knows?"

Joe agreed. "All we're going on is that one line she wrote—*some people died*. We just don't know enough. We need to get her to tell us more."

"Right," she said, doing another Google search. "But let me see if I can find what I found last night. Madison is smaller than Chicago, of course, and there was an unexplained murder there eleven days ago."

Joe's antennae went up because of the way she said it.

"Here," she said jabbing the screen. "From the *Capitol Times*. I'll print it out, but here's the headline: CONTROVERSIAL BLOGGER SLAIN."

It meant nothing to Joe, and he shrugged.

The printer purred, and she snatched out the sheet that slid out and handed it to Joe.

By Rob Thomas, Staff Writer

MADISON—Madison Police are looking for suspects in the alleged slaying of controversial anti-environmentalist blogger Aaron Reif, 38, author of "PlanetStupido.

com." According to MPD Spokesman Jim Weller, Reif's body was found Tuesday night in his studio apartment at 2701 University Avenue slumped over his computer. According to Weller, Reif had been shot twice in the head with a small-caliber weapon at point-blank range. Because there were no signs of forced entry, the police assume the alleged assailant may have been an acquaintance of Reif, according to police sources who asked to remain unnamed.

PlanetStupido.com attracted national and international notoriety last year when Reif publicly accused the proprietors of several international carbon-offset brokers of fraud and corporate malfeasance. Police sources refuse to speculate whether the alleged murder was connected with the website or Reif's high-profile activities.

Weller stated in a hastily called press conference at police headquarters that Reif's body was discovered at 9.47 P.M. by a pizza deliveryman who arrived at the apartment to deliver a pizza that Reif allegedly ordered, leading the police to believe that Reif was killed between 9.20 P.M. when the order was received and the time of delivery. The Madison Police Department urges citizens who may have been in the vicinity of 2701 University Avenue between 9.15 and 10.00 P.M. to report any suspicious persons, vehicles, or activities ...

"Interesting," Joe said. "I've never heard of this website, have you?"

"No, but when we get done here, I'm going to spend some time on it," she said. "But first I've got to show you something else."

She found no major crimes in Cheyenne or at Mount Rushmore, she said. But when she looked at the road atlas for South Dakota, she noted how many small communities there were around the monument. Hill City, Custer, Keystone, and Rapid City, the only city of any size.

"Keystone," Joe said, sitting up. "Wasn't that where—"

"Yes," she said, leaping in. "That's where that old couple from Iowa were found murdered a week ago in that RV park. Remember that they thought those poor old people had died because their motor home caught fire while they were sleeping, but they later found they'd been shot first?"

"With a small-caliber weapon," Joe finished for her.

He sat back, his head swimming.

"This proves nothing, I know," Marybeth said, spinning in her chair to face Joe, whipping her glasses off. "But you're right—we need to ask April more questions."

As they looked at each other they both came up with the same thought.

Marybeth returned to the keyboard and the Google home page, typed ASPEN + MURDER, and directed the search within the last twenty-four hours.

Joe observed her as she read the screen. Suddenly, she gasped, sat back in her chair, and covered her mouth with her hand.

He stood up and leaned across the desk. There were only four hits.

The first one, from the Aspen *Times* said:

MURDER IN ASPEN: COUPLE SLAIN ON EVE
OF WEDDING WEEKEND

9

Chicago, Two Weeks Before

STENKO HAD SAVED her. She owed him; she was loyal. Her journey from that frozen campground on fire in Wyoming to Chicago had been cruel and difficult, consisting of movement with no destination in mind. Until Stenko.

As Stenko and Robert argued back and forth in the front seat of the SUV while they drove north toward Wyoming again, she reviewed how she got to this place at this time and let their voices become nothing more than a discordant background soundtrack.

After the fire, after the raggedy soldiers of the Sovereigns had thrown her across the back of a snowmobile and raced away from that campsite under cover of smoke, confusion, and automatic weapons fire, she'd been bounced around the Midwest to family after family. Indiana, Iowa, Wisconsin, Minnesota, finally Illinois. All were Sovereign sympathizers, but that didn't mean they were necessarily sympathetic to *her*. She'd learned to expect nothing from anyone and to have no aspirations. She became what each family expected of her, which was a nonentity attached to a monthly check issued by the social services people. She'd had twenty or more "brothers" and "sisters" along the way. She matured early and was taller, softer featured, and more voluptuous than her mother had been, although when she looked into the mirror and squinted or made an angry face she saw the hard, flinty, cold-eyed gaze of her mother looking back, as if Mama were inside her trying to break out.

She'd smoked her first joint at age eleven and had sex for the first time at age twelve with foster brother Blake in Minnesota, who'd also taught her how to shoplift from Wal-Mart. The act took place in her basement bedroom while Blake's friends watched through the window well and hooted. It hurt, she hated it, and afterward she found out quick that most boys despised what they said they wanted most, and that was an important thing to learn. When her foster parents found out what happened they blamed her, called her names, shipped her out of there to the next family.

That's how she wound up with the Voricek family on the South Side of Chicago. The Voriceks supplemented their income by taking in foster children. She was one of ten. Ed Voricek, her foster father, was a pig-like man with a slight mustache and a comb-over, and he smelled of cigarettes, motor oil, and bacon. He held a series of jobs in the short time she was there, which turned out to be his pattern. He had so many jobs that if anyone at school asked her what her father did, she had to stop and think for a moment what uniform shirt he'd been wearing last. Midas? Grease Monkey? Jiffy Lube? He was chronically in and out of work. His wife Mary Ann was as stout as Ed but meaner, and the children lived in absolute fear of her. Any transgression— not making their beds, not eating every bit of food on their plates, talking back to her, sulking—was greeted with a threat to send them back to the agency. So she learned to do what she had to do, not talk, and live in her own head. Her only companion was a foster sister the same age who had come from the same place, and they used to sneak into each other's rooms and whisper about running away together. Her foster sister had stuck by her when she screwed up and protected her when a drunk Ed Voricek hovered outside their bedroom door one night when there was no good reason for him to be there. Not that Ed suggested anything or made any moves, but the fact that he was there, leaning against the wall next to their door, said enough in itself. She could still recall the stand her sister took when she opened the door, stared the man down, said, "Why don't you get the hell to bed?" Ed slunk away.

Ed Voricek was a gambler. She didn't understand very much about it at the time, but she and all the other children heard the furious arguments between Ed and Mary Ann about his losses. Mary Ann would scream at Ed, beat him with her fists, threaten to leave him if he ruined them, if the social workers found out that he'd lied about his employment status and took the children away.

She was surprised the evening Ed knocked on her bedroom door and told her to get dressed. "Wear something nice," he said. "Something cute."

So in her best second- or third-hand dress and sandals, she followed him out to his car. Although he'd told her not to pack a bag or bring anything along, she took a small leather pocketbook with a few papers and one-dollar bills—her savings. She knew Mary Ann was out for the evening—Thursday was her bingo night—and when she reached for the handle of the back door, Ed had said, "What're you doing? You can sit up front with me."

She thought she knew what would come next. She was wrong. But it turned out to be worse.

They drove through downtown Chicago and out the other side in Ed's rattletrap station wagon. They crossed the river to the west side, and she saw a battered street sign that read Division and she thought about that. She turned around in her seat and watched out the back window as the sun dropped and the buildings downtown burst with color, the glass and steel towers lighting up fire orange and magenta. The vibrancy of the colors reminded her of sunset in the mountain west and how long it had been since she'd seen one like that. Then, as suddenly as it started, the light and colors doused as if a curtain had been pulled and the buildings became buildings again. Dark, metal, and cold.

Ed was saying, "This is all for the best, all for the best."

"Are you taking me back to the agency?"

"Something like that," Ed said.

She was scared but resigned to whatever would happen next. She wished her foster sister were with her. But, as always, she was alone.

He parked on a street of old buildings. There were women in revealing clothes on the corners and knots of young black and Hispanic men on stoops and playing basketball on a cracked court with chain nets that sang when a ball passed through them. When she and Ed got out of the car, a couple of the boys saw her, stopped playing, and hooted like those friends of her "brother" outside the window well.

"Follow me," Ed said, taking her hand.

They went through a heavy door and up narrow stairs. At the top of the landing was a single bare bulb. She detected a new smell on Ed to go along with the cigarettes, motor oil, and bacon: whiskey. He held her hand too tightly, and she tried to jerk away.

He turned on her, his eyes blazing. *"Follow me,"* he said.

"You hurt me."

"Don't try to run," he said.

"Where would I run?"

"And cheer up. Try to look cute, like I told you. Wet your lips."

She licked her lips.

"Okay," he said.

At the top of the stairs Ed rapped out a series of taps on a door that could only have been some kind of code. She heard locks being thrown and the door opened.

"I'm Eddie V," Ed said. "I've got her with me."

A tall man in a suit with shallow, badly pockmarked cheeks ignored Ed and peered around him to look at her. But he didn't so much look at her as size her up, the way a man looks at a car he might buy. His eyes narrowed and he nodded to himself, humming. Then, "Come in."

The tall man shut the door behind them. The room was nothing like what the building and the hallway suggested it might be like. There were soft lights and empty chairs and couches upholstered in buttery leather. There was a desk with a green shade. Music played in the background from invisible speakers. A bar in the corner had dozens of bottles on it and the liquid in them looked warm and delicious.

The tall man continued to look her over. He walked around her, appraising.

"We can do business," the man said to Ed.

Ed let out his breath, obviously relieved. He turned to her and bent forward, lightly grasping her arms, and stared into her eyes.

"You're going to be staying here for a little while, do you understand?"

She nodded.

"We're doing this to protect you," Ed lied. "Mary Ann was going to send you back to the agency anyway. She feels threatened by you—she told me that a bunch of times. She doesn't like the way you look at her. This is for you. Do you understand? This way you can make some money and go on with your life."

She nodded.

"If anyone asks, you ran away," Ed said. "That's what we'll say, too. Do you understand? We'll even file a report with the agency people and the police to make it official."

She nodded.

"So don't even think of turning yourself in," Ed said, showing his yellow teeth. "Don't forget, we still have that special 'sister' of yours. You wouldn't want any harm to come to her, would you? Like sending her back so you'd never find her again? You wouldn't want that, would you?"

"No.

"Well, neither would I, kiddo."

Ed left her standing there in her dress and sandals while he and the tall man went through a door behind the desk. In a few moments, Ed came back out patting his breast through his jacket, as if he'd just put something there. She saw the corner of a thick white envelope as he passed by her. He said, "Take care of yourself, kid," and left.

"What's your name?" the tall man asked after the door closed and Ed went home with his pile of money.

She couldn't bring herself to speak. Her legs felt weak and her mouth was dry.

"Can't you talk?" the man asked her.

"Yes."

"Then what's your name? Don't worry, we can always change it."

She refused to say the name Voricek, or use the name they'd called her.

"April Keeley," she said.

"Nice," the tall man said. "And you're what, eighteen?"

She was confused. "No, I'm ..."

The man stepped forward shaking his head. "You're eighteen," he said with finality. "You just look younger. You have nice legs for your age, you know. And a good face. You need a manicure, though. We'll take care of that, don't worry."

She quickly hid her hands behind her back.

"That's a good look," the tall man said, "it makes your breasts stand out and makes you look all innocent." Then he chuckled and put his arm around her shoulders.

"We'll take good care of you here," he said. "We take good care of our girls. Ask them if you don't believe me. You'll be part of the family. And we take care of our family."

A door on the far wall opened and a man came out, adjusting his tie. He was heavy and his face was flushed. When he saw her, he stopped and looked her over.

The tall man said, "How was everything, Mr. Davis?"

Mr. Davis said, "Fantastic, Geno. Great as always. And who is this fresh-faced young flower?"

"Meet April Keeley," Geno said to Davis. "She's just joined the family."

Davis said, "Welcome aboard, April." Then to Geno, "They just keep getting younger, don't they?"

FOR THE FIRST week, she lived with the women in their rooms upstairs, which were nothing like the rooms down the hall from the reception area. Upstairs, the sleeping rooms were cozy, messy, personal, and feminine. There were posters of rock and rap bands on the walls and stuffed animals on the beds. During the daytime, they *were* a kind of family. They cooked for each other, went shopping, gossiped. Two of the women took a particular liking to her and bought her clothing and ice cream. One of them, a beautiful tan/black woman named Shawanna, did her hair and nails and told her to insist on protection no matter what and to never back down on that despite what the man said or offered or threatened.

"You're a sex worker," she told her, "you're not a whore."

Geno took fully clothed photos of her for the Internet site. He told her to wet her lips like Ed had and to pout and to pretend she was hungry. Shawanna urged her on, and the photo session was kind of fun as long as she didn't think ahead to how the photos might be used.

On the night of her debut—they called it her "debutante ball"—she wore a tight maroon dress and new high heels and she followed Shawanna out into the reception area with four other girls when the buzzer rang. She wondered if she would be chosen. They emerged to find a man squaring off with Geno. Shawanna whispered to her that the man was called Stenko. "He's a big man," Shawanna said. "He's one of the owners of this place."

The six girls were to lounge in the chairs and couch, see if Stenko was interested, let things develop from there. She stuck close to Shawanna. But Stenko barely looked at any of them.

Stenko said to Geno, "Why did you call them out? I didn't ask to see them." He sounded exasperated.

"I thought it might be a nice distraction," Geno said. There was a line of sweat that showed through his mustache. "I thought we could have our discussion afterward, when you're more relaxed."

Stenko was obviously worked up about something. His movements were stiff but sudden. His eyes darted around the room. At first, she was scared of him. He was big, his hands were huge, and his face was wide and fleshy. He kept

102

running his hand back through his thin hair in an angry way.

Stenko said to Geno, "I don't need to be relaxed. I want to cash out. I told you that, and I told the Carriciolis that. That is the only reason I'm here, Geno."

Geno looked nervous. She hadn't known him long, but she'd never seen him so pale, so furtive. Geno said, "Have a drink, relax. You look pretty good, Stenko. When I heard you were sick, I expected you'd look, you know, sick."

"I'm on meds," Stenko said, "and some days are better than others. But no matter what day it is, I can kick your skinny ass out that window if you don't cash me out of this operation." When he said it he gestured toward the girls without looking at them.

"I can't, Stenko," Geno said softly.

She could tell that the other girls were getting tense. There were no false smiles or purring, just quickly exchanged glances back and forth. She saw Shawanna mouth, *"Oh my God."*

Stenko said to Geno, "What do you mean you can't? I have an investment in this operation. I want it back. I'm not asking for principal plus profit, which is my due. I just want the principal back. Now."

Geno shook his head. "Stenko, you know what's going on. The feds are on us, too. We're not liquid right now. You know that."

Stenko said nothing, but his rage was building. It was as if he were getting larger. His presence seemed to fill the room, dominate it. She watched him clench and unclench his fists and stare down Geno. His stillness was more frightening than his words earlier.

Geno said, "What about your guy? The accountant? Is it true what I heard about him taking your money and the

103

Talich Brothers and hitting the road? Maybe you should be going after him instead of trying to shake me down."

Stenko just stood there, swelling in size. She found herself pressing back farther into the couch. She thought, *Shut up, Geno. Can't you see you're making him even angrier?*

"Get them out of here," Stenko said through clenched teeth.

The girls didn't wait to hear from Geno. They were up and rushing the door they had came through, stiletto heels snapping on the hardwood floor like castanets. Shawanna reached back and pulled her up by the hand, said, "Let's git, April."

She was nearly through the door when she heard Stenko say, "Who is that one?"

It was as if a bolt of electricity shot through her.

"April!" Geno shouted harshly. "Stay here." He seemed happy to change the subject.

Shawanna let go of her hand at the shout, and April stopped short of the open door. Before the door shut ahead of her, Shawanna said, "Sorry, girl," and sounded like she meant it. Alone again.

"Turn around," Stenko said. His voice was soft.

She turned, blinking through tears. She wished she could stop them. Geno was looking at her, angry, imploring her to *stop crying.*

Stenko looked at her and gently shook his head. There was something soft in his expression. Sympathy, pity. Or ... *recognition.* As if he knew her.

Geno said, "You want her? We can make a deal. She's absolutely fresh—the freshest. Inexperienced, though. No skills at all I know of. I just want you to know that up front."

"How old are you?" Stenko asked her, ignoring Geno.

"She's ..." Geno started to say.

"I'm fourteen," she said.

Geno stared daggers at her.

Stenko said to Geno, "Fourteen?"

Geno held his hands out, palms up. "Hey, she claimed she was eighteen earlier. I believed her. She *looks* like she could be eighteen."

"Look away, darling," Stenko said to her.

At first, she thought he was asking her to turn and pose. She hesitated.

"Avert your eyes," Stenko said. She turned. But in the reflection of a glass picture frame, she saw him reach behind his back under his jacket. That was the first time she saw the pistol. Stenko wheeled on Geno. There were two loud pops and Geno slapped his forehead like he'd just gotten a major idea instead of two bullet holes. Then Geno pitched forward onto the hardwood floor.

"Don't look," Stenko said, approaching her and taking her by the arm. "We're leaving, and I don't want you to see him."

THEY WENT OUT of the building the same way she'd come in, being pulled by her hand by a man saying, "Follow me."

There was a big dark SUV out front, double-parked. Some of the street boys had gathered around it, and they parted as Stenko came out with her. One of them said, "Nice ride, dude."

Stenko flashed his pistol, said, "None of you ever saw me here."

The boys scattered. She could hear a couple of them say, *"That's fuckin' Stenko!"* Recognizing him. Making her feel special despite her tears, despite the circumstances.

She climbed into the passenger seat and Stenko roared away. As he drove, she stole looks at him. He looked purposeful, determined. Like a man who knew where he was going and would stop at nothing to get there. She was scared, but only because she didn't know what would come next. And even though she'd seen what he could do, she wasn't sure she was in danger. For some reason, her intuition told her to calm down. But why would he single her out, take her like that?

He drove for a half an hour through the city, down streets she'd never seen, finally off the street into a park where there were dark leafy trees and a huge rounded ancient building with a sign reading GARFIELD PARK CONSERVATORY. He pulled over to the curb on the farthest corner of the lot from the conservatory. She looked around: they were completely alone. Whatever was going to happen, she thought, is going to happen now.

He turned toward her in his seat. She could feel his heat.

He said: "Don't worry. Don't be scared. Here, dry your eyes." He handed her a handkerchief from the breast pocket of his jacket. As she dabbed at her face, trying not to ruin her makeup, he said, "When I saw you in there it was like I was looking at a ghost—the ghost of my daughter. Her name was Carmen. What an angel she was. You could be her twin, I swear to God. Poor Carmen—she got mixed up with the wrong people. She ended up in a place like you just came from, but I wasn't there to rescue her. And on her last day on earth she called me twice on my cellphone, but I was in negotiations and I couldn't break free to call her back until that night. It was too late by then. She was gone."

She saw moisture in his eyes, and the corners of his mouth twitched.

He said, "We'd been on the outs and I was getting tired of her calling me only when she needed money. I blame myself for what she did that night, because I know in my

106

heart if I would have been there for her, I could have saved her. I could have checked her into rehab again ..." His voice trailed off. He stared out the window for a full minute before he turned back to her with a crooked smile. "But when I saw you there tonight I thought, *Damn! There she is again.* It's like I'm being given a second chance."

She didn't know what to say.

Said Stenko, "I'm going to treat you right. I'm going to feed you whatever you want to eat and buy you clothes you want. Like you're my daughter come back to earth, that's how it'll be. You'll stay in nice hotels and you'll never have to see the inside of a place like *that*"—he chinned in the general direction of where they'd come—"for the rest of your life."

She shook her head quickly, as if she'd imagined what he said, that he'd actually said something different.

"Really?" she asked.

He smiled. He had a nice smile. She thought if what he said was true—and it probably wasn't—the first thing she would want to do would be to rescue her special stepsister from the Voriceks. With money and a place to live, they could be together, care for each other.

"I will never touch you," Stenko said. "It isn't like that. I don't want you in a sexual kind of way."

"What, then?" she asked. Her voice sounded weak to her.

"I want to be kind to you," he said simply.

"Why?"

It took him a moment to answer, and he glanced outside at the trees, at the conservatory. "Because I haven't always been kind. I've hurt a lot of people—innocents, like Carmen. I didn't really think about what I was doing most of the time. But now I think about it every minute."

She asked, "Why now?"

He said, "I'm dying fast. It focuses the mind."

She didn't know what to say.

"Look," he said, "I know I can't really redeem myself. I don't have enough time. But when I die, I want someone to say, 'He was a kind man to me.' Believe me, it will be a lonely voice in the room. But it's one I just gotta know I might hear."

She was confused.

He said, "I don't expect you to understand all of this. I'm still sorting things out myself. I mean, it isn't unusual for a sixty-year-old man who can pound down an entire deep-dish to have digestive problems. But when you find out it isn't the pizza but advanced bladder cancer that's spread to your liver and you maybe have a month to live, well, like I said, it focuses the mind."

"That's why Geno said you were sick."

He nodded. "He never thought he'd see me again, either, that jerk. He never thought I'd show up at his place like I said I would.

"Anyway," he said, shaking his head, shaking away his thoughts about Geno, "forget what happened. I'm a little … volatile. The morphine and the meds keep me going, but I have the feeling that if I slow down and think about it, that'll be the end. So I gotta keep moving. And I gotta do things right, make things right with the Big Guy," he said, glancing upward.

"So," he said, "when that doctor told me nothing would help, that it was time to make peace with the world, I thought of two things right away. The first was to reconcile with my only son, Robert. That's step one. After we leave here, we're going to pick up Robert in Madison, Wisconsin. He has some kind of crazy-ass environmental foundation there he pays for through his trust fund …" She couldn't see that well in the dark, but she thought he rolled his eyes when he said it. He said, "I was a little surprised he agreed to see me, so I'm excited. I haven't even talked with him in a coon's age. But he said right away he's got a way for us to get back together. To become father and son again. And you—you're like Carmen. The three of us will do it all over again, and this time I'll make it right. This time there will be a happy ending. Ain't that cool?"

She nodded.

"You bet it is," Stenko said. "And the second thing is what we're doing now. Like I said, I want to be kind to you. I want to help you. No strings, April. Just let me be kind to you, okay?"

She nodded.

And he was.

10

Saddlestring

A MASSIVE BLACK full-sized Hummer with darkened windows blocked their driveway when Marybeth and Joe returned home. "Oh no," Marybeth said in an uncharacteristic whine. "Not now. This is *not* a good time."

Joe nodded toward his mother-in-law's vehicle with new vanity plates reading DUCHESS, said, "There never has been a good time."

The driver's window of the Hummer whirred down and there she was, on her cellphone, her free hand flapping at them, gesturing at them to park behind her, oblivious that she was blocking their entrance.

"Ram her," Joe said.

"That's not helpful ..."

Missy had never liked Joe, and the feeling was mutual. She thought her daughter could have done better for herself. Joe agreed with that, but didn't necessarily want to hear it from his mother-in-law. For a while, after he'd been fired from the Game and Fish Department, they'd lived in an old homestead on Missy and Bud Longbrake's ranch.

111

The close proximity had driven a wedge between Marybeth and her mother that had never healed. Joe had not discouraged the rift as it formed, grew, and hardened.

Marybeth said, "I'll try and get rid of her."

Joe said, "You'll need a cross and a wooden stake. I think I might have them in the garage."

"Joe, please. You're being worse than usual."

Missy terminated her call, tossed her phone aside and climbed out.

Missy was an attractive woman—sixty-seven but looked forty, a tiny, slim brunette with a heart-shaped porcelain face and perfectly highlighted and coifed hair. She may not look it, Joe thought, but she was the most relentless and challenging adversary he had ever encountered. Missy was a shark; she never stopped moving forward and she was always hungry, but not for food. In fact, Joe had been around her on the ranch when she ate no more than carrot sticks and celery *for days* if she gained a single pound. Missy was hungry for power, influence, and status. Her lifelong ambition to trade up, replacing husbands with those of greater power and means, had recently reached a new level that stunned the entire valley. He had not seen her since the coup took place several months before, and Marybeth was still beside herself with embarrassment and anger.

As she approached their van, Missy saw Joe, and she paused for a second, her eyes narrowing into slits, threatening to create a network of hairline fissures in the varnish of makeup on her face.

Joe got out, said, "Good to see you, too." He determined that a good part of his animosity was due to the after-effects of an astonishing dream he'd had one night in Baggs featuring ... *Missy*. The recollection of the dream made his scalp crawl, and he'd forgotten about it until he saw her in person.

Missy ignored him and said to Marybeth, "I was just calling your house. I knocked but nobody answered, even though I could hear loud music."

"Sheridan's home," Marybeth said, her voice chilly. "She gets dressed and listens to the radio. She probably couldn't hear you."

"I just got back," Missy said. "I've got some presents for the girls."

"Got back from where?" Marybeth asked without enthusiasm.

Missy went to the Hummer and gathered two packages wrapped in exotic foil wrapping paper. "Bali! It was wonderful."

"Bali?"

"Earl had a conference. We stayed in a hotel on the beach that was the most magnificent place I've ever been in. Who would think a Muslim country could be so wonderful and romantic with all that chopping off of heads and hands and all? But I miss it already."

Marybeth rolled her eyes.

Joe said, "I saw Bud a few weeks ago coming out of the Stockman's Bar. He looks like he's aged twenty years."

Missy fixed her coldest look of disapproval on him. "Was he with his friend?"

Joe shook his head, not understanding.

"His friend Jack Daniel's. The two are rarely apart these days. In fact, I think they're in love."

Six months ago, Bud Longbrake had returned from a bear-hunting trip to Alaska to find all the locks on their ranch house changed and his clothing in a steamer trunk on the front lawn. Missy had traded up again in breathtaking fashion.

They called Earl Alden the Earl of Lexington. Alden was a Southern multibillionaire media mogul who had owned what used to be the Scarlett Ranch. For several years, he'd divided his time among the ranch and three other residences in Lexington, Kentucky; New York City; and Chamonix, France. In an effort to be civic-minded, Alden had joined the library board, where he met its chairwoman, Missy Longbrake. From that moment on, Bud Longbrake's days were numbered, only he didn't know it.

"Duchess," Joe said, looking at her license place. "The Earl and the Duchess, got it."

Missy waggled her fingers. "One might as well have fun with it, right?"

"Who's next," Joe asked, "the president of France?"

Missy actually laughed. Then she composed herself and leveled her ice-blue eyes at him. "That would be going the wrong direction, my dear. Earl could buy and sell the president of France."

The divorce battle had been vicious. Missy had produced a prenuptial agreement signed by both parties that said in the event of a divorce the Longbrake Ranch would be divided evenly between them, even though the property had been owned by Longbrakes for three generations. Bud claimed he couldn't remember signing the document, and besides, if he had, he thought it was something else. Bud now lived in a log cabin that was once used for winter cowboys six miles from the main house. He lived there with his friend Jack Daniel's. Between the Earl and the Duchess, who had consolidated their holdings, they were now the largest landowners in northern Wyoming.

Joe shook his head. To Marybeth, he said, "I need to do some work inside."

He turned and headed for the front door.

Behind him, he heard Missy say, "Aren't you going to invite me in?"

114

"I'm really busy, Mom."

"Of course you are. But I have these gifts for the girls. Wait until you see them—they're beautiful. Hand-painted Indonesian batik boho skirts. You've never seen anything like them before. Lucy will look great in hers. She looks good in anything."

He heard Marybeth sigh.

"Eight hundred dollars each," Missy said, following Marybeth up the walk, "in case you were wondering."

Said Marybeth, "I wasn't."

Once inside, Joe quickly darted for their home office so he wouldn't have to see Missy when she came inside. He closed the door and reached for the road atlas.

He opened the book to the relief map of the U.S., tracing a route from Chicago to Madison on I-90, then continuing on the same interstate through Minnesota and across South Dakota to Keystone. It was a long drive, and there were hundreds of towns and cities en route. He wondered if there were other incidents besides the ones Marybeth had found.

From Rapid City he followed U.S. 18 south to Hot Springs, South Dakota, then south all the way to Cheyenne on U.S. 85. They could have stayed on 85 or jumped onto I-25 south through Denver to I-70 west, south on U.S. 24 past Vail, west on U.S. 82 to Aspen.

He sat back. A hell of a journey, he thought. But where were they headed next? What were they driving?

He hoped he would be present if April contacted Sheridan again so he could feed his daughter questions to ask. He made a list:

- Who is Robert?
- What is the name of Robert's father?

- Are there any others with you?
- What kind of car are you in?
- What do you mean when you say people died? How? When? Why?
- Where are you now?
- What is your destination?
- How did you get away from that compound six years ago?
- Are you willing to meet with me?

Through the door, he heard Missy say, "... and you need to quit telling people in town we're estranged. I hate that word. It makes it sound like *I'm* strange or something. It's not a good word."

Then, and he could visualize her gesturing toward his closed door, "Him I wouldn't mind being estranged from. But not you, Marybeth. You're my daughter."

He smiled grimly to himself. Sheridan had the right idea, he thought. He clicked on the radio to the local country station. Brad Paisley. He turned it up loud.

HIS FIRST CALL was to Duck Wallace, chief investigator for the Wyoming Game and Fish Department in Cheyenne. Wallace was good, and he was sometimes loaned out to other agencies, departments, the Division of Criminal Investigation, and local police departments because of his skill, knowledge, and rock-solid reputation. Duck was a Shoshone from the reservation, and so dark-skinned he was sometimes mistaken for black.

"Wallace," he said, answering on the first ring. He sounded bored and bureaucratic.

"Duck, Joe Pickett."

"Ah, Joe," he said, the inflection indicating he was already interested in what Joe would have to say and a little cautious because Joe only called when a situation was critical.

"Duck, I've got a situation. Without getting into specifics, can a text message be traced?"

"You mean to a certain number? That's easy. Look at the message, Joe."

"No, that's not what I mean. What I'm wondering is can a phone be traced to a physical location from a text message? Like a voice call can?"

Duck was silent for a long time. Joe knew it meant he was thinking, and he had no need to make conversation while he was thinking.

Duck said, "We can't take an old text message and determine where the location was that it was sent from. That just can't be done, I don't think. Of course, the feds have all sorts of tricks these days, especially Homeland Security, so I can't completely rule it out.

"Now if we're talking about tracing a phone to its geographic location when it's turned on or while it's being used, yes, that's possible."

Joe sat up. "How?"

"It's not easy. There's a way to do it, but it's beyond my capacity, Joe. I don't have the expertise. You need to go to the feds with this one. The FBI."

Joe winced. The agent in charge of the Cheyenne office, Tony Portenson, was still furious at Joe for letting Nate walk the year before. Portenson had threatened federal charges against Joe and would have had him arrested if the governor hadn't personally gotten involved and recruited the state's U.S. senators and congresswoman to lean on Homeland Security.

"Yeah, I know about your relationship with the FBI," Duck said. "But if you want this thing figured out, you'll need to go to them. They're the only ones with the expertise, equipment, and ability to get a quick subpoena from a judge to make it happen."

"Crap."

"Well put."

"Is there any way to do this, um, unofficially? Any equipment I can buy, anything like that?"

A long silence. "The only way to do it unofficially is to get many billions of dollars and buy up all the cellphone companies. That's the only way I can think of."

"Gee, thanks, Duck."

"You asked."

"Yeah."

"Can I ask why you're being so close to the vest with this? If it's an official investigation, I can run interference for you, maybe."

"It's not official, Duck. I really don't want to say any more than that."

"Okay," Duck said. Joe could almost feel the shrug through the phone. "I won't ask any more because I don't think I want to know."

"I appreciate that."

"Why is it I get the feeling that I may see the name Joe Pickett in the newspaper again? Why is it that I have that feeling?"

This time, Joe shrugged. Then Duck asked: "How's Marybeth and the girls?"

Joe said fine and asked about Duck's four kids. After ten minutes of trading family information, debating how well the Wyoming Cowboys football team would do this year (not well, they agreed), and discussing where and when each planned to hunt elk in a month, Joe hung up.

He sat back, tried to think of a way around the FBI to get what he needed. But there was no choice.

"Crap."

HE GOT UP and cracked the door. Missy was still out there, and Sheridan had joined them, standing in a robe with a towel on her head and looking uncomfortable. Missy was explaining, in the sweeping but definitive generalizations she used whenever she visited a new city or country and took a two-hour scenic motor coach tour given by a guide in native dress, everything there was to know about Bali. How the people were simple, content, and spiritual, telling them it was beautiful and the food was good and the staff at the hotel treated her like she was royalty, "like a real Duchess."

When Missy unveiled the painted skirts, Sheridan saw them and scowled, but Joe shut the door again and called the FBI office in Cheyenne.

He'd met Special Agent Chuck Coon several months earlier, when Coon was in the Little Snake River Valley investigating a cattle-rustling operation. Over beers in the cinder-block saloon once frequented by Butch Cassidy, Coon told Joe that since food prices had skyrocketed so had incidents of large-scale cattle rustling. "And this isn't like Western movie rustling," Coon explained, "where a couple of local outlaws change some brands. In terms of dollars, this is like stealing a whole damned street of houses."

The rustlers specialized in isolated areas like south-central Wyoming, where cattle were grazed on forest service and Bureau of Land Management land far from any town or highway, preventing suspicious activity from being seen. Using eighteen-wheelers and commercial cattle movers, the rustlers stole entire herds, hundreds of thousands of dollars of beef, in quick nighttime strikes. Coon was new to the job, new to Wyoming, boyish but enthusiastic. He wasn't aware of Joe's history and apparently had not been briefed about his supervisor Tony Portenson's animosity to Joe.

A few nights after meeting Coon, Joe was doing an antelope count in the Sierra Madre foothills when he saw a semi-truck on a remote two-track road in the distance, heading toward a series of forest service mountain meadows where cows grazed on leased grass. It seemed an odd time of year to move cattle, he thought, since the summer grass was lush and bad weather was still months ahead. Using his spotting scope, he was able to get the make and model of the truck as well as a partial plate. He called Coon with the info, and Coon was able to track the vehicle down to a used-truck outfit in New Mexico, who provided the name of the purchaser, who turned out to be an undocumented Mexican national suspected of cross-border rustling. The case was made, six men and two women were arrested, and Chuck Coon was responsible for nailing his first major case.

Coon was at his desk, and Joe ran through the same scenario he had with Duck.

Coon said, "Yeah, we could do it. We'd have to get subpoenas for the cellphone providers, and we'd have to move fast because the companies only keep texts on their servers for a few days before they delete them because the volume is unbelievable. Blame teenagers. But yes, we could do it. When I say 'could' that means we have the capability. That doesn't mean we will."

Joe said, "So you talked to Portenson, then?"

"Your name was in the warrant for the rustlers, Joe. Portenson saw it. When we finally scraped him off the ceiling, he told me his version of events. He doesn't exactly like you, Joe."

"I know."

"And I really can't get a procedure going like the one you're describing unless I've got more to go on," Coon said. "Somehow, we need ownership in this, a reason to go down the hall to see the judge. Judge Johnson doesn't go for fishing expeditions."

Joe knew telling Coon anything meant risking the chance the FBI might move in, take over, make him marginal. He thought of the last time the feds got involved in a situation that involved April and what happened. He didn't *dare* put her into harm's way again.

So he said it: "You owe me, Chuck."

He heard Coon sigh. "I was hoping you wouldn't play that card, Joe."

"Me, too. But believe me, I'd never bring it up if it weren't the most important thing in my life right now." He surprised himself—he'd said too much.

"Look," Joe said, "I'll work with you if you'll work with me. But I can't give you any details just yet. How about we have a meeting to discuss it? Outside your office, of course."

"Meaning away from Portenson," Coon said. "I understand. Yeah, I can do that. When?"

Joe said, "How about tomorrow afternoon? In Cheyenne?"

"You're in a hurry," Coon said.

"Yes, I am," Joe said, trying to figure out a way to give Coon something to go on without including the name April Keeley.

MISSY WAS OUTSIDE, starting up her Hummer, when Joe came out of his office.

Marybeth said, "Good timing."

He nodded. Sheridan was holding up the Indonesian skirt, turning it one way and the other, with bemused puzzlement.

121

"Where would I possibly wear this?" she asked rhetorically. As if to answer her own question, she dropped the skirt over the back of a chair and went down the hall to her room to get dressed.

To Marybeth, Joe said, "I need to go to Cheyenne and see the governor."

Marybeth nodded. "Well, it was good to see you."

That hurt. But she softened quickly. "Go," she said.

AS HE EMERGED from the shed with the eagle bound once again in his sweatshirt with duct tape, Sheridan came outside, and asked, "Where are you taking the bird?"

"Eagle rehabilitation center," Joe said, not meeting her eyes. "I can't get it to eat."

"She's stressed," Sheridan said. "There are stress lines in her feathers from the day she got shot. Feathers are like the rings in a tree—you can tell all sorts of things from them. She won't eat until she feels safe. So tell Nate hi for me."

Joe flinched.

"I'll keep my phone on," she said, "and I'll call you if I hear from April. I have a feeling it might be tonight."

"I've got a list of questions I want you to ask her," Joe said. "It's in on my desk. Of course, you'll need to do it casually, in that text-speak language you use. That's why I can't ask her. I don't know the code."

Sheridan nodded, keeping her eyes on him. "Dad?"

"Yes?"

"If you're going to go find her, I'm going with you."

Joe took a step back. The eagle screeched, sensing his angst. "You've got to be kidding," he said.

"Think about it," Sheridan said. "She's texting *me* on *my* phone. If I'm with you, we might be able to find her."

He started to object, but he knew she was making sense.

"Talk to your mother," he said. "We're talking about you missing some school, not to mention what else might happen."

She beamed. Her smile filled him with joy. "You'll need to talk with her, too."

"I will," Joe said.

"She wants you to find April more than anyone."

"Yup," said Joe.

Sheridan said, "I've been thinking about something, Dad. The last thing you guys told me the day April's mom came to school and took her was to watch over her. I didn't do it. I really feel bad about that."

"Don't," Joe said. "No one knew that would happen."

Sheridan shrugged. "Still ..."

"Look," Joe said. "April called you, Sheridan. Not your mom. Not me. She's doesn't blame you."

Sheridan looked at him, bored into him with her green eyes. "Do you realize what you just said?"

Joe shrugged.

"You said April. You didn't say 'whoever sent you those messages' or something. You said April."

"Slip of the tongue," he said, flushing. "You know what I meant."

"Yes," she said. "I know what you meant."

PART TWO

Future generations may well have occasion to ask themselves, "What were our parents thinking? Why didn't they wake up when they had a chance?" We have to hear that question from them, now.

—Al Gore, *An Inconvenient Truth*

11

Hole in the Wall, Wyoming

Hole in the Wall Canyon was on private ranch land west of Kaycee. It was an abrupt and harrowing scalpel slice through the heart of the high country sagebrush steppe rising toward the Bighorn Mountains. The single rough two-track passed by a ramshackle log home in a stand of cottonwood trees outside the town limits occupied by Large Merle, a bearded giant who was outside splitting wood when Joe approached in his Game and Fish truck. Hearing the vehicle, Merle stood up his entire seven feet and rested the ax on his shoulder and squinted. His bearing was pure intimidation, as was the lever action Winchester leaning against a tree but within Merle's reach. Out of habit Joe did a quick mental inventory of his weapons: .40 Glock on his hip, .308 carbine in the gun rack, 12-gauge Remington Wingmaster behind the seat.

Merle recognized him and nodded, and Joe waved back. To get to the Hole in the Wall, it was necessary to get Merle's nod. A hooded prairie falcon sat on a stump near Merle, a perfectly still sentinel Joe might have missed if it weren't for the rustling of feathers from the breeze.

Joe was always taken when he neared the canyon, not by what he could see but what he couldn't. From the road he couldn't discern the lip of the canyon or its far rim, but he could sense a void in the rolling landscape itself. That's where the canyon was. It couldn't be seen from the highway, the road he was on, or even from the other side in the foothills except for a jagged dark line in the prairie. To get there, one had to travel across the wide-open treeless plain for miles under the big sky, not a tree in sight. As he drove through the sagebrush and knee-high cheater grass, a heavy-winged squadron of sage grouse lifted off on both sides of him with the rhythmic thumping of miniature overweight helicopters. In the distance, a herd of pronghorn antelope were grazing, three dozen auburn bodies splashed with strategic patches of white that made them nearly invisible on the prairie among scattered drifts of snow in the winter and spring. It was impossible to sneak up on Hole in the Wall, which was why it had been the dedicated haunt of old west outlaw gangs, most famously Butch Cassidy and the Sundance Kid. Joe thought how odd it was that two days before he'd been in Baggs, where the old-timers swore that Butch lived among them into old age under an assumed name, and now he was at the place where Butch, Sundance, and the rest of their gang hid out between bank and train robberies with scores of other infamous Western outlaws.

Recently added to the list was Nate Romanowski.

THE TRAIL FROM the rim of the canyon was narrow, strewn with loose baseball-sized rocks, a sharp declination that switchbacked down. Joe carried the eagle in his arms like a baby, trying not to squeeze too hard when he misstepped on loose shale, lost his balance, and sat down hard with a thump that jarred his spine.

He stood up gingerly and dusted himself off, picked up the bird, and continued. It was usually at this depth into the canyon when he felt eyes on him and knew he wasn't alone.

Tough junipers rose on either side of the trail, and in the windless still air of the canyon they smelled sharp and musky. The Hole in the Wall, because of its vertical walls and the angry stream that coursed through the floor of it and kicked up waves of moisture, was a lush green oasis in the middle of high country desert. The bottom was thick with pines, ash, and ferns, and there were birds, including bluebirds and cardinals, and reptiles he'd rarely seen in the mountain west.

At a sharp switchback shadowed by a canopy of intermarried branches from a family of aspen, whose turning leaves were weeks behind those on the surface, Joe stopped, paused, and wiped the sweat from his face with the sleeve of his shirt. He studied the trail immediately in front of him until he saw it—the glint of the tripwire. He carefully stepped over it in an exaggerated movement. There was no way, he knew, he would have seen it if he hadn't known it was there. He had no idea what the wire connected to—bells? someone's toe?—but he didn't want to find out.

The unique feature of the canyon itself, and why outlaws loved it, was the naturally eroded caves in the opposite wall, their open mouths mostly hidden by brush. But from inside the caves looking out, the trail was in plain sight, a zigzag scar on the face of the canyon. In the daylight, no one could enter the canyon on the trail unobserved. And at night, there were the tripwires.

The roar of the stream increased in volume as he climbed down, and he could feel spray on his face and hands. There was a path through two-story boulders to the hissing whitewater, a crude footbridge, and the trail up the other side between the trunks of two massive ponderosa pine trees. Two hundred feet up the path, Nate Romanowski sat on a stump with his arms crossed in front of him, smirking.

"I watched you the whole time," Nate said. "That fall was kind of comical."

"I did it for your amusement," Joe said.

"Was Large Merle up there watching the road?"

"Yes, he was."

"And what did you bring me?"

"A bald eagle."

"Ah, that's what I thought."

Nate Romanowski was tall, lean, with intense ice-blue eyes, a hawk nose, and long ropy muscles. He was wearing a gray flannel henley shirt and a shoulder holster for his scoped .454 Casull revolver, the second most powerful handgun in the world. As always, Joe felt the sense of calm Nate projected, a calm that could erupt into brutal violence swiftly and naturally, the way a soaring raptor would suddenly collapse its wings and drop to kill its prey in an explosion of blood and snapped bones. After Joe had cleared Nate on trumped-up murder charges years before, Nate had vowed to help protect Joe's family. Their relationship had taken several odd and unsettling turns, but it held, and Nate was a man of his word.

"You remembered the tripwire this time," Nate said. "That's good, because I armed it with a shotgun."

Joe shook his head. "Now you tell me."

"Watch it on the way out, too."

"I will. Do you have room for this bird?"

"What's wrong with it?"

"A guy shot it with an arrow."

Nate's eyes narrowed. "Is the guy still alive?"

"I arrested him."

Nate mock spit into dirt beside his boots to show Joe what he thought of *that*.

JOE FOLLOWED NATE up the trail and through a thick greasy stand of caragana. The mouth of Nate's cave was obscured from the outside by curtains of military camouflage netting, and Nate pushed it aside so Joe could enter. Because the netting was translucent, the depths of the cave were lit in an otherworldly olive green glow, similar to what one saw through night-vision goggles. It took a moment for Joe's eyes to adjust.

"Here," Nate said, "let me see that bird."

Joe was grateful to hand the eagle over.

"You want your sweatshirt back?" Nate asked, pulling a wicked-looking eight-inch knife from a sheath on his belt and slicing through the duct tape.

"Yup."

"You want the sock back?"

"You can keep it."

"What would I want your sock for?" Nate asked.

Joe shrugged.

Nate talked to the eagle, telling her she was a pretty bird, a beautiful bird, that everything was going to be just fine now. Slowly, Nate removed the sock from her head and stared into her brilliant yellow eyes. The eagle opened her beak to screech, but Nate said, "None of that, none of that," and the eagle kept silent.

Joe was amazed, said, "*How* did you do that?"

Nate didn't respond. He was running his hands over the eagle, talking to her, acclimating her to his touch, keeping her calm.

"How do you know she's a she, for that matter?"

"I always know," Nate said. "I could tell when you were carrying her."

Joe didn't pursue it. He watched as Nate slipped the sweatshirt off the eagle, tossing it into a heap near Joe's feet, and continued running his hands over the bird, smoothing her feathers, pausing to feel the scarred-over entrance and exit wounds. From a bulging pocket in his cargo pants, Nate fished out leather jesses that he tied to her talons and a large tooled leather hood that he slipped over her head. He carried her to a heavy stoop made of branches with the bark still on and tied the jesses to the structure. Like a vintner slipping plastic webbing over wine bottles to keep them from clinking together in the sack, Nate gently fitted a sleeve of tight mesh over her body from her shoulders to her talons.

To Joe, he said, "She's going to be all right, I think. You did a good job binding her up like that so the broken bones could start to knit. We'll see in a few weeks if she can fly. This mesh sleeve will keep her from flapping her wings and breaking the bones again. Whether she can fly again will depend on how much other damage there is. I can't fix severed tendons."

"And if she can't fly?"

Nate used his index finger to simulate cutting his throat. "An eagle that can't fly is a deposed king: humiliated and useless to anybody or anything."

AS NATE BREWED cowboy coffee in an open pot on a Coleman stove, Joe took in the cave. It was as he remembered. Gasoline-powered generator, satellite Internet, bookshelves filled with battered tomes on falconry, volumes on warfare and world history, newer books on American Indian culture and spirituality. A table and ancient four-poster bed had been left by outlaws. Near the entrance of the cave were stacks of scarred military footlockers containing clothes, equipment, food, explosives. In an alcove near the cave entrance a skinned pronghorn antelope carcass hung from a hook, the backstraps and most of a hindquarter sliced away. Nate followed Joe's gaze and waggled his eyebrows.

Joe said, "At least you could have pretended you weren't poaching."

Nate said, "My life is an open book. You just don't want to read it."

Joe thought, *He's right.*

Nate handed Joe a cup of coffee, and Joe told Nate about the text messages. Nate had been there backing up Joe at the Sovereign camp that winter afternoon. As Joe talked, Nate's expression never changed.

Nate said, "I've always wondered about that day. I was pinning down the feds, as you know, but in my peripheral vision I saw maybe a dozen snowmobiles take off into the trees. A couple of them had two or three people on them, and I remember one in particular that had some small people clinging to it."

Joe paused. "Why didn't you tell me that before?"

"I never really thought about it," Nate said, shrugging. "You told me you saw April in the first trailer that burned down. I knew they had kids in that camp besides her, so why would I assume she was one of them on that snow-mobile?"

Joe conceded, took a sip.

"Now that I think about it," Nate said, letting the sentence drift away.

"Yeah."

"You feel guilty," Nate said. "You've always felt guilty. That's why you were crazy with rage and almost killed that FBI agent who fired the shot. It wasn't about him—it was about you."

Joe stared into his coffee cup, studied the film of oil on the top of the liquid. "What's your point?"

Nate said, "It isn't April out there. But you want it to be. You want to apologize and make things right. That's how you are, Joe. You're a good man."

"Shut up, Nate," Joe said wearily.

"I was there. You wanted to trust the system and the government. You wanted to believe the authorities would do the right thing. You never thought they'd fire and torch the Sovereign compound with all those people in it. You didn't realize then that the scariest thing on earth is a bureaucrat with a gun."

"Enough."

"HOW'S ALISHA DOING with the new baby?" Joe asked after a long while. They'd both been silent, each with their own thoughts about that afternoon in the campground.

Alisha Whiteplume was Nate's woman, a schoolteacher on the Wind River Indian Reservation, and the mention of her name produced a goofy, sloppy grin from Nate. Joe was still not used to seeing Nate's face light up.

"Still smitten, I see," Joe said.

"With both of them. I just don't see them enough, you know?"

"Believe me, I know."

"I hate having to hide out, Joe. I'm never turning myself in, but I hate hiding out. I'm starting to consider my options."

"You mean moving?" Joe didn't blame him, but Nate was a part of him now and he'd saved Joe's life more than once. And he was Sheridan's master falconer.

"Either that," Nate said, lowering his voice, speaking in his breathy Clint Eastwood cadence, "or taking out every damn one of them who is after me."

Joe groaned. "Nate, you forget I'm a peace officer who took an oath. I take that oath seriously. You just can't say things like that around me."

Nate smiled. "Sorry, I forgot." Then: "I've no plans yet. I won't just vanish."

"Good."

"Because it sounds like you might need me on this one."

Joe nodded.

"You want me to come with you now?"

"No, not yet. I'm going to be working closely with the people who want to throw you back into jail. You don't want to be around. *I* don't want you around."

"But you'll let me know if you need help." It was a statement, not a question.

"Yup. What's the best way the contact you? When I need your help, I might be too far away to come down and get you in this canyon."

Nate dug into his cargo pants and pulled out a satellite phone.

"You get a signal all the way down here?"

Nate shook his head. "Of course not. I don't even think the eyes in the sky can see down into this place. But twice a day I hike up the trail to the top to check for messages. And if for some reason I don't respond right away, call Large Merle and he'll let me know.

"Just send a text," Nate said. "You know how to do that, right?"

AS JOE PARTED the camo netting to leave, Nate said, "I never really thanked you for what you did for me last year, Joe. I bet your life has been hard since then."

Joe said, "If I trip over that wire on the way out and the shotgun goes off and I never find April, I'm really going to be pissed at you."

135

12

Craig, Colorado

T HREE HUNDRED MILES from Hole in the Wall Canyon, hours after Joe cleared the rim and hiked toward his pickup to drive to Cheyenne, she leaned against the stall of the gas station bathroom in Craig, Colorado, and listened to Stenko retching horribly in the men's next door. The sounds were awful, and she was frightened.

It had already been a long day. Stenko had awakened her deep into the night and hurried her out of the hotel in Aspen into the SUV. Robert was already inside the car. He was anxious, jittery, supercharged, thumping a rapid-fire beat with his hands on the dashboard like a drummer. "Go man go," Robert said to Stenko, "Go-go-go-go-go ..."

They drove north until dawn came pink and glorious, through still-sleeping Glenwood Springs and Rifle. Robert was still jazzed and had been talking incessantly about the need to change vehicles and tactics, but she tuned him out and went back to sleep. At a convenience store in Meeker, Robert pointed out a local Chevy Suburban parked and running while the driver was inside getting coffee. Stenko pulled to the side of the building while Robert got out, duck-walked to the Suburban, and drove it away. Stenko followed, cursing under his breath. A half hour out of town, when the terrain emptied of homes and buildings, Robert took a beat-up old dirt road and they bounced along it for what seemed like forever. Finally, the Suburban brake lights flashed and Stenko slowed to a stop.

Stenko addressed her by looking in the rear-view mirror. "April, you'll need to gather up all your things and take them to the Suburban. We're making a change."

"This isn't a hybrid, son," Stenko said as he climbed into Robert's car.

"I know," Robert grumbled. "These people out here give us no green options, but you'll just have to make it up on the other side."

The morning was cool and smelled of dust and sagebrush. After climbing into the far back seat of the Suburban, she watched with fascination as Robert sprayed lighter fluid on the seats of Stenko's SUV and tossed in a match. With the new Suburban, they pushed the burning vehicle over a cliff into a deep arroyo. The crash on the bottom was fantastic.

Their only other stop before arriving in Craig was at a roadside rest area, where Robert stole the plates off a car and replaced them with the plates from the Suburban.

SHE WAS STARING vacantly out the window when a cell-phone burred and for a moment she thought it was hers, thought she'd been betrayed. Had she forgotten to turn the ringer off?

But Robert didn't even turn around. To Stenko, he said, "Are you going to get that?"

"I forgot I even had it," Stenko said, slapping absently at his shirt pockets, then finally digging it out of his trousers.

He looked at it for a moment, said, "One of my friends in blue ..." and opened it up.

Stenko said very little, prompting the caller to continue with several "uh-huhs." Then he closed the phone and tossed it on the seat next to him.

"Who was it?" Robert asked.

"Like I said, one of my friends in blue."

"What's up?"

"Leo's wife called the station. She doesn't know where he is and she wants him found. She thinks he's taken up with a chippie and relocated to Wyoming."

Robert said, "Wyoming? What the hell's in Wyoming?"

Stenko said, "My ranch."

Robert did a dry spit take and the car weaved until he jerked it back into his lane. *You own a ranch?*

"I think I do, anyway. The more I think about how things went down with Leo, the more I become convinced I own a ranch." Stenko sat up in the seat and smacked his forehead with the heel of his hand. "That damned Leo. He always wanted to be a cowboy—he told me that once. Here's this little mousy guy who grew up on the South Side getting his lunch money stolen from him every day on the way to school, but he secretly wants to be a cowpoke. It used to crack me up."

Robert said, "You're drifting."

"No, I'm not," Stenko said. "I know where Leo is with all my money. He's on my ranch, the son-of-a-bitch." To her, he said, "Sorry for the language."

She shrugged, totally confused.

Robert shook his head, muttering, "*A ranch*. You own a ranch. What else do you own?"

Stenko said, "A lot."

SHE'D BEEN SLEEPING soundly in the roomy back seat

when she was awakened by Robert shouting, "Dad? Dad, what's wrong?"

AND SHE COULD hear Robert now, through the wall. Something about Stenko's morphine. "Then take more!" Robert yelled. "Take as much as you need to!"

She'd gotten a glimpse at Stenko as he staggered into the bathroom. He'd looked back at her. His face was white, his eyes rimmed red. His mouth was twisted in pain, but he still managed to smile at her and gesture with his hand that he'd be right back. The way he bent forward as he walked made her think it was his stomach that was hurting him.

The bathroom she was in was filthy, with grime on the floor, an overflowing trash can, and the strong ammonia smell of urine from the stall. She imagined the men's was just as dirty, and she felt sorry for Stenko, who sounded like he was probably clutching the toilet, knees on the floor.

She heard Robert say harshly, "For Christ's sake, Dad. Hang in there already. We've got too much to do here."

And she thought: What if he dies right there? What would Robert do with her? She thought about the look on his face that morning in the car, his wild eyes, the way he beat that drum solo on the dashboard. It was either that or long hours of pouting and sarcasm. Plus the way he sometimes leered at her, his eyes pausing on her breasts. She didn't want to be alone with Robert.

She fished the TracFone out of her jeans. She hadn't turned it on since the night before, when she'd made contact. It seemed like forever before the phone grabbed a signal, showed strong bars.

She typed:

Sherry, r u there?

13

Cheyenne

JOE HIT THE northern outskirts of Cheyenne mid-afternoon. He was traveling south on I-25 when he saw the first of many concentric circles of massive new homes. He also saw more grazing horses than had likely ever been there when the capital city was the hub of the Union Pacific and home to dozens of wealthy ranchers in the 1880s and 1890s, when the west was new.

He was running late. Too much time in the Hole in the Wall.

Special Agent Chuck Coon was getting up to leave and was obviously ticked off when Joe walked into The Albany downtown. The place was old and dark, with private booths. The building was in the shadow of the restored Union Pacific depot. Between the lunch and dinner crowds, The Albany was devoted to serious drinkers and none of them even turned around and looked at Joe as he said, "Sorry I'm late, Chuck, please sit back down."

Coon had stripped off his tie and loosened his collar, but Joe thought there was no one with a shred of intelligence in the bar who wouldn't look at him and say, "FBI." Coon had close-cropped brown hair, small features, and a boyish, alert face that didn't wear his impatience well.

Joe slid into the booth across from Coon.

"I can't spend much time," Coon said, looking nervously around the bar before sitting back down. "I told the secretary I had a podiatrist appointment. I don't know why I said that. There's nothing wrong with my feet."

"I won't waste your time then," Joe said. "Here's the number." He slipped a page from his notebook across the table with the number of April's cellphone.

Coon didn't pick it up. "I told you, Joe. I can't seek a tap unless we get approval to open up an investigation. I'm sorry you had to drive so far to hear that in person."

Joe nodded but forged on. "I've got other business this afternoon, but since I'm here at least you can answer some questions though, right? So I know more about this?" He tapped the notebook page.

Coon sighed, shot out his wrist, and looked at his watch.

"I'll be quick," Joe said. "First, tell me if it's possible to pinpoint the location of a cellphone user. I mean, assuming you've got the court order and everything's aboveboard."

"The short answer is yes," Coon said. "The long answer is what screws us up all the time."

"Meaning?"

"When a cellphone is turned on, it has to reach out and grab a signal before you can make a call. When it connects with a cell tower, it's referred to as a *ping*. The telephone providers can key on a specific number and they can pinpoint the location of the phone based on which cell tower got the ping."

"Great," Joe said, smiling.

"There is also a GPS feature in a lot of the newer phones.

Most people don't even know their phone is also a GPS device. We're waiting for someone to come up with software that blocks the signal, but so far no one's come up with an easy system. So we've got two ways to track down where a call comes from, the ping and the GPS if the phone has one."

"Even better," Joe said.

Coon looked around the bar again to see if anyone was listening to him. Satisfied, he leaned toward Joe. "The technology we've got is really good, but there are some real drawbacks out here in the middle of nowhere. Sometimes the cell towers are ten miles or more apart from each other. The mountains play havoc on the tower sight lines, for instance. It isn't like a city, where there are towers everywhere. So even though we might pick up the ping we've been waiting for, we often can't narrow the actual location of the phone down much more than a ten- or fifteen-mile radius of the tower. That's twenty or thirty square miles—a big area, Joe."

"What if the suspect is in a car?" Joe asked. "Can you track his movements by which cell towers get pinged along a highway?"

"Yes." Coon demonstrated by running his index finger along the table as if the Formica were a map. He flicked his finger every couple of inches, going, "Ping, ping, ping, ping, all the way to Denver."

"Let me ask you another question," Joe said. "If you were given a printout of a text thread and all the specifics of the exchange, could you go to the phone company and trace where each phone was at the time?"

Coon frowned. "It's possible, but it doesn't always work. Like I told you, the companies only keep text messages on their servers a short time. Once the texts are trashed, they're trashed."

The way Coon said it made Joe suspicious. Joe said, "Okay, that's the official FBI spin. But you can't tell me that if you really wanted to, if someone involved in counterterrorism, say, wanted to track down both parties even weeks after the conversation that they couldn't do it?"

Coon looked away. "I have no comment on that."

"Which tells me what I need to know," Joe said.

"I've got to get going, Joe. I'm sorry I can't help you more."

Joe said, "So the key is for the target to keep their cellphone on, even if they're not making calls all the time. If the phone is on, it's making these pings out there."

Coon sighed, "Right."

"What if the phone is only turned on to call or text, and then is turned off again?"

"That makes things real hard," Coon said. "It means we've got to be on top of it when that cellphone is turned on to track it immediately, as it's being used. Once it gets turned off, we lose any ability to know where it's going."

"What about the GPS feature?"

"Same thing. If the phone is off, the GPS is off."

"Hmmm," Joe said, rubbing his chin. He had a feeling April didn't keep her phone on because of how she'd warned Sheridan not to call. If April didn't want anyone to know she was in contact, she wouldn't risk an errant ring or even a wrong number that would tip them off. So it made sense she'd power it up only when she wanted to communicate.

"Who are you trying to find?" Coon asked.

Joe evaded the question. "How long does it take to get a subpoena if you've got probable cause?"

"Minutes, in some cases. As I mentioned, Judge Johnson is right down the hall."

"Wow—it's never that quick out in the real world."

144

"Who are you trying to find?" Coon asked again.

Before Joe could think of another way to avoid the question, his cellphone burred. He fumbled, found it in his breast pocket. Sheridan.

"Excuse me," Joe said to Coon, "It's my daughter."

"I'm out of here," Coon said, reaching for his jacket.

Joe held up his hand for Coon to wait, but Coon shook him off.

Sheridan said, "April texted me again."

Joe grabbed Coon's wrist. "Please, just a minute."

Coon conceded with a sigh.

To Sheridan, Joe said: "How long did you text back and forth?"

"Not long. Not more than a minute. She was in a big hurry. I think she's scared, Dad."

"What did she say?"

"Not much. She asked how I was."

"Did you get a chance to ask her any of the questions I left you?"

"Only one."

"Did she answer?"

"Yes."

"Give it to me."

"Okay. When I asked her 'Who is Robert?' she said, 'Stenko's son.'"

Joe grabbed the notebook sheet with April's number on it and uncapped his pen. "How is that spelled?"

"S-T-E-N-K-O."

Joe wrote it down. "Nothing else? No first name or anything?"

"That's all. Then she texted, 'Gotta go, later,' and that was all. I sent her a couple more messages but she didn't reply. I think she turned her phone off."

145

"Okay," Joe said. "Good job. Keep your phone on and call me if she gets back in contact."

"I will, Dad. Love you."

"Love you."

Joe snapped his phone shut. Coon hadn't left. In fact, Coon stood transfixed, staring at Joe.

"You're shitting me, right?" Coon said.

"What?"

"Stenko. You wrote down Stenko. Is that a joke?"

"No joke," Joe said.

"Stenko called your *daughter*?"

Joe could see in Coon's eyes that the name made bells ring. He didn't know which ones, of course, but it gave him the excuse to do an end-around, to keep April's name out of it.

"He didn't call," Joe said. "He sent a text."

"Is this Stenko from Chicago?"

Joe nodded.

"Do you have any idea who he is?"

"Nope."

"We do," Coon said, sitting back down.

JOE'S HEAD WAS still spinning when he went to see the governor. He bounded up the capitol steps and opened the heavy door just as the guard on the other side prepared to lock it.

"We close at five," the guard said.

"I'm here to see the governor," Joe said.

"Is he expecting you?"

"He told me to drop by any time I was in Cheyenne."

The guard laughed. "He tells everyone that."

"Really," Joe said. "It's urgent. If you don't believe me, go into his office and tell his receptionist Joe Pickett is here to see the governor. If he turns me away, I promise to go quietly."

The guard looked Joe over, noted the Game and Fish shirt, the J. PICKETT badge.

"You're really him, aren't you?" the guard said. "Wait here, Mr. Pickett."

For the first time in his life, Joe felt mildly famous. It was similar to a headache.

GOVERNOR SPENCER RULON was on the telephone. He cringed a greeting and waved Joe into a deep red leather chair. Joe removed his hat, put it crowndown in his lap, and waited.

Rulon was a big man in every way, with a round face like a hubcap, an untamed shock of silver-flecked brown hair, and eyes like brown laser pointers when he fixed them on a person or an object. He had the liquid grace big men had, and his movements were impatient, swift, and energetic. If the recent scandal allegations had affected him physically, Joe couldn't see it.

The last time Joe had been in the governor's office, Stella Ennis, Rulon's chief of staff, had been there along with the head of the state DCI. Tony Portenson of the FBI had also been present, and Rulon had successfully browbeaten him into releasing Nate Romanowski on Joe's request. That had not gone well.

Rulon was in the last year of his first term and he was running again. What should have been a walkover had turned into a race, primarily due to the Stella Ennis and Nate Romanowski scandals. His natural enemies were flush with newfound excitement and confidence, like journeymen boxers who had been beaten round after round but somehow landed a lucky punch that sent the champ reeling.

147

His opponent was Forrest Niffin, a Central Wyoming rancher with a handlebar mustache, who was mounted on a white horse in all of his campaign posters. Despite his rustic image, the challenger was a multimillionaire who had recently moved to Wyoming from upstate New York, where he'd founded a fashion empire. Oddly, Rulon had a framed photo of the challenger on his bookshelf behind his head.

Despite Rulon's eccentric and mercurial ways, like challenging the senate majority leader to a shooting contest to decide a bill or sending Joe on assignments "without portfolio" to maintain deniability, Joe knew that the governor had saved him and pulled him out of the bureaucratic netherworld. He owed him his job and his family's welfare.

"I understand," the governor said into the phone, "but if you permit one more well before your lawyers and my lawyers have a sit-down, I'm gonna sue your ass. That's right. And I'm going to call a press conference out in some scenic spot in the mountains to announce the suit so every photo has that pristine view behind me."

Joe could hear the caller say, "You're out of your mind."

Rulon nodded and waggled his eyebrows at Joe while he said into the phone, "That's pretty much the conclusion around here."

Smiling wolfishly, Rulon hit the speaker button on his phone and leaned back in his chair.

"You can't threaten me," the caller said. Joe thought the voice was vaguely familiar.

"I just did."

"Look, can't we discuss this more reasonably?"

"That's what I'm *trying* to do," Rulon said, grasping the phone set with both hands, pleading into it. "That's what I *proposed*."

Joe could hear the man sighing on the other end. "Okay. I'll have our legal guys call your people tomorrow."

"Lovely. Goodbye, Mr. Secretary."

Rulon punched off. Joe felt his scalp twitch.

"The Secretary of the Interior?" Joe asked.

Rulon nodded. In the west, the Secretary of the Interior was more important than whoever the President might be. And Rulon had just threatened to *"sue his ass."*

"Empty suit," Rulon declared.

Joe was confused. Did the governor mean the threatened legal action or the secretary himself?

"Both," Rulon said, reading Joe's face. "Now what is the occasion of your extremely rare visit to the very heart of the beast?"

Joe knew Rulon didn't like formalities or rhetoric, and Joe wasn't adept at either one anyway: "I want a leave of absence to pursue a case on my own. I might be in Wyoming, but I might also need to cross state lines. And this is the thing: I might need to call on you or the DCI for help at some point."

Rulon leveled his gaze. "You know how much trouble you got me in by letting Romanowski go?"

"Yes," Joe said. "I want to thank you for sticking your neck out for me last year. I know you didn't have to do that. I'm sorry about the heat you've taken."

Rulon said, "Goes with the territory. I'll survive. What can they do? Take my birthday away from me?" He gestured behind him at the photograph. "The people of Wyoming are smart. They'll flirt with that knucklehead Niffin at first, but they'll come to their senses."

"I hope so," Joe said.

"Besides, the Romanowski thing was peanuts compared to what Niffin's operatives are saying about me and Stella

149

Ennis." Rulon probed Joe's face, making him uncomfortable. Joe had known Stella two years before she showed up as the governor's chief of staff. He knew what kind of power she had over men. He doubted Mrs. Rulon would be so understanding.

Rulon said, "Nothing happened. And the stuff they're saying—that's not how we do politics in Wyoming."

Joe nodded.

"It could have. Hell, it should have. But it didn't."

"Okay."

"She left on her own accord."

"Okay," Joe said, squirming. He wasn't sure why Rulon felt the need to confess to him.

"Back to your request," Rulon said. "What's it concerning?"

Joe swallowed. "It's a family thing. I'd rather not say."

Rulon smiled slightly and shook his head, his eyes never leaving Joe. "You ask me things no one else would ask me," he said.

Joe nodded.

"Good thing I trust you," the governor said, standing up quickly. He was around the desk before Joe could react.

Rulon placed his hand on Joe's shoulder like a proud father. "Go, son. Do what you need to do."

"Thank you, sir," Joe said, taken aback.

"Do the right thing."

Joe said, "That's what you told me last time, and I let Nate escape."

Rulon chuckled. "I'll advise your new director that you'll be out of pocket for a while but that you're still on the payroll."

"Thank you."

"But Joe," Rulon said, leaning forward so he was nose to

nose with him, "if this thing, whatever it is, blows up—we did not discuss it here, did we?"

"No."

"And you can't expect me to bail you out again."

"I wouldn't even ask."

"So we're clear?"

"Yes, sir."

Rulon said, "I can tell from your eyes this is important to you. Go with God, but keep me out of it."

14

NORTH OF CHUGWATER on I-25, Joe remembered he had muted his cell while he met with the governor, and he checked it. Two messages—neither from Sheridan or Marybeth. He retrieved the earlier call because he recognized the Baggs prefix. It was the weary voice of Baggs deputy Rich Brokaw, saying Ron Connelly had been released on his own recognizance by the county judge and that Connelly had apparently skipped town. His neighbors reported seeing Connelly packing up his belongings into his pickup truck the night before. Brokaw had checked out the house—empty, garbage everywhere, holes punched in the drywall. The sheriff's office had issued an APB on Connelly, but so far there had been no credible sightings. Brokaw apologized for the way things turned out and said he'd keep Joe informed. Joe snorted angrily. Connelly didn't seem the type to have seen the error of his ways and split town to turn over a new leaf. He seemed the type, to Joe, to escalate into something worse. Men who thought nothing of killing or injuring animals for their pleasure were capable of anything. Connelly was like that; Joe could sense it. What was the judge thinking?

Joe made a mental note to be on the lookout for

Connelly's 4×4 with the Oklahoma plates. There weren't *that* many roads in Wyoming, and stranger things had happened.

The second call was from an unknown number that turned out to be Special Agent Chuck Coon's personal cellphone. "Joe, I looked up what we have on Stenko. You need to call me back as soon as you can. Call this number, not the office number."

Joe pulled off the highway within sight of Glendo Reservoir. The lake was still and glassy, mirroring the vibrant fuchsia streaks of dusk, and he could see the small twinkling lights of trolling fishing boats working near shore, trying to pick up walleyes.

He caught Coon at dinner with his family, and Joe offered to call later but Coon said, "Hold on." Joe could hear Coon tell his wife he'd be back in a minute, and a little boy say, "Where's Daddy going?" The little boy's voice made something inside him twang in a familiar way.

"Okay," Coon said in a moment, "I'm in the other room now."

"I'm on the highway headed north. There's a pretty sunset."

Coon ignored him. "Hey, I looked up Stenko, aka David Stenson of Chicago. I was right—we're interested in him."

"If his name is Stenson, why does he go by Stenko?"

"They do that," Coon said.

Joe said, "Oh. Who does that?"

"Chicago mobsters."

Joe took a breath and held it. The escalation from deviant game violators to … Chicago mobsters … made him suddenly light-headed. He said, "What do you mean you're *interested* in him?"

Joe could picture Coon hunching over with his back

154

toward the doorway so he could speak softly and not alarm his son. "Look, Joe, I can't just give you everything without getting something back. Like how is it a game warden in Wyoming is suddenly asking me questions about tracking down a cellphone involving some guy named Stenko? I mean, how do we get there from here?"

Joe felt a shiver run up his back. Coon's tone betrayed his intense interest, as did the fact that he'd left Joe his private number and asked him to call after hours. So who was this Stenko? And how was it April could be with him?

Joe said, "I'm not going to let you take over this investigation."

"*What?*" Coon sounded hurt, but it was a put-on, Joe thought.

"I know how the FBI operates," Joe said. "You move in. You take over. And most of the time I have to admit it's helpful because you guys have all the electronics, manpower, federal prosecutors, and heavy artillery. Hell, I can't even keep a poacher behind bars. But in this particular circumstance, I can't let you guys swoop in."

Coon said, "Look, Joe, I don't know what's going on, but you came to me. You threw out the bait and I took it. This can't be one way—me giving information to you. Whatever it is you're into, you *need* me. You're one guy in a red shirt in a state pickup. How in the hell are you ever going to track down Stenko?"

Joe thought, *You're right*. But he said, "I don't care about Stenko."

There was a long beat of silence. "Then what is this about?"

"I care about someone who might be with him," Joe said, hoping it wasn't too much information. "And the last time the feds showed up in a situation involving this particular person, really bad things happened. I can't let it happen again. Simple as that."

"I'm confused," Coon said. But he said it in a distracted way. In the background, Joe could hear Coon tapping away at a keyboard. Probably trying to find out what Joe was alluding to.

Joe said, "This is personal."

"If it involves Stenko, it's not personal, Joe. It's obstructing a federal investigation, and we could come down on you like a ton of bricks. Believe me, Portenson would *love* to do that. And it's the reason I'm not involving him at this stage. I'm doing you a favor, Joe, can't you get that?"

Joe believed him. Chicago mobsters? A federal investigation?

"Look, why can't we trade information?" Coon said. "You give me a little, I'll give you a little. It's not out of the realm of possibility that we can help each other out."

Joe watched a fishing boat do a slow circle in a bay out on the lake. "You start," he said.

Coon sighed. More tapping. Then: "Stenko's well known to our Chicago office. He's one of those guys who's flown under the radar for years because he's smart and careful, but his name just kept coming up over and over again in the background. We're talking real estate schemes, the Chicago political machine, downtown redevelopment, fast-food franchises, waste management contracts. There are allegations that he's been the mover and shaker behind quite a few Indian casinos as well, but it was hard to figure out if he was doing anything illegal. Finally, seven months ago the federal prosecutor had enough on him to convene a grand jury that indicted Stenko on twenty-four counts, including fraud, bribery, money laundering, extortion—the laundry list of white-collar crimes. No doubt the guy's intimately connected

156

to most of the stuff that goes on in Chicago, but he wasn't flamboyant or stupid like a lot of those guys. He made it a point not to get photos of himself with politicians and movie stars, for example. We had a hell of a time getting a valid photo and had to resort to DMV records. He was able to keep himself at arm's length from most of the hijinks and transactions because he had a really sharp accountant fronting his operations. I should say, he had a sharp accountant named Leo Dyekman. And the Talich Brothers."

Joe said, "Uh-huh," as if he knew whom Coon was talking about.

Coon said, "The Talich Brothers are ruthless leg-breakers of the highest order. Three of them: Corey, Chase, and Nathanial. Born a year apart: boom-boom-boom. One black-haired, one blond, one redhead, all built like cage-match wrestlers. They're famous in Chicago, from what I understand."

"Okay."

"So anyway," Coon said, getting into it, "after years of investigations and two trials that ended when lone jurors held out—call it the Chicago way—Stenko finally goes down. We arrest him in his real estate office with news crews covering it. Stenko gets thrown in the pokey and everything in his office is seized. But when our guys go to sweep up Leo the accountant and the Talich Brothers, they're nowhere to be found. They've flown the coop—disappeared. And so have the computers and financial records we were after to prove Stenko was worth millions. But we forge on, hoping to flip Stenko himself, hoping he'll turn on Leo and his crew who left him high and dry or the higher-ups in the Chicago scene. But Stenko lawyers up and gets his wife to sell five million dollars in real estate to pay his bond."

Joe was trying to keep up with Coon, trying to figure out where in all this April came in. If at all.

"So Stenko's out of jail and he misses a preliminary hearing because he suddenly claims he's sick. He claims he's dying, in fact. He gets a doctor to tell the judge Stenko's got liver and bladder cancer at the same time—which I guess is a death sentence. There's nothing the doctors can do when somebody has advanced forms of both and the end comes real fast. We don't believe Stenko's doc, and we ask the court that Stenko be evaluated by an independent expert. But Stenko doesn't make the appointment. This is two weeks ago or so."

Joe nodded, the time frame fitting.

"So Stenko is missing," Coon said. "He didn't even pack up. His wife claims she has no idea where he went—he didn't come home, hasn't called. We've got all the phones tapped, so we'd know. He vanished off the face of the earth. All we've got is an unsubstantiated rumor to follow up on—"

Coon cut himself off, probably realizing—as Joe did—he'd revealed more than he wanted to.

"Your turn," Coon said.

Joe sucked in air, trying to locate the words. Finally, "This is all news to me. Like I said, I don't really care about Stenko."

"Who do you care about, Joe?"

"Like I said, someone who may be with him. Maybe on the run with him."

Coon tried to keep the annoyance out of his voice, but he didn't succeed. "Someone with a cellphone? Someone who called you?"

"Actually, the text was sent to my daughter."

"Who is this person?"

"I won't say. I told you that."

"Where did the text come from?"

Joe hesitated. He needed to know what the rumor was. "Supposedly Aspen."

"Colorado?"

"Yup. That's what ... the caller ... claimed."

Alarm bells went off in his head. He almost said *she*.

"Male or female?"

"Whoever sent the text."

"Christ," Coon said. "I'm disappointed, Joe. I gave you a lot. You haven't given me anything I didn't know already."

"That's true," Joe said, his mind spinning, trying to figure out what to give without endangering April. But if she was somehow mixed up with this Stenko and these Talich Brothers? Maybe the best thing to do was to spill everything, let the FBI do what the FBI did best?

It didn't feel right yet. He said, "Okay, understand that this is speculation at this point, but it's all I've got."

"Go ahead."

"You should check out murders that were committed in the last two weeks. I don't have the exact dates in front of me, but all involve small-caliber handguns—probably the same weapon. As far as I can tell, no suspects have been arrested, suggesting the murders are random and not personal. The first was in Chicago, then Madison, then Keystone, South Dakota ..."

"Hold it, slow down ..." Coon said, obviously writing down the locations.

"... and Aspen, Colorado. Two days ago."

"Jesus."

"I said it was speculation, and I mean it," Joe said. "Those are locations given in the text messages. There could be more, or it all could be hooey."

Coon hesitated. "We need to put a device on your daughter's phone."

"No."

"Damn it, Joe."

"I told you the rules. And I already gave you the number to track. You have that number, don't you?"

"Yes. We can get an operation up and running tomorrow."

"Good."

"Will you let us look at the text messages?"

"Nope."

He knew he was risking the chance that the FBI would pinpoint the location of April's phone and close in on her without notifying him. But he doubted they'd be able to find her on their own, without his help. For one thing, they didn't know it was April. They also didn't know what kind of vehicle she was in or how many others she was with. The feds didn't have the manpower to flood a ten-to-fifteen-mile radius in the hope of running into Stenko, especially if he was on the move. It was a risk giving up the number, but one he was willing to take.

"You'll notify me if your daughter gets another text," Coon said. Not a question but a statement.

"I will," Joe said, "but only if you'll give me the location of the call if you're able to track it down."

"Deal," Coon said.

"I gave you something to run with," Joe said. "Now what was the rumor you referred to earlier?"

"It's just a rumor."

"I understand that."

Silence. Joe figured he could wait him out.

Finally, Coon sighed. "There is an unconfirmed report of a man matching Stenko's description coming out of a brothel in Chicago two weeks ago. Later, the brothel manager or

160

whatever he's called was found murdered upstairs. No witnesses to the killing."

"Small-caliber weapon?" Joe asked.

"Yes." He said it with the same bolt of realization Joe was experiencing—the two stories coming together.

"Anyone with him? With Stenko?"

"This is unconfirmed."

"Was anyone with him?"

"Calm down, Joe." Then: "He was supposedly with an unidentified female minor. Mid-teens or slightly older. Blond, five foot four, possibly one of the prostitutes."

Joe slunk against the door of the cab, his cheek on the window of the driver's side.

"Joe?"

15

Rawlins, Wyoming

STENKO WAS SICK, Robert was angry, and she was scared. They were in a parking lot outside Buy-Rite Pharmacy someplace in Wyoming in the car they'd stolen. There was only one other car in the lot, a muddy and dented Ford Taurus in a handicapped space. Through the afternoon the sky had darkened and now the wind gusted and rocked the car from side to side on its springs. A herd of tumbleweeds—perfectly yellow, round and hollow, like exoskeletons of large beach balls—swept from somewhere out on the high plains, rolled across the blacktop of the lot and piled up against a high chain-link fence that separated the Buy-Rite from a bank that was closed for the night.

That's me, she thought. *A tumbleweed caught in a fence.*

Stenko to Robert: "Morphine. You've heard of morphine. I need you to go in there and get me some."

Robert took his hands off the wheel and waved them in the air: "How? We need a damned prescription. And if I take those empty bottles from Chicago in there, the pharmacist might do some checking and find out they're looking for you. That would really screw up my life if we got caught in a hellhole like this." When he said it he gestured toward the Buy-Rite, toward the town in general. Robert was startled and gave a little cry when a tumbleweed smacked and flattened against the driver's side window before rolling up and over the hood toward the fence.

Stenko writhed in the front seat. She empathized and was an inch away from crying. She could smell his pain. It had a distinct odor as it oozed out through the sweat on his forehead and through his scalp. The poor man.

Stenko dug the gun out from under his seat and handed it to Robert butt-first. Robert didn't take it. Robert said, "I can't do that."

After a moment, the act of holding the gun seemed to exhaust Stenko, and he let it drop to the front seat. Stenko looked away from his son, out the window on the passenger side. "Then take me somewhere and leave me so I can die. I can't take this pain any longer. It's hell, son. I'm in hell already." His voice was pinched, and he hissed his words through clenched teeth. He wasn't angry. He was hurting.

Robert crossed his arms in front of him and shook his head like a four-year-old who didn't want to eat, she thought.

Stenko writhed again, twisted himself so he could rest his chin on the top of the front seat and look at her directly. His eyes were rheumy. Thick liquid gathered in the corners near his nose. He tried to smile. "I'm so sorry, April, but this may be the end of the road. I feel terrible it turned out this way—I thought I'd have longer. But it is what it is. Don't worry … I'll give you enough money to buy a plane ticket as soon as we can get somewhere with an airport. And I'll give you plenty extra because you'll need it."

For a moment, she was excited. This had turned out to be different than she thought it would be in every way. Now he was giving her a way out.

She said, "I'm not sure where I would go."

He winced, and she couldn't tell if it was from his stomach or what she said. He closed his eyes and the thick gel in them squeezed out and pooled on the tops of his cheeks like wet glue. "You think about it, April," he said. "You think about where you would want to go."

She thought, *No one should die like this, as if there were a brood of small fevered animals inside him trying to eat and claw their way out.*

Robert missed the exchange. As usual he was deep inside his own head, with his own problems. When he spoke his voice was high. "*You* do it," he said to Stenko. "This isn't what I do. This is what *you* do. This is what you've done your whole life. I'm along just to keep score and try to help you redeem yourself in the eyes of Mother Earth."

Stenko didn't respond. He seemed too spent to argue. Instead he turned around again and slunk down in his seat and talked softly to the windshield. "Do you know how to get to the ranch, Robert? On your own without my help?"

Robert nodded. "I can read a goddamned map."

Stenko raised one pale hand and wriggled his fingers in the air, a way of saying, *I don't want to battle with you.*

"What ranch?" she said.

Robert ignored her as he always did.

Stenko said, "You'll figure it out, son. Now, when you get there, you need to take that son-of-a-bitch Leo aside and make him give you all the account numbers. You may have to apply pressure because Leo can be real stubborn. There should be twenty-eight million in stocks, bonds, cash, and property. You won't get access to it all before the feds realize what you're doing, but if you pick the low-hanging fruit ..."

Robert went bug-eyed, shouted: "TWENTY-EIGHT MILLION! Jesus Christ, Dad!"

"Yeah, give or take," Stenko said, waving Robert away. "Now get that money and use it to pay down my debt. It's the only way because I'm running out of time. How much did you say was left on my balance sheet?"

Robert was frozen for a moment, frozen by $28 million. His mouth was hanging open.

"Robert?" Stenko prompted.

Robert shook his head and dug for his laptop. *Tap-tap-tap.* "Twenty-two million to go on your balance," he said. "So far, you've hardly put a dent in it because you really haven't done so well."

"I thought you said eighteen," Stenko wheezed. "I distinctly remember you saying eighteen after Aspen."

"I did some recalculating," Robert said, with a speed-glance toward her. It was what he did when he was lying, she thought.

"I bet you did," Stenko said without malice, "as soon as you heard what I have."

"Dad! Those Indian casinos use up a *ton* of energy! The lights, the air-conditioning, all the gambling machines ... think about it!"

"Sorry, son," Stenko said, reaching over and putting his hand on Robert's shoulder. Robert shoved it away.

"Really," Stenko said. "I'm sorry. I shouldn't have said that. Old suspicious habits die hard. Do you forgive me?"

After a beat, Robert said, "Mmmmmn."

"Okay then," Stenko hissed. "Then go get that money and pay down my debt. Use the rest for your cause. Plant entire rain forests or buy wind farms or whatever the hell it is you do."

It was quiet. She could see Robert thinking, probably shouting "TWENTY-EIGHT MILLION!" over and over to himself in his head.

An old woman with a headscarf pushed a walker out through the door of Buy-Rite and headed slowly for the Taurus. A white prescription bag was clutched in her hand.

Robert said, "Okay, I'll go in."

She watched Robert as he slammed the door shut and strode toward the pharmacy dodging tumbleweeds. He jammed the pistol into the back of his pants and made sure it was hidden by the hem of his jacket. At the door, he paused for a moment to rake his fingers through his hair, throw back his shoulders. Then he went in.

She said to Stenko, "Are you all right?"

He half-turned toward her, his face in profile. "Not really."

"If you give me some of that money, can I use it for something else?"

"Like what?"

She said, "I'd like to rescue my sister. She's not really my sister, but she's all I've got. She's still back in that house in Chicago with all the other kids. Can I use the money to get her out of there? To fly her to me?"

Stenko grimaced a smile. "Sure, April. Do anything you want."

She sat back, satisfied. For the first time in her life, she had a plan of her own and would soon have the means to carry it out. Thanks to Stenko.

"Thank you," she said.

"You're welcome."

Then Robert was back, throwing open the door against

the wind and heaving himself behind the wheel. He entered talking, "... We need to find another pharmacy. This one's no good."

Stenko said, "You didn't get the morphine?"

"Hell no," Robert said. "The pharmacist in there is a redneck. I'm sure he has a gun. And he just *stared* at me all suspicious, as if *daring* me to try something. He knows, Dad. Somehow he knows ... so I beat it out of there. We need to find another place."

Stenko looked away. Robert turned the key and started the engine. "These little towns give me the creeps anyway. They all just stare at you like you're from another planet. They're all inbred or something."

"I don't think there's another pharmacy," Stenko said in a near-whisper.

"Maybe not in this town," Robert said. "But there's bound to be one in a bigger place."

"It's after five," Stenko said.

She said, "Give me the gun."

AS SHE MADE her way up the aisle with the hood of her sweatshirt pulled up and the weight of the gun sagging in her front pocket, she gathered items into a shopping basket. Shampoo, deodorant, toothpaste, hair coloring, a new TracFone since the one she had was low on power. She thought about how Stenko had barked a sharp *"No!"* to her request, but Robert quickly warmed to it, handed over the gun, and said, "Maybe she can finally do something useful."

The jerk. She cared more about his father than he did.

The aisles were well lit, and they led the way toward a counter at the end of the store. Behind the counter was the pharmacist. He wore a white smock and had slicked-back hair and he pretended to busy himself with some kind of tiny project hidden under the cutout opening, but he was actually watching her closely. Robert was right about that. But she was the only customer—so why *wouldn't* he keep his eye on her?

She hoped no one else came into the store. Robert had agreed to tap on the horn outside if anyone showed up, but she didn't trust him to do it. If a police car turned into the lot, she was sure Robert would drive away and leave her in there.

She could hardly feel her legs and the shopping basket seemed weightless. She tried not to keep glancing at the pharmacist as she worked her way toward him, but she couldn't help it. There was a distinct ache in her chest that got worse as she got closer to him.

He said something to her that didn't register.

"What?"

"I said, can I help you find anything?"

What an opening. She knew she needed to decide right then whether or not to go through with it. Her instincts screamed at her to turn and run. But the image of Stenko's tortured face was stronger.

"Do you have morphine?" She could barely meet his eyes.

"Why yes!" the pharmacist said with sarcastic enthusiasm. "And would you like some other narcotics along with it? We have those, too!" And he grinned wolfishly, his eyes sparkling.

She was confused.

Then he reached across the counter and grabbed her wrist, squeezing it hard.

"Why do you have your hood up?" he said. "Is it so I can't see your face? Who are you and why do you want morphine?"

She struggled and pulled back but he gripped harder.

"Please, mister ..."

He reached for her face with his other hand to peel the hood back but she ducked under his arm. The shopping basket fell to the linoleum but didn't spill.

Then she noted that the pharmacist hesitated, that something or someone had diverted his attention. Suddenly her sweatshirt was lighter because the weight of the gun had been removed. Robert shot the pharmacist four times in his neck and chest. She screamed as his grip released on her wrist and she ripped her hand back. The pharmacist sagged out of view behind the counter, leaving a snail's track of blood on the wall behind him.

Robert said to her, "Shut the hell up and help me find the morphine."

16

Saddlestring

J OE AND MARYBETH were in bed but not sleeping. He'd arrived home after nine to find—pleasantly—that she'd saved him the last of the spaghetti and garlic bread they'd had earlier for dinner. While he ate, he'd outlined his day with Nate, the governor, and Coon. She nodded as he talked, seeing where it was going and becoming frightened by the inevitability of the situation ahead. Sheridan had already packed a Saddlestring Lady Wranglers duffel bag with clothes and placed it near the front door.

After they'd cleaned up the dishes, they'd continued the discussion about involving Sheridan, in his office with the door closed. He'd thought about the situation over and over while driving home, and each time he came to the same conclusion. He was more than willing to be talked out of the idea and hoped Marybeth could come up with a better way.

If another text came in while Joe was out in the field looking for April, it would be impossible for him to coach Sheridan into getting her foster sister to reveal her whereabouts. And even if Sheridan was able to get solid

171

information, she'd have to relay that to Joe at a distance—providing he could be reached and was not himself out of range of a cell tower—and hope he was in the vicinity of where the call came in. If those were the only obstacles, though, they could try to get around them. Marybeth could be there with Sheridan if a call came in, for example. She'd probably do a better job of coaching than Joe could do anyway.

But the fact was April had chosen to contact Sheridan. Not Joe, not Marybeth. And if April agreed to meet somewhere, it would be with Sheridan.

Marybeth talked it out, which is what she did. Joe listened. His wife came to the same conclusion he had, and they looked at each other with trepidation.

They went to bed before eleven but it was perfunctory.

OUTSIDE, A COLD wind rattled the bedroom window. Dried leaves that had been hanging from the cottonwood branches broke loose and ticked against the glass.

Marybeth rolled over and propped her head up by folding her pillow over on itself. She said, "I wish I could think of another way than to let Sheridan go with you, but I can't."

Joe grunted. While he welcomed the idea of his oldest daughter's companionship, he was terrified by the possibility that he couldn't keep her safe. This was his dilemma. This had always been his dilemma: keeping his family safe. Although there had been some horrific events and even more close calls, for the most part he'd been successful. Except once: April.

Joe turned to his wife in bed. "The last time she saw me, I was standing across the road with the local cops and the FBI who attacked the compound. I'm sure I

172

looked like I was on their side. What is she supposed to think of me?"

"Your actions can be explained," Marybeth said, "but not without gaining back her trust. And that won't be easy, I don't think. Not after all this time. And I'm sure I'm painted with same brush as far as she's concerned. It makes my heart ache to think of that poor girl being out there for six years thinking that the family that took her in betrayed her in the end. It just makes me want to *wail*.

"Our only hope is she trusts Sheridan to at least listen to her, and later to us. I can see from April's perspective that she assumes we chose not to try and find her after the fire. She probably doesn't even know we were convinced she was dead."

Joe stared at the ceiling, listened to the wind pound the window.

"If we somehow get through this," Joe said, "if everything falls into place somehow and we can talk to her ... would you want to take her back?"

"In a heartbeat, Joe."

He smiled.

"But of course it would be up to her."

After a long silence, Marybeth said, "Lucy wants to go, too."

Joe groaned.

"I'm not letting her, no matter how angry she gets. I know I'll hear plenty of, 'She's my sister, too,' but she'll just have to live with it."

Marybeth turned over on her back as well to stare at the same ceiling. Joe hoped she could gain more wisdom from the view than he had been able to get.

Joe said, finally, "How could April get caught up with a Chicago mobster? How could it even be April?"

There was a light knock on the door before it opened. Sheridan stood in profile from a hall night-light. Her phone glowed blue in the dark. She whispered, "It's her."

From: AK
sherry, u awake dude
ak
CB: 307-220-5038
Aug 26, 12.12 A.M.
Erase REPLY Options

yeah im awake. I've been waiting for u.
sorry. couldn't text earlier.
where r u?
same as always. in a car. ha.

Sheridan was sitting at her desk in her bedroom. Joe and Marybeth hovered behind her, reading the screen of her phone as Sheridan typed and scrolled. Tube had taken to sleeping in Sheridan's room, and he curled at her feet.

"Ask her if she's moving or stationary," Joe said.

Sheridan blew a breath. "Stationary? That's not the best word, Dad. Texting words are short and sweet. She'd know you're here."

"You know what I mean."

The list of questions he'd made out was on the desk. Marybeth gestured to it, and Sheridan nodded.

"I've got to be cool, you guys," Sheridan said. "April's always been pretty suspicious—she has a high-powered BS meter. So let me do this my way."

r u still in aspen?
na. we left last night.

174

where now?

some bar. middle of nowhere.

yre in a bar? cool.

na. im waiting outside in the car. bored.

where at?

not sure. cant remember.

no idea at all?

savage I think. y so many ????

Sheridan said, "See, I've got to be careful. She's starting to wonder."

Joe said, "Savage?" Then: "Not Savage Run? The canyon? That's the only Savage I know."

"Dad, please."

Marybeth shot him a look.

He mouthed, "Okay, okay."

im worried about u.

im ok. but kinda scared now.

?????

bad day. stenkos sick and we're going 2 some ranch.

r u scared of stenko?

na. robert. stenkos nice.

does robert. hurt u?

na. but he hurt some man 2day in a drug store.

?????

2 awful 2 say. later.

Said Marybeth, "Oh no—is that it? Did she sign off?"

"No, I don't think so," Sheridan said. "I think she means she'll tell me what happened later when she has more time. It's too much to text, in other words."

175

Joe said, "Ask her where the drugstore is. Ask her where the ranch is. Ask her if you can meet her there—"

"Dad, please."

"Joe, please."

"Sheesh," Joe said.

can I call u?

NO.

ok.

they cld come outside any minute.

ok. sorry. i want to hear yr voice again.

ya. me 2.

wheres this ranch?

not sure. black hills i heard stenko say.

can I c u?

id like that. me & my other sister.

Sheridan looked up. Joe and Marybeth shrugged.

there's 2 of you? or do u mean lucy?

id like 2 see luce 2. my other sister. chicago.

confused.

sorry. i got a sister in chicago i want to fly out 2 me.

how?

get her a plane ticket 2 me.

when?

as soon as stenko gives me the $. Lol. do u drive?

ive got a truck.

cool. u drive.

where? u name it.

not sure yet. ill let u know.

????
soon i hope.

"Okay," Sheridan said. "Here goes ..."

can i bring my dad?
NO.
what about mom?
NO.
????
just u. us sisters.

Marybeth reached over and squeezed Joe's hand. He looked up. Her eyes were moist with tears.

Joe thought, *Savage? What ranch? What sister?*

how bout 2morrow.
NO. do u miss maxine?
yes.
sad.
we have a new dog named tube.
can u bring him?
maybe 2morrow.
ill let you know.

Joe said, "See if you can get her to tell you what kind of car they're driving."

what kind of car u in?
just a car. no big whoop. what kind of dog is tube? is luce awake?

"Man," Joe said, "she's tough to crack."

Sheridan said, "Unless it's a cool car, girls don't know makes and models and things like that, Dad. I don't know what kind of van Mom drives and we've had it for years."

Joe shook his head.

lucys sleeping.

can u wake her up?

hold on. tube is a corgi/lab mix.

LOL!

Joe looked to Marybeth, puzzled.

"Laugh out loud," Marybeth said.

"Oh."

Suddenly:

here they come G2G bye.

"Is she gone now?" Marybeth asked.

Sheridan sat back. "Yes."

"Can you try again?"

Sheridan's tapped out several versions of "Are you there?" "Are you coming back?" "April?"

No reply.

"She probably turned her phone off again," Sheridan said.

"Why won't she let you call her?" Joe asked. "This text message back-and-forth takes forever. If you could just talk with her ..."

Sheridan said, "What she's doing makes sense to me in her situation. If Stenko or Robert come out of the bar and look at her in the car they'd see the phone if she was talking on it. You can always tell when someone's talking on a phone. But if she's texting the phone's in her lap and out of sight."

Joe saw the logic of that.

"That's what kids do at school," Sheridan said. "They text each other under their desks all day long."

"Really," Marybeth said.

Sheridan shrugged. "Not me, of course."

"Of course."

JOE WAS IN his office with a Wyoming highway map spread open. He could find no Savage, and there was no bar near Savage Run Canyon. Of course, he thought, she could still be somewhere in Colorado. Or Utah. Or New Mexico, Nebraska, Arizona, Kansas ... someplace up to twenty hours away from Aspen. That could be 700 road miles if they'd driven non-stop. He wished he knew when they'd left Aspen exactly so he could draw a radius. How many square miles would that be? Thousands.

But she'd mentioned black hills. *The* Black Hills were in western South Dakota and eastern Wyoming. She might know the Black Hills because she claimed to have been there in Keystone. Was there a Savage, South Dakota? He searched his bookshelves for a U.S. atlas and was following the tip of his finger through the cities, towns, and locations of the state to find a Savage. No luck: he'd need to do an Internet search.

His phone burred in his pocket and it startled him. He glanced at his watch: past one A.M. He retrieved his phone and looked at the display. It was the number of the FBI office in Cheyenne. He thought, "Ah ..."

"So you got the warrant," Joe said, opening the phone. "That was quick."

Coon said, "We had to interrupt Judge Johnson's dinner to get it. That didn't make him very happy, as you might guess."

"You said it would be tomorrow."

"I thought about it, Joe. I thought we couldn't risk missing your daughter getting a new call tonight and we were right, weren't we?"

"Yes."

"So, do you want to know where it came from?"

"What do you think?"

"First, give me the gist of the exchange."

Joe nodded. Coon had him.

Joe said, "The caller said they were sitting in a car outside a bar somewhere while Stenko and Robert were inside. We couldn't get a description of the vehicle. The only place names we could get were 'Black Hills' and 'Savage.' I've been looking over the map and I can't find any Savage. Oh—and it had been a very bad day. Robert allegedly hurt someone in a store."

Joe left out the part about the sister on purpose because he saw no way of not revealing April's identity if he went down that road.

"A store?" Coon asked. "What kind of store? And where was this?"

"We don't know. A drugstore. The text said a drugstore."

Coon paused. Joe knew the conversation was being taped. What he didn't know was how much Coon and the FBI knew. There was no doubt they were withholding information as well.

"Joe," Coon said, "the cellphone tower that got the ping is located between Pine Tree Junction and Gillette, Wyoming. On State Highway Fifty."

Joe brushed the atlas aside and stared at the Wyoming map. Savageton was seventeen miles north of Pine Tree Junction and thirty-five miles south of Gillette. The middle of nowhere. Was it even a town at all? Or was it like so

180

many place names on the Wyoming map—a location?

But every location in Wyoming had a bar.

Bingo.

He scanned the map. There were several south-to-north roads that could have been used from Aspen into Wyoming and on to Savageton in the northeast corner of the square state. There was WYO 789 through Baggs to I-80, WYO 130 or 230 through Saratoga to I-80, WYO 230 to Laramie. There were at least four other highways that could have been used to get to Savageton. If they were headed for the Black Hills, Stenko, Robert, and April would likely drive north through Gillette. From there, they would hop on I-90 East.

Joe's eyes narrowed as he stared at the map. If one were headed toward the Black Hills from Gillette, I-90 was, for twenty-five miles, the only road east. At Moorcroft, other options appeared on both sides of the interstate. But for twenty-six miles, 1-90 looked like a thin wrist that led to an extended hand with routes for each finger. And throughout the Black Hills, there was a spider's web network of rural roads.

So if Stenko was to be located, it would be either on that 1-90 stretch or before he got to Gillette on Highway 50 north of Savageton.

Marybeth came into his office looking puzzled. She'd heard him talking. He mouthed *"FBI"* and jabbed at Savageton on the map. Marybeth understood immediately, nodded, and turned in the threshold, said, "Sheridan ..."

On the other end of the line, Joe heard a voice in the background he recognized as Coon's boss, Tony Portenson. Portenson said, "Savageton!"

"We think we've found it," Coon told Joe.

"So Portenson is there?"

181

"Of course. He's my supervisor."

"Mmmm."

"Look," Coon said, "I know you two have history. But Agent Portenson is willing to look the other way right now. To quote him, Stenko is a bigger prize than you are a pain in the ass."

Joe smiled. He wondered how long it would take Portenson and Coon to coordinate a roadblock at the logical pinch point on I-90 with the Wyoming Highway Patrol. Then they'd order up their helicopter from the Cheyenne airport. He guessed it would take several hours at least to get the roadblock set up because there simply weren't enough troopers available to handle it themselves, which meant local sheriff and police departments would be asked to provide men and vehicles. And it would take a while to roust the chopper pilots and get clearances in order to fly north. It would be unlikely Coon, Portenson, and team would take off before dawn. That gave Joe a five- to eight-hour window.

The drive from Saddlestring to Savageton would be less than two. He could beat them there.

"What else?" Coon asked. Joe couldn't tell if Portenson was prompting him but he assumed so. "There has to be something else you can tell me. A twenty-minute text exchange and all you got was Savage, Black Hills, and Robert doing something bad in a drugstore?"

Joe felt his neck get hot. He didn't want to get into the sister thing. But then he asked, "Twenty minutes? What do you mean twenty minutes?"

"I told you, Joe," Coon said. "We have the ability to register the location of the phone from when it's turned on to when it's turned off. I have the printout right here in front of me, so don't hold anything back."

Joe said, "Hold on," and dropped his cell on the desk. He met Sheridan in the hallway. She had her duffel bag over her shoulder, ready to go. Marybeth was behind her looking concerned. Joe asked to borrow her phone and he took it back to his office.

"You're wrong," Joe said to Coon after opening Sheridan's phone and scrolling back through the exchange. "The first text came at 12.12 A.M. The last one came at 12.21 A.M. That's just nine minutes."

Nine long minutes of frustration while the two girls tapped out short messages to each other, sent and received, answered. So much could have been accomplished if April had allowed them to talk ...

"I see what I see, Joe," Coon said. Joe could hear paper rustling.

Then: "Oh, now I get it."

"What?"

"We were both right."

"What do you mean?"

"The phone was turned on for twenty minutes. But it looks like the first ten were to someplace else."

"Where?"

Joe heard muffled voices. Coon had obviously covered the mouthpiece. Portenson and who knows how many other agents were having a heated discussion.

Joe paced. Marybeth and Sheridan stood outside his office, looking at him cautiously.

Finally, Coon came back on. "We aren't at liberty to say right now."

Joe stopped. He wished he could reach through the phone and grab Coon by the throat.

"We suspect you're withholding information," Coon said, speaking as if he were being coached what to say. "If we're

183

going to be partners in this investigation, you've got to come clean. Like who it is you think is sending the texts. When we feel you've come clean, we'll do the same. Up until this moment, you've had the upper hand. But you forget, Joe. We *are* the upper hand."

It was as if Portenson had his hand up the back of Coon's shirt, using him like a ventriloquist's dummy.

Joe decided it wasn't worth it to reveal April. And while it was killing him to know whom she'd called before texting Sheridan, it might not be vital.

Joe said, "I guess I'll see you there."

"Where?" Coon said.

Joe snorted, "Chuck, you're a good guy, but you're not yet a good liar," and hung up.

He turned to Sheridan. "Ready?"

Sheridan nodded. Her face was deadly serious, but her eyes sparkled.

AS JOE EASED out of the driveway in his pickup, he looked at his house. Marybeth was in the front picture window with Lucy, who looked stricken. Through the glass, Joe could see her mouth, *She's my sister, too* … and it was like a knife through his heart.

Joe and Sheridan waved, and Sheridan hid her face from him while she cried.

17

Savageton

THE FULL MOON in the cloudless sky cast the prairie grass ghostly white/blue and threw impenetrable black shadows into the hollows of the hills and draws as Joe and Sheridan drove east on I-90 and crossed the Powder River. The river in the fall was no more than an exhausted stream marking time until winter came and put it out of its misery. Despite that, mule deer huddled on its banks and ancient cotton-woods sucked at the thin stream of water in order to provide the only shade and cover for miles.

Joe knew of a two-track ranch access road with an unlocked gate that would allow them to cut the corner of their journey and eventually intersect with Highway 50 and Savageton, although the likelihood of finding April still there seemed remote at best.

Although it was an interstate highway, there was no traffic at two-fifteen in the morning. Big semi-rigs were parked at pullouts with running lights on, and as they roared east, the twinkle of working oil and gas rigs dotted the prairie. This was the western frontier of the Powder River

Basin. Under the thin crust of dirt were underground mountains of coal, rivers of oil and natural gas, seams of uranium. A bald eagle nearly as big as the one he'd delivered to Nate fed on a road-killed pronghorn antelope on the shoulder of the highway, and the bird barely looked up as the pickup sizzled by.

Sheridan was wide awake and filled with manic energy that no doubt came from both fear and exhilaration. The moonlight kissed her cheeks, and Joe felt glad she was with him as well as concerned. Her cellphone was in her lap.

"Do you have a signal?" he asked.

"Three bars," she said.

"Good. Let me know if we start to get out of range. We can't afford to miss a call or a text."

"I've always wanted to do this," she said. "I mean, go on an investigation with you."

Joe said, "I know. But you'll have to be careful. You'll really have to listen to me. This isn't a game."

"I *know* that."

He nodded in the dark. She was miffed at him for stating the obvious, and he wondered why he'd felt the need to do so.

He kept the radio tuned to SALECS, which stood for State Assisted Law Enforcement Communication System, and listened as Coon and the FBI talked with the highway patrol. The HP had units in Gillette, Wright, Moorcroft, and Sundance, and all were rolling toward the checkpoint they'd agreed upon near Rozet, east of Gillette. The local police departments in Gillette, Moorcroft, and Hulett were sending officers as well. The operation was going smoothly, although the HP was obviously annoyed they didn't know what kind of vehicle they were looking for or who would be in it.

186

"Two male subjects and possibly more," Coon had said in response, giving a description for David Stenson, aka Stenko. Robert was described as Stenko's son, but Coon said there was no physical description yet. He said they thought they'd have a photo of him within the hour and they would e-mail it for distribution. Joe was intrigued. Where did they find a photo of Robert so quickly in the middle of the night? Did Robert have priors as well? If so, Marybeth had not found any arrests on her Internet search.

As he usually did in anticipation of a confrontation, Joe did a mental inventory of his gear in addition to his weapons. On his belt was pepper spray, handcuffs, spare Glock magazines, and his Leatherman tool. He was a poor pistol shot so he'd rely on the shotgun if he ran into Stenko and Robert. But he prayed it wouldn't come to that with Sheridan and possibly April present.

Joe maintained radio silence, but he was urged to grab the mike and tell the officers they should be looking for two adult males and one teenage female. He couldn't risk it. Not yet. As always, he doubted himself and fought against a compulsion to tell them what he knew. If Stenko, Robert, and April slipped through the checkpoint because the HP wasn't looking for a girl with them, the guilt would eat him alive. Not only that, he could be brought up on charges for withholding information. But if local cops, buzzed on coffee and adrenaline—*or* the Highway Patrol *or* the FBI—overreacted as they had six years before and April was injured or killed, he'd never forgive himself. He didn't realize he'd just moaned aloud until Sheridan asked him what was wrong.

"Nothing," he said. He slowed and eased to the right of the highway because he didn't want to shoot past the shortcut road.

"You can tell me," Sheridan said. "Is it that you want to tell them to look for April?"

Joe grunted.

"We can't," she said, shaking her head in a gesture that could have been Marybeth's. "Not yet. Not until I get a chance to see if it's really her. We can't let her down again."

"I know."

"I don't want her to think I snitched on her, too."

"Gotcha," Joe said, turning off the pavement toward a sagging wire gate. Sheridan climbed out, opened it, and closed it again after Joe pulled through. He used the opportunity to dig his shotgun out from behind the seat, check the loads, and prop it, muzzle down, between the seats. He watched Sheridan skip toward the pickup through a roll of dust turned incendiary by his brake lights.

The two-track cut through the knee-high dry grass, and the uneven surface of the ranch road rattled everything that wasn't secured in the cab of the pickup. Instinctively, Sheridan reached up and grasped the loop handle above the door and braced her other hand against the dashboard to steady herself.

"Do we have to listen to that?" Sheridan asked, gesturing to the radio. There was lots of chatter as law enforcement assembled on I-90.

"Yes."

"We can't listen to music?"

"No."

"I've got a question," she said.

"Shoot."

"Do you think that the day you stop listening to new music is the day you decide you're on the path to old age? Like you've given up on new stuff and you resign yourself to music you've already heard? Like you're through discovering and all you want to do is rummage through your old things?"

Joe jerked the steering wheel to the left to avoid a rabbit in the right track that refused to move. He said, "I don't know how to answer that."

Sheridan said, "I think I'm right. That's why I'm never going to listen to old music. I'm only going to listen to what's new on the radio."

"You might change your mind when you get older," Joe said. "Don't you think you'll miss the songs you're familiar with?"

She shrugged. "I don't know. Maybe the new songs will be better."

"It's possible. But don't you find that certain songs remind you of certain things in your life? That when you hear a specific song it takes you back to when you were listening to it?"

"Well, yeah," she said. "But then I'd be thinking backward and not forward. I'd be on the way to geezerhood."

"Like me," Joe said.

"Like you *and* Mom."

He smiled in the dark.

"I mean, Mom listens to that old stuff when she's in the car. People like Simon and Garfunkel, the Police, Loggins and Messina. I'm not saying it's all bad but it *is* old. Pretty sad, huh?"

"Not really," Joe said.

"Do you still have those CDs I made for you of new music?"

"Somewhere," Joe confessed. They might be in the console or glove box, he wasn't sure. Wherever they were, he hadn't listened to them recently. "Sorry," he said.

"See, you're the same way."

"I guess so."

She paused, then said what was obviously heavy on her mind. "What if it's April who's pulling the trigger?"

"What?"

"What if she's so messed up she's turned into some kind of teenage killer? Think about it. She has a lot to be messed up about. She might be a no-hoper."

"Sheridan, jeez ..."

"She used to be pretty mean," Sheridan said. "When she first came to live with us, I was kind of scared of her, but I never let her know that. It wasn't until the end that she kind of opened up. Don't you remember how mean she could be?"

Joe remembered. But they'd chalked it up to her transient childhood and to the presence of her on-again, off-again mother, Jeannie Keeley. April's hardness was a tactic against getting hurt or betrayed, they'd decided. April tested them early on with outbursts and rudeness, but Marybeth said she was simply probing to see where the boundaries were. Once April found out there were limits and rules in the family, she visibly softened and relaxed. April, Joe thought, was like a horse. She needed to know what was expected of her and where she fit in the herd. Once she knew both she was all right.

Sheridan said, "April scared her teachers, she told me that. Every kid wants to be feared by adults. And the truth is a lot of adults fear us. You can see it in their eyes. It gives us power, you know? We're like vampires. We feed off adults being scared of us. I could see April being pushed into hurting somebody."

He said, "Sheridan, let's not speculate too much until we have some kind of evidence, okay?"

Which didn't stop her. She said, "What if we find her and

190

she's so messed up we know she'll kill again? What do we do then?"

"Stop it," he said. "We don't know if she's done anything wrong in the first place."

Sheridan nodded, apparently thinking that over. She said, "No matter what, I miss her," she said. "Toward the end there, I was really starting to like her and I thought it was cool how she looked up to me. She must still feel that way or she never would have started texting me.

"I remember when she lived with us," Sheridan said, almost dreamily. "I came down the hall to get a drink of water at night and I heard you and Mom talking. I remember you saying you wondered if April was doomed."

"I don't remember saying that," Joe said, although he could vaguely recall similar conversations.

"What if *she* heard you say that? What if it stuck with her? Do you think that would mess her up?"

They crested a hill and the countryside opened up ahead of them. In the distance were the Pumpkin Buttes; four massive flat-topped cone-shaped land formations that dominated the southern horizon. They looked like crude sand castles formed by inverted God-sized buckets. Moonlight bathed the tops of the buttes, which shone like four blue disks.

"Wow," Sheridan said. "Those things are awesome-looking."

"I've been on top of them," Joe said, grateful to change the subject.

"What is it like up there?"

He told her how he'd climbed to the top of the middle butte and walked around. The surface was as flat as a tabletop, covered with short grass. Chippings from arrowheads and other tools winked in the grass like jewels, and there

191

were a half-dozen campfire and tipi rings where the Indians used to camp. The height of the buttes afforded them protection from other bands because the view was unparalleled: oceans of treeless prairie to the east, north, and south. He told Sheridan he could see until the land met the sky and vanished. To the west was the knotty blue spine of the Big Horn Mountains.

"I'd like to climb them someday," she said. "I've never found an arrowhead."

"Look," Joe said suddenly, "I've done and said things in the past I regret. I wish I could take some things back. You'll understand someday. But getting a second chance to save April means a lot to me right now. So let's concentrate on that, okay?"

Sheridan nodded. "Okay."

"No more speculating."

"Okay," she said, "I'll shut up."

"You don't have to shut up," Joe said. "Just quit bringing up things that give me a stomach ache. I've got to concentrate."

She laughed, "So what is your opinion about never listening to old music?"

AS THEY DESCENDED on the two-track, Joe pointed out the windshield at a tight cluster of blue lights on the prairie floor to the north-east. "See that?"

"Yes."

"That's Savageton."

"That's all there is?"

"Yup."

Joe's cellphone lit up and rang: Coon.

"Yes, Chuck?"

Joe could hear a roar in the background and recognized

192

it as the ascending whine of helicopter rotors. He was surprised how quickly the FBI had located their pilots and fueled the helicopter. It sounded like they were ready to scramble.

Coon had to shout: "Damn it, Joe. You're holding out on us."

"What are you talking about?" Joe asked, wondering if Coon and Portenson had learned about April.

"You know what I'm talking about," Coon yelled. "The subject fired up the cellphone a half hour ago. Are you telling me your daughter didn't get a call or a text?"

Joe slowed to a stop on the two-track and jammed the pickup into park. He glanced over at Sheridan, who'd heard Coon shouting.

Sheridan shrugged and checked her cell, just in case. "No new texts," she said, looking at the display, "and I still have a strong signal."

"I'm sorry," Joe said. "We've heard nothing. Do your contacts say calls are being made?"

"Yes, but we're not sure which numbers were called. We don't have that information yet," Coon said. "The night staff at the phone company isn't up on the tracing procedure, I'm afraid. But we do know the phone is on and starting to move."

Joe felt a tremor in his face muscles. So April had been at Savageton all this time? And was just now starting to drive away? He dug beneath his seat for his spotting scope while Coon said, "Yeah, we're tracking it going south on Highway Fifty, which is *the wrong way*! They're supposed to be headed north to I-Ninety, where we've got the roadblock set up!"

Without consulting the map, Joe knew 50 would intersect with Wyoming Highway 387, which went south-west to

193

north-east. On that road and several others, it would be possible for Stenko to access the Black Hills without ever putting his tires on the interstate. They'd all guessed wrong. He gave Stenko credit for being unpredictable in his movements.

Sheridan said, "I wonder why she turned her phone on."

"Hold on a second," Joe said to Coon and dropped his phone in his lap while he tightened the bracket of the spotting scope to the top of the driver's side window. He leaned into it, focusing on Savageton.

Savageton consisted of a single green corrugated metal building on a small rise two hundred yards from Highway 50. The sides of the structure had been battered by snow and wind over the years and the words SAVAGETON LOUNGE AND RESTAURANT could barely be read in the moonlight. The large gravel parking lot where energy trucks and semis parked during the day was empty and lit by four pole lights. He could see fifty-gallon drums that served as garbage barrels and large wooden spools that were used as makeshift outdoor tables. Two abandoned cars sagged on the side of the building. All the interior lights were on, but as Joe focused on them they went off one by one, from the back of the building to the front. Ten seconds later, the front door opened and a single large man came out, turned, and locked the front door. He was alone and obviously closing the place for the night. Joe was sure he couldn't be Stenko.

"There!" Sheridan said. "I see a car."

Joe looked to his right. Sheridan was pointing far to the south, where two tiny tail lights could be seen for a moment as the vehicle passed between two small hills. As the lights receded from left to right a brushy rise blocked them and they blinked out.

Joe grabbed the cell and put the pickup into gear. "We

have a visual," he said to Coon. "A single vehicle headed south on Highway Fifty."

"Can you see who's inside?"

"No."

"Make or model?"

"Too far," Joe said. "And I've got at least two miles of rough road in front of me before I hit the pavement."

"Stay on them!" It was Portenson, who had apparently snatched the phone from Coon. "Don't lose them!"

"Hi, Tony," Joe said.

"Don't 'Hi, Tony' me!" His voice was rapid-fire and angry. Joe could visualize Portenson standing in the dark on the tarmac with his salt-and-pepper hair flying in the prop wash and his scarred lip pulled back in a grimace. He shouted, "Catch up with Stenko and stay on him until we can get the chopper there or divert law enforcement from I-Ninety your way!"

Joe said, "I'll do my best."

But he'd lost the tail lights. Sheridan had, too, and looked over with a palms-up gesture.

"We can't see the vehicle right now," Joe said.

"You *can't* lose him!" Portenson said. "It's impossible. Christ, there's only one highway—"

Joe said, "This whole basin is covered with roads, Tony. This is where all the energy development up here is. There are gravel roads everywhere going to oil rigs, wells, gas lines ... and plenty of old ranch roads."

"JUST STAY ON HIM!"

Joe wasn't sure whether Portenson was yelling because of the increased motor noise from the helicopter or because his internal gaskets were blowing. Either way, Joe closed the phone.

"It's for his own good," Joe said to Sheridan.

195

She giggled as he tossed the phone aside and gripped the wheel with both hands. "Hold on," he said to Sheridan, and gunned it down the hill.

"WOO-HOO!" she howled, thrilled.

18

Powder River Basin

B Y THE TIME Joe launched up through a borrow ditch onto the stunning calm of the two-lane blacktop, he felt as if his bones had been rattled loose and his internal organs were sloshing around inside of him like loose pickles in a jar. He turned the pickup south on the highway and accelerated. The too-fast push down the butte and across the rutted steppe to the highway had been brutal, although Sheridan had shouted as if she were on a carnival ride.

"I feel like I just got tumble-dried!" Sheridan said, laughing. "That was cool!"

Unfortunately, the rough fast ride had jarred the glove box open and the contents—maps, papers, citation books, spent cartridges, spare handcuffs—had spilled all over the floorboards. As they sped down the highway, wind rushed in through the vents and sent papers flying through the air as if the cab of the vehicle were somehow gravity-free.

Worse: they'd lost sight of Stenko's car.

The terrain was rolling hills and shallow arroyos, as if the high plains were severely wrinkled. Every time Joe topped a hill, they looked into the distance for red tail lights before plunging back down into a low spot. Although there were plenty of static white lights on distant oil wells, there appeared to be no other traffic on the highway.

As they shot past gravel service roads that cut to the right and left of the highway, Joe and Sheridan tried to peer out into the murk for a glimpse of the car. As the minutes went by, Joe knew the odds of finding Stenko's car were tumbling. There were so many ways for them to get lost at night in terrain like this—taking an unexpected service road, pulling so far ahead that Joe couldn't see a vehicle, or simply pulling off the highway into the shadows of a depression and turning off their lights. If Stenko suspected Joe was chasing him—he could have easily seen Joe's headlights on top of the rise—he could be making evasive maneuvers.

Joe scanned the night sky for a glimpse of the FBI helicopter and wondered how many minutes away from the Pumpkin Buttes it was ...

"I just saw car lights!" Sheridan shouted, her face pressed to the passenger-side window. "Back there—we went right past them."

Joe slowed and craned around, trying to confirm what she'd seen. They'd shot by at least two gravel exits on the right. Stenko could have taken either of them.

"Where?" Joe asked, slamming the truck into reverse.

"Out there," Sheridan said, opening her window and waving generally to the west. "I saw tail lights way out there, I swear ..."

He nearly backed off the highway from going too fast, but he corrected the wheel and stayed on the pavement. Then he saw something on the second access road—an almost imperceptible roll of dust that lit up in the headlamps. He never would have seen the dust as they sped by, but in his brights the settling dust bloomed like a wilting flower in the road.

"They took this one," he said. "See the dust in the air?"

"Yeah ..."

He shut the lights off, and the gravel road vanished into darkness.

"Hey," she said. "How are we going to follow them in the dark?"

"An old Indian trick," Joe said while he reached under the dashboard and found the toggle switch for his sneak lights and turned them on. The sneak lights threw an orb of light down from under his front bumper into a pool immediately in front of the pickup. It was enough light to see to drive but because the beams pointed down into the dirt they were difficult to see from a distance. The sneak switch also disabled the taillights and brake lights, so that if he slowed or stopped, there would be no indication from flashing red.

"Hey," Sheridan said, "I didn't know you could do that."

"I've caught a lot of game violators over the years using these to follow vehicles or sneak up on poachers," he said. "I'm sure Stenko probably saw us earlier when we were coming down that rough road with the brights on. But he'll assume we went on down the highway, which is probably why he turned off here."

"Cool," she said. "How come you didn't ever tell me about these spy lights?"

Joe said, "I keep some of my tricks in reserve. There are lots of tricks you don't know about. You know, in case you ever decide to break any Game and Fish laws and I have to arrest you."

"Very funny," she said. "You'd never arrest your own daughter."

"You know I would," Joe said.

She sighed, said, "Yeah, I guess you probably would. But Mom would be mad at you."

He smiled, reached over and squeezed her shoulder. Then he shoved the pickup into drive and turned off the highway onto the unpaved road. The truck vibrated and shook as it had before as his tires ground over egg-sized gravel.

Sheridan said what Joe was thinking: "So what do we do if we catch them on this crappy road?" she asked.

Joe said, "I'm not sure."

He could feel her staring at him, waiting for a better answer. But she wouldn't get one. He didn't dare approach Stenko's vehicle too aggressively with Sheridan in his pickup and April with Stenko. The chance for a confrontation would be too great and he couldn't risk their lives. He was sure Sheridan would object so he didn't even want to discuss it with her.

He said, "We're going to maintain visual contact," Joe said. "That's all for now."

Sheridan didn't respond. He glanced over to see her furiously tapping a message on her phone.

"What are you doing?" he asked.

"I'm asking April what's going on."

"What if she can't answer?"

"Then she won't," Sheridan said, testy. "But if her phone's on like that man told us, maybe she'll get the text from me. She might be able to respond when Stenko or Robert aren't paying attention."

"So what are you sending her?" Joe asked.

"I'm asking her if they know we're back here."

Joe nodded. "It would be interesting to know that."

"Yeah, and she can text back with just a 'Y' or an 'N.' Easy."

Because the sneak lights drastically cut down on his field of vision, Joe proceeded much slower than he would have preferred. He hoped that if Stenko saw no headlights in his rear-view mirror, he'd have no reason to try and outrace him. He might even slow down or pull over to regroup. Joe and Sheridan topped a rise, and Joe saw the tail lights ahead in the distance less than a mile away.

"There they are," he said. He couldn't judge if Stenko had slowed or not before they plunged down into a hollow.

Halfway up the next incline, Sheridan's phone lit up and buzzed. Joe felt his stomach clench: April was responding.

Sheridan read the message in silence and lowered the phone to her lap. When Joe looked over for clarification he could see moisture rimming her eyes.

"What did she say?" he asked. "What's wrong?"

"She said something bad," Sheridan said, her mouth twisting into a pucker as if she was about to cry.

"What?"

"She said, 'Fuck you and the horse you rode in on.'"

Joe nearly drove off the road. He didn't know if he was more shocked by what April had written or the fact that Sheridan repeated it verbatim.

"Maybe somebody took her phone away from her and is using it to answer me," Sheridan said weakly, turning her head away.

Joe was instantly enraged at the idea of April—or whoever—talking to his daughter like that and he thought: *Things are going to get real Western here in a minute.*

IT WAS A car chase in slow motion: Joe fuming and driving under the duel handicaps of his anger and his sneak lights while the vehicle he was following ground on a half-mile ahead on the rough gravel road. Although they could only see Stenko's vehicle in short glimpses as they drove on the tops of rolling hills or Stenko did, Joe started to discern that Stenko (or Robert) was driving erratically—racing ahead, sagging back, taking stretches of the road too fast and other stretches with ridiculous caution. He'd also noticed tire tracks meandering off the gravel road to both the right and left before correcting.

His mind raced with situations to fit the facts as he knew them. The scenarios made his heart race, and he didn't want to share them with his daughter. She was smart, though, and he wouldn't be surprised if she was making the same speculations as well.

Was the driver injured or hurt, he wondered? Was there a fight going on inside the car, causing the driver to veer off the road and overcorrect? And he thought about that message Sheridan had received and he knew that whoever had sent it—whether it was a suddenly hostile April or someone who'd taken her phone away from her—the situation had changed drastically from what it was. He could only guess where it would lead, and he found it hard to imagine a narrative in which April would be perfectly safe.

He located his cellphone on the seat next to him, handed it to Sheridan and asked her to speed-dial Coon. When she connected she handed it over.

"Where are you guys?" Joe asked. "I've been following the subject vehicle for half an hour."

Joe could hear the roar of the props through the earpiece and he could barely make out Coon's voice. He heard Coon shouting to Portenson that, *"Pickett is still in hot pursuit."*

Then: "Joe, can you hear me?"

"Barely."

"I'd use the radio, but Agent Portenson thinks Stenko may have a scanner."

Joe shrugged.

"Anyway, the pilot says we're ten minutes from Pumpkin Buttes. That's where the cellphone pings have been coming from. Does that make any sense to you? I don't know the geography around here."

Joe nodded. "Yup. I'd be able to see the Buttes in my rear-view mirror if the sun was up. Right now, we're headed east on gravel roads through the oil field. I can't tell you what road we're on because I haven't seen a number or a sign. But if you tell the pilot to head due east-southeast from the middle butte you should soon be over the top of us."

Joe could hear Coon yelling the directions. While he did, Joe checked the coordinates from his dash-mounted GPS and read those to Coon.

"Okay," Coon said. "We've got you located. We're on our way."

"Hey," Joe said. "Are you tracking *my* cellphone as well?"

"Didn't I tell you?" Coon asked.

"No," Joe said, feeling his neck get hot. "You must have forgotten."

"Don't say anything inflammatory," Coon said. "I've got you up on speaker."

"Look," Joe said, "don't do anything crazy."

"Stenko is a dangerous man," Coon said.

And suddenly Joe visualized the helicopter swooping in over his pickup toward Stenko's car, guns blazing. Coon and Portenson would *love* to get Stenko. Capturing or killing a fugitive like Stenko might result in Portenson's promotion and transfer out of Wyoming, which was what he wanted most.

Joe and Sheridan exchanged glances. She said, "Don't tell them, Dad."

He put the phone face down on his thigh to cover the mike. "I might have to," he said.

She looked away.

To Coon, Joe said, "Promise me you'll make your presence known to them without any hijinks. Promise me you'll give them plenty of opportunity to pull over and give themselves up."

Muffled conversation on the other end. Joe muttered to Sheridan, "I've got nothing to bargain with right now. They know our location and Stenko's location. They can do anything they want and they know it."

Coon came back, said, "I give you my word."

Joe said, "What about Portenson?"

"He gives you his word, too."

Said Joe, "He did that once before. When he broke it he told me, 'Never trust a fed.' Put him on. I want to hear it for myself."

After a beat, Portenson said, "Damn it, Joe. We want Stenko alive and kicking. We need his testimony."

Joe felt a wave of relief, said, "Okay, then."

Suddenly, the cab of his truck exploded in white light as the helicopter bathed it with their halogen spotlights. They came swooping down with a roar. Sheridan covered her eyes with her hands and Joe squinted in order to see.

Just as quickly, the spotlights shot ahead up the two-track and found the fleeing vehicle, lighting it up as if it were daylight. Stenko was driving a battered silver SUV with Wyoming plates. Joe could see the silhouettes of two heads in the vehicle, one dark-haired and one light-haired, the dark-haired one driving.

Two people, not three, Joe thought. Who was missing or hiding? Robert?

"Is that April?" Sheridan shouted over the roar of the helicopter.

"Don't know," Joe yelled back, as the SUV took a sharp right off the road and bounced through untracked sagebrush. The spotlights lost it for a moment but found it again as the helicopter hovered overhead.

Portenson's sharp voice filled the night: *"You in the SUV ... this is the FBI. You need to pull that vehicle over right now and come out with your hands in the air. I repeat, this is the FBI and you need to stop the vehicle immediately and get out."*

Joe felt himself gasp as he saw something come out of the driver's side window—an arm, a hand, a gun in the hand ...

Three heavy concussions from the handgun and three orange fireballs into the sky. The helicopter banked sharply to the left and roared away, the spotlights crazily strobing the distant hillsides. The SUV plummeted into darkness as the aircraft fled.

"Oh no," Joe said. "I don't know if the helicopter got hit but Stenko's trying to get himself killed!"

"And April," Sheridan cried.

The shots had been wild, Joe knew. The driver couldn't have aimed so much as stuck the gun out the window and fired. Still, it was provocation enough for the FBI to return fire.

Joe turned off the gravel road into the brush. The tires heaved over sagebrush and Sheridan was tossed around inside, her arms flying. He thought if he could cut the corner and head off the SUV, Stenko might think he was surrounded and give up.

The chopper did a long arc through the sky and came back. In seconds it was once again back over the top of them, this time without the spotlights. Instead, Joe could see what looked like two red eyes dancing like fireflies on top of the SUV. He recognized them as laser sights that were likely mounted on automatic weapons. The FBI could open up any second and cut the SUV—and everyone in it—into pieces.

Panicked, Joe grabbed his cell—which was still connected to Coon and the speaker inside the copter—and shouted, *"They've got a hostage in the vehicle ... a minor."*

Silence. Joe knew what he'd done. Sheridan glared at him. Whether April was actually a hostage or was along for the ride could be sorted out later, he thought.

"A hostage? Who is the minor?" Coon asked, after no doubt being fed the question from Portenson. Joe noted that only one red eye remained on the top of the SUV. He guessed Coon had lowered his weapon while he questioned Joe. Which meant Portenson had not.

"Our foster daughter, April Keeley," Joe said in a rush of words. "She's the one who's been texting my daughter." In his peripheral vision he could see Sheridan slump into the door.

"Impossible!" Portenson shouted, once again apparently wresting the phone away from Coon. As he did, the second laser eye blinked out on the top of the SUV. "Is this your idea of a joke? Is this aimed at me because I was there when she died, Pickett? Are you trying to say she's alive and with David Stenson? Come on ... *I was there.*"

"I know you were," Joe said. "But she claims to be with Stenko. Which is why you can't attack that vehicle until we figure this out. Do you understand? If you do, the only way you'll ever get out of Wyoming is as a civilian because you completely botched this thing and got a teenage girl killed. And worse, you'll never see the end of *me.*"

Portenson sputtered something.

"I'm not kidding," Joe said. "Leave that vehicle alone until we can get a visual in the light and see for sure who is in it. We need to make them give it up without a fight so April can get away."

He tossed the phone aside. The helicopter spotlights came back on and lit up the SUV.

To Sheridan, he said, "I'm sorry. I couldn't think of any other way."

That's when the passenger door of the SUV opened and a female flew out into the dirt, arms out and hands clawing the air, blond hair flying like flames behind her in the harsh beams.

"DID YOU SEE that?" Coon shouted to Joe.

"Yup. I've got her," Joe said.

"Pick her up and we'll stay with the vehicle," Coon said.

Sheridan shouted, "Oh, no! I hope she's okay!"

Joe slowed down, hit his high beams, and cut the sneak lights. The scrub brush obscured where she'd landed. She'd not gotten up. Sheridan unbuckled her seat belt and shinnied halfway out of her open window, shouting, "April! It's me, Sheridan! Are you okay? April!"

Joe heard the *pop-pop-pop* of additional shots up ahead as Stenko or Robert fired wildly again at the helicopter, but he didn't look up. April was somewhere in the brush, possibly hurt, possibly dead.

The automatic weapons in the helicopter opened up and the sound was like twin buzz saws. Joe looked up to see angry streams of tracers pouring from the chopper into the SUV, raking it from hood to tailgate. Windows exploded and pellets of glass cascaded like droplets from a splash in a lake. The SUV lurched forward until one of the wheels dropped into a badger hole, where it stopped abruptly and

207

rocked. Plumes of radiator fluid rose from the undercarriage. The helicopter hovered, looking for signs of life, before slowly descending and kicking up dust.

"Dad!" Sheridan shouted, pointing to a thin figure rising from the brush like a specter. Joe braked and swung his hand spotlight in the direction Sheridan was pointing.

The woman was thin with scraggly blond hair, hollow cheeks, and haunted eyes. She wore an open flannel shirt that hung from her skeletal frame over a stained white tank top. She held her hands up and grimaced. Her open mouth revealed missing teeth. Even at that distance Joe knew a meth addict when he saw one. Sheridan slid back into the cab. Disappointed and confused, she said, "Who is *she*?" Then: "Oh my God, Dad, was April in the car?"

"I don't think so," Joe said, watching the skids of the chopper kiss the top of brush as it settled to earth. "I think April's long gone."

"Then what's going on? Why did those men in the helicopter say it was April's phone?"

Joe said, "Because it probably is."

19

ACCORDING TO A driver's license found in his bloody hip pocket, the body in the SUV belonged to one Francis "Bo" Skelton, thirty-four, of Moorcroft, Wyoming. A call via SALECS to dispatch in Cheyenne revealed Skelton had a significant rap sheet including multiple arrests for possession of methamphetamine, marijuana, and crack cocaine as well as one arrest for B&E that was withdrawn by the Crook County prosecutor when Skelton agreed to cooperate with authorities. Local law enforcement, who had been waiting in vain at the I-90 roadblock, knew Skelton as a rounder and informant who was working with a joint local/state task force to infiltrate methamphetamine traffic in northeastern Wyoming. When not doing drugs or informing, Skelton ran parts for oil well and gas supply companies based in Gillette.

The girlfriend of the deceased, Cyndi Rae Mote, thirty-eight, sat on Joe's pickup tailgate with a blanket wrapped around her to ward off the predawn chill. It didn't help much because the few teeth she had still chattered. She told Joe she'd ridden to the Savageton Bar that evening and they stayed until last call. As they left the bar she said the "alcohol caught up with her" and she staggered to a garbage barrel in the parking lot to throw up. The effort knocked her over and she was scrambling on all fours to get back on her feet when she found the cellphone in a stand of weeds.

"I couldn't believe it," she said. "It looked like a perfectly good phone. I was gonna turn it in to Badger in case someone wanted to claim it …"

Joe said, "Badger?"

"The manager. He's the bartender, too."

Joe scribbled the name into his notebook, even though he had his mini-cassette tape recorder running in his breast pocket for backup. "Do you have a last name?"

"Mote," she said, spelling it: "M-O-T-E."

"Not yours," Joe said patiently. "Badger's."

"Oh. No, I guess not."

Joe thought, *Badger should be easy to find.* He glanced up to locate agents Portenson and Coon, to see if he should call them in to participate in his interview with Cyndi Mote. He found them both where he expected them to be. Coon was circling the SUV with his flashlight, looking at the damage he'd helped inflict. Joe thought, *When Coon was talking to Joe the evening before from his kitchen table with his son chattering at him, neither one of them could have imagined how the night would end.* Joe felt bad for Coon. He knew Coon to be tightly wound but professional, basically good-hearted and honest. He doubted Coon had ever drawn his service weapon before, much less brandished an AR-15 with laser sights. Joe could only imagine what was going through his mind now that they'd confirmed that the entire incident, which resulted in a dead body, was all predicated on an error.

Meanwhile, Portenson was in the bubble of the helicopter making and taking calls. In a situation like this, Joe thought, raw priorities were revealed without pretense. While Coon was pensive, reflecting on what he'd done, Portenson was reaching out to people who could help bolster his case and save his job. Joe looked back to Cyndi Mote, assessing her. "Go ahead," he said.

She said, "Anyway, I was gonna turn it in but Bo looked at it and said it was one of those cheap-ass phones like the ones you get at Wal-Mart. He said somebody probably used it up and threw it away.

"He was right. When I turned it on the battery light was flashing," she said, "but I figured I'd get as many calls out of it as I could before it died."

Her version confirmed Coon's claim that the phone was being used to make other calls. It also explained the Wyoming area code and why the FBI hadn't instantly tracked down the phone number to a specific user. April had been using a TracFone that could be purchased anywhere, loaded with minutes from a calling card, and used like any phone. It was a favorite among those who didn't want or like long-term phone contracts, monthly bills, or the bells and whistles that came with more expensive phones. It was also the phone of choice among dealers and gangsters and others who didn't want to be pinned down or tracked, and it came with a kind of temporary anonymity since the number assigned to the phone wasn't assigned to a person but to the phone itself. But why had she thrown it away instead of recharging it or ordering more minutes? It didn't make sense. Joe asked, "Who'd you call?"

She grimaced again. Her lips peeled back and her eyes narrowed into slits. Joe realized it was actually her smile.

"I called every ex-boyfriend whose phone number I could remember and told them they were full of shit," she said, grinning/grimacing.

"Do you still have the phone?" Joe asked, thinking they

better check the call log to make sure it was the same phone April had used.

"I don't know where it is," Cyndi said, chewing on her nails. Joe saw that her nails were gnawed to the nub and bleeding. "It's probably somewhere in Bo's pickup. It's probably shot up all to hell, like poor Bo."

Joe said, "Why did Bo stick his gun out the window and start firing at the helicopter? Couldn't he hear them ordering him to pull over? If he had, none of this would have happened."

She shook her head and rolled her eyes as if to say, *Boys will be boys.* "I couldn't hear them neither," she said. "We kind of had the music up loud. Like full freakin' blast. We were just relaxing, you know? Driving down some roads Bo knew from work. All of a sudden the sky was full of light from that damned helicopter and all hell broke loose.

"I still can't believe Bo started shooting," Cyndi told Joe. "I knew he had a gun in the truck. I mean, who doesn't around here? But when that helicopter showed up out of nowhere, Bo went postal and started screaming and shooting."

She pulled her blanket tight and leaned forward, lowering her voice as if to tell Joe a secret. He bent toward her. The smell of cigarette smoke and souring alcohol was overwhelming. "See, he's officially helping the cops on some cases and he's not supposed to be messing with alcohol or drugs anymore. That's his part of the deal. And he's not supposed to have a gun. But when that helicopter showed up, he just lost it. He didn't want to get caught, I guess. I told him to stop but he pointed his gun at *me* and told me shut up." She said the last part indignantly, and Joe nodded.

"Back to the bar," he said.

"Okay."

"Who else was there? Anyone you didn't know?"

She shook her head, "Just energy guys. You know, hard-working Americans providing power for the rest of the country so they can all look down on us with their lights on. Oil guys, coal miners, gas guys. Some juggies and some surveyors loading up before they had to go home. Badger was there, of course."

"Mm-hmm," he said, scribbling, encouraging her to keep talking. A surprising number of witnesses loved to have their words inscribed, he'd found over the years. It made them feel important that their words mattered to someone. It was the same impulse some people had to immediately commence talking whenever a television camera was around.

"What I'm wondering," Joe said, "was if there was anyone in the bar you didn't recognize? Or maybe they just didn't fit?"

She gnawed on her fingers and looked up at the sky and closed her eyes. "Thinking," she said aloud. Then she snapped her fingers. "There were two guys sitting in back by themselves," she said. "I remember them now. One older guy and one handsome dude, but in an Eastern, kind of faggy bark-beetle way ..."

Joe interrupted. "What do you mean by that? Did he look homosexual?"

She laughed huskily and shook her head. "No, worse. He looked like an environmentalist. I can spot 'em a mile away. You know how some people have 'gay-dar' when it comes to picking out gay people? Bo said I had 'Gore-dar,' the ability to pick out whacko enviros. You know, after Al Gore."

"Got it," Joe said, suppressing a sigh.

"Anyway, they sat a back table keeping to themselves. I think they were arguing about something. Badger kept delivering them drinks. I noted they shut up every time he took drinks over to them, like they didn't want him to hear

213

what they were talking about. That was unusual because everybody around here knows everyone else's business. Well, they acted like they were having a big important discussion. The good-looking enviro had a laptop out, and he kept pointing at the screen to the old guy."

Joe paused. "Can you describe them a little better? I don't have Gore-dar."

She giggled. "Sure. The old guy was big—he had a big head and a big face. Dark hair, mustache. Mid- to late sixties, I guess. He was dressed pretty well in that he wasn't wearing Wranglers. Definitely not from around here. He had nice eyes—I remember that. Maybe six foot or a little over. Maybe, I don't know, two hundred and fifty pounds? The one with the laptop had wavy brown hair and his shirt was open too much for around here. Like I said, handsome in a faggy way."

Joe thought, *Stenko and Robert.*

"Was anyone with them?" he asked.

"Not that I can remember."

"A teenage girl, maybe?"

She barked a laugh. "Believe me, mister, if there was a teenage girl in that joint, I woulda known about her! I was the only female in the place!"

Joe nodded. "You mentioned you went outside a couple of times. Did you see anyone in any cars?"

She shook her head. "I didn't look," she said. "I was, you know, getting high."

He paused, thinking what to ask.

Then she said, "Hey, I remember something. Bo came back in once. He'd gone outside to piss. He likes—liked—to piss outside rather than inside. One of his quirks. Anyway, he sat down by me and said there was an underage girl out there in one of the cars who saw him pissing. He said she

214

was kinda cute. I smacked him. I thought he was shitting me about seeing a girl. You know, hallucinating. Are you saying he wasn't?"

PORTENSON MADE CALL after call with a satellite phone. He was lit by the green glow of the instrument panel. He looked distressed and angry. The pilot sat silently next to him but made it a point to look away as if he found something out in the dark sagebrush worth careful study. The pilot wore sunglasses and headphones. Joe guessed he'd wear a grocery bag on his head if one were available.

Coon stood for a long time looking at the body of Bo Skelton behind the wheel of the pickup and cursing. Joe asked Coon to watch his language in deference to Sheridan, who leaned against the grille of Joe's pickup with her arms crossed. Her cellphone, as always, was in her hand. Joe felt the need every ten minutes or so to approach her and give her a hug or a squeeze until she finally asked him to relax. She insisted she was okay, that the events of the night hadn't traumatized her in any way.

"Don't go near that SUV," Joe cautioned. He'd caught a glimpse of Skelton's body earlier. Machine-gun fire had practically gutted him and there were two bullet holes neatly spaced in his forehead like another set of eyes. Joe was thankful it had been a long time since he'd eaten anything or he likely would have lost it, like Coon had.

"I'll stay where I am," she said. "Should I call Mom and let her know we're okay?"

"Yes, please."

THERE WAS A thump on the inside of the Plexiglas bubble as Portenson smacked it with the heel of his hand. Joe looked up from where he was with Sheridan. Portenson was obviously furious and sharing his frustrations with the pilot, who listened without removing his sunglasses or headphones.

The FBI supervisor opened the hatch and climbed out. Joe said to Sheridan, "Hope he doesn't scorch your ears."

Sheridan said, "You are *so* protective."

Portenson paced and spoke as much to himself as to Coon in the distance. "We have to stay right here and wait. So forget trying to find Stenko for the time being. The powers that be are sending up an incident team from Denver, and our orders are to stay right here and not touch anything. Like we're a couple of suspects. Touch nothing! Hear that?"

Coon grunted in the dark.

"I think this was a righteous shoot," Portenson said. "I think we did everything by the book. Why that son of a bitch started firing at us, I'll never know. What the hell was wrong with him? Did he have a death wish or something?"

From the tailgate of Joe's pickup, Cyndi Mote said, "Bo was paranoid. But you didn't need to *kill* him for that."

Joe said, "I'll testify to what I saw. You guys handled everything the best you could. You had no reason to believe it wasn't Stenko. And Skelton did shoot first."

Portenson looked at Joe as if he'd forgotten he was there. The FBI agent sized him up, waiting for another shoe to drop. It didn't.

"Your action was justified," Joe said.

"I appreciate you saying you'd be willing to tell them what you saw and heard."

Joe said, "Yup."

"Because I know if you wanted to, you could hang me out to dry."

Joe said, "I could and maybe I should. But I saw what I

216

saw." He put his hand on Sheridan's shoulder. "*We* saw what we saw."

Portenson looked almost embarrassed. "Thank you, Joe."

TO THE EAST the sky took on a rosy cream color as dawn approached. Several Highway Patrol vehicles had found them and the troopers helped set up a perimeter. From whom, Joe wasn't certain. Local police from Gillette, Moorcroft, and Hulett drove out to look at the pickup, Skelton's body, and to count the bullet holes in the top of the SUV and whistle. Everyone waited for the FBI incident team to find them and clear the scene.

Coon wandered over and joined Joe and Sheridan leaning against Joe's pickup. He looked ten years older than when Joe had seen him the afternoon before.

"You okay?" Joe asked.

"What do you think?"

Joe didn't respond.

"Man, oh man," Coon said. "Why did that idiot shoot at us?"

Joe said, "Meth. We're drowning in it in rural Wyoming. Everyplace is."

Coon pushed himself up and away from the pickup. "I nearly forgot. There's something I need you two to look at. Come on, follow me."

"Me, too?" Sheridan asked.

Coon said, "Especially you."

COON OPENED THE passenger hatch of the helicopter and dug out his briefcase from under a seat. He unlatched it to reveal thick files and a sturdy government laptop. As he booted up the computer, he said, "I barely got a chance to see this before we took off. I downloaded it from the Carbon

217

County sheriff's department. From Rawlins, to be exact."

"What happened in Rawlins?" Joe asked.

"A pharmacy got robbed and the pharmacist was killed in the robbery. We're not sure what the bad guys took, but we're guessing it was cash and drugs. The sheriff's office is doing an inventory. The store had a closed-circuit camera, and they recovered the digital file. The quality's not so good and the angle kind of sucks, but you can see the crime going down. The sheriff sent it to us to see if we could help identify the assailants."

Joe and Sheridan exchanged looks, thinking: *"na. but he hurt some man 2day in a drug store."*

The static image was in black-and-white and it showed four empty aisles stocked with packaging.

"From what I understand," Coon said, "the camera is mounted on the ceiling behind the pharmacy counter. The view is basically what the pharmacist sees when he looks out into the store. As you can see, the store's deserted."

Joe felt Sheridan's hand find his. He didn't look down to draw Coon's attention away.

"Okay, here," Coon said, pointing at the screen, which showed a tall man with thick wavy hair entering the store and milling in the aisles. The man looked to be in his early to mid-thirties. Despite the poor quality of the transmission, Joe could see the man was fairly good-looking, with a prominent jaw and straight nose. He looked to Joe like an actor or an anchorman. The man was studying everything on the shelves with great interest, which struck Joe as discordant. No one was that interested in *every single item* on the shelves. His behavior was suspicious. Although there was no audio, it was obvious that someone—no doubt the pharmacist, who was out of view—asked the man a question because the man looked up with wide eyes and mouthed, "No."

218

Then the man turned and walked swiftly down the aisle and back out the door. The exchange between the pharmacist and the shopper was brief and odd, Joe thought. He said, "We ought to have Cyndi take a look at this. She might recognize that guy. My guess is he's Robert."

Coon nodded and reached for the laptop. "Okay, we will in a minute. But we're pretty sure it's Robert Stenson. The bureau has a few photos of him and we've got agents looking for more. But just a second while I advance this. See if you recognize someone else ..."

Joe felt Sheridan squeeze his hand.

The door in the store opened again and a second figure came in wearing a hooded sweatshirt with the hood up and cinched tight. There was enough shape to the profile to determine it was a thin female. A strand of light hair crept out from the hood, but because she kept her head down, her face couldn't be seen.

Joe watched transfixed as the girl dropped items into a shopping basket.

"She looks like she's really shopping," Joe said. "She's picking things out. It doesn't look random."

"I didn't think of that," Coon said. "Do you recognize her?"

"Not yet. I can't see her face."

"Sheridan?" Coon asked.

"She could be somebody," Sheridan said. "But I can't tell for sure yet."

Said Coon, "Keep watching."

The girl went from one aisle to the next, dropping more items in the shopping basket. One package was large, flat, and square, the kind of packaging used for electronics.

Joe said, "I think that's a TracFone."

Coon stopped the tape and tried to zoom in on the

package in the girl's hand. He couldn't get the controls to work. "We need to examine this on our hardware in Cheyenne," he said. "I don't know how to look closer. But if she's got a new phone, everything we've got goes out the window. We can't find her again unless she calls or sends a text to your daughter."

Joe grunted. Sheridan looked at her cellphone as if willing it to ring.

Coon gave up trying to zoom in on the package and let the tape roll. The girl got closer to the camera, to the counter. She flinched and Joe guessed the pharmacist had addressed her. She turned, and for a second she raised her head and he could get a glimpse of half of her face. The other half was still hidden in the hood.

What he could see: her face was angular, smooth, pale, and there was a slightly Oriental cast to her eye, which was widened in alarm.

He couldn't be sure.

Joe said to Sheridan, "Is that *her*?"

"I can't tell," Sheridan said quickly.

"Want to look again?" Coon asked. "It's the best shot we've got of her face on here."

Joe asked why. Coon said, "Watch."

Two things happened at once on the tape. A white-sleeved arm reached out from the bottom of the frame and grasped the girl by the arm and pulled her closer. Unfortunately, it was too close to the camera for the lens to focus. All that could be seen was the top of her hood, which was dark and blurred. She appeared to be struggling. At the same time in the background, Robert threw open the door and strode toward the camera. His face was a snarling mask. He bent into the girl and out of view and emerged a second later with a gun in his fist. He pointed it

220

below the eye of the camera and it bucked three times.

Sheridan gasped, "Did he shoot her?"

"No," Coon said, "he shot the pharmacist. Killed him. And if you want to wait for a minute here, I'll advance the tape to where you can see Robert and the girl leaving the store with the shopping basket and some rather large pill bottles. But their backs are turned to the camera, so we can't see their faces."

Joe realized that Sheridan was squeezing his hand so hard his fingers ached. He asked Coon to rerun the glimpse of her face again. They watched it over and over. He wanted to recognize April, but he was overwhelmed with the dark feeling that he couldn't remember her face except in abstract: a ghost at a trailer house window. He wished Marybeth were there to give her opinion.

Was it her? She'd certainly look different six years older. But was it her?

"I just don't know," Sheridan finally said. "It could be. But it might not be."

Coon sighed heavily, shook his head. "We can get that one shot blown up and printed. Maybe then?"

Sheridan shrugged.

"Man, I was hoping for better," he said.

Joe agreed. It bothered him immensely that April had been an eyewitness to Robert shooting the pharmacist to death. No matter what her role was, there was no reason for her to have to see that. She was fourteen. He despised Robert for what he'd done. Then: "What about April's cell-phone? Cyndi said she left it in Skelton's truck. Let's see if it's the right phone."

Coon didn't move.

"What?" Joe asked.

The FBI agent shook his head. "It got a direct hit. Maybe

two. The pieces are there, but I don't know if we can put them together to get anything out of it."

Joe said, "I'm sure there's a computer chip or something with the call log on it. Can't you guys find that and analyze it? Isn't that what you do?"

Coon nodded. "It may take a while."

"I'd suggest you speed it up."

Coon looked over at the SUV and his shoulders slumped. "If I'm not suspended."

THE FBI INCIDENT team arrived in two helicopters an hour after dawn. Eight men in suits and ties and sunglasses, so crisply and icily efficient that they'd cordoned off the SUV and separated the witnesses within minutes of landing. After Joe gave his statement, he declared himself free to go and was surprised there was no argument from the sandy-haired special agent who'd interviewed him. He was in his pickup with Sheridan and pointed back toward Savageton before someone else decided they needed him again.

In his rear-view mirror, he watched as Cyndi gesticulated for three stone-faced men, giving her version of events.

Sheridan was already sleeping hard, her head tilted back on the headrest. Joe reached over and gently lowered her to the bench seat and pulled his jacket over her.

As he drove out of the basin, he scanned the landscape. Oil wells, gas lines, survey stakes, metal signs adorned with the company logos of international energy conglomerates. He was exhausted and there was too much swirling in his head to make sense out of anything. But as he beheld the magnitude of the basin, the multimillion-dollar efforts being undertaken to extract fossil fuel from beneath the earth's crust in this particular place, he thought about energy, about power, about Cyndi's statement in regard to being looked down upon by people with their lights on.

He thought about the size of the carbon footprints in the basin from all that activity. Then something hit him.

What had April written when Sheridan asked her why she was in Aspen? *"Wedding & footprints."*

Joe thumped the steering wheel with the palm of his hand.

HOURS LATER, SHERIDAN moaned and woke up. "Where are we?" she asked. "I don't recognize this."

Joe said, "Ever hear of a place called Hole in the Wall? This is it."

"Why are we here?"

"We're gonna need some help, I think."

She nodded, and realization crossed her face. "Nate. Where you brought the eagle."

"Yup."

"This is where he is?"

"Not far from here. We'll need to do some hiking. Are you up for that?"

"Sure. What time is it?"

"Almost ten."

"Dad?"

"Yes?"

"Where's April?"

20

Bear Lodge Mountains, Wyoming

S HE OPENED HER eyes and tried to remember where she was. It was late dawn. They were parked off the road, hidden in a thick knot of pine trees on the side of a hill. It was cool and still in the dark rolling hills, but above in the big azure sky there was a lot going on, she thought, the way those clouds scudded across from horizon to horizon like traffic on a highway, like they were being called in for emergency duty somewhere else. Up there, things were happening.

On the ground they were, too. Or soon would be. She just wasn't sure about the details. Something about a ranch, a man named Leo, and the Talich Brothers. And about all that money.

THE NIGHT BEFORE, outside the bar, she'd decided to text Sheridan again and ask her to come and get her after all. The horrible incident in the drugstore haunted her. Up until that moment she'd assumed Stenko was in charge, that he'd protect her as he promised he would and give her the money he'd offered. And she still believed that was Stenko's intention. But when she saw that look on Robert's face as he aimed the gun at the pharmacist and pulled the trigger, she realized Robert had changed in front of her eyes. He was taking control as he hadn't before. She could see he was capable of anything, and Robert seemed to realize that as well. What had changed him so quickly? It was obvious: all that money Stenko had. That's what did it. Robert had a mission. And she needed to get away from him.

As she turned her phone on and waited for it to get a signal, she realized someone was standing outside the car in the parking lot watching her. For a moment she was terrified. Robert? If so, she didn't know what she'd say, how she'd get out of it. Maybe she'd just start running away in the dark. But Robert was fit. He'd catch her.

But it wasn't Robert. It was some drunk who'd come outside. He'd grinned at her while he urinated, and she was both disgusted and scared. But he'd seen her using the phone—she was sure of it. What if he went back inside and told Robert and Stenko? So once the drunk was gone, she pitched the phone toward the garbage barrels. It was nearly out of power, anyway, and she had a fresh one still in the package from the drugstore. Robert hadn't even looked in the basket. So if Stenko or Robert came out and asked her about a phone, she could honestly say she didn't have one on her. If Robert wanted to search her, she'd let him. And the new TracFone would stay in the package until she had some privacy and could activate it and text Sheridan.

ROBERT HAD TAKEN the keys from Stenko once they'd finally come out of the bar at Savageton. She was worried about him driving drunk, but since Stenko was no better—in fact, he was sleeping—there was no choice. She kept quiet and pretended to sleep. It took two or three hours to get to where they were. Once the smooth road turned into dirt, Stenko awoke and gave Robert directions. She could smell the pine in the air. It had the same smell as that campground where Stenko shot the old couple, and that brought back bad memories. It was like they'd gone full circle and returned to the scene of the crime.

She'd slept fitfully in the back seat. Stenko had slept on the front seat and his wracking snores often woke them both up. Robert had gone off into the trees with a sleeping bag and a bottle of whiskey. She'd watched him try to start a fire, but he had no talent in that regard and had given up and angrily kicked the pile of wood away.

WHEN THE SUN came up, she realized how hungry she was. They hadn't eaten dinner the night before and now they were in the middle of nowhere. She wished she had grabbed snacks at the drugstore and had some in the basket with her TracFone. Her stomach growled so loudly Stenko stirred and grunted in the front seat. In a few seconds his hand, like a bear paw, flopped over the back of the front seat and he gripped the headrest to pull himself up into a sitting position. His hair was askew and his eyes were red.

"Makers Mark and morphine doesn't mix well," he croaked. "How you doing?"

"I'm hungry."

He nodded. "Yeah, me too. And we don't have anything in the car. We'll have to try and get some breakfast at the ranch."

She said, "What ranch?"

Stenko chinned toward the hill that rose behind him. "Over the top," he said. "My money bought it."

"Why don't we go there now? I need a shower and a bathroom. I'm not used to sleeping in cars."

"We'll go soon enough. I need to scout it out first."

"For what?"

"For my old friend Leo. Leo was my accountant. Still is, as far as I'm concerned. Leo knows where all my money is."

She nodded. She could tell he wanted to say more.

"You know, April, I've learned a lot of important things in my life. It takes a while. When you're young, you think you're the only person to take this journey and you're going to do it better, smarter, and more thoughtfully than all the people who came before you. But as you get older, you start to gain wisdom. Wisdom is a lost commodity. And here's some wisdom in the form of a riddle: Who rules the world?"

"What do you mean?"

"Who really rules the world? Do you think it's politicians? Lawyers? Presidents of the bank?"

"I don't know," she said. "I guess I never thought about it. All I know is it isn't kids."

He laughed. "Maybe this world would be a better place if you did. But no, April, it's the accountants. Accountants rule the world. They can steal more with a pencil or a few clicks of a keyboard than a bank robber can with a gun or a politician can with a telephone. If the accountant is working for you and on your side, he can make you rich. But if he has his own dreams, well, he can secretly buy a ranch in Podunk, Wyoming, and live out his fantasy. He can be what he always wanted to be all those years in Chicago: a cowboy."

With that, he rolled his eyes.

They both watched as Robert awoke in his sleeping bag. He sat up and ran his fingers through his hair and stretched.

Stenko said, "You know, I've really come to admire Robert. He's still young enough to think he can change the world. He still has passion—maybe too much. I want to

228

enable that passion before I go. That's what this is all about."

"He shot that man in the drugstore," she said.

Stenko nodded. "He did it for me. So I could keep going."

So he could get the money, she thought.

SHE FOLLOWED STENKO and Robert as they hiked up the hill. Robert had the gun in his belt. A pair of binoculars dangled around his neck from a strap. Stenko's breath was labored from the climb, and he had to stop several times to steady himself against the trunk of a tree and rest.

When they reached the top, Stenko dropped to his knees, and for a moment she thought he'd collapsed. She reached out for him but Robert slapped her hands away. "Leave him alone—he's fine," Robert said. "Get down. We're crawling the rest of the way. We don't want them to see us."

She was angry with Robert for treating her that way, but she kept her mouth shut. She'd remember it, though.

The three of them wriggled through the dirt and over rocks until they reached the top. A lush wooded valley opened up before them.

"Wow," she said, pointing to a massive rock column in the distance. "What's that?"

"Devils Tower," Stenko whispered.

The column stood high above the forest like a primitive skyscraper. It was cylindrical with a flat top, and the sides were fluted.

She said, "I saw it in a movie once."

Robert said, "Yeah—*Close Encounters of the Third Kind.* That's where the aliens landed."

Stenko said, "The legend is better than the movie, though. See, the Indians say there were seven sisters and a giant bear came after them. The bear was a bastard and had caused all kinds of trouble with the tribe. Well, this bear

229

cornered the sisters and planned to kill and eat them, but they prayed to the Great Spirit, and as the bear got close, the earth started to rise. The sisters were on top as the column went up higher and higher into the sky. The bear got mad and still tried to get at them by trying to climb the tower. Those are supposedly his claw marks on the side. But he couldn't get them."

She asked, "How did they get down?"

Stenko turned to her. "They didn't. They went to the Great Spirit and turned into stars. Have you ever seen the seven sisters in the sky?"

"No."

"Me either," Stenko said. "But it's a good story. And you know how I know it?" he asked Robert. Before Robert could respond, Stenko said, "That damned Leo told me. This was eight, nine years ago. See, he wanted to buy a ranch out here that had a view of Devils Tower. He said land was always a good investment, and we had too much money tied up in the islands and in Indian casinos. He said we should consider something way out here as a quiet investment. He called it a 'retreat,' as if I'd ever retreated from anything. Apparently, Al Capone had a ranch out here in the Black Hills back in the thirties. So Leo made this pitch to me and when I asked him what the hell Devils Tower was he told me that crazy story. I don't know why I remember it, but I'm glad I did. Otherwise, I wouldn't have figured out where this place is."

Robert was focusing the binoculars down on the valley floor. She tried to see what he was looking at and for the first time noticed a light square of flat green as well as a red roof partially hidden by trees.

"Tennis court," Robert said, "and I see a couple of guys playing tennis. Unbelievable."

Stenko took the glasses. He snorted, "Nathanial and Corey Talich. And there's Chase standing off to the side like he's the referee. Damn! We've found it."

He swept the binoculars over the grounds of the ranch. "I don't see Leo, though. He must be in the house."

Robert said, "So how do we get through those guys to get to Leo?"

Stenko said, "We don't get through them, son. We recruit 'em."

Robert just stared at Stenko, shaking his head slowly as if witnessing the sad last act of a madman.

THEY TOOK THE car down into the valley. Stenko directed Robert to drive right by the ranch entrance that led to the front of the sprawling old Victorian home with the red roof. He told him to turn on a service road that led to the rear of the property where the tennis court was located. They saw no one.

"You're sure you want to do it this way?" Robert asked Stenko.

"I don't see that we have a choice," Stenko said. "We're outnumbered and outgunned. When that happens, you either run away or bull straight ahead. I always bull straight ahead."

"Any last words?" Robert asked with sarcasm.

"Yes," Stenko said. "Where's my morphine? I need another shot."

"I'LL STAY BACK and cover you," Robert said as he pulled off the road and parked. "You know them. I don't. They'd probably just as soon shoot me as look at me."

Stenko chuckled but didn't refute Robert. To her he said, "Do you want to go with me or stay here with Robert?"

It was an easy choice. Despite the danger, there was no doubt in her mind that she'd choose Stenko every time. Shooting an unarmed pharmacist in a white smock was one thing. Facing three tough men from Chicago was another. If things got rough, she was sure Robert would run. If it weren't for the possibility of getting the money, she thought he would have run already.

Robert dropped behind them as they walked into the trees toward the tennis court.

She asked, "What are they like?"

Stenko said, "The Talich Brothers worked for me for years. They're loyal if not imaginative. I always got along with them, but I didn't try to get too familiar. I just paid them well and that was enough."

She said, "But they're gangsters, right? I didn't know gangsters played tennis. It's just not right."

Stenko chuckled and patted her on the shoulder. She was familiar enough with him now to know the morphine was surging through him, cheering him up, making him feel strong. He said, "Gangsters do all sorts of normal things, April. We're just businessmen with a different kind of business. We marry, we have kids, and we paint the trim on our houses. We put snow tires on the car and go to PTA meetings. At least most of us do. My theory is we're all the same—the gangsters and the citizens—except maybe for one or two percent of our personalities. That one or two percent isn't much difference when you think about it. Of course, the really bad ones, the psychopaths who can't control themselves, well, with a few exceptions they don't last long.

"Besides," Stenko said, "what else are these guys going to do but play tennis? They're from the city. Are they going to ride broncs or something? Rope doggies? Sing around a campfire? At least they know tennis."

In the distance she heard the *thwack* of a tennis racket hitting a ball. Instead of another *thwack* she heard a man curse, "Shit!" and she imagined him missing it.

"There are three of them," Stenko said, lowering his voice. "Corey's the oldest. He has blond hair and he's the best looking of the bunch. He's smooth and does all the talking, usually. Chase is the middle brother, the one with black hair. Chase never smiles. Hardly talks, either. Chase is the one we send out to collect overdue loans because all he has to do is look at you with those black eyes and you start sweating bullets and reaching for your wallet. It's a gift he's got. On the rare occasion that he says something it's best to listen. The youngest is Nathanial. He's the redhead. He's the one who worries me the most because he's a hothead, and without his brothers' calming influence, he's known to explode. Don't stare at him, whatever you do. He doesn't like it. Plus, I don't think he likes females very much, based on the stories I've heard about what he's done to some of them. Frankly, he's found his calling as a killer."

She said, "They sound dangerous."

"I won't kid you—they are. That's why Robert hung back. He's heard of them. But I've got no animosity toward them, and as far as I know they've got none toward me. But anything can happen, April."

She stumbled on a root but didn't fall. She said, "When this is over ..."

"You want to leave?" Stenko said, barely hiding the hurt in his voice.

She nodded.

"Well, I can't say I blame you," he said. "This isn't what you bargained for, I'm sure. If everything goes well here, I can go out the way I want to go out. I'll get my debt paid

233

down below zero, Robert will get his funding, and you'll get to be with your sister."

She didn't ask what would happen if everything didn't go well. As they approached the tennis court, her legs got heavier and harder to move. It was difficult to get her breath and her stomach ached from more than hunger. She was getting tired of being terrified.

There was another sharp *thwack* and another curse and a man laughed, "You suck at tennis, Natty."

COREY, THE BLOND brother, was in the process of serving to Nathanial when they cleared the trees. He had just tossed the ball into the air and reared back when he saw them and froze in place. The ball dropped to the court and bounced between his feet. Then bounced again. Corey made no move to reach for it. Which made Chase, who stood at the side of the court and watched the match with dead black eyes, follow his brother's lead and turn his head to see Stenko and her. And slowly reach behind his back, for something in his belt.

Nathanial was still poised to receive the serve. To Corey, he said, "What was that about, just dropping the ball like that? Don't try to mind-fuck me, Corey. Just serve. Come on …"

Corey ignored Nathanial, said to Stenko, "I can't believe what I see."

"Me either," Stenko said, much more jolly than she thought possible. The sound of his voice made Nathanial snap his head around toward the source. Stenko said, "I never in my life thought I'd see the Talich Brothers playing *tennis* of all things. Target practice, maybe. Seeing who can hang the most men from a meathook in a day, sure. But *tennis*? Come on, you guys."

234

Corey laughed, repeated, *"Hang the most men from a meat-hook*. You still got it, Stenko. You can always crack me up."

"I never lost it," Stenko said.

Corey pointed at her with his tennis racket. "And who is this?" To her: "You look familiar. Where have I seen you before?"

She shrugged. She was pretty sure she'd never seen Corey or any of the Talich Brothers.

"She looks like someone," Corey said. "Who am I thinking of?"

Stenko said, "You're thinking of Carmen. That was a long time ago. This is April. You don't need to know any more about who she is."

"I'll bet," Nathanial said, spinning his racket and leering.

Stenko went cold the way he had back in that building in Chicago. Before he pulled his pistol and rescued her. He said, "I'm sure, Little Natty. And I think you should keep your mouth shut when it comes to her."

She was grateful Stenko had defended her that way, but she thought, *Isn't Natty the one Stenko described as a killer?*

Nathanial, surprisingly, broke off and looked away first. But his face and neck were red. For the first time, she saw the bundle of leather and metal on a bench on the other side of the court. She recognized the bundle as a pistol or two in holsters that he'd taken off in order to play tennis. He could get to the bundle in three steps. He was staring at it and fuming, but he didn't make a move. She found herself stepping closer to Stenko, reaching for his hand.

"Anyway," Corey said, "I'm very surprised to see you." To Nathanial, Corey said, "Calm down, little brother."

Nathanial took a deep breath, but his face was still red. He faced them squared up, taking deep breaths that made his nostrils flare out.

Stenko said to Corey, "I know. You figured I'd be in jail."

"No," Chase, the dark-haired one, said. "We figured you were fucking dead." The hand that had been around his back swung to the front again, empty.

"Is that what Leo told you?"

The three brothers exchanged looks, which confirmed that yes, that's what Leo had told them. She was surprised at their reaction. Despite the fact that the three brothers were bigger and younger than Stenko and at least two of them had guns, it seemed understood Stenko was their superior.

Stenko said, "Guys, Leo screwed you and he really screwed me. I suppose he told you the gig was up, that I was all but gone and I was singing to the feds. So the only thing you could all do was pack up what you could and move our base of operations out here away from Chicago and the cops. Does that sound about right?"

Chase nodded yes. Nathanial looked to his brothers for direction. Corey said, "Mr. Stenson, Leo has never steered us wrong before. He was, you know, your second-in-command. He said you were going down and everything you'd built together was going down with you. He said you were all remorseful and feeling guilty, and that you were out of your head with pain and drugs."

Stenko raised his arms and his eyebrows, said, "Is that how I look to you?

"Look," Stenko said, reading their faces one by one, "Leo saw this as his chance to cut and run. He'd been planning this for years behind my back and using my money to finance it. Since he thought I might be sending someone after him, he convinced you boys to come along with him for protection. He played you for suckers. Can you believe the disloyalty? The betrayal?"

"So you ain't even sick?" Nathanial asked.

"Oh, I'm sick," Stenko said, "but as you can see, I'm battling it. And I think I'm doing pretty well, considering. But Leo screwed me. He diverted all my holdings and closed the accounts I had access to. Have you ever heard of such a thing? Can you believe Leo tried to do this to me?"

Corey said the obvious, "So you came here to get your money back. To get back in business."

Stenko said, "Yes. And you boys can either help me or you can stand in my way. But if you help me, it'll be just like the old days. We can go home and go back to work. You can't tell me you like it here, can you?"

After he finished Stenko gave her a quick glance, signaling her he was lying to them. She was reassured.

Nathanial paused and appeared to be thinking over what Stenko said, then snorted and threw down his tennis racket as if it had suddenly become electric. It was a gesture that seemed to say he was throwing away the whole ranch as well.

Corey said, "The only one who likes this nature shit is Leo. We call him 'Hoss' behind his back because no matter how he dresses or acts like a cowboy, he's still just a little jerk-off accountant to us. He's the furthest guy you can think of for a *Hoss*."

Nathanial said, "There's nothing around here but trees and cows. There are *no* women unless you get really hot for fat divorcees, snuff queens, and barrel racers."

Chase reached back and this time drew the pistol. He racked the slide and said to Stenko, "Let's go see that son of a bitch Leo."

THE TALICH BROTHERS and Stenko walked across a shorn hay meadow toward the side of the old house. They walked

237

shoulder to shoulder, spaced evenly apart. Chase held his pistol loosely at his side. Nathanial had strapped on his shoulder holsters, and he held a gun in each hand.

Corey said, *"Gunfight at the OK Corral."*

Chase said, *"Tombstone."*

Nathanial said, "Fucking *Young Guns,* man."

She stayed a few feet behind Stenko. When she looked over her shoulder, she couldn't see Robert anywhere in the trees. She wasn't surprised. She guessed he was back at the car hoping he wouldn't hear any shots from the tennis court.

Stenko spoke softly to all three brothers, "Look, what I need most from Leo is information. Starting with where he keeps my cash hidden. Then account numbers, passwords, personal identification numbers. When I get all that info and check it out, then I don't care what you do with him."

Stenko scared her because he spoke with a coldness she wasn't familiar with. She considered turning and running herself. But what if Robert had left in the car? Or if he was so jumpy he might start firing at her from the trees when she got close?

Corey said to Stenko, "Leo just doesn't seem like the kind of guy to do this, you know? I mean, he never said a bad thing about you until the end. He was the most loyal guy I ever seen all those years, you know?"

Stenko grunted, "That's the kind you need to keep an eye on."

"That son of a bitch Leo," Nathanial said, echoing what Chase had said. "Son of a bitch Leo."

Stenko turned his head as he walked, said, "April, I don't want you here right now. I want you to go back with Robert."

"Robert is hiding," she said.

"Then go hide with him."

"I'm staying with you."

Nathanial kept talking, his words sounding like a mantra. "Son of a bitch Leo. A month out of my life, playing cowboy for no good reason. Son of a bitch Leo."

They were nearly to the porch when the screen door opened. A small man clomped onto the wood in high-heeled cowboy boots. He was looking off in the distance toward the road, away from the Talich Brothers and Stenko, who approached him from the side. He was slight and bald with a large nose, and he held a cowboy hat in his hands.

"Leo," Stenko said.

She could see Leo stiffen, his hands at his side. The cowboy hat dropped to the porch. Leo threw his shoulders back and raised his face to the sky in a reaction that was not unlike someone who'd just had an ice cube dropped down the back of his pants. Leo slowly looked over his shoulder at the four men who were now just ten feet away from him.

"Stenko, it's good to see you," Leo lied.

Stenko said, "Let's go inside, Hoss."

Hole in the Wall

21

Hole in the Wall

"I KNOW THAT name, Robert Stenson," Nate Romanowski said as the three of them hiked up out of the canyon. "If it's the same guy you're talking about, then he's familiar to me."

Sheridan had listened to her dad as he led the way up the trail, which was so narrow they had to climb single file. He'd been filling Nate in on the events that had taken place and what they'd learned since they'd last met. Her dad had ended his briefing with "and now we're stumped. All we can do is hope that Stenko, Robert, and April slip up and get caught somewhere and whoever catches them has the presence of mind to hold them in place. Either that, or April decides to start texting Sheridan again from a new phone.

"The wild card," her dad continued, "is whether or not Agent Coon will be available quickly and back on the case. He should be cleared—along with Portenson—but I don't know how long FBI shooting inquiries take before the agents under investigation are cut loose. Even if it's quick and Coon's back on the job, he'll have to start all over with

April's new cellphone number—going to the judge again, getting cooperation from the cellphone companies. There might be complications this time if the judge or phone company lawyers think the FBI will swoop down and smoke innocent citizens who just happen to pick up the wrong cellphone and use it like Bo Skelton and Cyndi Rae Mote did ..."

But that's when Nate interjected and said he knew Robert Stenson, which made her dad stop, turn, and glare at his friend. He asked Nate incredulously, "*How* do you know him?"

"It's not like I know him personally," Nate said, "I know *of* him."

"And how do you know of him?" her dad asked, his irritation showing.

"I know of his work. He's the owner of ClimateSavior. net, one of the flashier carbon-offset companies. Based in Madison, Wisconsin, just like you said your Robert Stenson came from, so it's probably one and the same guy. We've exchanged e-mails."

"What?"

Nate looked over his shoulder and winked at her. They both knew Nate was tweaking Joe by slowly doling out information her dad was desperate to hear.

"I sent him some money once," Nate said. "It was Alisha's idea. She's trying to save the planet. Me, I just want to hedge my bets."

Her dad briefly closed his eyes and breathed deeply to keep his impatience in check.

Sheridan looked from her dad to Nate and back.

"I have a different angle on him than you do," Nate said. "To you, he's just Stenko's crazy son along for the ride. I know of him in a different way."

"Not just that," her dad said. "He's a murderer. He shot and killed a pharmacist in Rawlins. It's on tape."

Nate whistled. "Then he's really stepping out. I never would have guessed he'd cross the line. I mean, he's very passionate and strident, but murder? Nah—that doesn't fit."

Her dad looked to Sheridan with exasperation, as if hoping she could translate Nate's language into something a game warden could understand. Sheridan shrugged and mouthed, *"Sorry."*

"Let's say they're the same Robert Stenson," her dad said to Nate. "How does that shed any light on what's going on? How does that get us closer to finding April?"

Said Nate, "I'm not sure it does."

"And if Robert's company has something to do with Stenko and the murders, why hasn't the FBI been working that angle?"

Nate said, "You give them too much credit."

"How do you always seem to have an angle I don't have?"

"Because," Nate said patiently as if explaining it to a child, "you think in a linear way and I don't. You've got that law enforcement thing going. I never have. But give yourself some credit, Joe. You're smart enough to reach out when you need help. That's an unusual trait and a rare one with men of your ilk. Now if you'll turn around and start climbing, we can eventually get out of this canyon and maybe we can put our heads together and find April Keeley."

Her dad sighed and turned and began striding up the trail. Nate started talking.

SHERIDAN WAS THRILLED but tried not to show it. In the last hour while Nate packed a daypack with clothes and equipment, she admired not only the recovering eagle but also Nate's other hunting birds—a male and female pere-grine falcon and a red-tailed hawk. She was fascinated by the cave where Nate now lived and awed that her dad had brought her there. She wanted to believe she was being thought of as part of the team, and she knew that as long as she had her cellphone she was integral in the search for her foster sister.

Nate had been a shadowy part of their family for six years. He'd arrived the same time April had. She didn't quite understand the partnership Nate and her dad had, but she found it exciting and reassuring. Nate had always been friendly to her, and she'd accepted his offer to be his appren-tice in falconry. Her mom had told her several times over the years not to put too much stock in Nate's presence, that she shouldn't be surprised if he simply vanished from their lives some day. For the past year, she assumed he had gone away. Now, to her astonishment, she'd learned not only that Nate was still in the picture, but also that her dad kept in contact with him. No doubt her mom knew about Nate's new home as well. That her parents had maintained the secret and kept it from Lucy and her surprised, angered, and impressed her.

Nate had a hooded prairie falcon in his gloved hand as he climbed and talked. He wore the shoulder holster for his .454 Casull revolver.

And as he talked, he made the case that it was the same Robert Stenson.

"I TRY TO live low-impact," Nate explained to her dad, "as much out of necessity as a sense of duty. Naturally, I'm concerned about the environment and my planet. The whole world is in a tizzy about global warming, but I never take these crises at face value. If I did, I'd never get any

244

sleep. Remember bird flu, swine flu, and mad cow disease? We were all gonna die from those, if you'll recall."

"What's bird flu?" Sheridan asked.

"Exactly my point," Nate said. "Sheridan doesn't even know that it was supposed to be a big-time pandemic and that no one would be safe. One great crisis steps forward and replaces the last one and we don't give it a second thought. Don't forget the millennium bug! Ha! And I distinctly remember when I was growing up that we were headed for a new ice age. Remember that? I remember reading about it at grade school. Seems like people always want to think they're doomed. It brings them some kind of black comfort, I guess. Anyway, since I've got that satellite Internet dish and plenty of time on my hands these days, I've been doing lots of research on climate change. I'm not sure what I believe yet. There's no doubt there's been an increase in temperature. Not much, but definitely real. The rub is whether it's our fault or a natural cycle. There are some pretty convincing arguments on both sides. The problem is the issue has moved from science into religion, with true believers on both sides. There isn't even debate anymore—both sides believe what they believe and their positions have hardened."

Sheridan observed her dad. She could tell he was getting antsy waiting for Nate to get to the point. The muscles in his jaw balled up and released, as if he were chewing gum. He always did that when he was annoyed.

Nate continued, "It makes sense to me that the temperature of the planet isn't stagnant. How could it be? How could it possibly remain at a single perfect temperature that never varies? That doesn't wash with what I know about nature. All you have to do is look around to know that's not right."

245

Nate stopped and kicked at the dirt on the side of the trail. "I could dig a few feet down from where we stand and find fossils of ferns and fish from when this canyon was a tropical swamp. Or I could dig a few feet further and find mammoth bones from when it was covered with ice. So there's no doubt the climate has changed and that logically it will change again.

"But at the same time," he said, hiking again, "I've got to believe that all the greenhouse gases we put into the air have to have some kind of overall effect. Again, it only makes sense that when you introduce all kinds of unnatural crap—including billions more people—into the ecosystem that you impact what's there. If nothing else, maybe we're accelerating a slow natural warming trend into something more serious, and if we can slow the trend, we should do it. Plus, it just goes against my grain to waste resources or use more energy than I have to. Like I said, I believe in living low-impact just because I want to. I don't want or need too much stuff. So I'm conflicted and I'm trying to figure out the best way to live."

Her dad grunted.

She didn't know if he was agreeing with Nate or simply grunting for Nate to get on with it.

"What's your take on man-made global warming, Joe?" Nate asked.

Joe said, "My take is I want to find April Keeley and bring her home safely."

Nate rubbed his chin, said, "That's an interesting take. Very Joe-like."

Her dad shrugged, as if to say, *Get on with it* ...

"Anyway," Nate said, "that's how I got to know of Robert Stenson and ClimateSavior. He's got one of those carbon-offset companies where you can pay to reduce your carbon footprint. In my research his name kept popping up. He's controversial because he's so outspoken and he's made a whole shitload of enemies. There was at least one website called PlanetStupido.com devoted strictly to attacking him and his company ..."

Her dad shot her a look over his shoulder. She wasn't sure why. Something Nate just said had jarred him.

Nate went on, "I sort of like the idea of being able to off-set my energy consumption and I wanted to hedge my bets, so I sent his company some money and he sent me back an e-mail with photos of some eucalyptus trees they'd planted on my behalf in Nicaragua and Thailand."

"How nice," Joe said.

"Dad..." Sheridan admonished him.

Nate said, "That pissed me off, those photos."

They were nearing the rim of the canyon. Sheridan was breathing hard from the climb.

Her dad said, "Why did eucalyptus trees you paid for make you mad? Isn't that the point?"

Nate slapped his thigh with his free hand. "No! See, what I found out was planting certain kinds of trees in the Third World does more harm than good, both morally and scientifically. See, some of these companies like Stenson's outfit plant trees like eucalyptus and pine—which are considered monocultures. Sure, those non-native trees suck up their share of carbon dioxide that comes from our fossil fuels. But I'm not sure I like the trade-off. Many of these companies not only take the land out of agricultural production for the locals, but they plant trees that gobble carbon dioxide but aren't even native to the area. So my dollars are helping to introduce alien plant life to unique ecosystems. Not only that, but those kinds of trees deplete the water table, increase acid in the soil, and put locals out of work. Just so

247

I'll feel good about myself."

They cleared the canyon. Her dad's green pickup was parked a hundred yards away.

Said Nate, "I hate polluters. I do. But you know who I hate even worse?"

Before Joe could respond Nate answered his own question. "I hate people who prey on the sincere goodwill of others. I hate false religious prophets who milk the savings from people who want to be healed or saved and I hate false environmental prophets who do the same damned thing."

Nate said, "I read where some of the tribes in the Amazon call these new plantings Devil's Orchards. So I sent an e-mail to Stenson's company and asked him what the hell he was doing with my money and raised all these issues. I expected some kind of reasoned response. But you know what I got back?"

Her dad said, "What?"

Nate said, "I quote: *'You either believe or you don't.'* Then he accused me of being a shill for the energy companies. Me!"

Her dad laughed. Nate continued, "You should see some of these websites, Joe. You can pay off your guilt for flying in a plane or taking a vacation. You can even offset the entire carbon footprint for your wedding!"

Sheridan felt *her* scalp twitch.

JOE STOPPED, FIXED his eyes on Nate, and said, "What did you just say about a wedding?"

Said Nate, "You can calculate how much of a carbon footprint a wedding will make due to the number of guests, the miles they travel, and so forth. Then using one of these companies like ClimateSavior, you can write a check to

248

offset the damage, and they'll go plant trees or buy up rain forest or something to offset the damage."

Joe said to Sheridan, "Are you thinking what I'm thinking?"

His daughter's eyes were wide, and she nodded without speaking.

To Nate, Joe said, "You've said some things that made bells go off in my head. The first was Robert's company. The second was the PlanetStupido website because the owner of it was murdered two weeks ago in Madison. The third was the wedding because April said they were at a wedding in Aspen where the bride and groom were murdered. This can't all be coincidence. It might just be a way to connect the murders."

Nate said, "So why would Robert's dad get involved? What's in it for him? And what's the deal with April? Are you sure it's even her?"

Joe kicked the dirt. "I don't know. But until now I thought Stenko was instigating this whole cross-country trip. I assumed he was running from the feds. Now I'm wondering if it isn't being driven by Robert."

WHILE NATE RELEASED his prairie falcon to the sky and Sheridan observed, Joe climbed into his pickup and tried to raise Special Agent Chuck Coon. When he didn't answer on the mutual aid channel, Joe called his cellphone. It went straight to voice mail.

Joe said, "We need to look closer at Robert Stenson. Forget about Stenko for a few minutes. Robert may be the key. What you learn may help us determine where they're going next."

He closed the phone and sat back. The late-summer sun was intense through the windshield, and it warmed him.

There was a dull ache at the back of his eyes from lack of sleep. He could use rest, and he knew Sheridan could, too. As he watched the prairie falcon climb slowly into the cloudless blue sky in wider and wider arcs, he heard a call come in on the radio from a local dispatcher based in Hulett, two hours to the north-east in the heart of the Wyoming Black Hills.

Someone had called 911, claiming he was dying of gunshot wounds. The alleged victim was a ranch owner named Leo Dyekman, who requested three ambulances to be sent to his ranch.

Joe sat up and increased the volume.

A scratchy response, probably from a Crook County sheriff's deputy: "Come again? Did you say three ambulances?"

"Affirmative. He requested three."

"We've only got one. You know that."

"Affirmative. I'm simply relaying his request. He said he was injured."

"Did he say what happened? Why he needed three?"

"Yes," the dispatcher said. "He said, *'One for me, one for the dead psycho, and one for more bodies outside.'*"

"Oh, man. What's the location of the ranch?"

"We're trying to determine that now. The line went dead. We've been calling him back, but no one answers. Ruth here knows the area, and she says she thinks it's in the Bear Lodge Mountains by Devils Tower. She says she heard some guy from back east named Leo bought it a few weeks ago."

Joe started the motor and opened his window, yelled to Nate and Sheridan, *"Let's go, let's go, let's GO!"*

250

22

South of Devils Tower

Blood everywhere. Hers.

Robert, shirtless, driving erratically. Screaming. Stenko in the front seat, yelling back at Robert.

They were driving too fast down a bad, bumpy road. Pine trees shot by on both sides, the sun strobing through them, reminding her of a bright bulb behind a rotating fan. Every time Robert hit a bump, the pain in her leg sent bolts of electricity piercing through her.

But she didn't cry. Yet. Not until they got out of this. Not until *she* got out of this.

Stenko yelling, "Watch where you're going, Robert! Watch the damned road or you'll kill us all."

Robert, panicked: "I'm watching the road! Stay out of my face. You're the one who got us into this, not me."

"You're looking more at the mirror than the road. Look at the goddamn road!"

"I'm looking for the Talich Brothers. I'm sure they're behind us. You know what they'll do if they catch us …"

Stenko: "If you drive off the road and kill us all, they

don't need to do anything, do they? Their job will be done. Now calm down, son. Calm down. Calm down."

Robert screaming: "Don't call me son. And HOW DO YOU EXPECT ME TO CALM DOWN?"

Stenko: "This is where you need to calm down. This is the kind of situation where you can't panic. It reminds me of that time we were at the place in Wisconsin and you saw the snake. Remember that? You screamed and cried like a girl until Carmen got a shovel and killed it. It was just a garden snake, not poisonous. But your reaction scared me and this scares me now. Calm down. Think. This is where you need to sit back and try to outthink them."

"Easy for you to say, Dad. You're a gangster."

"Ah, that again," Stenko sighed.

"I was wondering how long it would be before you brought up that damned snake."

She couldn't believe how much she'd bled, how much blood there had been inside her. How for a few frantic minutes all her blood was so eager to spill out of that hole in her leg.

IT HAD HAPPENED so quickly in a sudden eruption back on the ranch that she didn't see coming. She doubted anyone had.

After Stenko, the Talich Brothers, and the man they called Leo went into the house, she found herself alone on the front lawn. She had no idea how long they'd be inside and she really didn't want to go in there, but Robert didn't answer her calls for him. She wished she'd brought the cellphone so she could contact Sheridan and tell her to come get her now, please come get her now ...

Inside the house she heard deep voices and sharp skin-to-skin slaps. She hoped Stenko was okay and wasn't the

252

target of any of the violence, but at the same time she felt sick thinking that he was likely administering the blows. She knew he was capable of anything, but she tried to block that out, tried to pretend he'd left that part of him behind. Because how could a man who was so kind to her be like that?

She yelled for Robert. Either he couldn't hear her or he refused to answer.

The morning was cool, sunny, still. A beautiful high-mountain day that smelled of pine, grass, and clover. But from inside the house came the sounds of blows and shouts. And a maniacal laugh that gave her chills because she recognized the voice as belonging to Nathanial. The crazy one.

She tried to sit on a lawn chair and wait, but she couldn't. She was nervous and scared and she didn't like being alone, separated from Stenko. And who knew where Robert was? Robert and the TracFone, which she hadn't yet had the chance to use. As she stared at the sky, it dawned on her the blue was marred by the lines across it—lines from power poles that went into the house. *Phone lines.* She'd forgotten that old-fashioned telephones had to use phone lines.

She jumped to her feet. She'd go inside, find a phone, and call Sheridan, beg her to come get her.

So she opened the front screen door and stepped inside, letting the door close behind her on a spring.

She was repulsed by what she saw. The man named Leo sat behind a table, his back pressed against the wall, his hands on the tabletop. He was next to a large window that overlooked the back pasture. In the distance, Devils Tower shimmered in the cold morning sun. One of Leo's eyes was swelled shut and his lip was bleeding. Stenko sat across from him with his back to her. Nathanial stood next to Stenko, leaning across the table toward Leo. Chase was off to the side in the room, leaning back against a bookcase. Chase acknowledged her when she came in but turned back to Leo. Corey stood on the other side of Stenko facing Leo, his hands on his hips.

There was a phone on the wall of the dining room, past Corey Talich. No way she could get around him to use it. But there had to be another one somewhere, right? Maybe down the hall? Upstairs?

Nathanial saying, "You lied to us, Leo. You said the boss was dying and squealing to the feds. You said come with you and we'd be all right ..."

Stenko saying, "The money, Leo. My money. I know you well enough to know you've got cash here. I need that cash and I need all the account numbers and passwords so I can get the rest."

Corey saying, "I know where the safe is, Stenko. It's in his office under the desk. I seen it there."

She thought, *his office*. There would be a phone in the office. How to get there, though, without being noticed?

Leo saying, "I know I did the wrong thing, Stenko. I know now. I guess I panicked, you know? I shoulda trusted you to do the right thing, but ... you know. I mean, we all screw up at times, right? Everybody screws up. I'll come back—it'll be like it used to be ..."

Nathanial reaching over and slapping him again, hard.

"Jesus, Natty!" Leo complained, his voice cracking with a sob.

"Tell Stenko the fucking numbers for the safe!" Nathanial hissed, leaning in so close to Leo their foreheads were touching.

Leo sobbed out the combination.

Stenko pushed away from the table, saying, "I'll go get the cash, Leo. But you'll sit right here and write down the account numbers and the passwords to all the offshore accounts. ALL OF THEM. And you'll have them all written on that napkin by the time I get back."

Leo stared dumbly at the napkin and the pen on the table until Nathanial leaned over and cuffed him on the back of his head.

She felt sorry for Leo, who looked weak and soft. He didn't look evil. He just looked like a man being picked on by bullies. The concept of men hitting men distressed her. They were like overgrown children, no better than animals. She knew the world could be like this—and was—but she wanted no part of it. She wanted to grow up. She wanted to get away.

On the way to the office Stenko saw her standing there and for a brief moment she saw the face and eyes of a monster, a man she'd not seen since that evening in the campground. And although he softened when he saw her, the image lingered, hung in the air like a mask.

"I told you to stay outside," he said to her. "I don't want you to see this."

She didn't respond, but she hoped her being there would make him change his mind, rethink what he was doing.

It didn't.

"I'm coming with you," she said.

"No," Stenko said. "I don't want you around right now. Go outside, April. This will be over soon."

The way he said it sent a new chill through her.

She said, "I don't know where Robert is. I don't know where to go …"

"Out," Stenko said, raising his voice to her for the first time. "Out. Now." He paused to make sure she obeyed, and she turned for the door. As she crossed the floor toward the door, she looked over her shoulder to make sure he'd entered the office. He had. So instead of going out through the screen door, she pushed it open hard and let the spring bang it back. Stenko would think she was outside rather than down the hallway. She glanced back to see if the Talich Brothers were watching her. They weren't. She ducked into the dark hallway, looking for a phone.

While Leo scribbled numbers on a napkin at the table, she could hear him muttering to the Talich Brothers, saying now was their chance to take over the operation, that he'd show them how, that they could become equal partners in everything like they deserved to be, that they didn't have to answer to Stenko ever again, that it could all be theirs.

She paused and looked back down the hall into the dining room. She could tell Corey was listening. Chase, too. Both of them glanced toward the office where Stenko was, then exchanged looks.

Leo stopped writing. He knew he had their attention. His voice was more urgent. As he talked, blood from his broken mouth flecked the napkin on the table. He said, "Stenko is in his last act, like I told you. He plans to take the money and run. He'll probably give it all to his useless son. The whole operation—all the businesses, the casinos, the real estate—it'll all go away. You'll have to start over somewhere. Me, too. And we're too damn old to start over now ..."

She heard Chase ask Corey, "What do you think?"

And Corey say, "He has a point. Stenko doesn't look right. There's definitely something wrong with him."

They talked as if she weren't down the hall at all, like she was invisible. She had to find a phone, but she needed to warn Stenko. She couldn't let him come out of the office into a trap. But how to let him know?

Nathanial missed the exchange between his brothers, but

he'd heard Leo. He slapped him again, said, "How do I know you're not lying again, Leo?"

The slap must have stung, because there were tears in Leo's eyes. He glared at Nathanial and said, "Stop hitting me," in a little-boy voice.

Nathanial hit him again, this time with his fist. Leo's head snapped back and thumped the wall with enough force that a picture in a frame came loose and crashed to the ground.

"Natty!" Corey said sharply.

Nathanial ignored him and hit Leo again. "He's a lying little shit. He'll never turn anything over to us. He'll keep it all because everything's in his head. He's been planning this for years, Corey. He's not going to just hand it over to us now."

And he hit Leo again, knocking him to the floor.

Tears filled her eyes and she wanted to turn away, but she couldn't. She didn't know what to do.

Then Nathanial said, "Hey ..." and she saw that he was distracted by something he saw in the pasture outside the window. "Who is *this* asshole?"

"What asshole?" Corey asked.

"Some pretty-boy asshole," Nathanial said. "Creeping around out there in the bushes."

Leo managed to pull himself back up by grabbing the edge of the table. When he stood, he wobbled.

Nathanial said, "Who is that?"

Leo sighed, "It's Robert. Stenko's loser son. The one he's gonna give his money to. Robert thinks he wants to save the planet or some damned thing."

"What's he doing here?" Nathanial asked.

From the corner near the bookcase, Chase said: "Ambush."

The way he said it made a chill creep through her scalp.

Nathanial barked a laugh and tapped on the glass with

the muzzle of a .45. "Hey, you! Trust fund boy? What the fuck you doing in the bushes? You here to *ambush* us?"

There was a loud sharp *pop* from outside, and a pane of the window glass shattered. Nathanial grunted, *"Ung,"* and stepped back.

Pop-pop-pop-pop-pop. The window imploded.

Nathanial doubled over like someone had punched him in the stomach. Corey and Chase dived out of the way.

She didn't see Leo reach up under the table and pull a pistol loose that had been taped there all along, point it at the window, and start shooting. The pistol still had strips of tape on it. The shots were so loud inside the house that her ears rang from them.

Stenko materialized at the entrance to the hallway holding a large cardboard box that appeared heavy. He'd ducked and snatched the napkin from the table and it was crumpled in one of his fists. He saw her, yelled, "Run, April!" and started toward her. He spun and ran. There was a door at the end of the hallway with a window that streamed light, and she ran toward it. Stenko was behind her.

One of the Talich Brothers yelled, "Stenko! Stop!" but she felt him close in on her and she was relieved to find the outside door unlocked.

They ran across the lawn toward the trees. Behind them, in the house, she heard several more pops from Leo's gun, followed by a series of heavy booms. As they ran, Stenko pulled ahead and a few untethered bills fluttered out of the box he was carrying and settled into the grass behind him. Fifty yards ahead, Robert was running as well, his arms flapping wildly. He never looked back.

It didn't occur to her at the time that the reason Stenko was outrunning her was because something was wrong with her. She'd been hurt. She stopped and looked down, saw the bright red blood coursing down her right leg into her shoe, and when she saw the wound pulsing blood, she suddenly felt the pain and pitched forward into the grass.

She couldn't remember him carrying her through the trees all the way to the car, or Robert screaming at him because he didn't get the account numbers.

THEY'D DRIVEN A few miles like maniacs, Stenko yelling for Robert to pull over. When he finally did, Stenko said to Robert, "Take off your shirt."

"No! It's my favorite—"

Stenko bellowed, "TAKE OFF YOUR GODDAMNED SHIRT!" and Robert did, as fast as he could, and he watched in horror as Stenko cut it into strips.

Her head was slumped back against the seat, and she wasn't sure she could raise it. Her blood had soaked into the back seat fabric until the fabric was black. The sharp hot pain of the gunshot had faded some into a place that was empty, numb, and cold. It didn't make sense she was cold.

Stenko winced as if it hurt him to move her, to swing her legs toward him so he could work on the wound. He used the strips of Robert's shirt to tightly bind the wound. Robert watched from the front seat, making a face.

Stenko said to her, "There, I think I've got the bleeding stopped." He looked into her eyes and cupped his warm hand on the side of her face. "You'll make it now, I think. The bullet hit an artery but no bones or organs. As long as we stop the bleeding you should be okay. But we've got to get you to a hospital. You aren't hit anywhere else, are you?"

"No, I don't think so."

"The way Robert was blasting away, I'm surprised we all aren't dead."

Robert said, "It wasn't me who hit her. I never even saw her."

Stenko said, "Shut the hell up, Robert. Of course it was you. Bullets were flying everywhere. Did you ever think about maybe, you know, *aiming*?"

"Hey, I'm not the gangster in the family." Then, "Well, it wasn't on purpose." Petulant.

Stenko ignored his son and looked up at her, tears in his eyes. Said, "I'm so sorry, April. I'm so sorry you're hurt. It wasn't supposed to happen like this. I never saw it coming. I'd never seen Leo with a gun in his life. Leo is *scared* of guns, just like Robert used to be."

"YOU KNOW THEY'LL be after us," Stenko said to Robert after climbing back into the front seat and slamming the door shut. "They'll want their share of the money. And who knows how they'll be if their brother's dead? He was a loose cannon, but he was their brother. They'll want revenge."

Robert hit the gas and the car fishtailed gravel and a plume of dust. "I know," he said. "That's why I didn't want to stop."

"We had to. She was gonna bleed out."

A long pause. She pretended to sleep.

"What are we going to do with her, Dad?"

"We're gonna get her some help."

"How? For Christ's sake, look around you. There's nothing but trees and rocks for miles. And don't you think they'll be looking for us at all the local hospitals, or clinics, or whatever?"

"April needs a real doctor," Stenko said. "There might be infection in that leg—or hemorrhaging."

"We can't run the risk—"

"The hell we can't."

260

"Dad—"

"Shut up, Robert. I'd do the same for you."

"Look," Robert said, lowering his voice, "we could drop her off at a ranch or something. With some nice old couple. They'd call an ambulance and get her into the emergency ward."

"I'm not leaving her like that," Stenko said. "She'd been left places all her life. I told her I'd take care of her."

"This is insane!" Robert yelled. "You're insane! What is she to you? This is your son talking. Your real son!"

"I'm not leaving her."

SHE STARED AT her bandaged leg as they screamed down the old highway. He was right: the bleeding seemed to have stopped. Maybe, she thought, because she didn't have any more blood to lose. She was cold.

Robert was yelling, "Why did he threaten me at the window like that? It was like he was begging me to shoot him. And Jesus, I was pulling the trigger before I knew what was happening. I mean, it wasn't my plan. I didn't have a plan ..."

Stenko saying, "He's crazy, that Natty. Like you, he doesn't think things through. He just reacts. When he saw you outside the window, he probably thought we were trying to ambush them."

"Like we'd do *that*," Robert scoffed.

"Hard to tell you aren't when you just start shooting everything up."

"I was protecting you!"

"You were protecting yourself. You didn't even know where I was. The problem with you, Robert, is you don't hold yourself accountable for anything you do. It's always someone else's fault."

Robert screamed, "You made me what I am. *You made me what I am, Dad.*"

"Calm down."

ROBERT HAD BOTH of his hands on the steering wheel, squeezing it so tightly that his knuckles were white. She noticed that every time he shouted, he jerked the car one way or other.

"I wish I had more time with Leo," Stenko said, uncrumpling the napkin and looking at the series of numbers. The black ink had soaked into the paper and obscured the accounts. "I don't know where all these accounts are located or what Leo might have done to make sure only he could get to them. We still need Leo's help if we're going to get all the money for your cause."

"I think he might have been hit, too," Robert said.

Stenko groaned.

Said Robert, "How much cash did you get?"

"I don't know. A few hundred thousand, maybe more. I didn't take time to count it, Robert." Stenko sounded weary, beaten.

"Count it now."

"Robert ..."

"Count it now!"

"Don't grab at it, for Christ's sake. Just concentrate on your driving. *Robert!*"

And she felt the car careen off the pavement and into a ditch, heard the furious scratches of brush from the under-carriage, saw the rolls of yellow dust blossom in clouds from both sides of the car. She closed her eyes as the car turned and hit something big and solid, felt the vehicle leave the ground, hit on its side in an explosion of dirt and shattered glass, begin to roll ...

23

Bear Lodge Mountains

J OE SAW THE helicopter wink in the sunlight on the right side of Devils Tower as it bore down on the ranch in the foothills of the Bear Lodge Mountains. The mountains themselves had an entirely different look than Joe's Bighorns or the Sierra Madres he'd been in recently. Rather than vertical and severe with dirty glaciers sleeping the summer away in fissures, the Bear Lodges looked sedentary and relaxed, sleeping old dogs covered with a carpet of blue/black pine. The aircraft was miles away, a flyspeck on a massive blue screen, still far enough that the sound of rotors couldn't be heard. He knew Coon and Portenson were inside because he'd heard the chatter on the radio. Apparently, the preliminary investigation into the shooting had gone well enough to release them to the ranch call. Crook County sheriff's deputies were also en route. Joe guessed that all of them would converge at once on the location of the distress call.

They were on State Highway 14, north of Devils Tower Junction, looking for the ranch access that would take them east toward the mountains and the ranch headquarters. Dispatch had been quiet; whoever had placed the initial 911 call had dropped off the line and had never come back. Calls to the ranch house had gone unanswered, which didn't bode well.

Joe thought, *One for me, one for the dead psycho, and one for more bodies outside.*

Sheridan sat in the middle of bench seat clutching her cellphone, staring at it as if willing it to ring. Nate hung out the open passenger window, squinting at the sky with his blond ponytail undulating in the wind. He reminded Joe of Maxine, his old Labrador, who liked to stick her head out the window and let the wind flap her ears.

"See that chopper?" Nate said, pulling his head inside the cab.

"Yup."

"You had better let me off up here for a while. I don't think it would help anyone concerned if Portenson sees me."

"Agreed."

"Why not?" Sheridan asked.

"Because I'm on the run," Nate said, matter-of-fact.

"On the run?" she asked. "Like from the law?"

He nodded, said, "Thanks to your dad I'm not in jail right now."

Joe felt Sheridan's eyes on him, hoping for an explanation.

"Dad, I thought you put people in jail."

"I do."

"But ..."

"It's a long story."

"Are you going to tell it to me?"

"Not now."

264

"Nate?"

"Me either," Nate said, taking Joe's cue.

"There's a stand of trees up ahead on the right," Nate said, changing the direction of the conversation. "Maybe I can hang out over there and wait for you."

It was an old homestead. On the high desert that led toward the foothills, the only trees were those once planted by settlers trying to make a go of it. In nearly every case, they'd failed—overwhelmed by poor soil, harsh weather, isolation, and market conditions. All that remained of their efforts were rare stands of trees, usually cottonwoods, that had been put in for shade and to provide a windbreak.

The highway was a straight shot across the stunted high-country sage. Traffic was practically non-existent except for a single pickup ahead in Joe's lane. The vehicle crept along with its right wheels on the shoulder.

"Let me pass this guy and get up ahead out of his view," Joe said, "then I'll drop you off."

As he approached the slow vehicle—a late-model blue Dodge pickup with out-of-state plates and no passengers—and swung into the passing lane, Joe felt a rush of recognition. The Oklahoma plates—reading "Native America"—confirmed it.

The driver, Ron Connelly, looked over casually at first to see who was passing him as Joe shot by. Their eyes locked and Joe saw Connelly's nostrils flare as he recognized Joe as well. Connelly slammed on his brakes and Joe shot by him on the highway. But Connelly's face lingered as an afterimage and Joe was sure it was him.

Joe said, "Hang on—it's the Mad Archer!"

Nate said, "The mad *what*?"

"Brace yourselves," Joe said, flinging his right arm out to help protect Sheridan from flying forward as he hit the brakes.

265

Joe cursed himself for being careless and alerting Connelly, who'd been moving down the highway much too slowly and too far over on the shoulder with no apparent car problems or flashing emergency lights. He'd been cruising the road with all the characteristics of a road hunter—scanning the terrain out the passenger window for game animals to shoot illegally from the comfort of a public road. And since most wildlife became acclimated to the singing of traffic on the rural highway, they no longer followed their instincts for caution. Over the years, wildlife had learned not to look up unless a vehicle stopped. Unscrupulous road hunters like Connelly took advantage of the new paradigm and jumped out firing.

"Is he the one who shot Tube with an arrow?" Sheridan asked as Joe came to an abrupt stop in the middle of the highway.

"That's him," he said, throwing the transmission into reverse. To Nate: "He's the same one who shot your eagle."

"Let's get him," Sheridan said through gritted teeth.

Nate said, "Proceed."

Connelly had decided to run and was in the process of turning back the way he'd come, his back tires churning up fountains of dirt in the borrow pit, his front tires on the pavement. His pickup was bigger and newer, and Joe knew that on the open road Connelly could outrace him. He had to stop Connelly before he could get going.

Rather than turn around and give chase, Joe floored it in reverse. He was filled with sudden anger at Connelly, at Stenko and Robert, the choices he'd made that consumed him with guilt, at everything. Getting the Mad Archer would be another one in his good works column.

"Joe," Nate said calmly as the motor revved, "are you sure you want to do this?"

"Brace yourself," Joe said to Sheridan and Nate.

Joe used the rear bumper and tailgate of his pickup to T-bone Connelly's pickup on the passenger side as Connelly tried to make his turn. The impact knocked the Dodge six feet sidewise, and Joe saw Connelly's hat fly off and his arms wave in the air. The collision wasn't as severe in the Game and Fish pickup because they'd been accelerating straight backward, had braced themselves for the collision, and were cushioned by the seat.

"Got him!" Sheridan cried, raising a triumphant fist in the air.

"Not yet," Joe cautioned, swinging the pickup off the road into the ditch and aiming his grille at the Dodge.

Joe threw the transmission into park and launched himself out the door. He could see Connelly on the passenger side in his pickup instead of behind the wheel due to the impact on his passenger door, which had thrown him across the cab. Connelly sat stunned, shaking his head from side to side. Blood streamed down his face and into his mouth from a cut in his forehead.

Joe wanted to get to Connelly and subdue him before the Mad Archer tried to resist or run again. He was halfway there, his boots thumping on the asphalt, when Connelly looked up and saw Joe running in his direction. Connelly dove for the wheel and used it to pull himself back into the driver's seat. He righted himself and started fumbling for the gearshift.

The engine growled and the blue Dodge lurched forward. Connelly cackled and maniacally turned the wheel away from Joe, who pulled up and reached for his Glock as the bumper of Connelly's pickup grazed his thigh while it turned. "Later!" He laughed to Joe through a mouthful of bloody teeth.

The deep-throated concussions of Nate's .454 Casull coughed out once, twice, and seemed to briefly suck the air out of the morning. The blue Dodge bucked as if it had hit a set of hidden ditches head-on. The engine went silent and the truck rolled lazily forward off the road. The front tires bit into loose sand and it lurched to a stop. As intended, both slugs had penetrated the engine block. Green radiator fluid pooled on the dirt and plumes of it hissed and rose in the air, coating the windows of the Dodge.

Gun drawn, Joe ran to the driver's side of the pickup from the back. He yelled, "Thanks, Nate!"

"My pleasure," Nate said, standing wide-legged on the other side of the road, still holding his revolver in a two-handed grip. "I like killing cars."

Connelly opened his door cautiously. He looked at Joe coming at him. He turned his head to see Nate and his .454 in a cloud of green steam that made him look like an apparition from the Gates of Hell. Connelly was half in, half out of the cab. Joe could see only one of Connelly's hands, the one holding the handle of the door.

"Let me see 'em both," Joe said, raising the Glock and sighting down the barrel as he approached. He hoped he wouldn't have to shoot. Nate was not far out of his line of fire through the windshield, and ricochets could threaten Sheridan.

Connelly hadn't moved in or out an inch. He seemed to be weighing his options. Was his other hand gripping a gun?

"I said, show me your hands and climb out slowly," Joe said. "You're under arrest for skipping bond in Carbon County."

Connelly smiled slightly, said, "Don't you think this is excessive force? Since when is it okay for a damned game warden to injure a man and total his pickup for missing a hearing for a misdemeanor?"

Joe said, "Ever since you shot a dog with an arrow. Now shut up, get out, and get down on the ground."

Nate emerged from the steam and aimed his .454 at the side of Connelly's head. "Let me shoot him and tear his ears off, Joe. You know, for my collection."

Joe stifled a smile and watched as Connelly leaped out of his pickup empty-handed and eagerly threw himself face down into the sand.

As Joe snapped handcuffs on Connelly's wrists, Connelly said, "How in the *hell* did you find me all the way up here?"

Joe said, "Just good police work," and winked at Sheridan, who had watched the arrest openmouthed.

WITH RON CONNELLY cuffed to the front strut of his dead pickup on the side of the highway, Joe called in the arrest to central dispatch. In the days since the Mad Archer had vacated Baggs, he'd obtained a new compound bow and a set of broadhead arrows, as well as a Ruger Ranch Rifle and a stainless-steel .45 semi-auto. In the glove box were cartridges, a bloody knife still covered with deer hair, and plastic vials of crystal meth. Tim Curley, the game warden out of Sundance, heard the call and broke in.

"Joe, how the hell are you?"

"Fine," Joe said, remembering Curley as a big man with dark eyes, impressive jowls, and a gunfighter mustache. "Can you come get this guy?"

"This is the one they call the Mad Archer?"

"Yup."

"I thought I heard you already caught him and threw him in the pokey."

"I did. But that was last week. You know how it goes sometimes."

"What—a sympathetic judge who let him out on bond?"

"Tim, we're on the radio."

"Oh, yeah. Hey—you gonna stick around? It's been a while since we got caught up. I want to hear your version of what happened to Randy Pope."

"Nope," Joe said in answer to both questions. "I'll send you all the paperwork on Connelly later. You'll need to send a tow truck to the scene."

"Don't tell me you wrecked another departmental vehicle?" Curley laughed. Joe was infamous for holding the record for the destruction of departmental vehicles. No one else was close.

"Not mine, this time." But as he said it, he stepped away from the cab and gauged the damage he'd caused to the back of his pickup. Both tail lights were smashed. The back bumper was curled under the frame. His trailer hitch was flattened to the side and his tailgate hung open and out like the tongue of a dead animal. "Not enough that *I* need a tow truck, anyway," he said.

"What's going on? What are you doing in my district? Last I heard you were sentenced to Baggs."

Joe said, "I don't have time to explain right now. This arrest cost us ten minutes. I have to go, sorry."

Curley said, "Does this have something to do with that ranch deal that's been all over the radio this morning?"

Joe said, "I'll need to catch up with you later, Tim."

Sheridan and Nate were already in the cab, and Joe swung himself in, hung up the mike, and gunned it.

"That was a good one," Joe said to Nate and Sheridan as if they'd been privy to his earlier ruminations. He nodded at the view of Ron Connelly slumped against his pickup in his rear-view mirror. "That was worth the time it took to get that guy back into jail where he belongs. Yup, that makes me feel real good. That's one on the plus side, by golly."

Nate chuckled as he replaced the two spent cartridges in his five-shot revolver with fresh rounds the size of lipsticks.

Sheridan glared at Nate. "Your *collection*?"

Nate winked at her.

In the distance, they could see the helicopter begin its descent.

"There's the ranch," Nate said, gesturing toward the cottonwoods marking the abandoned homestead. "You can let me off here. I'll stay out of Tim Curley's way and watch for you when you come back out."

Joe said, "Do you finally have a cellphone so I can call you?"

Nate curled his upper lip. Nate hated cellphones. He once told Joe satellite phones were a necessity but cellphones made him feel that he was always on call.

"Here," Joe said. "Take mine. I'll let you know when we're coming."

Nate took it as if Joe was offering him a bar of feces. It was Sheridan's turn to wink.

24

Bear Lodge Mountains

THE RANCH YARD was a hive of activity; sheriff's department SUVs were parked at jaunty angles near the main house with their doors wide open, an ambulance driver was arguing with deputies to clear the way so he could back his vehicle in, and the FBI helicopter sat in a back pasture like a giant insect on a break. Joe drove his pickup to the other side of the yard near a Quonset hut filled with farm equipment.

"I want you to stay here," he told Sheridan.

"What about April?"

"Believe me," Joe said, "if April's in there, I'll come running." Thinking, *Unless she's in bad shape.*

"Why don't you get your mother on the phone?" he said. "Let her know what's going on and that we're both okay. I'm sure she's going crazy."

"I'm sure she is."

TWO SHERIFF'S DEPUTIES stopped Joe from entering the house, saying they were under orders to keep everyone out.

Joe asked who to talk to and one of the deputies said the FBI was in charge and both agents were inside. "When one of them comes out," the deputy said, "you can talk to him."

Joe considered rushing them, but they were both bigger as well as filled with the official hubris that always resulted when there was a multiple homicide in a single-digit crime rate county. Their blood was running hot with purpose. He knew better than to try and get through them.

Instead, he circled the house hoping he could see inside. If he saw April, he decided, he was going in even if he had to fight his way inside. He walked on the lawn around the left side of the house and saw a side door with another deputy stationed at it. Joe waved and kept walking, looking in every window and seeing nothing out of the ordinary. He walked the length of the back of the house and around the side. He was noting a broken window to what looked like the kitchen when the tip of his boot ticked something metallic. He stopped and looked down. Spent cartridges from a handgun blinked in the sun. He counted eight before he stopped counting, then stepped back and away so he wouldn't crush them into the ground. From the location of the spent shells, he could imagine a gunman standing just outside the kitchen and firing inside. It bolstered his theory when he noted there was no broken glass under the window in the flowerbed—the glass had been blown inside the house. He wanted to show the FBI agents what he'd found.

Coon was exiting the front door of the ranch house, struggling with the removal of a pair of latex gloves. As Joe approached, Coon held up a gloved hand made a sick yellow by the latex covering and said, "I'd suggest you stay where you are. Agent Portenson just gave the order to seal up the crime scene as soon as we get more photos of the victims taken out of there."

"Who are the victims?" Joe asked, feeling his chest constrict.

Coon said, "An adult male DOA in the kitchen. Another adult male in critical condition. The EMTs are loading him on a gurney as we speak."

"Anyone else?"

Coon frowned. "Should there be?"

"The nine-one-one call mentioned bodies outside. Is there a girl in there?"

"No."

"Can I look?"

"I said …"

"Stay the hell out," Portenson interrupted, appearing behind Coon. He was red-faced. "Why are you always around, anyway?"

Joe sighed in frustration. "Can you at least describe the scene to me? What's your best guess what happened in there?"

Portenson rolled his eyes and shouldered past Coon toward the helicopter, making it clear he didn't have time to waste with Joe. Over his shoulder, he said, "I want Stenko. I want his head on a platter."

When Portenson was out of earshot, Coon said, "He is not a happy man."

"He never has been. What's going on?"

Coon said. "Tony is in big trouble because of that incident earlier today. Our bosses don't like that kind of thing anymore because it attracts the wrong kind of attention in the press and in Washington. We're supposed to be counterterrorism these days except for the occasional slam-dunk mob arrest. And when we screw up like we did this morning, the shit rolls downhill."

Joe nodded.

"I think you know that all Agent Portenson really wants is to get out of Wyoming. What happened earlier doesn't help. Neither one of us is out of the woods yet. Hell, I don't mind whatever happens. I like it here and so does my family. But Tony ..."

"... wants out," Joe said. "I know. He wants to run with the big dogs."

Coon nodded. "The only way he can make amends is to nail Stenko."

Joe gave it a beat. "So what's it look like inside?"

Coon finally got his right glove pulled off with a sharp snap. "As I said, two victims. One under the broken kitchen window. Male, thirties, dressed in tennis togs, if you can believe that. His ID said he was Nathanial Talich from Chicago. He was the youngest of the three brothers and considered to be the craziest ..."

"The psycho," Joe said, repeating the term from the call.

Coon nodded. "Multiple gunshot wounds. I could see one right below his eye, but my guess is he took at least a few more in the belly the way he was curled up."

"The other guy?"

"The sheriff said he's the owner of the ranch. A guy named Leo Dyekman. Also of Chicago," he said, raising a single eyebrow. "We think he's a known associate of Stenko. His money man, we think. Portenson is in communication with Washington now to confirm that."

"Can you tell what happened?"

Coon shrugged. "It looks like a gunfight. They were both armed and I'm guessing they shot each other."

Joe shook his head. "I doubt that. Can Dyekman talk?"

Coon narrowed his eye, not pleased by the Joe's casual disregard of their theory. "Why? What do *you* think?"

"I'll show you in a minute. Can Dyekman talk?"

"I'd be surprised if Dyekman ever talks, judging by the amount of blood he lost. I don't think his wound was fatal—it looks like he got hit on the side of the neck—but he might have bled out after he made the call. There is a *lot* of blood in that house."

Joe hoped none of it was April's.

Coon said, "That's the problem with living out here in the middle of nowhere. The EMTs can't get to you in time."

"So why do you think the two guys shot each other up?" Joe asked.

"Because that's what it looks like, Joe. But that's why we called in forensics. They might be able to figure out what the hell happened in there."

"So why did Dyekman refer to more bodies?"

Coon shrugged. "Who knows?"

"Was there any other blood anywhere?"

"I told you, Joe, there's blood all over the place. It looks like a slaughterhouse."

"So why is the kitchen window broken?"

Coon gave Joe a big-eyed exasperated expression. "I don't know, Joe," he said with annoyance. "That's why we called in our team."

"I can't wait for your team," Joe said. "Look, there's brass on the side of the house outside the kitchen window. I tried not to disturb it much. But what it looks like is that somebody stood outside and started blasting."

Coon stared at Joe skeptically.

Joe said, "April's not here. Every minute we wait for your team she gets farther away."

Coon threw up his hands, said, "We don't even know that she was ever here, Joe. Come on …"

Joe held up his hand and extended a finger for every point: "One, she said she was going to a ranch in the Black

Hills. Two, these guys are associated with Stenko. Three, the caller said there were people who might be injured. Four, someone who is *not* on the floor in there stood outside the house and fired inside. Which says to me they got away from here and they probably took April, who might be hurt."

"Is there a five?" Coon asked sarcastically.

"Five, where else could she be?"

"Go home, Joe," Coon said. "For once, I agree with Portenson. We've got this handled. There's nothing you can do. Plus—"

Joe waited. Coon didn't finish. Instead, he stepped out of the way of the EMTs who came crashing through the door with a body on a gurney. Joe stepped aside as well and walked alongside the gurney, hoping the slight middle-aged man beneath the sheet would open his eyes. The man—Leo Dyekman—was ghostly white. Swinging plastic units of blood coursed into both arms as they wheeled him toward the open ambulance. Joe recognized the stitched brown cowboy shirt Dyekman was wearing as one he'd seen on a Western wear store clearance rack.

"Leo, talk to me," Joe said, prodding Leo's chest.

"Please don't touch him," a bearded EMT warned.

"Leo, where's April?"

"Man ..." the EMT said, shaking his head.

"Leo!"

And Leo's eyes shot open.

"Jesus," the EMT said, as surprised as Joe.

Joe reached out and stopped the gurney and leaned over the victim. His eyes were open but there was no expression on his face. "Can you hear me?"

Dyekman groaned.

"Leo, who shot you?"

"Fuck. I'm gonna die."

"No you're not. You'll be fine. Now who shot you?"

Dyekman rolled his head to the side. "I think Robert. But it could have been Natty. Lots of shots."

"Robert Stenson?"

"Who else?" As he said it, his eyes drooped. Joe didn't think Dyekman would be conscious much longer.

"Was there a girl in the house?"

"Stenko," Dyekman said. "That damned Stenko got the cash."

"Clear the way," the bearded EMT said to Joe. "We need to get going. You can talk to him later in the hospital." He pushed on the gurney and the lead EMT pulled. Joe walked alongside.

"What about the girl?" Joe asked again.

"What about her?"

He felt a thrill. "So there *was* a girl. Do you know who she was?"

Dyekman's face contorted with pain.

Joe slapped him. The bearded EMT said, "Hey!" One of the sheriff's deputies guarding the front door broke away and started jogging toward them, his hand on his weapon.

"Did you see what he just did?" the EMT said to the deputy.

"Clear the hell away, mister," the deputy growled.

But the slap had opened Dyekman's eyes again. Joe cocked his hand as if to do it again.

Dyekman said, "I didn't get her name!"

"Blond? Fourteen?"

"Could be."

The deputy bear-hugged Joe while the EMTs rolled Dyekman into the ambulance.

"Man, what's wrong with you?" the deputy hissed into Joe's ear.

"Let me down," Joe said. "I got what I needed."

When the deputy released him, Joe turned toward his pickup near the Quonset hut. Sheridan had watched the altercation and looked to him with pleading eyes. He knew what she was asking: Was April here? He nodded: *"Yes."*

"SHE WAS HERE," Joe told Marybeth on Sheridan's cell-phone. "I just know it."

Marybeth was calm, he thought. Calmer than he was. It always amazed him how pragmatic she became when events seemed out of control.

"But Sheridan said she might be hurt," she said.

"We don't know. They won't let me inside the house. But she's gone—that we know."

"Did someone identify her?"

"Maybe. I couldn't get much out of him."

Marybeth sighed. "This is tough, Joe. It's tough that you're gone with Sheridan. And I understand you went and got Nate. I don't know—is she ready for this? Is she okay?"

Joe assessed his daughter, who leaned against the door of the pickup pretending she wasn't listening to every word. What he saw was a young woman who was lucid, calm, but worried. She'd never been out in the field on an investigation with him. All she knew were the results. She'd never been in the middle of a chaotic crime scene like this one with uniformed men cursing at each other and running around, the jockeying for status and position, the clash of jurisdictions among personnel from different agencies, the baseless speculation thrown around in regard to what might have happened. He wondered if she was questioning his acumen and clearly seeing his fallibility. Lord knows he was fallible. But he was her dad. He knew she always thought he had special abilities. Now, he thought, she'd know that

280

he didn't. That he could run around and speculate with the best of them.

"I think so," he answered Marybeth, trying not to tip off the question.

But Sheridan sensed it and mouthed, *"I'm fine, Dad."*

There was a long pause on the other end of the line. Then: "Maybe it's time to bring her home, Joe. There haven't been any calls from April. I know she'd rather be with you and Nate, but I'm not sure that's the best idea."

He looked up to see Sheridan glaring at him. He wondered if his face betrayed Marybeth's question, and he tried to deaden his expression. "You may be right," he said. And for Sheridan's benefit: "I'm exhausted. We haven't gotten any sleep for I don't know how many nights. We would both probably welcome being in our own beds." He nodded as he talked and looked to his daughter for agreement. The glare didn't waver.

He turned away. "How's Lucy doing?" he asked in a whisper.

"She's not happy. She wishes she were with you and Sheridan. This morning at breakfast she looked at your empty chairs and said, 'I'm sick of being the baby in the family.'"

"She said *that*?"

Before she could answer, there was a chirp on the phone that he disregarded. He assumed it was a bad cell connection.

"Yes, Joe. She's growing up. She's an interesting child. She observes the rest of us and makes up her own mind. And I've found when she says something, I'd better listen."

"I can't imagine being out here with the both of them," Joe mumbled. "Especially with Nate."

"Yes," Marybeth said, "I heard about the ear collection."

Joe cringed. "You know he really doesn't have one, right? That it's his way of joking?"

"I knew that. But does Sheridan?"

"I think so." What was he doing to his daughter?

"Don't worry," Marybeth said, as if reading his mind. "Sheridan might just have a better understanding of Nate than either of us. She's almost grown up with him around."

He chuckled, despite himself. And the phone chirped again.

"Hold on," he said to Marybeth. Cupping the mike, he said to Sheridan, "Your phone is making a funny beep. Does that mean you have to charge it or something?"

Her eyes shot open. "No, Dad. That means there's a call coming in. Or a *text*."

It took a moment to realize what she meant. But Joe quickly said to Marybeth, "Look, I've got to go."

"What?"

He snapped the phone closed. He felt bad doing that to Marybeth, but he knew he could always call her back and explain. Quickly, he handed the phone to Sheridan, who took it and looked at the display.

She said, "It's a number I don't recognize. There's no text or message. It says I missed two calls."

Joe thought, *April took a fresh TracFone from the pharmacy in Rawlins.* It would have a new number. And if it was April, her situation was desperate enough that she finally decided to call, not text.

"I *know*," Sheridan said, again reading his mind, again staring at her phone. Again, willing it to ring.

Although Joe had told her to stay in the truck, she jammed the phone into her pocket and stalked away into the meadow to regroup. Joe didn't stop her.

"JOE, THIS ROBERT angle you suggested may have legs," Coon said. Joe hadn't seen him walk over from the helicopter, and his sudden presence jarred him. "I just talked to our team in Washington. They're going crazy with the linkages. I can't believe we weren't looking in his direction before this. Stenko's such a big fat target that we didn't really move the spotlight off him."

Joe turned away from Sheridan and her cellphone, hoping Coon wouldn't pick up on what might be happening.

"Sometimes we think in too much of a linear way in law enforcement," Joe said, echoing Nate.

"What?"

"Never mind." Joe was preoccupied. If all Portenson wanted was Stenko's head on a platter, as he said, April could once again end up being collateral damage. Joe refused to open up that possibility. Which meant he couldn't yet confide in Coon regarding the incoming calls. They were back to square one.

Coon said, "The dead guy in Madison, Reif? Apparently, he was Robert's nemesis. The two of them used to work together at one point and they founded the carbon-offset company together. But they had a falling out. Reif got disillusioned with either Robert or the cause or both, because he left ClimateSavior and spent all his time ripping our boy and the company on his own blog. He hated Robert and no doubt he damaged the credibility of Robert's company and his cause. And then he turns up dead and Robert's nowhere to be found."

Joe said, "You guys need to run the spent casings on the lawn over there against casings found in Madison."

"Already on it," Coon said. "But there's more. Like a double homicide in South Dakota of a couple with a giant RV. Robert had a thing against those big vehicles and he railed about it on his website. In fact, he tried to urge his fans to sabotage them."

Joe said, "Keystone. That poor old couple."

"Yeah."

"And the Aspen wedding?"

Coon said, "Two trust fund kids with high profiles on the society and gossip pages. Two great big huge carbon footprints."

Joe shook his head.

Coon said, "I don't want to believe what it's looking like. Plus, I believe in global warming and climate change. I don't want this to screw up the effort. It's up to all of us, you know. These guys could give it all a bad name."

Joe grunted.

"There's something else," Coon said, stepping in closer and looking over his shoulder.

"What? Are you worried about your boss overhearing you?"

Coon leveled his gaze at Joe until Joe was uncomfortable.

Coon said, "I was watching your truck through my binoculars as we came in earlier. I saw you pull over and let somebody out."

Joe looked away.

"Some big guy with a blond ponytail got out," Coon said, taking another step toward Joe until they were inches apart. "That wouldn't have been Nate Romanowski, would it?"

Joe said, "Who?" But he knew his face was flushed.

"So it was him," Coon said. "You are a really lousy liar."

Joe didn't respond.

"If Portenson knew he was around, you would both be in a world of hurt," Coon said. "Not that I told him what I saw."

Joe nodded. He was grateful Coon hadn't told his boss. And wished he were a better liar.

"What are you going to do if you find her, Joe?" Coon asked.

"I'm not sure."

"Do you think you can save her?"

Joe met his eyes again. "I don't know."

Coon asked, "What *do* you know?"

Joe shook his head. "Not much. But I know she deserves better than what's happened to her. She needs to know somebody cares."

Coon started to speak but stopped himself. Instead, he tilted his head back and looked at the big blue autumn sky. Finally, he said, "That's admirable. It may not be protocol, but it's admirable."

He wasn't sure how to respond.

"If she calls again," Coon said, "you need to give me the number. I'll help you track her down."

Joe made a decision. He said, "It's a deal."

Coon walked away.

In the meadow, Sheridan kicked through ankle-deep cheatgrass toward a wall of trees. She had no destination other than to have a few minutes to herself. She didn't want to simply go home. Not without April. The grass was dry and stiff and crunched underfoot. She noted she wasn't the only person to have recently walked through it. There were two parallel tracks heading from the house toward the trees—one heavier than the other. Then she saw the blood flecked across the stalks of grass and yelled, "Dad!"

He came running.

While she waited for him there was another chirp. She pulled out her cellphone and read the message.

As her dad approached and saw the blood on the grass, Sheridan said, "It's her."

SHE HANDED THE phone to Joe. He looked at the display and his stomach clenched.

285

It read:

From: AK

im hurt and its getting bad. im in the woods. the car is crashed. i need u 2 come get me now. i think there r some men coming 2 get me. i hear them. idont know what theyll do 2 me. plz come get me sherry. take me home. plz help me.

ak

CB: 307-220-4439

Aug 26, 11.18 A.M.

Erase REPLY Options

25

South of Devils Tower

S HE COULD HEAR them coming.

Far above her, in the trees. They were working their way down the steep slope and occasionally one of them stepped on and snapped a dry branch or dislodged a rock that tumbled down. They were certainly taking their time. A half hour before, while she was texting Sheridan, she'd heard the sound of an engine and the crunch of tires on gravel far above her on the road. Then the sound of two car doors slamming.

She had no doubt they'd find her. Although the hillside was extremely steep, the trail leading to her was obvious. Far above, as far as she could see, there was a gap in the brush near the road where the car had torn through. It had rolled to the bottom, snapping off pine trees and churning up the ground. The car now rested upside down on its hood, wheels in the air. The motor had finally stopped ticking. She was grateful it hadn't burst into flames like cars did on television when they crashed and rolled down a mountain. Instead, it was immensely quiet. The only sounds were the buzz of insects, the watery sound of a breeze in the treetops, and footfalls as they got closer.

She'd tried to stand but the pain in her leg wouldn't let her. Her hands and face were covered with tiny cuts and her neck and shoulder ached from where the seat belt had bitten into her. She was too weak to crawl any farther from the car than to the base of a huge dark pine. She sat slumped against it.

Waiting.

SHE TRIED TO recall the events of the last half hour but they came to her in bits and pieces. She remembered the car rolling, her head either pressed against the inside of the roof as it dented down farther with every rotation or being slammed back again to the back seat. Robert was screaming the whole time, holding his hands in the air as if to stop the hood from collapsing on his head. The sounds of snapping trees were like gunshots and there were glittery jewels floating through the air. No, not jewels—tiny cubes of safety glass from the windows as they shattered. She'd picked some of the glass out of her hair and from folds of her clothing. Her leg had begun to bleed again.

She'd faded in and out of consciousness, but she knew both Robert and Stenko had somehow survived the crash as she had. She remembered Stenko moaning—something about his ribs—and Robert pulling him out of the car through the open windshield. When Robert crawled back into the interior of car to get his computer case and Stenko's daypack, she'd opened her eyes. He scowled at her but didn't speak, as if she weren't worth his words, as if he just wished she'd go away. She seemed to be floating in the air upside down, and she realized she was hanging suspended from the seat belt.

Later—she wasn't sure when—she heard Robert imploring Stenko to take more morphine.

Robert saying, "Come on, Dad. We've got to walk. You can walk downhill, can't you? They're gonna find us here if we stay. And if they find us, they'll butcher me. You need to take more of that stuff so you can function."

"What about April?" Stenko had asked, his voice slurred like he was drunk.

She had wanted to answer, to call out. But she was in shock and nothing worked. The only words she could express were in her own head.

"She's dead in there," Robert had said. "I'm sorry."

She remembered wondering if she *was* dead.

Stenko started sobbing. The recollection of the sound brought tears to her eyes now.

"It's okay," Robert had told him. "She couldn't have walked out of here anyway with her leg and all. You never should have brought her, Dad. You never should have brought her. She isn't Carmen and she never was."

Sloppy, racking sobs from Stenko.

"Come on, Dad. We can't stay. We'll go downhill until we run into a road or a ranch where we can get a car."

Stenko said, "She was innocent. She never hurt anyone. I was trying to save her, Robert. Every time I try to do something right it seems like they end up getting hurt ..."

Robert: "Get the box of cash. We need to take that with us. And you still have that napkin with the account numbers on it, don't you?"

"Didn't you hear what I said?" Stenko cried.

Robert's voice was shrill. "Yeah, I heard. Like you need to tell *me* you screw up the lives of those around you.

Sheesh. Like *that's* news to me. It's a freaking wonder I'm so well adjusted, you know?"

Then silence. They were gone.

FROM A RESERVE she didn't know she had in her, she managed to find the buckle of the seat belt and release it. When it opened, she dropped a few inches. Although she was hurting everywhere, no bones seemed to be broken, and she crawled out of the car through the gaping rear window. She'd found the cellphone a few feet away from the vehicle but not the card she'd need to load minutes.

In the shade of the big pine tree, she tore at the packaging with her teeth and powered the phone. There was an automatic ten minutes of airtime on the phone to enable the user to call and load it with more time. Instead, she tried to call Sheridan, who didn't answer, so she sent a text.

SHE HEARD A voice.

"Chase, down here." She recognized the voice as Corey Talich, the oldest brother. It came from above in the trees and to her left. It was a whisper/yell. He was being cautious.

"What do you see?" Chase asked in the same tone. He was above to her right. The brothers were descending the mountain on either side of the churned-up ground the rolling car had made.

"An upside-down car. I can see the tires. It's got to be them."

Then she heard something else. Either a rock dislodging or a car door slamming.

She breathed deeply and closed her eyes. If she lay still, maybe they wouldn't see her against the tree. Or, like Robert, they'd think she was dead.

"D'you see anybody?" Chase asked, his voice low but

bolder, as if he was starting to believe there were no survivors.

"Nobody I can see."

"I hope Robert isn't dead," Chase said, "because I want to kill him."

Corey laughed harshly. He was very close. She cracked an eye and saw him as he pushed into the clearing through a pine bough on the other side of the car.

"Jesus," he said. "How many times did it roll over to get all the way down here?"

"Not enough," Chase said. "Are Robert and Stenko in there? Is our money in there?"

She knew they wouldn't let her live if they found her. She just hoped they'd just kill her and nothing else.

She thought of her sisters and how much she'd like to see them again. How she never would. She wished Stenko would come back. Even Robert. No, not Robert.

"The car's empty!" Corey hissed. She couldn't see him and she assumed he'd dropped to all fours on the other side of the vehicle to look inside.

"You're kidding!" Chase said, emerging from the trees on the right side. He had a gun in his hand.

"No, man, I'm not kidding. There's no Stenko, no Robert, no money. Even that girl is gone. Where in the *hell* did they go? How in the hell did they get out?"

"*Shit,*" Chase barked. "This is why I hate seat belts."

Corey stood up and she could feel his eyes lock with hers. He raised his hand and pointed. "There's the girl."

"What?"

"I see that girl. She's over against that big tree."

"Where?"

Corey shook his finger at her. "There."

She'd never felt more helpless.

"I bet she knows where those bastards went," Chase said, walking around the car toward her. His face was expressionless, his eyes dark coals. The lack of feeling or emotion on his face scared her more than if he'd been snarling, because he approached her as if he had a routine job to do and wanted to finish it so he could go on to the next task.

When he was ten feet away he raised his pistol and she could see the black O of the muzzle.

"Where'd they go, bitch?" Chase said. Corey walked up behind him. It was obvious by the way Corey looked at her expectantly that he had no intention of stopping what was about to happen. Especially if she didn't talk.

She moaned and felt hot tears cut through the grime on her cheeks.

And suddenly there was a red fist-sized hole in Chase's chest accompanied by a massive *BOOM* that seemed to shake the earth. Blood, bone, and tissue spattered the grass. Chase's eyes rolled up in his head and he dropped straight down as if he were a mountain climber whose rope had been severed.

Corey cursed and wheeled around, fumbling at the back of his pants for a pistol grip.

"Freeze and put your hands up where I can see 'em!" a man shouted as he came out from under the branches of a tree in a crouch. He had a rifle or a shotgun—a shotgun—and he wore a red shirt and a gray cowboy hat. There was a badge on his breast that caught a glint from the sun.

Corey stiffened and slowly released his hold on the gun behind his back. He said, "Okay, okay, you don't have to shoot."

The man with the hat and badge stood up and walked stiff-legged toward Corey, aiming at him down the barrel of his shotgun as he closed the distance between them. His face was white, and he looked determined. His eyes were hard, but there was something pleasant and a little sad about his face.

"Get down on the ground on your belly," he said to Corey, "hands on the top of your head, fingers laced."

"My brother," Corey said, his voice a plaintive cry, *"you killed my brother."*

"Wasn't me," the man said. "Now get down like I told you."

At the same time a blond man appeared from the trees holding a giant silver revolver with both hands. He was bigger than the man with the shotgun.

Corey dropped to his knees, then flopped forward with his hands on his head. The man in the hat was quickly on top of him, flinging Corey's gun into the brush and yanking on one wrist at a time to snap on handcuffs.

Only when he was done and he was sure Corey Talich had no more weapons on him did he pause and look up at her.

She managed to say, "Thank you." Her voice was a croak.

The expression on his face was anguished. He said, "Who are *you*? Where's April?"

The blond man with the ponytail slowly shook his head.

The heavy beat of helicopter rotors coming over the mountain drowned out any more questions.

PART THREE

People will kill their puppies to stop global warming these days.

—*Dave Snyder*, transportation policy director,
San Francisco Planning + Urban Research
Association, 2007

26

Rapid City, South Dakota

Marybeth was the only one allowed by the hospital staff to go see the girl who had been admitted that afternoon under the name of Janie Doe. A nurse told Joe that unknown female patients under the age of eighteen received that moniker at Rapid City Regional Hospital.

He sat with Sheridan and Lucy in the reception room. Not until he realized he'd read the front page of the *Rapid City Journal* for the fourth time without retaining anything did he toss it aside. His eyes burned with lack of sleep, and he was dirty, tired, depressed, and thoroughly flummoxed. Sheridan slept fitfully on a couch, overcome by exhaustion and emotion. Once, when she was crying in her sleep, Lucy went over and sat next to her and put her hand on her older sister's head and stroked her hair.

The late-summer sun was ballooning outside the west windows and throwing discordantly festive peach-colored light into the room. Joe refused to be impressed. As it got later and the sun went behind the Black Hills, the hospital seemed to rest as well. Others in the reception area left one by one after visiting whomever they were there to see.

Joe smiled at Lucy. "Hungry? It's past dinnertime."

Lucy, who was always hungry, shook her head no.

"How are you doing?" he asked her.

She shrugged and pursed her lips, the precursor to crying herself. "I'm sorry I got so mad at you and Mom," she said.

"It's okay. You just wanted to help."

"I wanted to see April again," she said, and the tears came.

Joe said, "Come here," and held out his hand. She slid away from Sheridan and sat next to him and burrowed into his side. He put his arm around her and his muscle memory told him it wasn't Lucy at all but a much older girl. The Lucy he remembered was small, a thin stalk with downy white-blond hair. It was as if she'd grown into an adolescent overnight.

"How can it not be her?" Lucy asked after a while.

"I don't know."

"Does it mean April is still out there somewhere? Is this the wrong girl you found?"

He squeezed her tighter. "I don't know who she is or why she said she told us she was April. I don't know if the real April is out there or not. For whatever reason, she pretended to be April to all of us."

"It's just so unfair," Lucy said. "To make us believe like that."

Joe said, "There has to be a reason, but we don't know what it is. Maybe your mom will find out something."

"I hope so. If anyone can, it's Mom."

WHEN MARYBETH AND Lucy had arrived in Marybeth's van, he'd had a few moments alone with his wife without Sheridan or Lucy. Marybeth's first thought, that they'd simply located the wrong girl, was dispelled when Joe explained what had happened. How he'd called out the new cellphone number to Coon, how Coon had been able to get his people in Cheyenne to contact the phone company and track it under the original judicial authorization. "For once," Joe had told Marybeth, "she didn't turn her phone off right away after she sent the text. The FBI was able to pinpoint a tower. Luckily, there was only one road in the area and we were able to get there fast. Fifteen more minutes and ..." he left the sentence to hang there with meaning.

Coon and Portenson had loaded the girl on their chopper and taken off en route to the nearest large medical facility: Rapid City. According to Coon, Janie Doe had lost consciousness in the air. The Crook County Sheriff's Department arrested Corey Talich and sent for a state helicopter to airlift Chase's body to town. Joe had climbed back up the mountainside, dreading Sheridan's reaction when he told her.

"What about Nate?" Marybeth asked him. "Where is he?"

Joe said, "As soon as the chopper came over, Nate vanished. He didn't want Portenson to see him and grab him. He knew we had to get April—or whoever she is—out of there fast."

"Where is he now?"

Joe shrugged. "You know Nate. He's probably hiding out with some falconer buddy of his. Those guys take care of each other."

WHILE THEY WAITED for Marybeth to return, Joe looked up at the silent wall-mounted television and was surprised to see a visual of Leo Dyekman's ranch house. He didn't need to turn up the volume to follow the story. A local correspondent did a stand-up on the front lawn of the ranch house and theatrically gestured behind him. The camera zoomed in on the front door and panned across the crime scene tape. The initial on-the-scene report was followed by a clip of Portenson, flanked by local law enforcement, speaking behind a podium. Coon was at his left, avoiding the camera lens and looking uncomfortable. There was a photo of a handsome older man in a tuxedo identified as David Stenson, aka "Stenko," who looked remarkably like Ernest Hemingway, Joe thought. Then came a grainy, poor-resolution photo of Robert standing in what looked like a rain forest. Joe guessed the image had been taken from the ClimateSavior.net website. A graphic read ARMIED and DANGEROUS. Joe guessed "armied" instead of "armed" was a result of the news staff's hastily assembling the report.

The reporter on Dyekman's lawn threw it back to the anchor, an attractive brunette who looked all of twenty-five years old and was obviously reading from a teleprompter by the way her eyes tracked across the screen. The face of Leo Dyekman filled the screen, followed by a Chicago Police Department booking photo of Nathanial Talich.

There was a long-distance helicopter shot of the mountains that zoomed in on the overturned vehicle on the floor of the canyon. Under the graphic IN CUSTODY was an old booking photo of Corey Talich.

Joe waited, hoping there would be news of the arrest of Stenko and Robert. Instead, the local news switched to an interview with a rancher complaining about his fences being knocked down by buffalo from Custer State Park.

MARYBETH FINALLY CAME back shaking her head, her face ashen.

Joe and Lucy looked up expectantly.

"She could almost be April," Marybeth said. "She's

fourteen, fifteen, sixteen, it's hard to tell. But she's blond, tall, and attractive. I tried to convince myself that it might be her, that her looks had just changed as she got older. But no, it's not her. Not at all."

Joe said, "Is she awake?"

Marybeth was stoic. "No. She's just out of surgery for her leg injury so she's still under. But it isn't the bullet wound that's the problem. It's the loss of blood. The doctor said blood loss was severe."

Joe waited for a beat, said, "Is she going to be okay, then?"

Marybeth's face twitched and her eyes filled with tears. "Maybe. Doubtful. They don't know for sure. The emergency doctors said the blood loss could create something called hypovolemic shock. That's when not enough blood flows through the organs. It made her heart beat too quickly and made her blood pressure drop. It could have long-term effects on her brain. When someone loses that much blood … they just don't know what kind of internal damage was caused. It could be days before she wakes up, if she wakes up at all. And if she does, well, they just don't know."

Sheridan stirred and sat up rubbing sleep from her eyes. She said, "Who is she?"

"We don't know," Marybeth said. "She had no identification on her of any kind."

Said Sheridan, "Why did she chose me? Why did she even start sending me texts?"

There was no answer to that.

"I mean, she knew all about us. Our pets, Lucy, everything. How could she know all that if she isn't April?"

Joe and Marybeth exchanged looks. Joe hoped Marybeth had an answer.

Marybeth said, "I've been thinking about it. April wasn't the only child in the Sovereign Camp that day. Maybe this

301

girl knew April. Maybe they were friends and April told her all about us."

Sheridan hugged herself, unconvinced. "Okay, but why would she text me? Doesn't this girl have family of her own? Why me? Why us? And why would she wait so long after April told her about us to contact me?"

"There's only one way we're going to find out," Joe said. "She'll have to tell us."

Lucy had listened to everything but said nothing. Finally, she declared, "April is still alive. This girl knows where she is."

Marybeth sat on the couch next to Joe and Lucy and ran her fingers through Lucy's hair. "If only it were so," Marybeth said sadly.

JOE AND MARYBETH sent Sheridan and Lucy to the cafeteria so they could get dinner before it closed. It also gave them a chance to talk without the girls around.

Marybeth said, "One thing I do know is this girl, whoever she is, is all alone. Maybe someone somewhere has reported her missing, but we don't know that. I have a feeling she's been on her own for quite some time, though. I can't ascribe her contacting Sheridan as some kind of malice on her part. I never even considered the possibility. She needs our help, Joe. Maybe this was her very strange way of asking."

Joe said, "I was wondering how long it would take for you to say that." He still couldn't get over the shock of finally finding April, only to find out she was someone else.

Marybeth took both of Joe's hands in hers and looked deeply into his eyes. "We've got to help her, Joe. Even if she's not conscious, she needs to know we're here and we care about her. Can you imagine waking up in a hospital and having no one—I mean no one—there to hold you?"

302

He shook his head. It *was* unimaginable.

She said softly, "Maybe it was supposed to happen this way. Maybe we're being given a second chance to make up for what happened to April."

Joe didn't know what to say. The implications of Marybeth's statement made it suddenly hard to breathe.

"Are you here for Janie Doe?" someone asked.

Joe and Marybeth looked over to find an overweight woman in an ill-fitting business suit carrying a clipboard. Her face was a facsimile of sympathy and understanding. Joe didn't resent her for her show of false concern and expression of faux familiarity. He thought it must be tough to be her.

"Yes," Marybeth said. "We're here for her."

"So you're the parents?"

"We're not her parents," Marybeth said, shaking her head. "We're here as, well, what are we, Joe?"

Joe shrugged. "We thought she was someone else," he said to the hospital staffer.

The staffer, whose hospital ID read Sara McDougal, waited for more explanation with her eyebrows arched.

"I'm sorry," McDougal said, finally, "so you're not related or friends with Janie Doe in any way?"

Joe and Marybeth shook their heads, but Marybeth said, "We want to be here for her, though."

"Even though you say you don't know her?" McDougal said gently, trying to tamp down the doubt and suspicion that lurked beneath her question.

"That's correct," Marybeth said.

"Well, that's interesting."

Joe said, "Yup."

McDougal made a point of reading the document on her clipboard studiously, although it was apparent she was really trying to figure out which way she wanted to go with the discussion. She said, "I hate to ask you at a time like this, especially given your, um, lack of a relationship with Janie Doe, but do you know who is responsible for paying for her medical care? Does she have insurance?"

"We have no idea," Marybeth said flatly.

"Is she a resident of the county?"

Marybeth said, "I doubt it. We heard a rumor she might be from Chicago, but we've got no proof of that."

"Does she qualify for Medicare? Medicaid? Does the State of Illinois have some kind of insurance for its residents?"

"*I don't know,*" Marybeth said, steel in her voice.

"How are we going to resolve this?" McDougal asked. "Someone's got to be responsible."

"I'm losing my patience with you," Marybeth said to her. "I know you have a form to fill out, but this is a very difficult situation without easy answers. We'll work something out, I'm sure."

After McDougal walked away, her heels clicking down the hallway, Joe asked Marybeth, "Work it out how? This is going to cost thousands of dollars. And if she requires long-term care … how can we help her?"

He was surprised when Marybeth responded with a slight conspiratorial smile. "I've got an idea," she said.

Before she could explain, Coon stormed down the hallway. "Joe, there you are. Stenko and Robert's trail has gone cold and we need to talk. Do you have a minute?"

"Slow down," Joe said to Coon. "Let me introduce my wife, Marybeth. Marybeth, this is Special Agent Chuck Coon of the FBI."

Coon took a breath and said to her, "I'm sorry I was rude. I have better manners than that."

"It's nice to meet you," she said. "Thank you for what

304

you did to rescue the … girl in here."

Joe could tell she struggled through the last few words.

Coon was confused and looked to Joe for an explanation.

"It's not April Keeley," Joe said. "We don't know who she is and we won't know unless she comes out of her coma."

"What?" Coon cried, and bent forward at the waist with his palms out, as if someone had delivered a blow to the back of his neck. "I was hoping she could help us find Stenko. She's the only one who knows what they're up to or what they might do next."

"She can't talk," Joe said.

"She may never talk," Marybeth added softly. "She has very little brain activity. They don't know if they can bring her back."

He turned and walked away, cupping the top of his head with his hand, saying, "Jesus, help us."

Joe said to Marybeth, "I'll just be a minute."

"Take your time," she said. "I'm not going anywhere."

JOE FOLLOWED COON down the stairs and out through a heavy door marked EMERGENCY EXIT—DO NOT OPEN into a side parking lot of the hospital. The night was crisp and cool, the stars beaming through light cloud cover.

Coon fished a pack of cigarettes out of his sport coat and tapped one out.

"I didn't know you smoked," Joe said.

"Officially, I don't," Coon said, lighting up. "I haven't for the past year. Want one?"

"No thanks."

"So did she say anything at all before she went under?" Coon asked. "Anything at all?"

Joe shook his head.

"Man, this is terrible. Portenson sent me here to question her. We need to know what she knows."

"Sorry."

"Yeah, me too. Like I said, Stenko's trail has gone cold. Portenson's pulled out all the stops to find him as fast as we can. His name and photo is out nationwide, and he's doing press conferences and interviews one after the other. We've got the national cable news networks interested, and they're lining up."

Joe said, "I saw it on the news. I was surprised you guys went so high-profile so fast."

Coon nodded and sucked on his cigarette. "Yeah, me too. We've really got our necks out there this time. With all the stuff that's been happening with the Bureau in general and our incident this morning in particular, we can't afford to screw this up worse than it's already been screwed up. And my boss is nearly crazed. He knows if he doesn't deliver Stenko within twenty-four hours and make that incident this morning peripheral to the big arrest, he'll look like an idiot. We'll all look like idiots."

"But if you find him," Joe said, "it may turn out to be Portenson's ticket out of here."

"That's what he's thinking," Coon said. "You know how the bureaucracy works. He doesn't even want to consider any other outcome at this point. Which brings us back to the situation at hand. Is there anything we can do to get that girl to talk?"

Joe said, "You're starting to piss me off, Chuck. There's an unknown teenage girl in there fighting for her life. As far as we know she's completely innocent—maybe even a kidnap victim. My family's been turned upside down. Show a little compassion, will you?"

Coon stopped pacing and looked Joe over. He said, "I'm

306

sorry. You're right. But I'm not sure what to do. Every minute Stenko is getting farther away and we don't even know what direction."

Joe leaned back against the brick wall of the hospital and bent a knee so his boot rested against it as well. "Are you searching the area of the crash?"

Coon said, "The sheriff has his people all over it. Your governor agreed to send troopers and DCI personnel. So far, no one's reported anything."

"Have they checked with all the local ranchers? Found out if they saw Stenko or Robert?"

"Yeah, all of that. Not all the ranchers were there, though, which leads us to believe that maybe the Stensons found a vehicle somewhere and took the owner with them."

Joe whistled. He knew it would be a matter of time before someone local reported a missing person. But given the isolation of the area where residents might not see each other for days—or realize someone was not there—the delay could be fatal to the investigation.

"The pressure's on," Coon said needlessly, tossing the cigarette aside and digging for another. "When we left the crash scene with the injured girl, we might have lost our chance to get on top of Stenko and Robert. They couldn't have gotten very far at that point. We might have been able to run them down."

"You did the right thing," Joe said. "You saved her life bringing her here."

Coon snorted. "Fat lot of good that's going to do me now." Then, looking up, "I'm sorry I just said that. Really. You're right, Joe. But you don't have to be the one to tell Portenson what's happened."

"I'd like you to find them, too," Joe said. "The only way we might be able to learn about who is up there in that hospital room is to find out from Stenko."

"I might need a couple of drinks before I tell Portenson," Coon said. "I've seen him blow up a couple of times and it's not a good experience. I think my skin actually blistered the last time."

Joe barely heard the last part of the sentence. He was recalling what Marybeth had asked him about Nate, and how he'd assured her Nate would be just fine. But would Nate, being Nate, seek sanctuary so he could hole up? Or would he ...

Joe said, "Give me your cellphone. I might know how to find them."

27

South of Devils Tower

Earlier that afternoon, as the thumping bass beat of the FBI helicopter faded away into the sky miles behind him, Nate Romanowski crossed a shallow creek and saw that someone had been there before him.

He was halfway across the creek, hopping from one exposed river rock to another to keep his boots dry, when he noticed that the side of the basketball-sized rock he was about to step on was glistening with moisture. It had been splashed as if someone had stepped on it, slid off, and wetted it. He paused and looked carefully downstream and up the creek. The water was cold and clear if not more than four inches deep, and there were sandy pockets downstream from the cluster of river rocks he was using to cross. The creek was perfect habitat for brook trout. He *should* have seen them shooting from the sandy pockets to the shadows like small dark comets as he loomed above them. But there were no fish to be seen. Which meant someone had already spooked them.

And in the mud on the far bank was a fresh footprint

with chocolate-colored water swirling in the depression of a half-moon-shaped heel.

He bent down and studied it. The shoe that had made the print had a smooth sole and a squared-off toe. Not cowboy boots or Vibram hikers. A city shoe.

He stood up and rubbed his chin.

His intention before seeing the footprint was to continue down the creek until it joined a stream and to follow that stream to Sundance. He had an old friend in Sundance, a falconer and Special Forces operative he'd not seen in years but who would take him in.

But when he thought about it, and he looked at the moisture on the rock and the city shoe print in the mud, he changed his mind and his destination. And he checked the loads in his .454 Casull.

ONCE HE WAS on them, their tracks became more glaring. Aspen leaves covering the trail were crushed into the ground by the prints, and spider's webs that had been spun knee high had been breached and halved so that the threads seemed to reach across the opening in an effort to rejoin. There were two men ahead of him, all right. They were taking an old game trail south, mashing old and new deer tracks and mountain lion tracks. Different shoes; the squaretoed hipster shoe that had left the track on the creek bank and a more traditional businessman's shoe—worn heels, a rounded toe—that sank deeper into the ground because the wearer was heavier. The businessman's stride was inconsistent, the right foot flaring off the game trail with regularity, while the square-toed shoe proceeded relentlessly down the middle of the trail.

Stenko and Robert.

As he tracked them and observed their path, Nate paused often to stop and listen. They weren't that far ahead of him. But he heard no voices or sounds.

The tracks stopped at a rusted three-strand barbed-wire fence stapled to gnarled pitch wood posts. On the base of the nearest post there was a collection of old C-shaped staples on the ground in the grass, indicating that they'd stepped on the wires like stairs to climb over the barrier, but weight—probably Stenko's—had overburdened the staples and popped them out. Because the wires were now free, it was easy to press them down and throw a leg over and continue.

The boughs of the old-growth pine trees closed over his head, and he walked in shadow. Following their trail was simple now, as the forest floor was carpeted with dry yellowed pine needles that had scattered on the periphery of every footfall.

Ahead, less than a quarter mile, sunlight poured through the trees. There was an opening.

The afternoon suddenly filled with the sharp barking of dogs. Nate dropped to his haunches. The eruption of barks echoed through the timber and originated a quarter mile or so ahead of him. Nate imagined the scenario: Stenko and Robert had just broken from the trees and were approaching a ranch house. Most ranches had a small pack of dogs roaming the premises whose purpose was to alert the rancher to the appearance of strangers.

THROUGH THE SCOPE of his .454, Nate watched the proceedings. He was looking for a good shot.

The ranch itself was ancient. Front and center was an unpainted clapboard house with shutters and shake shingles on the roof so weathered they were the color of concrete.

There were several dark and sagging outbuildings to the side of the main house and a post-and-rail corral. In the corral near the barn three steers and a swaybacked blue roan grazed on haphazard piles of hay. The barn on the grounds sagged as well, and what little white paint remained on it curled from the siding like dried worms. The dogs he had heard barking all sat in front of the ripped screen door on a porch, looking at the opening as if awaiting someone to open it and throw food to them. He could see no human activity.

Next to the barn, in sharp contrast to the buildings, was a new-model black Ford F-350 pickup crew cab.

He thought: Stenko and Robert are inside with whoever lives here. And like all ranchers, no matter the circumstances, the owner drove a state-of-the-art pickup truck. Priorities.

THE DOGS BACKPEDALED comically as the screen door was pushed out, clearing the way for whoever was inside to exit. Nate thumbed back the hammer on his revolver and squinted through the scope.

The first person he saw was an older bald man in his sixties or seventies wearing a pearl-snap-button yellow shirt, suspenders, and worn Wranglers. The man was unshaven and bespectacled in yellowed horn-rimmed glasses. His bald head was paper white on top and there was a clear line mid-forehead where his absent hat shielded the sun, while the rest of his face and neck were nut-brown. He held his hands out in front of him like he didn't know where they should go.

Nate swiveled his weapon slightly to the right and his scope filled with the handsome, square-jawed face of Robert Stenson, who was immediately behind the rancher. But as he swept his weapon, he saw the pistol Robert held and the muzzle of it was pressed into the back of the neck of the rancher as he guided him outside. Nate's finger tightened on the trigger but the rancher stopped on the porch and backed up into the crosshairs.

"Shit," Nate whispered to himself.

The rancher was saying something over his shoulder to Robert. Nate peered above the scope. He couldn't hear what the discussion was about, but he knew it was an argument. Without the aid of the telescopic site, he could see that Robert and the rancher were nose to nose, yapping.

"Step aside," Nate whispered to the rancher. "Give me a clean shot and I'll lend you money for paint."

But the rancher kept it up until Robert closed in, lowered his gun and shoved the rancher ahead of him toward the pickup. Immediately behind them, an older man appeared in the doorway: *Stenko*.

Nate rotated his weapon again and peered through the scope. For a moment, the crosshairs kissed Stenko's forehead. Until he ducked and Nate could see only the shadowed interior of the ranch house.

Again, Nate sat back and glared.

Stenko was doubled over, both hands on his belly. Nate could hear him moan. Despite that, Robert pushed the old rancher toward the pickup, staying so close behind him they looked like their belts were fastened together. Whatever dispute they had was over. Robert was in charge.

The two of them were now blocked by the pickup. Nate heard the door open and saw Robert push the rancher into the cab. Stenko was right behind them, still bent over, and he vanished into the back seat of the cab before Nate could fire.

The motor ground and took, and the pickup did a fast turn in the ranch yard toward a weathered two-track.

And they were gone.

NATE HOLSTERED HIS gun and jogged across the ranch yard toward the barn and outbuildings. Ranchers always had extra vehicles, and in his experience the keys were usually in them. His boots crunched through the gravel and he got a glimpse of machinery in the shadows of the barn so he veered toward it.

Which was when he heard a muffled squeal, and a crash inside the house.

He paused. In the barn was a vehicle he could borrow so he could stay close to Stenko and Robert and the kidnapped rancher. But someone or something was in the house. The dogs watched him from the front porch as if wondering what his decision could be. That they didn't bark at him seemed unremarkable at the time. For his entire life, he'd had an odd, tranquilizing effect on some animals. He had no explanation for it.

Nate sighed, shooed the dogs aside, and entered the old ranch house. It smelled of cooked meat and old people. The décor looked frozen in time from 1972—avocado-colored appliances, gold shag carpeting, a digital clock radio on the kitchen counter with large red numerals.

In the living room, a large woman in a floral printed dress was on her side on the floor in a hardback chair in the living room. Her arms were bound behind her back and her bare mottled ankles were tied to the chair legs with duct tape. The hem of her dress was pulled up because of her fall, exposing a meaty white leg. She had white hair, metal-framed glasses that made her big eyes look even bigger, and a sock in her mouth. She squirmed against her bindings, which consisted of shrugging her shoulders and wagging her head from side to side. He could see where she'd managed to wriggle across the carpeted floor and overturn a small telephone stand by banging it with her head. The phone lay useless near her hair. The cord had been cut.

The way she glanced down at her leg said to Nate she was embarrassed by the exposure.

"Are you okay?" he asked.

She said, "Ooof."

Nate said, "Don't worry, I'm one of the good guys. I'm not going to hurt you. Who put the sock in your mouth?"

He flipped her dress back down and righted her chair before cutting the tape free with his Buck knife. She came up flailing and talking.

"They took him, they took Walter with them. They tied me to that chair and left me like that. I could have suffocated and died. The dogs could have come in through the screen and eaten me! It might have been days before anyone found me. And they marched Walter out of here at the point of a gun."

Said Nate, "Do you have any idea where they're going?"

She shook her head, "No. They didn't say."

"Do you have a car I could use? A truck?"

"In the barn," she said, gesturing outside. "*Walter!* They took him. I just can't believe he's gone. He has a doctor's appointment in Rapid City tomorrow. He's been having, you know, *incontinence* issues. He's not a well man, and it's taken me months to convince him to go to the doctor at all—and now this!"

She reached out with both hands and squeezed Nate's forearm. "He could die out there, you know. He doesn't get out much. It's been years since he's been any farther away than Rapid City."

315

"Call the sheriff," Nate said. "Let them know what happened and give them a good description of your pickup, including the license number. I've got to go."

"They cut the cord," she said, shaking her head with disgust. "We have another phone in the bedroom and they cut that, too. Why did those men do this to us? Are they outlaws or something? The older one seemed kind of nice. The younger one—he gave me the willies."

Nate remembered the cellphone Joe had given him and pulled it out of his pocket and flipped it open.

"Forget *that*," she said. "We don't have cell service here."

She was right—it read No Signal.

"Who are you, anyway? Why are you here?"

"Long story," Nate said.

"Where's my Walter? What are they going to do with him? He has a doctor's appointment in Rapid City tomorrow."

"You mentioned that," Nate said, turning toward the screen door. "Look, I'll send somebody here for you since you don't have a phone. And I'll do my best to find Walter."

"Please, please," she said, hugging herself. "He's all I've got. And he's got that appointment—I don't want him to miss it."

The screen door banged behind him.

THERE WERE PICKUP trucks from the seventies, eighties, and nineties parked side by side in the barn as well as a huge sedan with tailfins. The keys were in them, but none of them would start. The pickup from the nineties wouldn't even turn over because the battery had been cannibalized for use somewhere else. Nate kicked the bumper in anger, then ran back in the house. Walter's wife was sitting at the table, still stunned.

316

"I'm not having any luck out there," Nate said. "Can I borrow whatever it is you drive?"

"I don't drive," she said, "haven't for years. When I need to go to town Walter drives me. I guess I could learn but I keep putting it off ..."

"Do you have anything that runs?" Nate asked, cutting in.

"The tractor runs," she said.

"No, something faster."

She tapped her chin with her index finger. "Well, Walter keeps his dirt bike out in the shed for irrigating. That runs."

"Thanks," Nate said, banging the door again.

THE DIRT BIKE was stripped down, battered, and muddy. A squared-off irrigation shovel was mounted into a PVC pipe Walter had fashioned and wired to the frame. The key was in it and Nate got it going on the third kick. The motor revved and popped is if were spitting mad, and the shed filled with acrid blue exhaust.

He guided it out through the door into the ranch yard and sat back in the saddle, getting used to the feel of it. The speedometer was broken, the dial frozen at 58 miles per hour. The gas gauge showed empty, but he hoped it was broken as well. The tachometer worked, as did the headlamp. As he raced through the gears he shot a backward glance over his shoulder.

Walter's wife stood at the screen door, dabbing her face with a handkerchief with one hand, waving goodbye to him with her other.

He didn't know Walter, but he wanted to return him unharmed. He had a doctor's appointment, after all.

NATE'S TOUGHEST DECISION was when he reached the T of the two-lane highway. Robert and Stenko had either turned north, toward Devils Tower, or south, away from it. Nate knew if he didn't make the correct choice, it was the difference between tailing them and possibly saving Walter or losing them forever. He turned south on U.S. 85 and opened up the throttle. The shovel head hummed in the wind and chunks of dried mud shook loose from under the dented fenders of the bike.

A lime-green Volkswagen beetle was in his lane. As he passed it, the faces of two college-age girls rotated toward him. The back of their car was crammed with boxes, pillows, lamps. Kids on their way to school to start the fall semester.

He read in their puzzled expressions that he must look like a demented farmer who'd lost his way.

NATE TORE THROUGH Newcastle and didn't stop. The dirt bike was starting to wear him down. His face stung from airborne insects that felt like pinpricks when they hit his skin. His hands and arms quivered from the hard vibration of the handlebars. The insides of his thighs burned because the motor was running so hot. He wondered if Walter had ever even taken the bike out on the open road and doubted the rancher had ever run it at highway speeds. It was like riding an electric razor.

A lone convenience store and gas station squatted in the desert brush at Mule Creek Junction. Nate glanced down at his gas gauge—still showing empty—and swung into the gravel lot.

He filled the tank and rubbed his face with his shaking free hand. If there was a car or truck of any kind for sale at Mule Creek Junction, he swore he'd buy it for cash or steal it if necessary. But the only vehicle—a dark red Ford Ranger pickup with bald tires—belonged to the attendant, a shockingly white middle-aged man with a dark maroon pompadour. When Nate went in to pay for the gas, the store was dark and crowded with ubiquitous snack racks and low-priced merchandise found at every truck stop in America. The owner apparently had a pawnshop operation going as well and had a wall filled with used firearms, auto parts, CDs, golf clubs, and dozens of other items tagged and stacked in two piles. He contemplated buying one of the AK-47s on the wall to take with him, but the idea of roaring down the highway in his shoulder holster and an AK strapped to his back was just too *Mad Max*.

The attendant arched his eyebrows like a fellow conspirator and said, "Don't assume the AK can't be converted to full auto by someone who knows what they're doing."

Nate said, "I know that. I've done it. But I'm not interested right now. Just the gas, please." He dug into his wallet and handed the attendant a $100 bill from a stack of them. "Unless you're looking to sell your Ranger out front?"

The attendant looked up. "Then how would I get home?"

"I'm riding a bike. I'll leave it. I won't even deduct it from the balance."

"I'm afraid I can't sell the Ranger to you. It ain't mine. It belongs to my intended, Jenny Lee. I'm just keeping it running until she gets out of the women's prison in Lusk. Sorry."

Nate shrugged.

The attendant said, "You look lost, mister. Can I help you with directions?"

Nate glared at him. "I'm not lost."

The attendant nodded at the dirt bike outside. "Thought maybe you were looking for a motocross track or something. There's one over by Edgemont."

"No. I'm looking for a black Ford pickup."

The attendant paused while he made change. "F-350? Crew cab? Crook County plates?"

Nate's voice raised a click when he said, "Yes."

The man nodded. "They were through here a half hour or so ago. Saw an old rancher type inside without a hat. You can always tell a rancher by his tan line. And then some Dapper Dan type comes in and gives me a $100 bill, just like you did. I ain't seen two $100 bills in a single day since, well, I don't know."

Narrowing his eyes, Nate said, "Did you see anyone else in the truck?"

The attendant pursed his lips and looked at the ceiling for a moment. "I had the impression there was someone in the back seat. I didn't see him outright, but the Dapper Dan guy turned around in the front seat and it looked like he was talking to someone before he came in."

"Did the rancher look okay?"

"He looked old and crabby. Typical rancher."

Nate nodded. "They were still headed south on Eighty-five?" He asked because at the junction there was a road back into South Dakota.

"Yup, south," the man said. "Mind if I ask you why you're chasin' them on a dirt bike?"

Said Nate, "Yeah, I mind."

"Okay, okay, calm down," the man said, raising both of his palms to Nate.

"I'm perfectly calm."

Nate asked the attendant to call the sheriff after he left. "There's a woman all alone in a ranch house between Upton and Osage, about six miles from the highway. Her phone is out and she might need help. Her husband's name is Walter, but I didn't get a last name. You might ask the sheriff to swing by there to check on her."

The man studied him for a beat, said, "I can do that." Then: "You have bugs on your face. Doesn't that hurt when

320

they hit?" If there wasn't genuine sympathy in the attendant's tone, Nate thought he might have been tempted to pistol-whip him.

"Yeah, it hurts," he admitted.

"I heard a story once," the attendant said, leaning on the counter with $82 of Nate's change still in his hand. "This guy was riding without protection like you and he ran square into a big old bumblebee. The bee struck him right in the forehead," the man said, putting the tip of his finger on his own forehead as if Nate didn't know where it was, "and it was just like a bullet, the impact of that damned bee. He never knew what hit him. The force of that bee knocked him silly and he spun out. He died a few days later in the hospital. Never even woke up." As he ended his story, the attendant widened his eyes for emphasis.

Nate reached out for his change. "If he didn't know what hit him and he died, how in the hell do you know it was a bee?"

The attendant nodded wisely. "It's just a story I heard. I wasn't there. What I was getting at is, do you wanna buy a helmet?"

NORTH OF LUSK in his new German army helmet fitted with a darkened plastic face mask, Nate braced himself and cranked the hand-grip accelerator back as far as it would go. The motor went into a high-pitched whine, and he prepared for the bike to shake apart. But he needed to locate the black Ford before it got to Lusk to see what direction it would head. There were three choices: west on US 18 toward Manville and I-25; east to Chadron, Nebraska; on US 20; or farther south on 85 toward Fort Laramie and Rangeland. Although he'd been trying to think it through, he had no idea at all where Robert and Stenko were going. He wasn't sure even they knew.

Maybe a hospital, he thought. Stenko was obviously in pain.

Dusk threw gold light over the tops of the rolling hills and deep shadows into the draws. It was getting cooler. His back ached and his muscles were screaming at him from the constant vibration. His right inside calf was soaked with hot oil the motor was throwing off.

He topped a hill so fast he caught a few inches of air. The lights of the town of Lusk were splayed out ahead of him at the bottom of the rise. And the brake lights of a black Ford F-350 winked a mile ahead as the pickup slowed down at the town limits.

Because of the whine and the wind, Nate almost didn't feel the burring of Joe's cellphone in his front jeans pocket.

28

North of Rangeland, Wyoming

Aᴛᴇʀ ᴀɴ ʜᴏᴜʀ of smoldering silence, Robert said, "I blame you for everything bad that's happened." Although he held the gun on his lap and the muzzle was pointed generally at the rancher, who drove, Robert was speaking directly to his father in the back seat.

Stenko, through gritted teeth, said, "I'm shocked." Despite his condition, he still managed to project sarcasm. Maybe sarcasm was the last thing to go, he hoped.

The fight they'd had was vicious. It started when Stenko studied the numbers Leo had written on the napkin and said, "That rotten son of a bitch. These aren't account numbers. These are the phone numbers of all of my Indian casinos. He just didn't put hyphens in the numbers so you can't tell at first. That rotten son of a bitch."

And Robert realized what Stenko was saying—that the $28 million was out of reach.

"When I say everything, I mean everything," Robert said bitterly. "I'm not just talking about the last two weeks when you corrupted me and made me see and do things I'd never even imagined. I'm not just talking about your great friend Leo who gave us worthless phone numbers. I'm talking about my whole life. Not to mention my entire generation. You people have ruined everything for us with your greed and your predatory consumption of all the resources of the planet. It's like you were a bunch of drunks on the greatest bender of all time. You sucked everything dry and left us nothing but shit. When I think about it now, where I am, I think, *How fucking selfish can you be?*"

Stenko took it all like lashes that didn't really hurt. Instead, he sat up enough to see clearly out of the window near his feet. Man, what a night. The long vibrant Technicolor dusk that dominated the western half of the sky for a half hour had faded into an exhausted twilight of blue-grays and midnight blue. Hard pitiless stars grew in intensity as the sky went black. The sliver of a moon looked like an after-thought.

"Do you ever think about what you left us?" Robert asked, his voice higher than normal.

Stenko said, "Doesn't it matter that I'm doing everything I can to make it up to you?"

"It's not enough," Robert said with a snarl. "There are too many sins of the father."

He was angry, manic. Stenko figured Robert was going to vent at him until he could reach some kind of equilibrium and calm back down. In the meantime, though, Stenko just let it roll. He threw his attention toward the dregs of the big western sunset and thought about how few sunsets he'd actually studied in his lifetime and what he'd missed. To think that this fireworks display occurred every night of the year—amazing. And there was no cost of admission. All one had to do was watch it. The thought of that—just watching the sunsets—hit him like a hammer. So simple. And it had taken more than six decades to experience the joy of a great sunset. How could that be possible?

It was then he knew this was it. It was crushingly disappointing for him to think that his last actual thoughts on earth might be about how beautiful the sunsets could be in Wyoming. He wanted more than that. He wanted some kind of reward, some measure of wisdom. Something from heaven. But maybe, he thought, God had priorities and a pathetic gangster from Chicago was pretty low on the list. He could live with that, so to speak. But in his hope for wisdom, he was stuck on how mundane his insights were. And when he put them into words, ah!—it was awful. They tended to resemble the phrases on the posters mounted to the ceiling he used to read in agony while on his back in the dental hygienist's office. Crap like:

HAPPY IS THE HEART THAT HOLDS A FRIEND.

HE WHO LAUGHS ... LASTS!

HARD WORK IS THE YEAST THAT RAISES THE DOUGH.

On it went. Sappy bromides from another era. Crap from hayseed publications like *Grit Magazine*, the only subscription his mother ever had.

Now here he was, wondering if he'd seen his last sunset and wondering if they'd always been that great. He doubted it. He wanted to think 99 percent of the time the sunsets sucked and no one noticed. That maybe this one was special.

And he almost completely tuned out Robert going on and on and on about how it was all *his* fault that Robert was wretched.

Stenko was ready to take responsibility for Robert's wretchedness. It was just that he'd rather do so on his own terms. What a mistake it had been to try and reunite the family. How ridiculous it was that he'd fallen into a kind of pathetic role-reversal: the father desperately trying to gain some kind of approval from the son. Stenko realized how stupid it had been, how quixotic. To think that he could pick up the son who hated his guts and a girl who resembled Carmen and to somehow assemble them into what he remembered fondly as his only real family ... was a failure. April/Carmen died once again and Robert turned violent and then lost his mind. Stenko smiled with cynicism when he contemplated how badly it had gone. All Robert cared about was his silly website and his vapid efforts to save the planet. He didn't know what April had wanted, and that continued to haunt him. April was special. What had happened to her was unfair. That she'd died in the crash Robert had carelessly instigated by grabbing for the cash in the box was more than tragic.

His attention drifted back over to Robert, who was still yammering.

"Al Gore said something recently that sounded like he was talking directly to me," Robert said, "as if he were a human oracle who could anticipate my problems and address them directly."

Stenko said, "A *Gore*-acle."

The rancher chuckled and quickly looked away.

"What?" Robert asked.

"Never mind," Stenko said. "What did he say?"

Robert snorted triumphantly. Stenko thought it was one of the five Robert gestures that at least came across as sincere.

Robert looked him in the eyes and said, "'*Future generations may well have occasion to ask themselves, "What were our parents thinking? Why didn't they wake up when they had a chance?" We have to hear that question from them, now.*'"

Finally, after several moments, Stenko said, "So do you want an answer or do you just want to ask the question?"

Robert narrowed his eyes. "What is your answer, Father?" Sarcasm dripped.

"My answer is I was too goddamned busy to contemplate the question. Not everyone has the time to sit around and be bitter like your generation of thumb-suckers, Robert."

Again, the rancher chortled.

Robert angrily raised his pistol and pointed it at the rancher's temple. "You stay out of this. This is between me and my dad."

"Don't shoot him," Stenko said lazily from the back seat. "If you shoot him, we'll crash again. One car crash a day is my limit."

Walter the rancher said, "Can I ask how far you boys are going to take me from home?"

Robert said, "As far as we want to. Now shut the hell up and drive."

Stenko didn't like the dismissive way Robert talked to the old rancher. He also knew Robert wouldn't want to leave a witness who could tell the cops which way they were headed and describe the vehicle. Robert had turned out to be much more cold-blooded than Stenko thought possible. And so damned bitter.

"I've got a question for you," Stenko said to Robert. "Why in the hell is it you feel like you're entitled to a perfect world? No other generation ever thought they were, I don't think. What's so special about yours that you can blame me for your misery?"

Robert rolled his eyes with contempt. "Maybe because no other generation was handed a planet ready to burn up. Maybe because we're better informed and we know that."

Stenko said, "So if you're all so smart with your computers and iPhones and technology, why don't you fix the problems you're complaining about? You just want to blame

327

other people—me—and bitch and moan. It's your turn now, so why don't you solve all these problems?"

"What do you think we've been doing, Dad?" Robert said as if talking to a child. "It's hard to make up for a lifetime of abuse in a couple of weeks, you old fool."

Stenko decided he didn't want to argue anymore. His son's words cut him deeper than he thought possible. No one had ever called him a fool, or to his knowledge ever thought of him as one. It hurt.

Robert was what he was, thought what he thought, believed what he believed. Stenko gritted his teeth and said, "So how much do I still have on my balance? I assume you're going to apply the cash to my debt. How much is left?"

"Why are you asking?"

"Because I don't know how much longer I'm going to be around, son. I feel like my insides are on fire. I've taken so much morphine, I'm an inch away from killing myself with an overdose. I want to know what my balance is."

Robert said, "Twenty-four million."

Stenko was suddenly angry again. "That's ridiculous. It keeps growing the more I do to offset it. How can that be?"

Robert wheeled around in his seat, his eyes flashing. "Goddammit, Dad, haven't you listened to a thing I've been saying to you? Your lifestyle is such that your carbon footprint just keeps growing. You still own the casinos, right? You still own all of the real estate in Chicago and down south, right? And you don't have access to your own cash. Every minute that goes by, your footprint gets bigger. You haven't done enough or paid enough to offset the damage you've caused."

Stenko sighed and let his head drop back into the cushions. "But I've done everything I can," he said. "I've run around the country doing all these things. I killed for you—"

Robert cut him off. "That wasn't for me, Dad. It isn't my debt. It's yours. Don't you *dare* say what you did was for me. It was for you, so you could try to get to below zero, remember?"

"But you're the one keeping score," Stenko said. "You're the one I'm trying to get to forgive me."

"Don't give me that role. I didn't ask for it."

Stenko closed his eyes and tried not to grind his teeth against the pain.

In the front seat, he heard Robert ask the rancher, "What the hell is that out there on the prairie? It's lit up like an obscene riverboat or something. But it's not a boat, is it?"

The rancher said, "That's a power plant."

"What kind is it?"

"Coal-fired," the rancher said. "Coal trains come down from Gillette."

Suddenly, Robert was talking to Stenko again. He said excitedly, "Dad, we might have just found it. We might have just found your way to salvation. It's a miracle because there it is out there, right when and where we need it."

Stenko had no idea what Robert was talking about. He didn't care. He wondered if he would last the night.

"How long has that single headlight been behind us?" Robert asked the rancher.

"Since Lusk," the rancher said.

"Why didn't you say anything?"

"Why should I? You think the sheriff is chasin' us on a motorcycle? Is that what you think?"

"You know, I don't have any problem putting a bullet in your brain. You're a damned rancher. You're as much of a problem to the planet as my dad. I think you're both use-less."

The rancher said nothing.

Robert said, "Take that exit. I want to check something out."

29

Rapid City

J OE ENTERED THE reception area after his discussion with Coon and strode over to Marybeth where she sat in an armchair. She looked up expectantly, and he squatted down beside her. Both Sheridan and Lucy were asleep on vinyl couches, and he didn't want to wake them up if he could help it.

His voice was soft but urgent. "Coon managed to track the location of my cellphone. Nate is just about to enter the town of Rangeland from the north."

Marybeth said, "Rangeland? What's in Rangeland?"

"Other than Stenko and Robert, I don't know."

"That's enough, isn't it?"

He nodded. "I'm going with them. They're getting their helicopter ready at the airport, and we're leaving in five minutes."

"Any idea how long you'll be gone?"

He shook his head. "I'm not sure. But I think this will all be over soon."

She reached out and touched his cheek with her finger-tips and glided them over his stubble. He knew she was thinking of Janie Doe when she said, "I hope Stenko can help us. When I think of that poor girl in there, I want to cry. It's like she's no one. No name, no anything. We've got to find out who she is, Joe."

"Maybe Stenko ..." he said.

"Let's hope so."

"Have the doctors said anything more?"

She pursed her lips. "I talked to one of them a few minutes ago. He said there's been some brain activity, but it's sporadic. She may or may not regain consciousness."

Joe waited a beat while the significance of what Marybeth said gained hold. "Ever?" he asked.

"Maybe," she said. "It's possible she might come out of it. It's happened before, I guess. This is where doctors become observers instead of experts—they're hoping for a miracle just like we are. But he said there's nothing they can do other than keep a close eye on her."

Joe stood. "Maybe you should take the girls to a hotel. They shouldn't be sleeping here."

"I'll wait awhile," she said. "In case Janie wakes up. But yes, I'll find a place near here and get the girls a decent place to sleep."

He put his hand behind her head and gently pulled her toward him and kissed her. He wasn't sure what to say.

"Let me know as soon as you find out something," she said.

"I will," he said. "You, too."

On the way out of the room, Joe lightly brushed Sheridan and Lucy with his hand so as not to wake them.

But Sheridan opened her eyes. She said, "You're leaving without me?"

"Yes."

She blinked back sudden tears.

Said Joe, "We make a good team. You were great, darling."

"But you're leaving me behind."

"This time, yes." He said, trying not to look over at Marybeth, who was no doubt watching the exchange with concern.

Sheridan turned away and stared out the window into the dark.

Joe squeezed her shoulder as he left.

THE LAST TIME he'd been in a helicopter, Joe recalled, was when he was doing an elk trend count north of Buffalo. The experience had been harrowing and he'd been violently airsick, much to the amusement of the contract pilot who, he thought, made many unnecessary swoops and fast turns.

The feeling all came rushing back as the aircraft roared, lifted and the lights of Rapid City started to rush by outside his window. Instinctively, he shifted his weight toward the center of the craft. He tried not to look down.

There were four seats in the chopper. The pilot and Portenson were up front behind the Plexiglas bubble, and Joe and Coon were directly behind them. All were strapped in, and Joe was the only one without a headset. It was too loud inside to talk normally, so he observed. He was curious why they'd invited him along and suspected Portenson was up to something. The senior agent had not stopped talking on his headset since they lifted off. Coon was listening in, adding things, scanning the ground as it shot by. The wash of lights from town was soon behind them. He gripped the armrests with all of his strength and tried not to notice that his stomach was churning. Stars and the sliver of moon filled the Plexiglas and framed the pilot. The flight deck was awash in ambient-lighted gauges and digital numerical readouts.

He jumped when Coon tapped him on the hand. Joe looked over and saw Coon gesturing toward a headset hung up on the back of Portenson's seat. Still gripping the chair with his right hand, Joe put his hat, crown down, on his lap and fumbled with the headset until it was free, and managed to adjust it on his head. Coon reached over and clicked a switch on Joe's armrest to channel A, which was internal to the craft.

"You okay?" Coon asked. His voice was clear, if detached. It seemed odd to be talking through electronics to someone three feet away.

"I hate flying."

"I can tell."

"How long before we get there?"

"Thirty minutes, maybe."

Joe groaned.

"Joe, there's a lot going on right now. Agent Portenson is in contact with the Rangeland PD and Platte County Sheriff's Office. They know Stenko and Robert are in town, but we've asked them not to intercept them yet until we can figure out what they might be doing. For all we know, they're going to a hospital or getting a room at a motel. We don't want the Stensons to know we're on to them."

"Okay," Joe said.

"I'm also in contact with our HQ. Your cellphone has stopped moving. It's been pinging the same tower for ten minutes. That might mean the Stensons have stopped moving, too. But we need to find out."

Joe nodded, seeing where this was going.

"We need you to make a call to your phone and get some information."

Joe shot a glance in front of him to confirm his suspicion that Portenson had stopped talking to the Rangeland PD and was listening in. Yup, he was. And now he knew the reason they'd brought him along.

"I'll call on one condition," Joe said. "That the two of you swear that you'll confine your actions to apprehending the Stensons and nothing beyond that."

"I knew it," Portenson said, breaking in. "You've got Nate Romanowski down there."

"I didn't say that."

"Who the hell else would it be?" Portenson spat.

Coon and Joe exchanged looks. Joe could tell Coon would make the deal. Portenson was the wild card.

"He's a fugitive," Portenson said. "And he pisses me off."

Joe didn't push. He waited. He ran the scenario through his mind.

Finally, he saw Portenson fire a punch through the air and heard him say, "Okay, damn you. We'll confine our operations to the Stensons only. We won't even think about who is down there with your cellphone."

"You've burned me before," Joe said. "You better not dream of doing it again. Remember when you told me, *'Never trust a fed'?*"

"In a moment of triumph," Portenson conceded. "I used to have them. They've pretty much gone away since I met Joe Pickett and Nate Romanowski."

Joe chuckled at that. "So it's a deal? I have your word?"

Coon said, "Yes."

Portenson sighed and said, "Yes."

Joe said, "I'll make the call. Show me how to do it on this headset."

Coon switched the channel again and gestured toward a keypad. Joe punched in the numbers. He heard the phone ring. As it did, he looked up and saw that Portenson had switched to the same channel so he could listen in. Joe reached up and snatched the headphones off Portenson's head and shook them at Coon to warn him against trying the same thing.

Nate said, "Speak."

"It's Joe. I'm in the FBI chopper on the way to Rangeland. Do you have the Stensons in sight?" He turned his head so Portenson couldn't read his lips. The agent was furious.

Nate hesitated.

"It's okay," Joe said. "I have a deal with Portenson not to arrest you."

He heard Nate snort. Then: "I've got the Stensons under surveillance. They've got an old rancher with them, too. They stole his truck, made him drive. I followed them all the way."

"Great work. What are they doing now?"

"They're parked outside a bar. The old rancher and Stenko are still in the truck. Robert went inside."

"What's he doing?"

"How should I know?"

"Nate, the girl isn't April. We don't know who she is or if April's alive. Stenko is the only man who could shed some light on it, so we need to keep him in one piece."

"Gotcha."

"Look," Joe said, speaking very slowly and deliberately. He suspected someone might be listening in, perhaps at FBI headquarters. He chose his words carefully. "The feds have locked in on my cellphone. They know *exactly* where you are. Do you understand what I'm telling you?"

A beat. "Yes."

"We're thirty minutes away."

Nate said, "I'll be ready."

Joe hoped so.

He killed the connection and handed Portenson's headphones back to him. Portenson angrily jammed them on his head, switched to the internal channel, and mouthed, "That was a rotten thing to do."

Joe didn't hear it because he hadn't switched back to channel A.

A FEW MINUTES later, Joe could see that Portenson was in an animated conversation with someone. The way the agent nodded and gesticulated, it was obvious he was excited. Even over the engine noise, he heard Portenson say, "*That's* what I'm talking about," and again pump his fist in the air.

Joe looked to Coon, who indicated that Joe should switch back to channel A.

"What's he so cranked up about?" Joe asked. "Did they locate the Stensons?"

"Not yet."

"Then what's the deal?"

Coon's expression was noncommittal. "Our analysts suggest that the Stensons might have picked Rangeland for a reason, that their stopping there might not be random."

"Yes?"

"If your theory holds up, that the Stensons are picking targets with large carbon footprints—with the exception of Rawlins and the ranch, where the reason was drugs and money—then Rangeland has quite a big prize."

"It does?" Then it came to him. North of Rangeland was Esterbrook River Station—a power plant with three cooling towers that emerged from the sprawling high-grass prairie. "The power plant?"

Coon nodded his head and shot a glance toward Portenson to make sure his boss didn't see them talking.

"I've been listening in on the calls," Coon said, consulting his legal pad where he'd been jotting down notes. "Our guys and gals have been working hard. According to them, the Esterbrook River Station is a 1,650-megawatt power plant fueled by 135 coal cars per day. The coal is from Gillette and it's shipped down here 24/7. The plant burns 135 train cars of coal—that's 24,000 tons—*a day*."

Joe had seen the coal trains for years parallel to I-25. He'd been oblivious to the fact that they all had a single destination.

Coon said, "The plant provides power to two million people in Wyoming, Montana, the Dakotas, Colorado, Nebraska, Minnesota, and Iowa and feeds two of the three national power grids. But this is what may interest Robert: ERS emits approximately *thirteen million* metric tons of CO_2 per year."

Joe stared at him.

"Yeah, I said thirteen million metric tons per year. That's a lot. And that doesn't include the carbon produced by the coal trains or the coal mines."

Joe looked out the window. The lights of Rangeland were a creamy wash on the southern horizon. But out across the dark terrain as far as he could see were individual ranch and farmhouses, single pole lights, outbuildings with lights on. If something happened to the power plant, everything would go dark. "So what's Portenson so happy about?" Joe asked.

Coon waited a few seconds to speak, as if choosing his words carefully. "If the Stensons are going after that plant, it's domestic terrorism. That's what the FBI is supposed to be doing these days. It's Job One. If Portenson can turn around the debacle this morning into stopping a massive act of domestic terrorism—"

Joe finished Coon's thought: "He can write his ticket out of here to anyplace he wants to go."

"Right."

"What if Stenko and Robert just stopped to get gas?"

"Please don't mention that possibility to my boss right now."

Joe had been to Rangeland several times. It was a small agricultural town of not quite 4,000 people. It was low in elevation compared to most of the state, which was why there were farms instead of ranches. The terrain was flat and fertile all the way east to the Nebraska border.

As they roared south, Joe again looked down at what made Portenson so energized. The power plant was isolated but lit up like a Christmas display against the dark prairie. The three towers reached high into the sky and were illuminated in the darkness. He could see a train filled with coal heading toward it, and another train just behind the first. This is where it began, he thought. Coal was burned to superheat boilers, which turned river water into steam. The steam turned giant turbines that generated electricity and sent it screaming through transmission lines toward end users in eight states. Most of those users—like Joe—rarely thought about how the electricity got to his home or how it came about. All they—and he—knew was that when they flipped a switch, the light came on. The power came from *somewhere,* and he was looking at it.

Except when it didn't.

Joe frowned to himself, said to Coon, "How in the hell could two guys from Chicago sabotage a power plant?"

Coon shrugged, said, "We don't know. But we're going to stop them before they do."

And Joe realized what *really* made Portenson so happy. Thanks to Joe's initial theory, the FBI had focused on Robert and the environmental angle. Things had fallen into place. The analysts were not only connecting the crimes, they were anticipating what the Stensons would do next. Coal-fired power plants with massive carbon dioxide emissions were a natural target. It all played out and fit the pattern. And Portenson was in the catbird seat. He'd be able to avert the plot before anything bad happened. He'd get the credit. Even if the Stensons *were* in Rangeland to buy gas.

The fly in the ointment, Joe thought, was if Stenko or Robert started talking after they were arrested and threw too much doubt on the FBI's theories. If they denied ever targeting the power plant. Then Joe realized what else worked in Portenson's favor. He was pretty sure that the Stensons wouldn't be alive to talk. Not with Robert's new propensity to try and shoot his way out of every situation and Stenko's fatal cancer.

Which meant that Joe would need to get to Stenko before Portenson did.

AS THE PILOT negotiated with the Rangeland sheriff on where to land and Coon arranged for vehicles with the police department, Portenson turned in his seat and said to Joe, "You've got a call on channel C."

His stomach knotted as he turned the dial two clicks. Joe thought: *Marybeth. Janie Doe has taken a turn for the worse.*

Governor Rulon said, "Finding you was not so easy. How is it going?"

"Not great."

"You don't have to tell me that. I got a briefing from DCI and between these bad guys you're chasing and the FBI, there are bodies all over my state from Rawlins to Devils Tower." He didn't sound like he was in a good mood.

"It's been rough," Joe said. "But we may finally be closing in on them."

Rulon acted like he didn't hear Joe. He continued, "Tell Agent Portenson that Wyoming has the smallest population of all the states. He and his minions are doing serious damage on our census count. Those are citizens and voters. I mean they *were* citizens and voters. At this rate we'll lose a seat in Congress *and* our federal funding if he keeps up with all the bodies."

By the set of Portenson's jaw, Joe could tell he was once again listening in.

"He just heard you," Joe said.

"Good! I figured he might be eavesdropping on a private conversation without a warrant."

This time, Portenson ripped his own headphones off.

"He's gone," Joe said.

"So tell me, did you find the girl you were looking for?"

Joe briefed him on the situation.

Rulon said, "Unbelievable. So you think these bad guys might know where the girl you're looking for is located?"

"Maybe," Joe said.

"So where are you now?"

"We just got cleared to land in Rangeland. The FBI thinks the Stensons may be going after the power plant."

"Jesus Christ! They had better not be!"

"I don't see it," Joe said, making sure Coon wasn't listening in, either. He wasn't. "I just can't imagine they can waltz their way in there and disrupt the electricity. These Stensons are not geniuses, and one of them may be terminally sick. But that doesn't mean somebody might not get hurt."

"But the feds are coordinating with local law enforcement?"

"They appear to be."

"Will miracles never cease."

Joe shot glances at Coon, who was obviously engaged in another conversation, and Portenson, who took a cue from Coon and was adjusting his headset back on. Joe saw Portenson switch channels to Coon's frequency. They were getting information from someone that was making them both sit up straight.

"Something's going on," Joe said. "Coon and Portenson are getting new information."

"What?"

"I think I know, but I can't say."

Rulon said, "My lights are still on. So the Stensons haven't done anything to the power plant."

The ground rose up and Joe felt one of the skids touch the field. They were landing on the north side of town in an empty cornfield. He could see several police department vehicles parked on a service road beyond a barbed-wire fence.

"Sir," Joe said, "we've landed. I'll call you back as soon as I have something to report."

"Keep the lights on, Joe. When the power goes out, bad things happen. Streetlights go out; computers go down; home oxygen units fail. Innocent people die, Joe."

"Got it."

"Plus, I'm watching a football game."

"I'll do my best," Joe said, rolling his eyes.

Rulon said, "I hope you find your girl."

"Me too, sir. Thank you again for letting me pursue this."

"Don't mention it. Besides, it sounds like it's turning into something much bigger than anticipated, something you seem to have a penchant for. I bet being a normal game warden sounds pretty good to you right now."

"It does. But I nailed the Mad Archer yesterday."

Rulon said, "Again? Good work!"

WHEN BOTH SKIDS were firmly on the ground, Portenson turned in his seat and gestured for Joe to get out first. He was happy to comply. He almost didn't notice that Coon hadn't unbuckled his safety belt or that the pilot wasn't turning off the rotors.

His boots thumped the ground, and he clamped his hat on his head with his hand to save it from the rotor wash. He felt more than heard the hatch close behind him.

He turned as the motor roared and the helicopter lifted off. Behind the Plexiglas, Portenson waggled his eyebrows and waved goodbye with a sardonic smile on his face. Coon looked away, embarrassed.

Behind him on the edge of the field, the Rangeland police officers scrambled back into their cars and pulled out one by one and U-turned onto a gravel road that headed south. Joe sank to his haunches with one hand on his hat. He watched the taillights of the cars get smaller down the county road and the chopper move across the sky. He didn't stand until it became quiet, as the *thump-thump-thump* of the rotors faded out.

Joe rubbed dust from his eyes and sighed a heavy sigh. Then he heard a dirt bike motor cough and come to life. A single headlight blinked through a hedgerow and turned toward him once the rider found an opening in the brush. Joe started walking toward the headlight.

Nate was wearing a ridiculous helmet that looked like German army issue. His face shield was pushed up on top but spattered with starbursts of insects. He looped around Joe and stopped the bike just ahead of him. The motor popped and spat as Nate gestured to Joe to get on behind him.

Joe threw a leg over the saddle and tried to balance himself without having to hold on to Nate.

Joe said, "I was hoping you'd have a car or a truck."

"Nope. I'm actually starting to like this thing."

"Are Stenko and Robert still here?"

Nate nodded. "They were when I left them."

"And my phone?"

Nate turned and grinned. "I found a bread truck at the truck stop gassing up. I opened the back and tossed it inside amongst the buns. The last I saw of it, the truck was headed south on I-Twenty-five toward Cheyenne."

Joe nodded. He figured he and Nate would have no more than fifteen minutes before Portenson realized what had happened and turned back around.

30

Rangeland

STENKO WATCHED THROUGH pain-slitted eyes as his son emerged from the bar with a grin on his face. Robert twirled something on a string or chain. He'd been gone a long time, it seemed. Stenko had taken the rest of the morphine, and the spent plastic pill bottles lay open on the floor of the car near his feet.

Robert threw the door open and jumped in. He was ebullient. He said, "So are you ready for one great and glorious last act?" His smile was maniacal.

Stenko grunted. It hurt to talk.

"Hey," Robert said, suddenly alarmed. "Where's that rancher?"

"Got away."

"You let him get away? You old fool. What's wrong with you?"

"Sorry," Stenko moaned. But he wasn't. Ten minutes before, he'd turned to Walter and told him to get the hell out of there. The rancher had asked about his truck. Stenko had said, "Run, you idiot, before my son comes back and puts a bullet in your head."

Reluctantly, Walter had gotten out and done a stiff-legged jog in the general direction of the interstate highway.

"He's going to talk," Robert said. "I was going to make sure he kept quiet."

"He overpowered me," Stenko lied. "He's a strong old fart."

"Christ, is there *anything* you can do right?"

Stenko thought: *The role reversal is now complete.*

He said, "Guess not."

"SO THE TOUGH thing for me," Robert said, starting the motor and backing out of the gravel parking lot, "has been to reconcile myself to the fact that once again you're not going to come through for me. I have to wrap my mind around the fact that all the money is out of reach and we can't use it to save the planet your generation trashed and left us with. You'd think after thirty years of living around you, I'd be used to crushing disappointment, right? But damn if I still don't keep coming. This time, you really had me for a while. But in the end, well, in the end it's like it always has been. A big fat zero."

"You've got some cash," Stenko said, his voice thin. "And we did some things."

Robert swung out on the dark road. A passing street-light reflected blue on his bare teeth. "Yeah, we did some things. But in the end, Dad, it was just jerking off. There were no bold strokes. No real blows were struck. Christ, you ended up with a bigger footprint than when we *started*."

"That's because you were keeping track. You saw it as a way to get all my money," Stenko said, regretting the words as soon as they came out of his mouth.

"That's right," Robert said. "Blame me. Blame your son.

Just like always. Blame your kids while you make the world a worse place to live."

Stenko reached over and put his hand on Robert's shoulder. He said, "I don't want to argue anymore, son. I don't. You can say whatever you want. I'll take it. I don't have the strength to fight."

Robert shook his hand off and it dropped to the seat. He drove silently, pouting. Robert was always the angriest when Stenko said something true about him. But now was not the time to remind Robert of that.

Stenko said, "The fight went out of me when April died in that crash back there. That poor girl. I had my chance with her, to do something good. And look what happened."

Robert snorted, said, "Her again. You're just like you were about Carmen. Have you ever thought about maybe using some of those feelings toward the kid you have who's still alive? The *real* son? Not the dead daughter or *fake* daughter?"

"Really, son. I don't want to fight."

More pouting.

Changing the subject, Stenko said, "What was that thing you were twirling when you came out of the bar?"

"Oh this?" Robert said, handing it over, his smile returning. "This little old thing?"

Stenko took it. It was a large laminated card strung from a lanyard. He pulled it close to his eyes. There was a photo on it, a magnetic strip on the back, and a name: Lucy Annette Turek.

"Who is Lucy Turek?" Stenko asked.

"She's my new girlfriend," Robert said.

"That was quick."

"Dad, if you haven't noticed, I'm a pretty good catch."

Stenko bit his tongue. Then: "What does she have to do with this last act you mentioned?"

347

Robert cleared town and turned onto a service road that went north. Old cottonwoods laced their branches over the top of the road and formed a tunnel. At the end of the tunnel was a faint glow of light.

Robert said, "Here's what I was thinking. That big coal-fired power plant must have a lot of local employees. It turns out they have three hundred workers, and it made sense to me that a few of them would be in the bar closest to the plant. Damned if I wasn't right.

"So I sit at the bar and start talking to a pretty one next to me. That's her key card you hold in your hand: Lucy Turek. I start asking her about what it's like to work at the power plant, what she does, blah-blah-blah. Like I'm interested in getting a job there myself or something. She answers every question. Finally, when she begins to trust me because she wants me to take her home, I ask her how much access she has to the plant. That really gets her going, because she tells me how she's got a senior clearance that can get her into the control room and she can even take the security elevators to the top of the boilers, which apparently is some kind of big deal. I get her to explain to me how the power plant works, and she goes on and on and I keep buying her drinks. I don't really care how it works. I know what it does: it consumes tons of fossil fuel and churns out tons of carbon into the atmosphere that will eventually heat up our planet and kill us all."

Stenko looked from the key card to Robert and back. The glow at the end of the tree tunnel was getting brighter.

Robert said, "So I ask her, kind of playful, how she'd get back at the company if they fired her for no good reason. Lucy is kind of feisty and I'm sure she'd be a little tiger in the sack, so I knew if they fired her, she wouldn't take it lying down. So she tells me about these gigantic boilers they have. Five-thousand-ton hanging boilers made up of miles of superheated tubing that rise over three stories tall. That's where they heat the water to drive the turbines or some kind of shit like that. Anyway, Lucy said the boilers have to run on negative pressure. That didn't make any sense to me either, but I kept pressing. Finally, she got to the point. If the doors to the hanging boilers are opened and the pressure escapes—the boilers fail. That shuts down the plant in a serious way. Millions of people would lose all their power, and the company would lose millions of dollars while all the repairs were made. It might take down the entire power grid. It could take them days or weeks to get the thing running again. That's how she said she'd get back at them—in the wallet."

Stenko nodded.

Robert gestured toward the trees through the windshield. "And for however long it took, the planet would get a break. Carbon wouldn't be pouring up through the stacks. The offset would be tons and tons of carbon not going into the atmosphere."

Stenko said, "Lucy told you a lot."

"As I said, she likes me. She's my new girlfriend, even though I'll probably never see her again."

"And she gave you her key card?" Stenko asked.

"Well, not exactly," Robert said, not looking over. "I followed her into the restroom and hit her head against the wall and took the lanyard from around her neck."

"My God," Stenko said. And as he said it, they cleared the tunnel of trees and the massive power plant filled the northern sky, lights blazing.

"So if you ever meet Lucy Turek," Robert said, "be sure to thank her. She's the sweetie who made it possible for you to go out in a great blaze of glory. Because of her, you may just be able to get to below zero after all."

The headlights lit up a ten-foot chain-link fence that now bordered the road. Ahead, Stenko could see a dark guardhouse. There was a metal lockbox with a slit to slide the key card in to open the steel-mesh gate.

"She said there wouldn't be a guard this late," Robert said. "Cool. Now all you have to do is go inside wearing that lanyard. You can get anywhere you want to by swiping that card through the readers. Find the security elevators and go to the top floor. That's where the hatches to the hanging boilers are located. If someone tries to stop you, just shove them off the catwalk. The boiler hatch opens by turning a big wheel, according to my sweet Lucy. Open the hatch and jump in. The open door and the presence of your body will shut down the whole system and you'll leave this planet as a hero."

"Are you coming in with me?" Stenko asked.

Robert said, "Are you kidding? This isn't *my* problem you're trying to solve."

Stenko sighed, "Of course not."

"Think of what you're doing as a gift to me and the younger generation," Robert said. "After a lifetime of committing environmental crimes, you're sacrificing yourself for us. For me. It would make me happy, Dad. It's the one thing you can do for me to make up for everything else. You can go out a martyr for Mother Earth."

Stenko's eyes flooded with tears. They were tears from the pure physical pain that laced his guts, but also because of April and her innocence and how she was gone. But most of all the tears were because of Robert and what he'd turned into.

"Are you really this broken?" Stenko asked. Oh, how it hurt to talk.

Robert glanced over. His eyes were cold. "What are you babbling about, old man?"

"You're not very sentimental, are you?"

"I learned from the best about selfishness, Dad."

Robert looked up at the rearview mirror and made a face. "There's that damned single headlight behind us again. What's up with *that*?"

Rapid City

Sheridan rolled over and yawned and remembered she was in a hospital and why she was there. She sat up and rubbed her eyes, then looked over at Lucy, who was still sleeping, and her mother, who'd finally dozed off.

There had been a sound that had jarred her awake. She looked down the hall, assuming it was a nurse or staffer who'd passed by, but she couldn't see anyone. She stood and looked out the window at the night and the still parking lot below.

Then she heard it again: the rapping of knuckles on glass.

She turned and saw him, a cop in a khaki uniform on the landing of the emergency exit that went to the stairs. He gestured at her and pointed at the handle of the door. She thought he looked vaguely familiar, and when she opened the door she recognized him from earlier that day. He'd been one of the deputies who'd arrived at the scene of April/Janie Doe's crash.

"I'm sorry to bother you," he said, stepping into the hallway. His hat was clamped under his arm and he carried a plastic grocery sack. "They shut the elevator down to visitors at night, I just found out. Anyway, the sheriff sent me over here to talk to Agent Portenson and Agent Coon, but I don't see them anywhere."

"They're gone," Sheridan's mom said from her chair. "Is there anything we can do?"

351

The deputy shrugged. "Is Joe Pickett here?"

"He's with them," her mom said.

The deputy's face fell. He clearly didn't know what he should do next. He said, "We found some personal items in the wreckage of that car. The sheriff bagged them up and asked me to deliver them to the FBI, thinking they might help somehow. Now I'm not sure who to give them to."

"What kind of personal items?" her mom asked cautiously.

The agent flushed. "Just some feminine things, you know. Underwear, tampons, that kind of thing." When he said the words, he looked away from Sheridan. "Plus, a pocketbook thing. Do either of you know a girl named Vicki?"

Sheridan felt the skin of her scalp pull back. "No," she said, "but I think I know where she is."

Her mom asked, "What's her full name?"

"Damn, I forgot. Let me look it up," the deputy said, digging into the plastic bag and pulling out a small leather purse with a metal clasp. He opened the clasp and drew out a small stack of papers, photos, and cards. "This here is a library card from Chicago, Illinois. It says it belongs to Vicki Burgess."

Her mom covered her open mouth with her hand.

Even though it seemed like alarm bells were going off inside her head, Sheridan said to the deputy, "Can we look at what else is in the purse?"

Thinking: *Who is Vicki Burgess?*

How did she get my name and number?

The deputy straightened the stack of papers to put them back into the purse when he said, "Oh, there's a photo. Two girls in it. I bet one of them is this Vicki Burgess ..."

Rangeland

Nate leaned forward on the handlebars of the dirt bike and

opened it up. Joe bent with him. The electric steel-mesh gate Stenko and Robert had just passed through was closing. Joe squinted over Nate's shoulder as the bike sped up, trying to gauge whether they could really get through the opening in time. He didn't think so.

He hollered, *"Stop—we won't make it!"* then barely had time to duck his head into Nate's back as they shot through the gap, the edges of the gate and steel receiver frame less than an inch each from the widest part of the handlebars.

Incredulous, Joe looked over his shoulder to see the gate lock shut behind them. He hadn't imagined what had just happened after all.

"How did you do that?" Joe asked Nate, but it sounded more like an accusation than a question.

"Don't know," Nate yelled back. "I just opened up all the way and closed my eyes."

"You closed your eyes?"

The taillights they'd been following were less than 200 yards ahead of them now. The vehicle had slowed and was swinging into a parking lot outside the front vestibule door of the power plant.

"Here," Nate said, handing back his .454 to Joe. "You might need this to start blasting as we go. I think Robert might have seen us, and you know how he is."

"Remember," Joe said. "We need Stenko alive."

And it was if someone had flipped on a switch for the sun. Joe, Nate, and the bike were bathed in brilliant white light. They hadn't heard the helicopter coming because of the whine of the dirt bike engine.

"Not us, you idiots!" Joe yelled, looking back into the blinding lights and pointing ahead of them with the muzzle of Nate's .454. "Put the light on Stenko and Robert! They're up ahead of us!"

And thinking what a bad idea it was to be waving a handgun in the air at an FBI chopper that had already gunned down a man just that morning who did the same exact thing …

ROBERT SAID, "SHIT. They're all over us."

Although the spotlight had yet to find them in the parking lot, it was bright enough behind them to illuminate the few rows of cars and trucks that belonged to the midnight shift. Instead of parking the car, Robert killed his lights and roared forward across a small lawn toward the front doors.

He said to Stenko, "That helicopter is going to find us any second, Dad, and I see flashing lights out on the road coming from town! *Get out, get out, get out … get inside.*"

But Stenko wouldn't move. He slumped against the passenger window, his cheek pressed to the glass. His eyes were wide open, but without expression. Robert saw the open empty morphine bottles on the floor of the car, said, "Stupid old man," and shoved Stenko in the arm hard, trying to wake him. Stenko's head lolled back, his mouth open, a string of saliva like a slug trail connecting his upper and lower lips. The front doors of the vestibule were right outside his window now, and Robert braked.

"Ten steps, Dad," Robert pleaded, his voice cracking. "*Get out.* Ten steps and you're in."

But Stenko refused to move, and he disappointed Robert once again.

Robert cursed and ripped the lanyard out of his father's fist. He'd do it himself. Get inside, take the elevator to the top, and open the hatch to the hanging boilers. But he wouldn't jump in. Opening the hatch would do enough damage. Robert had his life and his mission still ahead of him. What good would it do anyone to become a martyr for the cause? He wasn't like his old man, after all.

He threw open the door and bounded up the front steps, rejoicing that the spotlight on the helicopter hadn't found him yet. As he approached the vestibule, he looked over his shoulder and saw the beam flashing over the cars in the parking lot like the vengeful eye of a Cyclops.

He swiped the key card, and a red light on the box switched to green. But the door didn't give when he yanked on it. That's when he saw the dial pad on the side of the lockbox and the LED display that flashed ENTER THREE-DIGIT CODE. Damn that Lucy, he thought. She hadn't mentioned a code.

He said to no one in particular, "Fucked again! *Stenko fucked me again!*" and tried combination after combination on the box with one hand while digging for the pistol in the back of his belt with the other. He tried the most obvious codes first. After all, how complicated would they make it for a bunch of power plant workers? He tried "1-2-3" and "3-2-1" and "1-1-1" and "2-2-2."

The night was suddenly incredibly loud and obtrusive. There was the thumping of the blades from the helicopter that still hadn't located him, the sirens of every cop car in Rangeland bearing down on the power plant, and a high whine getting higher by the second.

When he keyed "6-6-6" he heard the lock click open.

As he reached for the handle he looked over his shoulder and saw the bike coming straight at him from the parking lot. The driver wore a war helmet and had blond hair streaming behind. Instead of slowing down for the three concrete steps to the vestibule landing, the bike veered to the right toward a handicap ramp incline and then sped up. Someone dropped off the back of the machine and rolled away. And before he could untangle his pistol from his shirttail, his vision was suddenly filled with an extreme close-up of a muddy, knobbed tire …

JOE ROLLED TO his belly and looked up as Nate shot up the stairs and jumped the bike full speed into Robert standing in front of the glass doors as if pausing before he entered. The impact made a fat hollow sound followed immediately by broken glass as Robert's body was hurled through the vestibule into the reception area inside. Both Nate and the bike lay in heaps on the landing. The alarm system in the power plant whooped, and emergency lights on the walls flashed.

Getting his legs under him, Joe stood up uneasily in the grass. He brushed gravel and dust off his shirt and spit a pebble out of his mouth. Nate's gun was near his feet, and he picked it up and cocked it.

Inside the building, he could see the soles of Robert's splayed shoes on the floor. Robert was flat on his back and not moving. As Joe approached, he saw the blood—rivers of it running across the marble floor from gaping, pulsing holes in Robert's throat, neck, and groin where he'd been slashed by the broken glass. The distinct impression of a motorcycle tire could be seen on Robert's face, which was dented in. His pistol had been thrown to the far side of the room and was under a chair, well out of his reach.

"Is he dead?" Nate asked, scrambling to his feet and standing shoulder to shoulder with Joe on the landing.

"If he isn't, he soon will be. We need to get him to the Rangeland ER."

"Bullshit," Nate said, taking his revolver back from Joe. "He sure as hell didn't get April to the ER when she was bleeding to death. And he planted all those damned euca-lyptus trees …" With one swift movement he straightened

356

his arm and fired, blowing the top of Robert's head across the marble tiles.

"Oh, man ..." Joe moaned.

"Go find Stenko," Nate said, holstering his gun and ignoring Joe's pained expression. "I gotta get out of here before Portenson finds me."

Nate righted the dirt bike, kicked it twice to start it, grinned when the motor fired up, and roared away.

THE CHOPPER WAS touching down on the far side of the parking lot and the Rangeland cops and county sheriff's convoy was pulsing through the front gate when Joe found Stenko's dead body slumped over in the front seat of the stolen car.

Joe threw open the door and reached in and grasped Stenko's neck and shook the body anyway, saying, "Who is she, damn you? Where did you find her?"

Stenko's head flopped from side to side, and his eyes were cold and dead. His body seemed light and unsubstantial— the shell of the man who'd once worn tuxedos to Chicago charity events and who once bore a resemblance to a virile Ernest Hemingway.

Joe let him drop to the seat cushion.

"Damn you," he said again.

Rapid City

Sheridan handed the battered photograph to her mother. The image of the two girls had been cut with scissors or a knife from a larger photo. Because of the clothes they were wearing and their formal smiles and the sliced-off heads, arms, and dresses of others who had been standing close to them, she thought the original might have been a family portrait of some kind.

357

There were two of them in the photo, two blond girls. They looked like sisters, but they weren't.

The deputy said, "Do you recognize either of these two girls to be Vicki Burgess?"

Sheridan's mouth was so dry she had trouble saying, "Yes. The one on the right."

But it wasn't Vicki Burgess's likeness that had shocked her.

Her mother took the photo and her eyes widened. She whispered, "Oh, my God."

Lucy reached up and took it from her mother. Her eyes moved from one figure in the photograph to the other.

She said, "That's April," and tapped her finger on the girl on Vicki's left. "She's alive," Lucy said.

Her mom walked away, digging her cellphone out of her purse to call her dad.

Rangeland

Joe sat in the open doorway of the silent helicopter with his head in his hands. The parking lot and vestibule area were whooping with red and blue wigwag lights from the dozen PD and sheriff's department vehicles that surrounded the death scene. Portenson was ecstatic, running from place to place, firing off orders, alerting the brass in Washington, D.C., what had happened, physically moving local law enforcement away from where they were gawking at the body of Robert in the reception area. Men and women from the midnight shift inside the plant had wandered down to the front as well and were being herded back toward the elevators before they could track blood across the floor.

Coon walked over and leaned against the aircraft next to Joe.

"I've got one happy boss right now," he said. "Do you

know what he screamed at me when we saw it was Robert inside the building? He said, *'Hello, D.C.! Here I come!'* "

Joe grunted. "Can't say I'll miss him."

"Me either."

A minute passed by. Bruises Joe didn't know he had from falling off the dirt bike began to ache on his legs, ribs, and butt.

Coon said, "Should I even ask who it was driving the bike?"

"Nope."

"Didn't think so. Any idea which way he headed?"

Joe shrugged. *Hole in the Wall,* he thought.

Coon said, "You've never seen a guy more scared than that bread truck driver when we landed the helicopter in front of him on the highway. I think the bureau will need to pay for some dry cleaning."

Joe didn't respond.

"That was a pretty good trick," Coon said. "You want your phone back?"

As Joe reached for it, the phone lit up and burred.

Marybeth.

31

Chicago

Two days later, Joe, Marybeth, and Lucy occupied the middle seat of a black GMC Suburban with U.S. government plates as it cruised slowly down a residential street in an old South Side neighborhood. Sheridan was in the seat behind them. The street was narrow, the sidewalks cracked. Homes that looked fifty or sixty years old lined up one after the other on both sides of the road. Most had enclosed porches and neat, close-cropped lawns. Parked cars had Bulls, Bears, and Blackhawks bumper stickers. Towering leafy hardwood trees blocked out the sky. The morning was cold and dark, and the wind that had cut through Joe earlier while he opened the car door to let his family in reminded him that no matter how cold it got in the mountain west, it was colder and damper in the Midwest. Maybe, he thought, it was why they were so damned tough.

The Suburban was full of people. Coon sat in the front seat next to the Chicago-based FBI agent driver and the Chicago Police Department liaison. In the third seat with Sheridan were two senior representatives from the Illinois

Child Welfare Agency. They'd introduced themselves at the airport as Leslie Doran and Jane Dickenson.

Joe was a red ball of raw nerves. He found it hard to let go of Marybeth's hand in the car. He needed her; she was stronger about this. He wore a jacket and tie with his Wranglers and Stetson as well as a light raincoat he'd owned for fifteen years. Sheridan and Lucy wore dresses and tights, and Marybeth wore a dark business suit. Joe reached up and worked a finger between his neck and collar and tried to loosen it.

"This is exciting," Lucy said. "It feels like we're going to church."

"Yes it kind of does, honey," Marybeth said.

"That's ridiculous," Sheridan said to Lucy under her breath from the back. "You should just stop talking."

"Oooh," Lucy purred. "Someone is very *prickly* today."

"Girls," Marybeth said.

The liaison, a beefy square-jawed man with gray-flecked red hair named Matt Donnell, winked at Joe and Marybeth with empathy that said, *Been there*, then told Coon, "We've got four cruisers in the neighborhood within a minute of the Voricek home ready to move in on my call. I doubt we'll need them, but they'll be ready."

Coon nodded, said, "Good. Do we know who's in the house right now?"

"Ed's there. He's a piece of work. From what we understand he's between jobs again, so he's home. His wife, Mary Ann, is always home. And we're lucky today because it's an in-service training day for the school district." He raised his eyebrows.

Coon said, "Which means she's there."

"Should be."

"Have your guys actually seen her?"

362

"There's a girl who matches the description. We checked her description against the school yearbook. She's there, all right. Goes by April Voricek. Problem is, there is no known birth certificate for April Voricek, and no legal record of a name change from Keeley. It's her," Donnell said.

Joe felt Marybeth's eyes on him and felt her squeeze his hand.

Lucy said, "I thought Chicago would be, you know, big buildings. Skyscrapers and stuff like that."

Jane Dickenson chuckled in the back seat. "It does look like that downtown, honey. We're a long way from the Loop."

"This just looks like houses," Lucy said, disappointed.

"Where do you think people in big cities live?" Sheridan asked her sister, annoyed.

Lucy shrugged. "I thought they all lived in apartments a hundred floors up. You know, cool places, like on TV."

Joe thought, *What if April hated the sight of him? What if she refused to come back because of what she thought he'd done? What if she was so damaged by what had happened that they didn't even know her?*

STARTING OUT WITH the photograph, library card, stubs for the "El," and a middle school girls basketball schedule, the FBI had been able to pinpoint the likely location of April Keeley Voricek within a day and a half. Joe had been suitably impressed at what the Bureau could do with their technology, manpower, and a competent leader running the investigation: Special Agent Chuck Coon. Portenson, Coon said, was happy to turn over the case and get out of the way since he had bigger fish to fry: press conferences, conference calls filled with accolades from Governor Rulon, the acting head of U.S. Homeland Security, his superiors in Washington.

Coon said Portenson had already listed his home in Cheyenne for sale.

JANE DICKENSON TALKED over the heads of the Picketts to Agent Coon.

Dickenson said, "We're finding out all sorts of things about the Sovereign network. There are a lot more of them out there scattered across the country than we thought. And since they completely distrust the government, they've been operating their own child placement operation for years. To be honest, most of the kids seem to be doing pretty well. But in some instances, they've shuffled kids from family to family across the country. And because it's all privately funded—secretly funded, to be more accurate— the kids are under our radar. They're out of the social welfare system, so we simply don't know how many there are or where they are. We're learning a lot, though."

Coon asked, "How much do you know about Ed and Mary Ann Voricek?"

Joe and Marybeth followed the exchange in silence.

"We have a file on them," Dickenson said. "But until yesterday it wasn't high priority. A few years ago a neighbor made a call saying it seemed like there were a lot of children coming and going in that house. A caseworker visited them and saw no signs of neglect or abuse. Since our workload is massive and some of the things we have to deal with are horrendous, we concentrate on the high-priority cases. We just don't have the manpower to snoop around a house when everything seems in order and the children seem to be on the right track."

Leslie Doran opened a folder. "The Voriceks seem to take in these kids solely for the money. That's my take on them, anyway. Neither Ed nor Mary Ann seems to be very committed to the Sovereign movement or survivalist cause. Ed might have had some peripheral contacts with them, but I doubt they're true believers. If Ed sold Vicki to a brothel like you people say he did, he must have been in a desperate situation because we don't have any record of similar allegations on him in the file."

Donnell said, "Ed's a gambler. He's got debts to cover. And from what I've heard, he's scared to death of Mary Ann finding out he's still gambling. That may have been his motivation, the slimeball."

Coon nodded. "What do we know about Vicki Burgess?"

"Not much. But we think she was in that campground six years ago. We think she might have known April Keeley then. The fact that they apparently reunited here in Chicago is providence."

Joe closed his eyes.

COON TURNED TO Marybeth. "What's Vicki's condition?"

"More hopeful," she said, managing a smile. "There has been some brain activity, which is encouraging. The doctors are being cautious but they've upped her odds to sixty-forty for a full recovery. But there will no doubt be psychological issues to deal with if she comes out of her coma. And thanks to the Bureau, Vicki's grandparents were located and have agreed to take her in."

Coon whistled. "That's fantastic. She's still in Rapid City?"

Marybeth shook her head. "She's been transferred to the Mayo Clinic in Minnesota. She's got the very best care."

Coon looked puzzled. Joe smiled inwardly.

"My mother," Marybeth explained. "She recently came into quite a bit of money. I asked her to step up and help with the medical expenses."

Coon looked to Joe and said, "Your mother-in-law is a very generous woman."

Sheridan stifled a laugh and covered her mouth with her hand. Marybeth shot her a look.

Joe said, "She's a peach, all right."

"That she'd agree to pay for the care of a girl she didn't even know," Coon said, "I'd call her an angel."

"Oh, she is," Marybeth said, straight-faced.

Joe had been in his office and overheard Marybeth talking to her mother about Vicki at the kitchen table. When Marybeth suggested Missy step in, her mother had demurred by pointing out she'd never even met the girl. Joe thought the topic was settled when Marybeth went on to other things. Then, five minutes later, he heard his wife say:

"Is Earl aware that you're ten years older than you told him you were and that you have four ex-husbands instead of two?"

Missy asked icily, "Why are you doing this?"

"I bet it would be a shock to him if he found out the truth," Marybeth said conversationally. "Of course, he'd never need to find out if you and the Earl of Lexington performed a particular act of kindness."

Joe always knew Marybeth could play hardball. She knew no bounds when her maternal instincts took over. Even Missy, who continued to surprise Joe with her ruthlessness, must have felt that she'd finally encountered a worthy opponent in her very own daughter.

THEY WATCHED FROM the Suburban as the liaison, Doran, Dickenson, and two uniforms knocked on the front door of 18310 Kilpatrick. Sleet had begun to fall and it smeared the windows of the SUV and made all of the dark-clad bodies near the door undulate.

The woman who opened the door was tall and wide and angry. She yelled, "Ed!" over her shoulder.

Ed appeared behind her. He was overweight with a perfectly round bald head and a comb-over that started just above his ear. He wore an open flannel shirt over a black wife-beater, and when he saw the police he went still and turned white.

Joe could see Mary Ann yell at him to do something. Ed didn't do anything. He looked down at his slippers and stood aside for them to enter. Mary Ann continued to harangue him, but Ed looked beaten.

"That was easy," Coon said to no one in particular.

In a few minutes, Jane Dickenson stepped back out of the front door and gestured a thumbs-up to the SUV.

"She's here," Marybeth whispered. "Are you girls still okay with this?"

Sheridan nodded grimly.

Joe said, "Your mother can go in there with you to talk to her. You don't have to do this alone."

"We *want* to do it alone," Sheridan said. "If she's going to talk to anybody, it'll be us."

Lucy said, "Do you think they'll let me use their bathroom?"

IT WAS A long half hour for Joe and Marybeth. While they waited, Dickenson and Doran organized a team of their colleagues to lead children from the house into waiting cars. Joe noted that the children looked well fed and well clothed and normal, and he felt sorry for them. It wasn't their fault their parents or guardians were Sovereigns and had opted to place them within their network of survivalists rather than government-sponsored foster programs. He hoped they would do as well or better wherever they wound up.

Mary Ann Voricek was brought out with her hands cuffed behind her and stuffed into the back seat of a cruiser. Her face was red and angry. Ed came out more passively. When the police officers led him toward the car Mary Ann was in, Ed stopped and gestured to another one. The officers exchanged smirks and complied.

When Sheridan finally came out the door and made her way toward the SUV, Marybeth sat up straight in her seat.

Coon said, "If you'll excuse me a minute, I'll give you folks some privacy."

"Thank you," Joe said.

Sheridan climbed in and shut the door. "I can't believe it's her, but it is," she said, flashing a grin. "She's April, all right."

"Thank God," Marybeth said.

Joe felt as if something inside of him had been released.

"Lucy and April are sitting in there catching up," Sheridan said. "She's got lots of questions."

"So do we," Marybeth said.

Sheridan nodded. "She's really worried about Vicki, though. She wants to go see her if she can. She said Vicki called her last week and told her what she'd done and that it would be just a couple of days before we'd all be together— April, Vicki, Lucy, and me. She told April we could all be sisters together."

Marybeth shook her head. There was moisture in her eyes.

"It's sad, Mom," Sheridan said. "Vicki sort of worshipped April and April told her everything about our family, including our phone number. Vicki told April on the phone that she wanted to get us all together again—plus her. She just wanted to be a part of a real family. Isn't that crazy? So when Stenko took her away from here, Vicki said she pretended to be April because April was the strongest girl she knew and she wanted to be strong, too. She told April that Stenko was nice to her and was going to give her money for plane tickets so we could all be together in a place without adults. I don't know what she was thinking, but I think Vicki had had it with adults," Sheridan said, grimly looking at Joe and Marybeth.

"My God," Marybeth said. "I can see why she didn't trust adults, but …"

Joe rubbed his eyes.

"But why didn't April ever contact us herself?" Marybeth asked.

Joe knew what was coming by the way Sheridan avoided his eyes.

"She said that the last thing she remembered seeing in the campground that day was Dad standing across the road with all the other cops. She said she thought he was there to save her, but he didn't. She thought we'd all just thrown her away. You can imagine how that felt to her."

"That's so sad," Marybeth said. "And did you tell her the truth?"

Sheridan nodded.

"Does she believe you?"

"I think so. It helped that it was just Lucy and I. She trusts us."

Marybeth paused for a long time. She said, "So will she come back with us?"

"I'm not sure, but she doesn't know where else she will go."

After Sheridan left and went back in the Voricek house, Marybeth said to Joe, "This may turn out badly. We've got to prepare ourselves for that. If she comes out of that house, we'll need to set up counseling at the very least. There will likely be some really tough days ahead. That girl has been through things we can't imagine, both before we took her in and for sure the last six years.

"And I'm worried, Joe," she said, turning away from him, speaking to the rain-moist window. "Can I love her again like she's mine? Can you?"

Joe said, "I don't know."

"Doing the right thing is so hard sometimes."

APRIL KEELEY AND Lucy and Sheridan came out through the front door one by one. When they were all outside on the porch, they stood shoulder to shoulder. April was in the middle. Joe could see Sheridan watching April closely. Lucy, too. April looked straight ahead, toward the SUV.

Joe noticed that the cops, social workers, and Coon stopped whatever they were doing and looked at the three blond girls.

Marybeth got out first. Joe could tell by the way she jammed her hands into her coat pockets that she didn't want anyone to see they were shaking. He got out and stood behind her.

"April," Marybeth called, "can I see you?"

April was frozen. Joe studied her without appearing to stare. She was taller, more angular. She had sharp cheek-bones and white skin and acne on her cheeks and forehead. Her face was stoic, a mask that revealed nothing, the way it was when they'd first taken her in. She'd looked older than her years then and now her body had grown into the somewhat surly, defiant attitude that had come with her. He remembered how Marybeth described it at the time as a shell of self-protection. In the months before the Sovereigns arrived, the shell had shown cracks. Now, Joe thought, it was harder than ever.

"Go ahead," Lucy said, reaching up and tugging gently on April's hand.

April let go and started to walk forward. Marybeth cried

370

out and ran until the two of them embraced. They held each other for a long time.

Joe didn't move. He waited until April finally raised her head over Marybeth's shoulder and looked at him. For a moment their eyes locked. For Joe, it was like looking into the eyes of one of Nate's falcons. Whatever was going on behind those blue eyes was hidden from him and unknowable.

He mouthed, *"I'm sorry."*

She blinked as if momentarily touched by his words—a crack in the shell?—and buried her head in Marybeth again. Sheridan and Lucy walked up and hugged them both.

Lucy said, "Come on, let's go. Wait until you meet Tube. He's our new dog."

ACKNOWLEDGMENTS

THE AUTHOR WOULD like to sincerely thank those who contributed to the research and construction of this novel, including Sherry Merryman, Bill Stafford, Richard Bower, Mark and Mari Nelson, Todd Scott, and Kevin Guilfoyle. Kudos to the terrific Putnam and Berkley team, including Rachel Kahan, Ivan Held, Michael Barson, and Summer Smith. Thanks to Don Hajicek for www.cjbox.net. And my deep appreciation to Molly, Becky, and Laurie Box and Ann Rittenberg for their careful reading and invaluable suggestions.

AND NOW
AN EXCLUSIVE PREVIEW OF
NOWHERE TO RUN
THE NEXT JOE PICKETT NOVEL
BY ACCLAIMED MYSTERY WRITER
C. J. BOX

THREE HOURS SINCE he'd broken camp, repacked, and pushed his horses higher into the mountain range, Wyoming game warden Joe Pickett paused on the lip of a wide hollow basin and dug in his saddlebag for his notebook. The bow hunters had described where they'd tracked the wounded elk, and he matched the topography against their description.

He glassed the basin with binoculars, and noted the fingers of pine trees reaching down through the grassy swale and the craterlike depressions in the hollow they'd described. This, he determined, was the place.

He'd settled into a familiar routine of riding until his muscles got stiff and his knees hurt. Then he'd climb down and lead his geldings Buddy and Blue Roanie—a packhorse he'd named unimaginatively—until he could loosen up and work the kinks out. He checked his gear and the panniers on Roanie often to make sure the load was well balanced, and he'd stop so he and his horses could rest and get a drink of water. The second day of riding brought back all the old aches, but they seemed closer to the surface now that he was in his mid-forties.

Shifting his weight in the saddle toward the basin, he

clicked his tongue and touched Buddy's sides with his spurs. The horse balked.

"C'mon, Buddy," Joe said, "Let's go now, you knuckle-head."

Instead, Buddy turned his head back and seemed to implore Joe not to proceed.

"Don't be ridiculous. *Go.*"

Only when he dug his spurs in did Buddy shudder, sigh, and start the descent.

"You act like I'm making you march to your death like a beef cow," Joe said. "Knock it off, now." He turned to check that his packhorse was coming along as well. "You doing okay, Blue Roanie? Don't pay any attention to Buddy. He's a knucklehead."

But on the way down into the basin, Joe instinctively reached back and touched the butt of his shotgun in the saddle scabbard to assure himself it was there. Then he untied the leather thong that held it fast.

IT WAS TO have been a five-day horseback patrol before the summer gave way to fall and the hunting season began in earnest—before a new game warden was assigned the district to take over from Joe, who, after a year in exile, was finally going home. He was more than ready.

He'd spent the previous weekend packing up his house and shed and making plans to ride into the mountains on Monday, descend on Friday, and clean out his state-owned home in Baggs for the arrival of the new game warden the first of next week. Baggs ("Home of the Baggs Rattlers!") was a tough, beautiful, raggedy mountain town as old as the state itself. The community sprawled through the Little Snake River valley on the same unpaved streets Butch Cassidy used to walk. Baggs was so isolated it was known within the department as the "warden's graveyard"—the district where game wardens were sent to quit or die. Governor Spencer Rulon had hidden Joe there for his past transgressions, but after Rulon had won a second term in a landslide, he'd sent word through his people that Joe was no longer a liability. As luck had it, at the same time, Phil Kiner in Saddlestring took a new district in Cody and Joe quickly applied for—and received—his old district north in the Bighorns in Twelve Sleep County, where his family was.

Despite his almost giddy excitement about moving back to his wife, Marybeth, and his daughters, he couldn't in good conscience vacate the area without investigating the complaint about the butchered elk. That wouldn't be fair to the new game warden, whoever he or she would be. He'd leave the other reported crimes to the sheriff.

JOE PICKETT WAS lean, of medium height and medium build. His gray Stetson Rancher was stained with sweat and red dirt. A few silver hairs caught the sunlight on his temples and unshaved chin. He wore faded Wranglers, scuffed lace-up outfitter boots with stubby spurs, a red uniform shirt with the pronghorn antelope patch on the shoulder, and a badge over his breast pocket with the designation GF-54. A tooled leather belt that identified him as "Joe" held handcuffs, bear spray, and a service issue .40 Glock semi-automatic.

With every mile of his last patrol of the Sierra Madre of Southern Wyoming, Joe felt as if he were going back into time and to a place of immense and unnatural silence. With each muffled hoofbeat, the sense of foreboding got stronger until it enveloped him in a calm, dark dread that made the hair prick up on the back of his neck and on his forearms and that set his nerves on edge.

The silence was disconcerting. It was late August but the normal alpine soundtrack was switched to mute. There were no insects humming in the grass, no squirrels chattering in the trees to signal his approach, no marmots standing up in the rocks on their hind legs and whistling, no deer or elk rustling in the shadows of the trees rimming the meadows where they fed, no grouse clucking or flushing. Yet he continued on, as if being pulled by a gravitational force. It was as if the front door of a dark and abandoned house slowly opened by itself before he could reach for the handle, and the welcome was anything but warm. Despite the brilliant greens of the meadows or the subdued fireworks of alpine flowers, the sun-fused late summer morning seemed ten degrees cooler than it actually was.

"Stop spooking yourself," he said aloud and with authority.

But it wasn't just him. His horses were unusually twitchy and emotional. He could feel Buddy's tension through the saddle. Buddy's muscles were tight and balled, he breathed rapid, shallow breaths, and his ears were up and alert. The old game trail he took was untracked and covered with a thin sheet of pine needles, but it had a switchback up the mountain, and as they rose, the sky broke through the canopy and sent shafts of light like jail bars to the forest floor. Joe had to keep nudging and kissing at Buddy to keep him going up the face of the mountain into the thick forest. Finally deep into the trees, he yearned for open places where he could see.

JOE WAS STILL unnerved by a brief conversation he'd had with a dubious local named Dave Farkus the day before at the trailhead.

Joe was pulling the cinch tight on Buddy when Farkus emerged from the brush with a spinning rod in his hand. Short and wiry with muttonchop sideburns and a slack expression on his face, Farkus had opened with, "So you're really goin' up there?"

Joe said, "Yup."

The fisherman said, "All I know for sure is I drink beer at the Dixon Club Bar with about four old-timers who were here long before the energy workers got here and were a hell of a lot longer than you. A couple of these guys are old enough they forgot more about these mountains than either of us will ever know. They ran cattle up there and they hunted up there for years. But you know what?"

Joe felt a clench in his belly from the way Farkus had asked. He said, "What?"

"None of them old fellers will go up there anymore. Ever since that runner vanished, they say something just feels wrong."

Joe said, "Feelings aren't a lot to go on."

"That ain't all," said Farkus. "What about all the break-ins at cabins in the area and parked cars getting their windows smashed in at the trailheads? There's been a lot of that lately."

"I heard," Joe said. "Sheriff Baird is looking into that, I believe."

Farkus snorted.

"Is there something you're not telling me?" Joe asked.

"No. But we all heard some of the rumors. You know, camps being looted. Tents getting slashed. I heard there were a couple of bow hunters who tried to poach an elk before the season opened. They hit one, followed the blood trail for miles to the top, but when they finally found the animal it had already been butchered and the meat all hauled away. Is that true?"

Like most hunters who had broken the law, the bow hunters had come to Joe's office and turned themselves in.

Joe had cited them for hunting elk out of season, but had been intrigued by their story. They seemed genuinely creeped out by what had happened. "That was their story."

Farkus widened his eyes. "So it's true after all. And that's what you're up to, isn't it? You're going up there to find whoever took their elk if you can. Well, I hope you do. Man, nobody likes the idea of somebody stealing another man's meat. That's beyond the pale. And this Wendigo crap— where did that come from? Bunch of Indian mumbo-jumbo. Evil spirits, flesh eaters, I tell you. This ain't Canada, thank God. Wendigos are up there, not here, if they even exist. *Heh-heh.*"

It was not much of a laugh, Joe thought. More like a nervous tic. A way of saying he didn't necessarily believe a word of what he'd just said—unless Joe did.

Joe said, *"Wendigos?"*

JOE BROKE THROUGH the trees and emerged onto a tree-less meadow walled by dark timber, and he stopped to look and listen. He squinted, looking for whatever was spooking his horses and him, hoping reluctantly to see a bear, a mountain lion, a wolverine, even a snake. But what he saw were mountains that tumbled like frozen ocean waves all the way south into Colorado, wispy puffball clouds that scudded over him, immodestly showing their vulnerable white bellies, and his own mark left behind in the ankle-deep grass: parallel horse tracks, steaming piles of manure. There were no human structures of any kind in view and hadn't been for a full day. No power lines, microwave stations, or cellphone towers. The only proof that he was not riding across the same wilderness in the 1880s were the jet trails looking like snail tracks high in the sky.

*

THE RANGE RAN south to north. He planned to summit the Sierra Madre by Wednesday, day three, and cross the 10,000-foot Continental Divide near Battle Pass. This was where the bow hunters said their elk had been cut up. Then he would head down toward No Name Creek on the west side of the divide and arrive at his pickup and horse trailer by midday Friday—if all went well.

THE TERRAIN GOT rougher the higher he rode, wild and unfamiliar. What he knew of it he'd seen from a helicopter and from aerial survey photos. The mountain range was severe and spectacular, with canyon after canyon, toothy rimrock ridges, and dense old-growth forests that had never been timbered because cutting logging roads into them would have been too technical and expensive to be worth it. The vistas from the summit were like scenery overkill: mountains to the horizon in every direction, veins of aspen in the folds already turning gold, high alpine lakes and cirques like blue poker chips tossed on green felt, hundreds of miles of lodgepole pine trees, many of which were in the throes of dying due to bark beetles and had turned the color of advanced rust.

The cirques—semicircular hollows with steep walls filled with snowmelt and big enough to boat across—stair-stepped their way up the mountains. Those with outlets birthed tiny creeks, and water sought water and melded into streams. Other cirques were self-contained: bathtubs that would fill, freeze during winter, and never drain out.

PRIOR TO THE five-day trek, Joe had been near the spine of the mountains only once, years before, when he was a participant in the massive search-and-rescue effort for the runner Farkus had mentioned, Olympic hopeful Diane

Shober, who'd parked her car at the trailhead and vanished on a long-distance run on the canyon trail. Her body had never been found. Her face was haunting and ubiquitous, though, because it peered out from hundreds of homemade handbills posted by her parents throughout Wyoming and Colorado. Joe kept her disappearance in mind as he rode, always alert for scraps of clothing, bones, or hair.

Since he'd been assigned districts all over the State of Wyoming as both a game warden and Governor Rulon's point man, Joe ascribed certain personality traits to mountain ranges. He conceded that his impressions were often unfair and partially based on his mood at the time or things he was going through. Rarely, though, had he changed his mind about a mountain range once he'd established its quirks and rhythms in his mind. The Tetons were flashy, cold, bloodless Eurotrash mountains—too spectacular for their own good. They were the mountain equivalent of supermodels. The Gros Ventres were a rich graveyard of human history—both American Indian and early white— that held their secrets close and refused to accommodate the modern era. The Wind River Mountains were what the Tetons wanted to be: towering, incredibly wealthy with scenery and wildlife, vast, and spiritual. The Bighorns, Joe's mountains in northern Wyoming where his family still was waiting for him, were comfortable, rounded, and wry—a retired All-Pro linebacker who still had it.

But the Sierra Madre was still a mystery. He couldn't yet warm to the mountains, and he fought against being intimidated by their danger, isolation, and heartless beauty. The fruitless search for Diane Shober had planted the seed in his mind. These mountains were like a glimpse of a beautiful and exotic woman in a passing car, a gun on her lap, who refused to make eye contact.

HE DISMOUNTED ONCE he was on the floor of the basin to ease the pain in his knees and let his horses rest. As always, he wondered how horsemen and horsewomen of the past stayed mounted for hours on end and day after day. No wonder they drank so much whiskey, he thought.

Joe led his horses through a stand of widely spaced lodgepole pines that gradually melded into a pocket of rare and twisted knotty pine. Trunks and branches were bizarre in shape and direction, with softball-sized joints like swollen knees. The knotty pine stand covered less than a quarter mile of the forest, just as the elk hunters had described. As he stood on the perimeter of the stand, he slowly turned and noted the horizon of the basin that rose like the rim of a bowl in every direction. This was the first cirque. He was struck by how many locations in the mountains looked alike, how without man-made landmarks like power lines or radio towers, wilderness could turn into a maelstrom of green and rocky sameness. He wished the bow hunters had given him precise GPS coordinates so he could be sure this was the place, but the hunters were purists and had not carried Garmins. Still, though, they'd accurately described the basin and the cirque, as well as the knotty pine stand in the floor of it.

In the back of his mind, Joe thought that if there really were men hiding out in these mountains stealing elk and vandalizing cabins and cars, they would likely be refugees of the man camps. Over the past few years, as natural gas fields were drilled north of town, the energy companies had established man camps—clumps of adjoining temporary mobile housing in the middle of sagebrush flats—for their employees. The men—and it was only men—lived practically shoulder to shoulder. Obviously, it took a certain kind of person to stay there. Most of the temporary residents had traveled hundreds and thousands of miles to the most remote part of the least-populated state to work in the natural gas fields and live in a man camp. The men were rough, independent, well-armed, and flush with cash when they came to town. And when they did, it was the New Wild West. For months at a time, Joe had been called just about every Saturday night to assist the local police and sheriff's deputies with breaking up fights.

When the price of natural gas plummeted and drilling was no longer encouraged, the employees were let go. A half-dozen man camps sat deserted in the sagebrush desert. No one knew where the men went any more than they knew where they'd come from in the first place. That a few of the unemployed refugees of the man camps had stuck around in the game-rich mountains seemed plausible—even likely—to Joe.

He secured his animals and walked the floor of the basin looking for remains of the elk. Although predators would have quickly moved in on the carcass and stripped it of its meat and scattered the bones, there should be unmistakable evidence of hide, hair, and antlers. The bow hunters said the wounded bull had seven-point antlers on each beam, so the antlers should be nearby as well.

As he surveyed the ground for signs, something in his peripheral vision struck him as discordant. He paused and carefully looked from side to side, visually backtracking. In nature, he thought, nothing is perfect. And something he'd seen—or thought he'd seen—was too vertical or horizontal or straight or unblemished to belong here.

"What was it?" he asked aloud. Through the trees, his horses raised their heads and stared at him, uncomprehending.

After turning back around and retracing his steps, Joe saw it. At first glance, he reprimanded himself. It was just a stick jutting out from a tree trunk twenty feet off his path. But on closer inspection, it wasn't a stick at all, but an arrow stuck in the trunk of a tree. The shaft of the arrow was hand-crafted, not from a factory, but it was straight, smooth, and shorn of bark, with feather fletching on the end. The only place he'd ever seen a primitive arrow like this was in a museum. He photographed the arrow with his digital camera, then pulled on a pair of latex gloves, grasped it by the shaft, and pushed hard up and down while pulling on it. After a moment, the arrow popped free and Joe studied it. The point was obsidian and delicately flaked and attached to the shaft with animal sinew. The fletching was made of wild turkey feathers.

It made no sense. The bow hunters he'd interviewed were serious sportsmen, even if they'd hunted prior to the season opener. But even they didn't make their own arrows from natural materials. No one did. Who had lost this arrow?

He felt a chill roll through him. Slowly, he rotated and looked behind him in the trees. He wouldn't have been surprised to see Cheyenne or Sioux warriors approaching.

HE FOUND THE remains of the seven-point bull elk ten minutes later. Even though coyotes and ravens had been feeding on the carcass, it was obvious this was the elk the bow hunters had wounded and pursued. The hindquarters were gone and the backstraps had been sliced away. Exactly like the hunters described.

So who had taken the meat?

Joe photographed the carcass from multiple angles.

JOE WALKED BACK to his horses with the arrow he'd found. He wrapped the point of it in a spare sock and the shaft in a T-shirt and put it in a pannier. He caught Buddy staring at him.

387

"Evidence," he said. "Something strange is going on up here. We might get some fingerprints off this arrow."

Buddy snorted. Joe was sure it was a coincidence.

AS HE RODE out of the basin, he frequently glanced over his shoulder and couldn't shake a feeling that he was being watched. Once he reached the rim and was back on top, the air was thin and the sun was relentless. Rivulets of sweat snaked down his spine beneath his uniform shirt.

Miles to the southeast, a mottled gray pillow cloud and rain column of a thunderstorm connected the horizon with the sky. It seemed to be coming his way. He welcomed rain that would cool down the afternoon and settle the dust from his horses.

But he couldn't stop thinking about the carcass he'd found. Or the arrow.

THAT NIGHT, HE camped on the shoreline of a half-moon-shaped alpine lake and picketed the horses within sight of his tent in lush ankle-high grass. As the sun went down and the temperature dropped into the forties, he caught five trout with his 4-weight fly rod, kept one, and ate it with fried potatoes over a small fire. After dinner, he cleaned his dishes by the light of a headlamp and uncased his satellite phone from a pannier. Because of the trouble he'd had communicating several years before while temporarily stationed in Jackson Hole, he'd vowed to call home every night no matter what. Even if there was no news from either side, it was the mundane that mattered, that kept him in touch with his family and kept Marybeth with him.

The satellite phone was bulky compared to a mobile, and he had to remove his hat to use it because the antenna bumped into the brim. The signal was good, though, and the call went through. Straight to voicemail. He sighed and was slightly annoyed before he remembered Marybeth had said she was taking the girls to the last summer concert in the town park. He'd hoped to hear her voice.

When the message prompt beeped, he said, "Hello, ladies. I hope you had a good time tonight. I wish I could have gone with you, even though I don't like concerts. Right now, I'm high in the mountains, and it's a beautiful and lonely place. The moon's so bright I can see fish rising in the lake. A half hour ago, a bull moose walked from the trees into the lake and stood there knee-deep in the water for a while. It's the only animal I've seen, which I find remarkably strange. I watched him take a drink."

He paused, and felt a little silly for the long message. He rarely talked that much to them in person. He said, "Well, I'm just checking in. Your horses are doing fine and so am I. I miss you all."

HE UNDRESSED AND slipped into his sleeping bag in the tent. He read a few pages of A. B. Guthrie's *The Big Sky*, which had turned into his camping book, then extinguished his headlamp. He lay awake with his hands beneath his head and stared at the inside of the dark tent fabric. His service weapon was rolled up in the holster in a ball near his head. After an hour, he got up and pulled the bag and the Therm-a-Rest pad out through the tent flap. There were still no clouds, and the stars and moon were bright and hard. Out in the lake, the moose had returned and stood in silhouette bordered by blue moon splash.

God, he thought, *I love this. I love it so.*

And he felt guilty for loving it so much.

C.J. BOX

THE JOE PICKETT SERIES

|1

|2

|3

|4

|5

|6

|7

|8

|9

|10

|11

ORDINARY MAN EXTRAORDINARY HERO

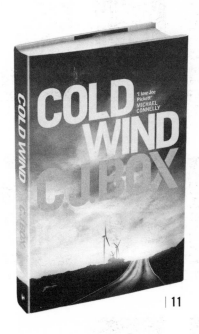

JOE PICKETT, Wyoming game warden, has taken on eco-terrorists, rogue federal land managers, animal mutilators, corrupt bureaucrats, crazed hitmen, homicidal animal rights advocates – all in the pursuit of justice.

COLD WIND available in hardback Christmas 2011

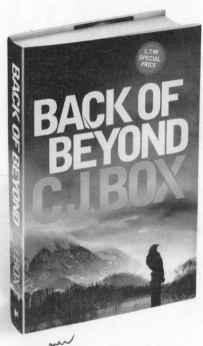